Changing Shapes in Mid-Stream

"Wren!" Titch shouted. Then he saw the tangle of wet cloth snagged in the branches in the stream. Something twisted inside the cloth. An eye rolled, white teeth flashed. An otter caught in human clothing could not swim . . .

At least she was still alive. Teeth a-chatter, he plunged into the current to free her. The otter, terrified, bit at his hands; Titch grabbed her by the scruff of her neck.

The otter heaved, and of a sudden, 'twas a brown duck, pummeling him with her wings. Her blunt bill stabbed at his face, then she shifted again. Feathers vanished, and he felt smooth scales instead. The salmon heaved, wriggling free of tangled cloth.

As he struggled to hold her, Titch's frozen toes slipped on the rocky stream bottom. He went under. He tried to stand, but he couldn't with his arms full of the salmon. But if he let go of her now, how would Wren ever find her own shape again?

By Susan Dexter
Published by Ballantine Books:

THE RING OF ALLAIRE

THE WIZARD'S SHADOW

The Warhorse of Esdragon
THE PRINCE OF ILL-LUCK
THE WIND-WITCH
THE TRUE KNIGHT

THE TRUE KNIGHT

Book Three of
The Warhorse of Esdragon

Susan Dexter

A Del Rey® Book
BALLANTINE BOOKS • NEW YORK

A Del Rey® Book
Published by Ballantine Books

Copyright © 1995 by Susan Dexter

All rights reserved under International and Pan-American Copyright Conventions. Published in the United States by Ballantine
Books, a division of Random House, Inc., New York, and simul-
taneously in Canada by Random House of Canada Limited, To-
ronto.

Library of Congress Catalog Card Number: 95-92519

ISBN 0-345-39345-7

Manufactured in the United States of America

First Edition: January 1996

10 9 8 7 6 5 4 3 2

THIS BOOK IS FOR:

Ryan, whose heart is brave and true.

Champ and Shadow—your worth was measured by the size of the empty places you left behind you.

And I herewith recognize some members of the Society for Creative Anachronism, to wit:

Duncan, an excellent juggler.

The games master who taught me—most patiently—to play Tafl.

The Druid Chirurgeon who went down on one knee to kiss my hand in the baggage claim area of the Pittsburgh airport—doing that while wearing a backpack was certainly above and beyond the call of anyone's chivalry.

Contents

Prolog

THE LADY DRUYAN of Splaine Garth and the duke's post riders gave the Eral freebooters cause to think twice and thrice upon the wisdom of raiding into the Duchy of Esdragon, but the kingdoms of Clandara enjoyed no such unity and boasted few such fortunate heroes. The Eral assailed those kingdoms freely for a generation and more, hacking out footholds on the shores of Heil and Josten, then acquiring horses through theft and tribute, and thrusting farther inland than warships or men's feet could easily venture, soon settling permanently in the lands they began to call Calandra. The raiders prospered in their new ventures, making most of the petty kingdoms their own through conquest and expedient intermarriage within a generation.

Esdragon managed to keep her own borders, in small part due to caprices of geography, in larger measure owing to the warhorse Valadan, who served a succession of noble masters over the turbulent years. His fabled fleetness never waned with time's passage, and his storm-black coat was yet unsullied by so much as a single white hair. Magic had made him long ago. It showed most plainly in his eyes, which flashed as if the costliest of gemstones were hidden therein.

A River of Tears

THE PRINCESS SAVRIN knew her life was forfeit when she beheld the trophy that hung—the royal blood still dripping sluggishly out of it—from her royal stepmother's iron-clad stirrup. It was not so much that she recognized her father's dead face. The battered head looked nothing like the gentle man she had known as her sire. But she knew well that if Melcia the warrior-queen had come upon them, it could only be because Savrin's father was dead, and once that was established, the identity of the wretched head became obvious.

Savrin's own mother, Zorana, screamed at the sight. The throat-tearing shriek hurt to hear, but Savrin herself only stared stony-eyed at her father's severed head, twisting slowly to and fro on the makeshift rope of his long, flax-pale hair. His eyes were closed, but the features about them were twisted as if he yet felt pain. There was a red bruise on one cheek, got bare moments before his death. That tugged worse at her heart than the unreal rest of it, somehow—that bruise which would neither swell nor purple.

After an endless moment, Savrin shifted her gaze a trifle, but only to the snorting warhorse that loomed over her, its scarlet mouth dragged wide open by the cruel bit between its frothing jaws and the crueller hand upon its crimson-dyed reins. Savrin stared at the iron-gray destrier. She could not make herself look higher, at her father's lawful wife seated on the charger's back, under a banner the hue of fresh-shed blood.

No one spoke, but there was hardly silence. Other horsemen rode up to flank their armor-clad queen, so hooves pounded, bits jingled, leather creaked. Grunts and snortings came from the horses, bursts of speech and orders from the knights upon their backs. Man by man, the victorious army surrounded the two women afoot. One by one, their own loyal retainers were dragged away. Most went without a struggle, stunned by disaster, but once, then twice, Savrin heard the sound of blows, of some protest ruthlessly dealt with.

"My husband shall stray from my side to yours no more, Lady," a harsh voice proclaimed. Savrin thought of ravens croaking over the battle-slain, as in the ballads. "Our armies clashed, and then Kenric chose to end the slaughter with a single combat."

Impossible, to think of that grisly trophy as her father. Savrin felt it would be better not to try. Kenric was the huge bulk against the warm sun that scooped her up in strong arms, held her close to a face that was all beard-prickles and white teeth. He was the sun and the moon, every song and legend come to vivid life. He was the king of all the land, her mother's lord, her own father. The thing that hung from the stirrup was nothing to do with any of that. Savrin watched the patterns the blood made, dripping darkly down into the rank bleached grass, the thoughts dripping likewise from her mind, emptying. If she watched with sufficient intensity, perchance all the rest would go away, fade back into the dark realm of nightmares, where the queen had always dwelt . . .

"Your continued existence is an insult I will not bear," the raven voice rasped.

"My death comes welcome," Zorana declared, unafraid. "You have slain my lord, and I will follow him gladly into the afterworld. But spare Kenric's child—Savrin bears no blame for my crimes against you, or her father's. She is innocent of all."

"*Innocent?* The reminder that my wedded lord left my side to consort with you? She bears his guilt stamped on her very face!" The queen jerked her reins in a spasm of fury, and her warhorse rose half onto its hind legs, swinging its great head from side to side, fighting its royal rider.

Savrin, her attention drawn by the commotion, looked up into the contorted face.

She had never beheld it ere that dreadful day, but it looked exactly as she had always imagined it. Savrin distinguished rage, anger—and surging beneath those, pain and wounded pride. There was dirt, as well, and blood, and cleaner places where sweat had run through. She took note of the queen's weapons, the sword-edge still stained, the long shield showing the scars of combat on its gules paint.

She fought him, Savrin realized. *Herself. He betrayed her, and she took his life from him.*

Savrin had been taught always to expect no mercy from the woman before her, this queen and lawful wife. She had never been encouraged to think of Melcia as a woman at all, but merely as the stuff of dread nightmares. And always her father had stood firmly between her and those terrors, a mighty bulwark. The danger had been real when she had been very small, when her father had been wed to two women, one for the kingdom and one for his heart, when the first must not be allowed to know of the second. The danger of discovery ended when Kenric broke with Melcia and claimed Zorana openly, but no safety had followed. Instead, declarations of war, marching armies, endless shuttling about in the midst of wholesale destruction—and now, ultimate disaster.

The queen pronounced her sentence, in her ruined voice. One or two of the armed men behind Savrin made startled exclamations, which they prudently stifled.

Savrin's mother was weeping, twin waterfalls of tears coursing down her flawless face. She did not cling to—did not even reach out to—her daughter. After the one brave plea for her child's life, she seemed to have forgotten her entirely. When Zorana all at once lunged forward, it was to clasp the bloody head to her breast, ignoring the risk of trampling by the startled warhorse as she sought to give the king's dead lips one last kiss. Dismounted knights snatched her back, closed around her, led her away. The swollen river, fed by days of weeping rain, was only a few paces distant. Earlier, Zorana's little party had hoped to gain

safety by crossing it, but its flood had held them prisoner
on the shore instead, until escape no longer mattered.

When Savrin's turn for execution came, she thought to
struggle, but she saw there would be little point. To attempt
escape would merely force the men ranged about her to lay
hands on her—whereas if she willingly went with them,
they permitted her to walk free, as a king's child ought. Bereft of all else save her dignity, Savrin clung to it with
trembling fingers and unswerving determination.

Only when she reached the river's washy edge did she
pause, to turn and look back at the woman on the blood-
spattered horse. The Red Queen seemed a league away, the
day's fading light gone weird as night came on.

They had drawn her mother's drowned body from the
river already—one of the knights cursed the men whose
thoughtlessness let Savrin see that. But her gaze did not lin-
ger on the poor wet heap of clothing, which was no more
her mother than was that lopped head her sire. Savrin
stood, staring at the dark water sliding past her, barely a
yard from her toes.

The Red Queen croaked an order at her liegeman. *Haste.
No pity.*

"I'm sorry," the nearest knight said, and put a gauntleted
hand upon Savrin's shoulder.

She nodded gravely, a courtesy born of meticulously les-
soned manners, and stepped obediently forward into the sable water. Cold, so very cold it was, like a midwinter's
night when the fire had died early, and her nurse, asleep,
had not put fresh logs on. The chill lapped her ankles,
dragged at her skirts. Next stumbling step, it was above her
knees. She bumped her toes on shifting rocks and tottered.

Savrin wondered if it would hurt, to drown, or if the cold
would numb her first, so that she knew naught. She faltered, then felt the implacable if unwilling hands on her
shoulders. In another moment, they would thrust her beneath the cold dark surface, hold her down till her lungs
failed and the king's illicit daughter ceased to exist. One
more step . . .

Over the far shore, the first star pricked out in the deep
lavender of the sky. Savrin fixed her gaze upon it, and a

single tear sprang to each of her eyes. As she stumbled forward into death and despair, her tears ran like quicksilver down her cold cheeks, till they met the river water surging upward.

The knight thought there was no recompense his queen could offer him for this deed. He despised his duty, hated himself for his obedience. But the girl went so unquestioningly, he might cling to the hope that grief and terror had unhinged her, that she had no idea what was happening to her. Her mother had gone to her death blank-faced with shock—he did not dare look to see whether this tainted princess did likewise. As it was, the one glimpse he'd had of her face would haunt him all the rest of his days . . .

When he thrust her beneath the water, the trance seemed to snap, and she began to struggle. The knight sought to tighten his grip. A quick death was the nearest to mercy he could offer the girl, and he thought he owed an innocent that much. But the more the knight sought to grasp, the more she melted out of his hold, like ice dissolving. He tangled his fingers in her cloak, ready to push down when she tried to surface, seeking air—but she did nothing like that, and all at once he realized that he held nothing more than the sodden cloak. He reached, searched, but he could find nothing more of her.

The river otter went downstream fast as thought, her wriggle of escape extending effortlessly into swimming. She went deep with one long ripple of her body, nose to tail, and stayed deep, skimming just over silvery pebbles and streaming water weed. By the time she needed air, she was far downstream, and night was falling swiftly.

Ford of Disaster

HE WAS UNDOUBTEDLY overmatched.

Titch suspected that unpleasant fact the moment the stranger hove into view, riding at a slow jog toward the ford. The man wore his gear with an air of easy authority, and even the least bit of it spoke as eloquently of costly quality as of its owner's prowess. His helm was plain, so as to allow an attacking blade to slide freely and safely off, but all the rest was ornamented wherever it could be, whether by chasing or by patterns of brass rivets. The rider wore a shirt of mail beneath his dyed leather jazerant, and both garments were dust-filmed from travel, but the visible links of the hauberk glinted in a way that vowed they'd been scrupulously preserved from rust—and the sleeve-ends showed. Such a length suggested they'd been crafted to the man's long-limbed measure, an extra expense. His lances were straight-shafted and borne so he could lay hands on them readily. Nothing was encumbering his scarlet-gauntleted sword hand. He was big, well equipped, and alert. He appeared to enjoy excellent health.

A fair match, and a fitting trial of Titch's prowess. That was the rub—at this stage of his career, Titch was properly more interested in the profits from the sure thing than the risks attendant on a fair fight. The strength of his own body was not in question. The days when 'twas apt that he was called after the smallest possible kitchen measure were long gone. Titch would never be reckoned a tall man, but he'd grown up hard—and ahorse, he was as high-headed as any man. Patient practice swinging a heavy blade in attack and defense had given him better arms and shoulders than the

7

blacksmith's beefy son boasted of to all and sundry on market day.

Nor was the strength of his will at issue—it was equally tough. Not all the combats he had seen had been strictly friendly in nature. He'd won his armor and weapons in such contests, and had been practical enough to sell off the glittery stuff for hard coin, prudent enough to keep the plain and the useful for himself. Though he was not accoutered to the stranger's costly level, Titch would scarcely call himself ill-equipped.

But to offer a challenge would be ill-considered. A calculated risk was a risk nonetheless, and Titch had plans a-hatching. Gambling recklessly his first day out was no part of them. The sensible thing to do would be to let this undeniably puissant stranger cross unmolested over the ford and go his way, whether to tourney or on some lord's business, and be on about his *own* affairs. Challenging such a personification of chivalry would be sheerest idiocy.

The trouble was, Titch wanted the horse.

The beast the stranger rode was the color of midnight at midwinter, without the slightest speckling of stars or dusting of snow. If there lurked a white hair anywhere on the creature, it would have to be under the tack, where Titch couldn't spy it out. Not that the stallion's color mattered in the slightest. What took Titch's love-blinded eye was the way the horse came toward him, neck arched and chin tucked in obedience to the bit, each step delicate and deliberate as a deer's, or a dancer's. The road ran along the river for a way before finally descending to the ford. Titch had time for a good, long look, and the winter-bare trees did nothing to spoil the superior view.

It was by no means a tall horse, not one of the great and somewhat unwieldy destriers that could break a line of foot soldiers simply by trotting at it—but what there was of it was put together exquisitely. A small clean head carried on the supple neck, wide at the jaw and tapered at the muzzle. It was the same thing from the front as in the profile—a very wide forehead dwindling to a muzzle that would fit in his palm with room to spare. Little ears alert to every bird-chirp, the slightest leaf-crunch. A shoulder perfectly sloped, a short back and powerful quarters under the high-set tail. A round barrel, strong loins. Legs clean as a stag's, with generous flat joints. The stallion's conformation gave him a way of using himself, even at the walk, that put Titch's heart into his throat. He could imagine the other gaits, and the exercise dizzied him.

He leaned forward, patted Gray's winter-shaggy shoulder just ahead of his own left knee. "No offense, old friend, but I think I'm in love. And you deserve an honorable retirement." Gray answered him with a snort and a head-dip. "No, that wasn't the plan," Titch agreed. "But when fortune winks—"

The plan had been to ride out from the village that morning, cross this very ford, and make his way deeper into Heil, to a holding where tourneys of repute were conducted during each of the winter months. It was a sensible plan— there was no way Titch could achieve either fortune or fame by continuing to spar against the same locals he'd grown up with, in the friendly combats at large the Eral men-at-arms used to hone their war skills over the fallow months when there was no true war being fought. No one on the local scene was good for a decent ransom, and he'd already won all he was going to get from them by way of gear and weapons. His late father had bequeathed him the best horse and the best sword in the district. If he wanted more—and Titch devoutly did—he needs must go after it.

And now, perversely, here it came, walking deliberately toward him. He could so easily imagine how such a horse would look running. How it would feel, to bestride such an incomparable beast. What such a steed would mean to him in combat. Speed, power, agility—Titch gave Gray another pat, feeling guilty and intensely disloyal. The old warhorse was, in some ways, his second father. They had been together every day of Titch's life, at least the parts that Titch had clear memories of—they were of an age, in truth.

But twenty years to a man meant Titch was just entering into his fighting prime, whereas the gray gelding was well past his and sliding farther from it in the opposite direction every day. They were nowhere near balanced, ability-wise. And it was no kindness to his old friend to keep pushing the horse on just because Titch himself had no other options.

The Eral philosophy as regarded combat was simple—might made its own right. Beat a man in a fair fight, and you got whatever of his gear and goods you fancied. Weapons, armor—or his horse. Titch had been buying his bread for years by bartering off his prizes, but if he could get this horse, he'd never part with it, not for goods or even gold coin. And he'd risk whatever he must in pursuit of this new goal.

He fished back behind the cantle of his saddle, caught up the steel helm that hung there while he traveled and had little need of it. He scowled at the crooked nasal bar, which invariably rubbed a raw spot across the bridge of his not-inconsiderable nose, and settled the helmet firmly onto his head, over the leather coif and the padded skullcap. It served, and the freckling of rust spots, the dents he hadn't been able to pound wholly out, only made the cap a true match for the rest of his accouterments. From gauntlets to boots, every item he wore was mismatched and had a piecemeal look to it—how else should it be, when he'd won it bit by bit, then been forced too often to sell the better stuff for the hacksilver it would bring him, the food and lodging? But a good horse—*this* horse—could go a long way to changing some of that sad circumstance. At a larger tourney, there'd be rich ransoms to be won. And one day, when he distinguished himself in front of the right noble lord, he'd win himself a knighthood and the grant of land that went along with it.

All he had to do was get past this first step.

Titch pulled the laces of the gorget at his neck snug, then adjusted the bullhide collar that further protected his throat. He tugged on his gauntlets of padded leather and linkmail—right, then left. He flexed his fingers, gathered his reins, settled deeper into his creaking saddle. Then, just as the stranger put the black horse at the downslope that led to the ford, he legged Gray out into plain view.

Black ears pricked and scarlet nostrils flared wide. The horse spotted him first, though maybe it had already known that Gray was among the trees. Titch gave his full attention to the rider. The man's helm had cheekpieces as well as a nasal, but Titch could still see the blue eyes go wide with startlement. He could also see, at closer range, how big the man was—probably four-stone over Titch's own weight.

The strange knight reined hard, and the black stallion responded with a half rear before halting. As it plunged, its mane rose and fell, a dark inrushing tide upon its neck. Its tail plumed into a sable banner flaunted behind it. Even with all four of its hooves planted on the dull earth, it seemed to be in motion, so alert and responsive it was as it stood at the halt.

Gods above, he wanted that horse!

"Planning to cross here?" Titch inquired, his voice steady. His knees shook, but Gray disregarded what might have been confusing signals.

The stranger eyed him, nothing alarmed, deigned to make an answer. "I am that. What is it to you?"

"You haven't the right of passage." Titch lifted his lance just a trifle.

Consternation, then the merest hint of a sneer. The helm let that show. "You mean you expect me to fight *you* for the passage?" The stranger looked at the ford, which seemed nothing anyone would care about contesting.

Titch shrugged. "It's the only crossing for three leagues, unless you like winter swims. And on the main track into Heil, too. Your choice."

"What terms?" the man asked, voice edged with irritation.

Titch swallowed, allowed himself no further hesitation. "Your horse."

"My—" The blue eyes went amazed. "You're daft."

"No." Titch shook his head, feigning that he was casual, confident. "I'm challenging you. If you want to cross here, you have to fight me. And if I best you, your horse is your forfeit."

"In a run with lances?" The polished helm swiveled left, then right, sharply. "I don't think so. You want to try for my horse, then it will be with swords. Or you back off, boy!"

Titch tossed his lance carefully to one side, into the

brush, and drew his father's sword from its patched and mended scabbard. "Swords it is, then." He legged Gray forward.

Lances would have been better, from his perspective. If you were skilled, and lucky, too, such a contest could be concluded successfully in a hundred heartbeats. Arriving at a conclusion with blades took a lot longer, and favored a bigger, more experienced opponent. It wasn't a contest Titch should have—or would have—sought. But it was fair, he had to concede that. Such a horse was too valuable to be wagered on something as chancy as a joust with a suspiciously met stranger. He didn't think he'd have risked Gray on such an adventure, if he hadn't been the one to initiate it.

He'd want to be careful this man didn't get past him, or behind him. No reason he couldn't trade a few blows, then spur his way through the ford and keep going. The rules of combat were shifty and malleable as beeswax—especially those of informal challenges such as this one.

No drop of the marshal's baton to signal a fair beginning. Titch caught a flash of sunlight as the knight's spurs moved against the black stallion's flanks—that was all the warning he got that the challenge was accepted, that the combat was under way. He sent Gray forward at the best speed the gelding's old legs—especially the foreleg prone to swell if Titch didn't keep it wrapped—could manage. They flew forward like a goshawk launched from a falconer's fist, and gravel was hurled backward in their wake.

If he dodged sharp to his left, he'd be able to strike at the knight's sword arm, and neither horse would be in the way of his blows. But that action would leave his own right side open—and worse, leave the path to the ford clear, with Gray running full tilt the opposite way and the black horse galloping even more rapidly straight at it. Titch steered his course so the horses would pass near side to near side, and raised his shield in readiness, while he held his sword high.

He would be at a disadvantage as to momentum, Titch was sure. Gray had a respectable early turn of speed, but the ground favored the other horse, and the black was closing like a stooping falcon. If his rider timed his sword stroke precisely, he could tumble Titch out of his saddle very handily. He wouldn't even require his sword—his shield's edge would do just as neatly, shove the upstart away like a clod from a plowshare. He could see the knight thinking it.

What Titch needed to do was to allow the knight's shield to slide along his own instead of encountering it solidly. And then get in a couple of good blows with the flat of his sword, while keeping the horses in close contact so the black couldn't make another run at him, because he might be caught flatfooted if that happened, unable to turn Gray quickly enough to counter. A shoving match as much as bladework, and the first man on the ground lost. The thunder of hooves was so loud, Titch couldn't tell any longer which were Gray's, which the black's. He let his reins fall onto Gray's neck, so his shield arm was free for fullest motion, and held tight to its straps. He picked a target for his blade and drew his arm back.

At the last instant, the knight swung the black straight over into them. The stallion's shoulder met Titch's knee and Gray's side at the same moment the wooden shields crashed together like a battering ram against a castle gate. Titch swung his blade into empty air. Instantly he tried to wrap his legs about Gray's belly, to sink deep into his saddle like a stone falling to the bottom of a pond, all the tricks. It didn't matter. Gray staggered from the impact, and Titch realized as the scenery shifted position that he wasn't in his saddle any longer.

He didn't land on his head, particularly—Titch arrived abruptly and flat on his back, with sufficient impact that he suspected he was imbedded two inches deep in the streamside gravel. His eyes were both wide open, but he couldn't really see. He couldn't move, either. Couldn't breathe. Wasn't sure he cared about any of it, just then.

"Lady Moon, not *another* one—" Heavy boots crunched the gravel, stopped just beside him. Titch was surprised his ears worked. He blinked, trying to discover whether he could clear his sight, as well.

"Are you all right? Speak to me—"

The voice seemed to echo, as if one of them was down

a well. Fingers unstrapped his helm, dragged the metal cap from Titch's head, the cloth skullcap after it. The air was chill on his bared scalp.

"Alive," the voice decided, relieved and amazed both, Titch thought. He took a shallow breath, coughed it violently out, gasped another and another, alternating with more coughs. Sensation came back in an unwelcome rush as he sat up, then doubled over, still fighting for his breath. Pain flashed through his head, his back. Something dripped onto his hand. His nose was running. Some of it was blood, bright scarlet as poppies. Titch stared at his fingers.

"Hurt?" the voice asked him, from about a league off by his ears' report.

"Oh, yes," Titch agreed faintly. Quite true. Everything hurt, from breathing on up.

"I said, are you hurt?" the voice boomed. "Can you hear me?"

He could, actually, once the coughing subsided. Titch wiped the back of his hand across his upper lip. He shook his head to the first question. The pain was general, but nothing hurt much worse than anything else, and none of it seemed to worsen as he moved. Breathing was becoming marginally easier as he practiced it.

Of course, the worst of the disaster wasn't physical, but financial. He'd just wagered everything of value that he possessed in the world—and lost it. Gray, who'd wandered back into sight and dropped his nose down to snuffle the gravel, reminded him painfully of that new reality.

The stranger saw where Titch was looking. "That horse is too old for this business, you know," he said angrily. "It's cruel."

Titch wiped his nose again. Less blood this time, he noted dispassionately. And his sight had cleared, save for a few floating purple dots. "It's his last time," he explained. "If I'd won, I'd have myself a better horse and wouldn't need to use Gray for this. If I lost . . . well, you already *have* a better horse, so you wouldn't work Gray hard, either. No matter what, Gray makes out."

"What addled logic!" The stranger dragged his own helm off, revealing cropped brown hair, dark with dampness and flattened by the cap's padding. "Not the first time someone's dropped you on your head, is it?"

"You've won my horse," Titch answered angrily. "You don't need to insult me into the bargain."

The man smiled. The teeth splitting his ruddy face were astonishingly white. And numerous. Accident and disease had by some miracle passed them by, every one. "I don't *want* your horse. I don't need him, and I refuse to put myself out finding fodder for an elderly plowhorse, just to salve what's left of *your* pride. All I truly desire from anyone hereabouts is to learn where a fellow might buy a decent meal—not that you look as if you'd know."

He didn't want Gray? The reversals of his fortunes were making Titch's head spin quite as much as ever his fall had. He hadn't lost Gray after all? He struggled to keep his focus on the conversation, to make a proper answer.

"I know," he said. "And they'll serve *you*, never fear." Titch decided to concede the difference in status as well as ability. "I'll show you, sir." He got to his feet, suppressing a moan, and limped two steps toward Gray, pausing to scoop up his helm and his sword along the way.

The stranger regarded his progress with sympathy. "The resilience of youth! If I'd come off like that, I'd be in pieces! Or are you just used to it?"

Titch swallowed the insult. With his gullet already well stretched by his pride going down, 'twas nothing. He said the same—nothing—but took hold of Gray's bridle.

The two men studied one another—the one tall and quite wide enough to balance his height, with the broad regular features in his squarish face arranged well enough to please the minstrels. The other—the battered one—nowhere near tall but solidly built about the shoulders and sturdy everywhere else, his hands especially wide and strong. His face gave the contrary impression of narrowness, despite prominent cheekbones—Titch's chin was sharp, and his nose thrust forward like the beak of a hawk. His eyes being flecked with many colors, it was hard to choose one and let it take precedence over the others, so they were brown or gray or green, by turns and tricks of the light. He kept them narrowed anyway—respectful, but wary as a wild fox. He

had done the best he could to approximate a helm-cut by
slicing off any dark locks that poked out beneath his steel
cap's rim. The usual style was to shave the area, but that
was difficult to do for oneself, so Titch had compromised,
and fretted that the difference was obvious and marked him
as an amateur.

The knight was better barbered—carefully scissored short
in the front for unobscured vision, with the long hair at the
back bound neatly into a tail. As the breeze dried it, sun-
bleached glints appeared in the hair, gold against brown. He
smiled again, affable. "I am Gerein, of Kendillin," he said.

"Titch," the younger man volunteered, painfully aware
that he could claim nothing more by way of title. Not even
the name of the village, which belonged to another.

"Titch who—if our match is judged to be now honorably
concluded—knows the location of an inn?"

Titch nodded, as much to keep his sore neck from stiffening as anything else, he told himself.

The knight dazzled him with another smile. "Then lead
on! If the fare's passable, I'll stand you a meal. If it's bad,
I'll feed you my share, as well, for a punishment—so have
a care."

Titch inspected Gray's girth, to see whether he'd loosened
anything when he came out of the saddle. By the time he'd
finished, the bright-haired knight was already ahorse. Titch
sighed to himself over the loss of the black warhorse. But
then, he reminded himself, he'd stood to lose far more. And
if he had not, some gratitude was owed, whether to this
generous knight or to the gods. Gratitude—and shame. Gerein might intend it as a kindness, to allow Titch to keep
horse and weapons, but Titch saw it as a token of his own
worthlessness as compared against a true knight's chivalry.
The gesture, however well intentioned, stung. He headed
Gray toward the little village he had left but a few hours before and motioned silently for the knight to follow him.

There was room on the track for two horses to walk
abreast. The black caught Gray up, matched strides with
him. To do so without passing him, the stallion needed to
slow its own chosen pace a trifle, Titch suspected. He
frowned, jiggled his reins to make Gray take notice, gave a

squeeze of his calves so the old horse would pay more heed to how he carried himself. That was sense anyway—Gray was apt to stumble if Titch didn't keep him well on the bit, more balanced and engaged than Gray's laziness made natural for the horse. Titch kept his gaze fixed between the white ears ahead of him, refusing even a single covetous sidelong look at the ebony neck, the sculptured black head that nodded alongside Gray's.

"Are you bound for a tourney, sir?" he asked, trying to be polite on a safe subject.

"Tourney? Yes, I might be. Doesn't Wystan host one at the turn of the midwinter moon? I might set myself for that, if the prizes are good."

"A manned falcon, and sometimes a golden cup," Titch supplied. "Kendillin's not near here," he added, fishing.

"No," the knight agreed evenly. "It's in Esdragon. What the earth possessed you to challenge me for my horse?"

Obviously, he was taking the act for evidence of insanity. Titch swallowed that, too. His stomach was upset with him, overloaded. "I wanted him. He's a fine horse," Titch answered—an understatement of high degree.

Gerein chuckled. "So fine that he moved you to attempt suicide! Envy I can understand—it's the scope of your ambition that astounds me. Do all the young peasants hereabouts harbor such desires? Will there be one popping out from behind every tree?"

Titch set his jaw, counted silently to twelve before he answered. "I am no peasant. My father was a knight like you, and my mother came of an old Clandaran family." He was forced to be willing to be despised, but not for even less than he was, Titch resolved grimly.

"Are your parents aware you spend your days assaulting chance-met travelers? Sorry—" The knight lifted a gauntlet. "It *was* a fair challenge, if a foolish one. But do they know of this martial career of yours?"

"I'm sure they wish me the very best, and bend the gods' ears whenever they can, in the afterlife," Titch said stiffly. "My father died of wounds when I was ten, my mother in childbed six months later."

"So, it's an ambitious orphan!"

"My father was knighted," Titch repeated, feeling Gray's quick step as his clenching of the reins confused the gelding. "He gave his lord service in arms in return for his lands. I was too young to be invested with those lands when he died, and they went to another, but I have the right to offer service in return for holding lands of my own." He made his fingers relax, and Gray settled back into a more comfortable stride.

"You want to be a knight," Gerein said, pleased, as if he'd just worked out a difficult puzzle. He frowned. "A knight needs a warhorse. That's what a knight *is*—a warrior trained to fight on horseback."

"I *have* a horse," Titch answered testily. "My father couldn't give me lands, but he left me his horse and his sword."

"That was a horse five years ago," Gerein pointed out gently. "Now it's sentiment. I assume the sword is better preserved?"

"Gray's not *that* old!" Titch protested, trying with all his might to keep his hand *away* from his sword. "I didn't try for your horse because I thought Gray was worthless. I just—"

"You were tempted." Gerein ran his eye over the black's head, stretching before him. Most men would have patted the horse while they discussed it—Gerein kept his hands carefully still on his reins, which struck Titch as odd, though in what way odd he could not quite have said. "It's been known to happen."

Again, oddness, something amiss. Titch essayed another avenue of conversation. "If you didn't come purposely for Wystan's tourney, what did bring you this way, sir?"

"I'm looking for a woman," Gerein replied absently, still watching the stallion's ears. Most horses flick an ear back if their rider speaks. The black's ears stayed trained straight ahead.

"Well—" Titch hesitated, thinking hard and coming to a decision. "I could probably find you one of those, too—"

"Bless your kind heart." Gerein turned that smile on him once more. "A *particular* woman."

"Aren't they all? Sir?"

Gerein shook his head, sighed. "Do I take it you are yourself bound for this tourney of Wystan's?"

Titch nodded to affirm that, though his misadventure had taken the gloss off of setting out tournamentward that day. "If I want to take service, I need to make a name for myself. I can't do that here."

"You've exhausted the local supply of opponents?" the knight surmised. "Are you sure you're ready for others?"

Titch smiled, without humor, just stretching his lips a little. "Oh, yes. I have learned something from every man I've fought, every man I've watched fighting others, and there will be very few at the tourney who will have a horse like that one of yours. I can hold my own against anyone mounted on less." He said it quietly, because it was not knightly to brag and boast—but nonetheless it was true.

"I tender you my heartiest good wishes," Gerein said solemnly, tongue perhaps in his cheek. "Is that the inn?"

He had to ask, Titch supposed. There was no signboard, and a stranger couldn't be expected to know that the straggling hamlet boasted no other structure with a full second story. Smoke and steam were rising into the cool air— Katlin was outside boiling the laundry. She looked up, startled, when Gray clopped into the yard and stopped by habit as much as instruction.

"Change your mind about leaving?" She looked at the white horse, then at the sky. "He's not lame, and it's not raining—"

Titch waved her quiet as he dismounted. "I brought you a paying customer, Kat. What do you have over a fire besides the washing? He's hungry."

"Stew from the latest hen to quit laying. But it's nowhere ready," Kat answered, flustered. "There's the last from supper—" She put down the paddle and headed for the door.

Titch trailed her into the kitchen. "Don't be afraid to charge him dear," he whispered. "He's rich. Did you see the horse he's got under him?"

"And for the sake of such a horse, I should submit myself to robbery?" a voice inquired sweetly from over Titch's shoulder. Gerein had come in the door just behind him, lightfooted as a cat.

Katlin squealed and fled to the far side of the hearth, but Titch stood his ground, refusing even to flush with shame. "Her idea of charging you dear would be to ask *half* what you'd pay anywhere else. The beds are clean, the roof doesn't leak, and the food's decent."

"Best be—your stomach's most at risk." Gerein shifted his sky blue gaze to Katlin and illuminated her with a smile.

" 'Tis only rabbit pie," she faltered, looking hopelessly at Titch. "And it isn't even hot—"

Titch drew off a flagon of ale, and took it and Gerein to a small table near the warmth of the fire in the common room. "I'll put your horse up, sir," he offered.

"Leave him bridled," the knight ordered, sipping ale.

Titch raised a brow. "I was thinking to let him have a flake of hay." Was the man planning to ride out the instant he'd met his own needs, uncaring for his transportation? 'Twas too early in the day for either of them to look as they did, unless they'd been riding all night. And there was nowhere else they might have stopped the night before that.

"And you certainly may." Gerein made a face at the ale, which Titch knew the brew did not deserve. "But the bit stays in his mouth. He can eat around it."

"Hard to bridle, is he?" Titch hated to believe it, but no horse was without some fault. "I can get it back on him, never fear, sir. There's no horse comes in here doesn't have a vice or two."

"Leave the bit in. No more backchat. I don't particularly care what you're used to."

Titch nodded, perplexed but certainly clear enough as to his orders, and went out. He reminded himself he'd no right to take offense, as he led the black into the widest stall the inn's low-roofed stable boasted. There were no other tenants at that moment, Katlin's pied cow being out at whatever grass she could find. Gray walked to his accustomed place at the rear and waited. Titch pulled the gelding's tack off and stowed it, then turned to the stallion. Nothing had been said about the saddle, so he slipped the double girth and put the gear and its matching panniers onto a rack. His own gear began to get in his way, so he paused to divest himself of helm and knee-length, split-skirted jazerant. Inside the stable, his undertunic and trews were warm enough. He leaned the knight's spears in a corner and picked up a bit of rough sacking. Gray nickered to him expectantly.

"Guests first," Titch said, apologetic. He'd had to say it often enough. Katlin's inn was the nearest thing he could claim to a home—her widowed mother had taken him in after his own mother had died of a hard birth and lingering grief. That same winter had brought a persistant fever that had taken Kat's father and a score of others. The village folk left living had tended to clump together into new families that never quite took the place of the old. Titch worked as Kat's hostler in return for his and Gray's keep, whenever there were mounted travelers passing through. And while Gray was first in his own heart, Titch always had to leave him for last when it came to the matter of feeding and grooming. Anything else would have been thievery.

He rubbed the sacking over the sweat marks the saddle had left, and the black stallion leaned against his hands, relishing the massage. Still, Titch knew to watch himself. Stallions bit and struck, even when you were doing something they ought to enjoy. They meant nothing by it, usually, but it was a good idea to stand wary. You didn't get hurt that way. The saddle marks yielded slowly to his ministrations—Titch guessed it had been some time since the saddle was last removed. He searched carefully for galls and was pleased to find none, but obviously the horse had been ridden hard and probably long.

Esdragon. Titch knit his brow and struggled to call to mind where that land lay. Somewhere the other side of a wide reach of hilly forest. He'd never been into that country, which held few settlements and no tourneys, and he had no notion what lay beyond it except for overhearing the odd song or story in the common room. He turned his attention to the stallion's legs, rubbed away the mud that had dried on them below knees and hocks. The horse was very good about not trying to stomp him while he worked. It stood quietly, ears relaxed, head drooping. Under saddle it hadn't seemed so placid, but he wouldn't wonder if the beast was weary. The mud on its lower legs was of more than one color, as if it had traveled great distances over difficult country.

Gray, who hadn't been saddled long or ridden enough to work up a sweat even beneath his winter-shaggy coat, got a lick and a promise, and then Titch collected the hayfork and steeled himself for the trip to the mow. Just a dozen rungs up a sturdy wooden ladder, but he would sooner have fought unarmed against a dozen men or faced a dragon armed only with the same wooden fork. He clung to the side rails so tightly, it was all he could do to shift his feet to the next rung, and the rough wood marked his palms with an exact pattern of its grain. He felt no relief once he'd gained the top—sweat stood out all over his body while he gathered forkfuls of hay and pitched them down for distribution to the horses. No matter how wary he was of the edge, how far back he stayed from it, Titch was mortally certain he'd topple over.

He had no idea whence the paralyzing fear sprang. Being atop a tall horse didn't distress Titch, but any perch much loftier than that unavoidably did. He could go comfortably up the stairs of the inn, but he couldn't bear to look out a window once he attained the upper floor. When the roof needed patching, it had been Kat who'd done the work, and he'd gone green just trying to watch her. Maybe he'd taken a tumble out of a forgotten tree, or escaped his mother's eye and gone out on his own cottage roof when he was just a tot, so long ago he couldn't remember it—all Titch could be sure of was the dread, which he had to subdue each time the horses required fodder. He came back down the ladder with his eyes tight shut, holding his breath till his chest hurt.

Once he'd steadied himself, Titch edged toward the stallion's head with an armload of fragrant hay. This was when an ill-mannered stallion was apt to hurt him—reach back making a grab for the hay and slam him into the wall. Not even malice, just disregard. But the black did not stir beyond the flick of an ear as he spread the fodder in the manger before it. The dark eyes regarded him mildly. Titch held a hand out to be sniffed and blown upon, then scratched carefully beneath the bridle's wide cheekpiece. He could feel dried sweat in the hair, and knew from Gray's joy at having his own hairy jawbone rubbed that the matted hair itched. What was that foolishness about leaving the black bridled to eat? It would only take a moment to put the tack back on, and both horse and leather needed to be cleaned, which could not readily be done while one was touching the other.

Titch made a face and reached for the buckle that fastened the throatlatch.

"Don't even think about it!"

Titch jumped back. The wall stung his shoulder but held him up, as well. He slid along it to escape the stall, as the stallion kicked out furiously. Gerein stood scowling at him, and Titch glared right back.

"That's a good way to get a person killed!" he exclaimed hotly. "Startle a horse that way—"

"You'd have deserved it," the knight said, unyielding. "I told you to leave the bridle on him."

"So dirty tack can rub him raw?" Titch protested. "I don't understand you! A horse like that deserves—"

"You hear me, boy!" Gerein grabbed him by both shoulders, held him helpless against the stable's rough wall, jerked him once for emphasis. "That horse is demon-bred! Depend on it, a cold iron bit's all that keeps him safe to be around. Take it out of his mouth and he'll go berserk. Tear your throat out quick as thought, and be off breathing chimera-flame all the way to the horizon!"

Titch stared. Could the man be serious?

"Hear me!" A shake hard enough to rattle Titch's molars, just in case his attention was wandering. "That bit stays in his mouth—waking, sleeping, eating—"

As if to punctuate what Gerein had accused him of, the black slashed back with both heels again, with force enough to splinter the stall boards.

"You understand me?" The knight's eyes were blue as the edges of flames.

Slowly Titch nodded.

An Escape by Night

IT WOULD HAVE been warmer and more comfortable to sleep in the haymow, with sweet fodder for his pillow and his blankets—but of course Titch could do no such thing. He knew full well he'd never have been able to shut both eyes at once while he lay so far above the ground. Not shut them to sleep, anyway. If the night was particularly cold, Kat might coax him to sleep in the kitchen, in front of the banked fire. But there were other guests besides the knight, chapmen come in with a train of half a dozen mules and ponies, and the villagers whiling away a long winter's evening, so there'd be no peace in the kitchen until very late, and Titch was in no mood to endure an evening's wait for his sleep. He had sat awhile watching a bathed and barbered Gerein charm Kat, drying the boots he'd soaked fetching the hot bathwater up to the knight's room, wondering how long 'twould be ere strong ale coaxed forth the tale of his misadventure and humiliation for the general amusement of all and sundry. Finally, he chose to return to the stable's quiet and minimal comforts.

The barn was every bit as crowded as the common room, but the horses and mules went to sleep—or at least fed quietly—once the sun set. They didn't swill ale, and they didn't sing. They didn't quarrel loudly. They didn't make a joke of his future. There was no stall left empty for his bed, but there still remained a narrow space created by small eccentricities of masonry long ago that Titch could squeeze himself and a blanket into. It was already half filled with emptied grain sacks, which provided him with warm bedding, a sort of a mattress.

The refuge lay just back of the last two stalls on the left-hand side. Titch edged past Gray, slipping the horse a bit of woody carrot he'd brought from the kitchen, and clambered over the rough boards into the coffin-size gap betwixt the back of the stall and the outside wall. Feeling a draft, he stuffed a sack into the likeliest chink to shut out the cold and tried to settle himself for sleep.

He heard a snort from the stall next to Gray and thought he caught the glint of an eye in the dimness. He certainly heard the sound of teeth working on a bit. There was no mistaking that.

Sleep so close to a demon-bred horse? He would, Titch thought, and probably sleep sound, too, because he was worn out from caring for the last-minute influx of ponies and mules, and his bruises stopped hurting him when he stopped moving. If he lay still, snuggled in the warm sacking, he'd be out before he had leisure to wonder about demons and whether iron truly safeguarded one from them.

Titch wasn't sure what woke him—the horses stamping as they were disturbed, the sudden blast of chill air that told him the stable door was open, Gray's questioning whicker close at hand. He blinked, uncertain for an instant just where he was. He'd been dreaming of riding, among white-trunked trees, and there'd been something about a dark horse, a horse that breathed flame out its nostrils . . .

Then he heard the voices.

"There! The Warhorse!" An excited whisper.

"And where the Warhorse is, Gerein will be, also," another voice replied, pleased. "Go fetch Cullum and the others. If you get back by sunup, we can likely take him while he sleeps. I'll bide here, to keep a watch on him."

Titch's eyes stretched wide, though the effort was useless in the darkness. At the first realization that the voices were those of strangers, he'd suspected thieves, after the chapmen's goods. But very plainly, this was something else. Someone wanted to take the knight captive, by any means they could.

He heard the door close behind the man sent to fetch the reinforcements. Straining his ears, Titch could just make out the sound of hoofbeats, dwindling. Then he picked up the soft scrape of boots on the packed earth of the aisle. They came near, then halted. Titch held his breath. Reminded himself he couldn't be seen. He was hidden by more than darkness.

The boots went restlessly away again, back toward the door. Halted again. The pacing bothered the mules, which began to shift about in their places, rustling bedding, and Titch couldn't hear the footfalls any longer. Thinking furiously, he gathered one of the sacks into his hand, felt about till he found a length of twine among the others he was nestled in. Whatever was afoot, the men were about it in the dead of night, which said nothing pleasant about their motives. He needed to stop them, if he could, by warning their intended victim. It was no less than his duty, surely.

Gray was lying down, but the mules' fuss had plainly disturbed him, so that he would feel safer on his feet. Titch saw him raise his head, read the intention, and as the gelding heaved himself upward, Titch threw himself over the partition, into the stall alongside the horse. Then he waited silently for the footsteps to come close again, making sure of the sack and the twine while he waited.

All he could make out was a hulking shape against the dimness. Titch felt carefully for Gray's water pail, which was nearly empty. He waited till he was fairly certain the man in the aisle had his back to him, then jumped out and swung the wooden pail hard into the back of his head.

There was a dull ringing sound as the wood met the metal of a helmet. But the dark shape staggered from the blow and, when Titch followed up his attack by leaping on him, fell to the floor. Titch hit him a second time with the heavy pail, then pulled the sack over his head.

The man wasn't stunned—he began struggling at once—but Titch was able to truss him securely before he could overcome what must have been considerable surprise, and the sack muffled his protests. He bound the man's hands behind him with the cord, used the man's own belt to secure his booted ankles. Then Titch bundled his prisoner over the partition, dropped him facefirst into the sacking, and threw a large bag of turnips in on top of him. He heard a grunt and a rustle, but nothing more. Between the sack over his head and the others he'd been flung into, the man probably didn't have air enough for more of an outcry.

Titch made quickly for the kitchen door of the inn, then the dark stairs. No question that a personage such as the knight would have been given Katlin's best room, the one that overlooked the quiet back garden rather than the often-noisy yard. He'd been there well ahead of the chapmen, who must be the cause of the rafter-rattling snoring in the chamber Titch was passing. The little room next, tucked into the corner by the chimney, was Katlin's. And then the door Titch sought.

It was latched, but none of the inn's latches were much of a barrier to anyone familiar with them. Titch had the door open—silently—in a dozen heartbeats. He crept across the splintery floor, to the bed.

"Sir?"

He reached down to touch the knight's shoulder and found his wrist seized. There came a sleepy chuckle from the bed. "And just who's this? M'lady Innkeeper?"

"No," Titch hissed, offended and outraged for Kat's sake.

The grip tightened till his bones protested. Titch decided to state his business before they broke. "Sir, it's Titch. I was sleeping in the stable, and two men came in, looking for you."

Gerein loosed his wrist and leapt from the bed with the same nimbleness a fighting man used to spring to his saddle, an oath on his lips. "What men? Where are they now?" The first thing he made sure of was his sword, Titch noticed, and then the knight glanced at the door, which Titch had closed behind him.

"The only name I heard besides yours was Cullum," Titch confessed. "But he wasn't here. One of the men left to fetch him, and I tied the other one up."

"Good lad!" The knight smote him hard on the back and scooped up his shield with the remainder of the motion. "So they didn't touch the horse?"

Titch shook his head, forgetting the murkiness of the room. "No, sir. They recognized him, but that was all. I think they didn't want to start anything until the others could get here."

"I should think not! Hark, boy, can I get out that window there without breaking my neck?"

The kitchen roof lay just under it. Titch said so, trying not to think about the height of the drop from kitchen to ground. A man used to scaling battlements would likely think naught of it. "I'll go saddle your horse, while you arm yourself," he offered.

"Someone'll hear you," the knight protested, alarmed.

Titch shook his head again. "Only if I try going out the window, too," he said, and vanished silently back out the door.

Titch risked lighting the stable's lantern—he could have tacked Gray up by feel, but he wanted the use of his eyes before he tried to put someone else's gear on a demon-bred horse. Not that the stallion seemed much bothered at being disturbed. He made no protest about the saddle, nor the panniers that Titch lashed into place behind it, did not so much as stamp when Titch tightened the padded leather girth—though he did swish his tail once, almost lashing it. The prisoner behind the partition made more fuss, managing to thump his heels once on the wall before he accidentally worked himself into a less useful position and his struggles were muffled once again.

Titch lifted Gray's head away from the last stems of his hay and made him open his mouth for the bit. His common sense asserted itself as he lifted his saddle to the horse's back, though. The inner voice, which told him things a father or mother would have, spoke up. *You don't have to make this fellow's trouble yours, Titch.*

But if he did, surely this noble, knightly, and desperate Gerein would be grateful. And such gratitude might translate into a useful sponsorship at some future time. When else might such a chance wander his way?

A chance to get yourself killed, the voice observed. *Those men mean business. Nasty business.*

Which also meant the knight *would* be grateful for real help. And Titch could give it to him—he was the only one of any of them, pursuers or pursued, who knew the country well, who could find the swiftest, most secret ways to cross it. Anyway, a knight so foully set upon was entitled to any aid another fighting man could give him, even if it meant leaving home in the middle of the night . . .

The door opened a crack, and Gerein, armed, slipped in. He looked askance at the second saddled horse.

"I'll guide you," Titch said quickly. "And they're looking for a man riding alone, aren't they? So they may have a harder time tracking you if there are two of us." His heart exulted—this was a finer adventure than any tourney Wystan had ever hosted.

There was snow on the ground, but it was not fresh-fallen. Because it had lain long, it was very well marked in many places, and Titch kept to those obsessively, so long as they lay in the direction he wanted to take them. He *thought* he had made out the departing rider's trail, and deduced from it the way he'd been heading toward the rest of his company, so that he himself could guide Gerein another way entirely. After some while they were forced to take to more open country, but the fact that the snow was unmarked was a reassurance by then. They'd be leaving a trail, but no one would be on it for a long while, if the gods were kind—or sleeping.

The going got hilly, and they slowed to a walk to let the horses breathe easier for a space. The night air was very cold, but exercise had warmed them all—steam rose from Gray's neck, poured from Titch's mouth. When they crested the hill, they halted just past the ridge—so as not to show themselves against the sky—and surveyed their back-trail. The elevation wasn't sufficient to disturb Titch.

"It appears you were right about knowing the best ways to travel undetected," the knight said, pleased. "There's no sign of Cullum or his men."

"I don't know how far away he was," Titch pointed out. "The man who left said something about trying to be back by dawn, to catch you sleeping. They may not be back at the inn yet, or know you've left it." He peered at what ought to be the sunward sky. It was a shade paler than the sable of the rest of the reach overhead, closer to a dark blue than pure black.

"He should have a hard time picking up the trail, thanks to you." The knight took a feel of his reins, and the stallion snorted. Its coat looked an even deeper black than the sky. "Can you keep on guiding me so well?"

"I think so." Titch considered, secretly pleased the knight wasn't wasting time trying to send him back with naught but a word of thanks. "I don't know the country from here quite so well, but I've been over it. I'll do my best."

"I've no notion of it at all." The knight stared back the way they'd come. "Do you know where there's a manor called Faircam?"

Titch stretched one leg out straight in the stirrup, to ease a knee that was threatening to go stiff. Gray sighed and shifted his own weight. The dark-blue sky was going purple, and translucent. "Faircam? I've heard the name, I think. Near the sea, but not quite on it?"

"Are you trying to tell me we're nowhere near it?" The knight murmured an oath, something about swords and blood.

"We'll need to circle around," Titch said soothingly. "That's a good plan anyway—make straight for something, and men following you find ways to get there ahead of you."

The knight nodded grimly. "How far away are we?"

Titch reckoned it in his head. "Two days riding if we don't get more snow. Might not matter all that much if we *do*—we won't be on roads much." He gathered his reins and checked his direction. The sun was finally poking its golden head up over the distant purple horizon, so he could be more precise. "I take it this Cullum hasn't any idea you might be making for Faircam?"

The black stallion moved out beside Gray in an easy trot. "No. He's as much a stranger in these parts as I am," the knight said. "But I am acquainted with the Lady Ailin and have cause to believe she will shelter me."

Titch was stealing glances at the black stallion alongside him, and his heart was aching within his chest, as if he were being thrust through with a red-hot blade. The stallion trod the snow so lightly, he couldn't believe it was leaving tracks. If he looked back, there would be only a single set, Gray's. The stallion moved like a night breeze. To have such a horse—

"You have not asked why I should be running from Cullum."

Titch had supposed it none of his business, when he hadn't been busy coveting the horse. "Is he your enemy?" he guessed. It would be that, or Gerein's lord's enemy.

"Now. A week ago he was my friend. Or at least my sword-brother." The sun was up enough to throw their shadows before them, suddenly. "Before Cullum decided I was guilty of Olvan's death."

The ground turned rough, and both horses had to slow for safety, picking a way through wind-tattered weeds and frozen puddles.

"Olvan was a squire," Gerein went on. "And a close cousin of Cullum's. He was learning the arts of war by serving the duke's knights, as all squires do. Is it not so here in Clandara, as well?"

"Mostly," Titch agreed, leaving his own case out of it. There'd been no knight about for him to serve as a squire, but he knew how the system worked. "What happened to Olvan?"

"We were sparring with swords, a friendly bout. He hit me a stinging blow, and I was angry—I admit that. I hadn't even wanted to fight him, but he'd been pestering me, and I yielded to shut him up. I struck him back, and probably harder than was fair. Olvan wasn't a trained warrior yet, and I was. I had the advantage of reach and weight, not to mention skill. But I hit him with the flat of the blade, not the edge. He shouldn't have been hurt—though I was sure I'd knock him down. Only . . . his helm split with the blow, and he fell without a sound. I expected him to get up in a moment, but he never moved. We all went to him, to see what the trouble was, but he was dead. Just like that."

Titch remembered the fear in Gerein's voice after he'd been unhorsed. Small wonder he'd been concerned!

"It was an accident," Gerein went on. "A tragedy. But Cullum has sworn vengeance all the same."

"What about your friends? Won't they help you get justice?" Titch frowned. "What about your lord? Your duke? If it was an accident—"

"I haven't any friends left," Gerein said. "They were all Olvan's friends, you see. He was very well liked, and a lot of them were his kin, too. So I declined to submit myself to their mercy and fled Esdragon instead."

Bog of Betrayal

FAIRCAM'S TOWER WAS a lookout, not a defensive structure. It was tall, and thin as a finger, single rooms stacked one atop another like honeycakes till the topmost was of a height to let one have a view of the distant sea. The original purpose had been to spy Eral raiders landing, so the inhabitants might gather their goods and livestock and hide inland till the raid was over. Once the Eral came to stay, such needle towers were useless, offering protection to neither their inhabitants nor the straggle of buildings ranged about them.

Still, if times were peaceful, the place would be just as fair as its name implied. Every window would give a pretty view of either the soft hills or the blue sea, and the upper floors would be warm in the winter, escaping the damps of ground level, capturing the rising heat of the hearths below. Tapestries and carpets would soften the round stone walls, brighten dark winter days.

Faircam's lady brightened the heart no less. Ailin was tall and slender like her tower, and her hair was a shade paler than wheat ready for the reapers, while her eyes were the same blue as spring's shy violets. And she had welcomed Gerein with evident pleasure.

Music drifted from the tower, into the evening air. Sweet notes from pipes and strings wafted, reaching even so far as the stable where Titch was drowsily mending a frayed spot at the edge of Gray's saddle cloth. Not for him the festivities. Regret was tempered slightly by reality—the lighted windows showed the revelry to be taking place on one of the tower's higher floors, where he'd scarcely have been able to concentrate on the music. A lady as fair as Ailin

33

might have distracted him, but she was plainly Gerein's. No one had suggested he join them. He had been granted a plain supper in the kitchen, had watched while dainties were readied for the lady and her guest.

Well, 'twas only food and music. Titch reserved his envy for the knight's possession of the black stallion. The horse stood in a loose box next to a white-maned dapple gray palfrey, while Gray had been squeezed in hard by the milch cows. Gray was dozing, head adroop and resting a leg, and the palfrey was busy with her hay, but the black had abandoned his manger and put his head out over the door, his ears pricked as if he hearkened to the wandering notes of the music. He seemed to notice Titch watching him and tossed his head sharply, so that the fittings of the heavy bit jangled.

He might have been sculptured of ebony, rubbed to a high polish. The lines of his head seemed too refined to be formed by mortal flesh stretched over common bone. His eyes were dark as obsidian, so black that the pupils of them could not be distinguished at all. Sometimes Titch thought his own eyes must grow weary of the unrelieved darkness, for he'd have sworn he saw sparks of light within, bright brief reds and fleeting golds, flashes of sapphire and amethyst, swirls of emerald. But no horse had eyes like that. No creature he'd ever heard of did, save maybe dragons, which were said in songs to ensorcel with their gaze. He didn't know anyone who'd ever eyeballed a dragon and come back to sing about it.

Titch sighed. He ought not to be wasting his time in longing for the horse, mooning like a lovesick boy under a lady's window. He'd do far better to figure himself a quick route back to Wystan's lands. He'd missed a portion of the tourney, but there'd be some action still to be had, even as late as the next week. He'd done all that Gerein wanted of him—guided the knight to a safe haven. There probably wasn't any way he could contrive to stay on. He wasn't needed, and the shelter Faircam's lady would extend to a noble knight she was well acquainted with wouldn't stretch to include him unless Gerein requested it—and whyever should the man do that? He'd already granted Titch a boon, allowing him to keep his horse and arms even in defeat. That must content him, and if Titch needed a lesson in gratitude, he need only think how he'd fare horseless and weaponless. He might well have been Katlin's hostler for the rest of his days.

It would not be so very hard to leave Gerein, but abandoning the stallion was another matter. So long as it was under his eye, Titch might dream that some twist of fortune would yet bring it his way—if only because he wanted it so. If need and desire alone had been sufficient for magic—

The horse watched him as if it knew his thoughts. Watched intently, as if it either expected or desired some action from him. And the obsidian eyes still seemed to glitter with colors as impossible as his own hopes. Titch sighed and folded the mended blanket. All his yearning had achieved was four pricked fingers, when he'd had his eyes too much on the horse and too seldom on his needle.

No one at Faircam mistook Titch for quality, so he slept on the tower's lowest floor, among the grainsacks back behind the stair's last spiral. Pallets stuffed with dusty grasses and faded herbs made beds for the unwed men of the holding—cramped enough without a guest thrown among them. Someone offered Titch a tankard of ale, and he drank it straight down, striving for sleep's quick oblivion.

Snores kept disturbing him all the same, so the voices pierced what was at best a light doze.

"Ailin, hush now—"

"*Hush?* I will *not* hush! And you shall not tarry here one instant longer, knave! *Hide you,* you beg me—on your knees you pled, as if this were one of my minstrel's lays—but only until the first moment you can desert me to go elsewhere! Well, go! *Begone!*"

"Sweetling, you surely know I cannot stay the winter here—"

"You shall not stay one instant longer than it takes for you to climb onto your horse! And no more of your honeyed words! They are false as lead, false as every word you have spoken to me since you came here, since we *met*, forsooth! Begone, before I have the dogs set on you—" The narrow tower made the voices echo.

"You mistake me, Ailin. I would stay forever with you if I but could. 'Tis unsafe here, for you, too, if I stay. I must get a reach of sea between me and Esdragon—"

"You only wanted to be safe while you had your pleasure of me, you wretch! And having taken it, you go now seeking other pleasures elsewhere! Well, I am not the lovesick fool you once knew! If Cullum and his men ride this way, I will set them on your track, quick as the wind! And then I will ask a boon of them—that they bring your black heart to me, Gerein—if they can find it!"

All the snores roundabout had ceased—Titch was not the only one wakened by the row. He was, though, the only one to get to his feet. He scrambled into his boots, turning an ear to the footsteps coming erratically down the stairs. They paused once, and there was a crash as something was hurled down from above. From the tinkle of falling glass, it might have been a hand mirror. The tempo of the footsteps quickened markedly.

Gerein reached the end of the stair and stepped onto the rough boards, with a curse as a splinter jabbed his bare foot. From above came sobs, and he looked up once—only to dodge hastily as his left boot was hurled down at him. He stepped out into view long enough to lure the right boot, as well, then flinched back and bumped into Titch. "Is that you, boy?"

"It is, sir," Titch said.

"I think we're leaving now, if you'd be so good as to saddle the horses. And we won't want to waste any time."

"No," Titch agreed soberly.

"I told the lady I would not be staying. Other vital business, her own safety . . . she took it ill."

"Yes," Titch agreed again, straight-faced.

The way the land rolled, if they were unlucky, the pursuit could be very close and they'd never know it. Perchance the riders wouldn't visit Faircam, but even if they did not, it hardly improved matters. The snow was a great trouble—wherever they went, they left a trail that could easily be read. The two horsemen paused, resting their mounts and trying to draft a plan that was not all flight and forced re-action.

"The thing is, Heil is too near to Esdragon. I thought I might be safe with Ailin, but only till I found a ship. How well do you know Josten?" Gerein fussed with his cloak, to thwart the wind seeking passage to chill his skin.

Titch considered. "Only what I've heard, and that's not much. It's an Eral kingdom now, of course."

"So's all of Clandara. And perchance the local king won't take kindly to a band of strange men riding in to drag another man out. Usurping his authority. Cullum might have to turn back," the knight finished with satisfaction.

"Do you think she'll really send him after you, sir?" Titch took another look back at their too-visible progress through the snow.

"I fear she will—especially if he should arrive hard on our heels. Ailin's temper is a match for her looks, and she feels I wronged her."

Ladies were high and baffling matters. Titch supposed he should have listened better to *all* the minstrels' songs, not just the ballads of battles and combats. The knight seemed accepting, but surely the lady was wrong to act so—he had come to her for protection, had done her no harm or discourtesy . . .

"Josten it shall be. What's the country between like? Settled or wild?"

"Lots of it's forested," Titch replied, struggling to remember specifics out of things heard too long before. "Not many folk about in the forests, especially in the deep of winter. There's only one road crosses the woodland, but if you stay off that you might not meet a soul."

"So I'd just vanish, confounding Cullum as if I'd ridden into one of those haunted rings of hanging stones the songs tell of? That appeals. Of course, he might still track me, especially if my trail's the lone one. Cursed snow. Have to find a way round that." Gerein stared at the white landscape, waiting for inspiration. The sky was grayish, holding the promise of more snowfall, but it might not cover his tracks in time. He wouldn't be able to depend on it. Toward the horizon, a dark smudge showed where the forest began. It was a rather obvious choice for cover, even without the snow advertising an entrance.

"I think I've an idea," the knight said. "But only if you agree."

"If *I* agree?" Titch frowned. What difference did his opinion make?

"I want you to lay a false trail in open country, while I go through the forest to Josten."

Titch was astonished. It was one thing to guide a fugitive. It was quite another to deliberately take the whole pursuit onto his own shoulders. "And just why should I want to do that? What happens if they catch *me*?"

"Most likely nothing," Gerein assured him. "They'd just have been following the wrong traveler. They may question you, but so far from the duke's authority, they'll dare no more. They'll be frustrated. But I shall be very grateful to you."

"*How* grateful?" Titch refused to drop his suspicion.

The left corner of Gerein's mouth lifted. "Let's just leave it that I know what you want."

Titch's eyes flicked to the black horse. He couldn't help himself. The wind lifted the long mane like a sheet of dark flame. The stallion was restless with being made to stand still and pawed fiercely at the snow, bending his neck and tucking his head, seeking relief from the bit's pressure.

Titch nodded his own head. Folly or not, risk or not, he couldn't lose such a chance, not and live with himself after. "All right. Where will we settle up?"

"If Cullum should overtake you, I'd rather you didn't know anything too specific." Gerein frowned, thinking. "Let's say that if you ask at the tourneys in Josten, you'll come to me quick enough."

It also made it easy for Gerein to dodge making payment as he was dodging the unseen Cullum and his horsemen. *But only if I let him,* Titch told himself. And if the horse was to be his payment, he'd search out Gerein if he'd gone to the end of the earth. Depend on it. Such contingency plans were unworthy—a true knight's word was his bond, his honor was his very life.

And so the knight's steed was as good as his, Titch concluded cheerfully. All that separated him from his goal was a handful of days' time and a few leagues of snowy ground.

The river wound out of the hilly woodland, swift-flowing enough not to have frozen completely over. The horsemen parted company there. Gerein rode carefully up the riverbed, the stallion picking its way nimbly over gray gravel bars and between snow-dappled boulders, leaving no track that any creature save a fish could spy. Titch simply crossed the stream without any care except for Gray's footing and rode unconcernedly away across open, rolling ground. When he turned to look back, the black horse and his rider were just vanishing into the gloom of the winter forest, still following the winding streambed.

At about the same moment, it began to snow. Great flakes like goose feathers drifted down, soon lying in a thick layer along the crest of Gray's neck, the back of Titch's hands and forearms, his shoulders and his thighs. He put up his cloak's hood for protection as Gray plodded on into whiteness thick as any twilight.

It was no mere squall of snow—the storm went on softly for hours, at least until nightfall. Visibility was so poor, Titch wasn't quite sure when night formally descended—he had been riding slower and slower, hoping to come to something resembling shelter—and he halted only when Gray's stumbles suggested the gelding was too weary to be watching his feet any longer. They actually had been climbing just a trifle—a dark mass ahead resolved into bushes clinging to an outcropping of rock, which seemed sited to break the force of the freshening wind.

The flakes were smaller by then, more icy, but still as incessant. Skeins of them blew into his firelight, then vanished once more into the darkness. Gray put his tail to the wind, and Titch sat with his back to it, his head on his drawn-up knees, his cloak spread to make a very small tent over him. He was too chilled to sleep easily, too fearful he would never wake at all if he let slumber woo him. He warmed himself by spinning fantasies of what his life would be like when he owned the black stallion. He would, for one thing, be looked at with never less than the deepest respect. He'd be able to show off his skill at arms in the very highest levels of every tourney. He'd be noticed there. Kings would vie for his fighting skills and deed him some of the lands they held in their royal hands. And before that he'd have won such prizes: robes of silk, and snow-white falcons, golden plates and bejeweled cups . . .

Titch lifted his head, blinking sleep-sand from his eyes. The sky was milky, rose and gold at one edge. Gray was browsing industriously at the bare bushes, sending down secondhand showers of snow, but otherwise the fall had ceased. Impossible to tell how deep the accumulation was till he went out onto open ground, but there'd been a cubit at least, he guessed. Titch stirred the fire to life and cooked himself a little porridge out of pounded oats and melted snow.

Would the weather have thrown off his pursuit? Made his mission useless? That depended on how far back it was, Titch supposed—and if they'd ever gotten onto following him in the first place. He gave Gray a good feed of oats, then saddled him and set off, with many a backward glance.

At sun-high, Titch first suspected a dark speck on the far horizon. But he couldn't locate it when he looked back over his shoulder, and the sun glaring on the snow had him seeing specks everywhere. Horsemen *could* have been hidden by a far-off roll of the ground, after that first brief sighting. Or they might never have been there at all.

At least he was taking them—if he was taking anyone— far from the forest. And snow wouldn't settle so heavily in woodland. Gerein might be making better progress, never mind that he had a better horse for the task, too. Titch got down at intervals to check the wrapping he'd put on Gray's left foreleg to give the tendon some extra support—snow made the bandage heavy, wet and inclined to slip. Poor Gray had done a day's work before sun-high, but they dared not halt.

Finally they came to ground the wind had scoured well. Instead of reaching nearly to Gray's knees, the snow barely topped his shaggy pasterns. Titch let him walk easy awhile, then gave a gentle squeeze with his calves and an encouraging cluck with his tongue. Obediently Gray moved out into a heavy canter, the gait becoming smoother after a dozen strides.

Not too far, Titch silently promised the weary horse—but Gray could manage a league, tired as he was, and by then they might have reached some sort of shelter. Or a road. He hadn't been forbidden to use the roads, there'd just been none convenient. Maybe he'd chance on one of the tracks the chapmen used to travel town to town. With most of the snow blown off, those ought to be easy to see.

Gray was sweating. Titch could feel the heat coming off him, through blanket and saddle and his own heavy clothing. But the gelding's breathing was still reasonably unlabored, and they were headed downhill, though not precipitously. Titch glanced back again, though he knew there was small point to that—anything close enough to see at that moment would be *so* close he'd scarcely need his eyes. He'd hear it, smell it, horse-sweat and rusty armor.

He could not, though, shake the notion that sound was carrying over the wide open landscape. Could he truly hear the faint echo of other hoofbeats above Gray's? Had that been the cry of a hawk somewhere high in the sky—or the far-off shout of a huntsman sighting the quarry? There was nothing to be a landmark in any direction—not a tree, not a rock tall enough to poke out of the snow. The white ground seemed as boundless as the pale sky above, and Titch felt hopelessly exposed, like a flea caught on a bedsheet. And reassurances or not, he wasn't sure he *wanted* to be overtaken by anyone who had pursued Gerein so far. Vengeance with such a long arm had a heavy hand.

The sun was slightly veiled, but still the snow was bright to look upon. It tricked the eye—was that a darkness, as of woodland very far ahead of him? Or might it be a still more distant range of mountains? Was it shelter, or merely a deceptive bank of dark cloud? Gray loped onward, nearer to whatever it was with each leap, and Titch patted his steaming neck. He'd have a job to do getting the horse cooled and dried that night, that was sure. Trouble was, the air wasn't all that cold despite the snow, and warm temperatures coupled with a heavy coat and exercise meant a lot of sweat. Even if he went at a walk—

Just then, the most horrifying sound imaginable reached Titch's ears—the cracking of thin ice beneath the innocent white caul of snow. Gray lurched forward wildly, stumbling, sinking, tripping onto his nose. Titch went headlong over the horse's off shoulder, hurtling toward that treacherous whiteness.

He expected to land in cold water. Instead he encountered something that bore him up briefly before letting him sink into it, rather like a chilly featherbed. *Mud,* Titch realized, struggling to rise. It hadn't been too bad to fall into—he hadn't even had his wind knocked out of him, though his heart was racing. Now if only Gray was equally unharmed . . .

A frantic squeal, followed by loud splashes and ominous sucking sounds, told him that wouldn't be the case. The mud felt bottomless, but Titch could, if he used care, stand in it, balancing and sinking not much deeper, Gray, who weighed a great deal more and yet had legs as thin as most men's under him, could not copy his master. The horse's momentum had carried him the gods knew how far into the muck, and he had naturally struggled the first moment he realized his trouble. But struggle only forced his four hooves deeper into the yielding mud—by the time Titch gained his feet, the old gelding was mired to knees and hocks, white-eyed with the beginning of panic as he realized he was trapped.

Seeing him about to plunge uselessly again, Titch struggled to Gray's head, grasping a cheekpiece of the bridle with either hand. He held the gelding's head down, whispered calming words into the shaggy white ear. The horse's nostrils were red as gaping wounds, and great puffs of steam escaped them at too-frequent intervals. He trembled, almost ready to break out of Titch's control, to yield to panic.

"Steady, Gray. Trust me, now. I'll get you out," Titch pledged him. Only he'd no idea how to manage that. Titch was sinking himself, though with the slow inevitability of a nightmare. He felt icy fingers of either mud or water delving into his boots, for by then he was in a little over his knees. He didn't have a rope, and if he had, there was nothing near to tie it to anyway. Gray's next struggle might land him belly-deep, and there'd be no getting him out then. The horse was exhausted already. How much longer before he'd be unable to move at all? Or unwilling—weary, hopeless horses gave up even if they were entangled only in a poorly tied rope; he had seen it.

The thing to do was to find the bog's nearest edge. Titch rubbed Gray's jaw soothingly, still whispering reassurances to the horse. Slowly the brown eyes calmed, lost their rings of white. The nostrils gave up their flaming color. Titch fished about in the pack, offered a handful of grain. Gray nibbled it gratefully, to Titch's relief. Nothing much wrong with him if he'd eat. He was scared, he was tired, but he wasn't dying.

"All right. You just wait here now. Nothing silly—I'm not leaving you. I only want to see how we have to do this—" Titch dragged a few splashing steps away, seeking firm ground. Not ahead, that was sure. Unless this was merely a thin tongue of soggy ground along a watercourse, there was no use to that. And now that he looked—*really* looked—he could make out a sort of flatness ahead of them, with a few sticks poking out of its expanse. Reeds, those would be. He must be at the marshy edge of a pond. Maybe 'twas spring-fed, and he was in the worst, wettest spot. The snow cover was smooth and white and perfect, save where Gray had churned it and brought up black muck.

Sucking in his lip, Titch traced their course into disaster. Valiant creature that he was, Gray had stayed up for a dozen yards after that first lurch when the footing went bad. He hadn't fallen, which might have killed them both, but he'd gotten himself a long way into trouble. They had to maneuver him back to solid ground, and the nearest seemed to be that which they'd left a dozen yards back.

Trouble was, Titch would have to turn Gray before he could aim for it. There was no way he could make the old gelding leap and plunge *backward*. He wasn't certain a horse *could* do that, much less that Gray would attempt it under present conditions, even for the master he trusted.

He squelched back to his horse. Gray pricked his ears at him, certainly a heartening sign. "It'll be all right," Titch said, giving more pats. "Not easy, but you can do it. I'll be beside you, every step."

First thing, he undid the girths and took the saddle and packs to firm ground. They gave him something to aim for, and the less Gray had encumbering him, the better. Titch was amazed at how much deeper he himself sank under the gear's weight. And Gray weighed ever so much more. This wasn't going to be easy, not at all. He'd dealt with cast horses, colicked horses, downed cows, but a horse mired in a winter bog was a thousand times worse than any of those minor difficulties.

Pulling the reins over Gray's head, Titch positioned himself beside the gelding's right shoulder. The mud seemed fractionally less deep, ever so slightly less gluelike, to him on that side, better for the hardest part, which was turning the horse about. He clucked to Gray and pulled gently, firmly upon the reins. He couldn't drag the horse over, even if he had sufficient strength, even if the reins held under such abuse. The bit would tear Gray's mouth apart. But he could encourage . . .

Gray sighed, gathered himself, and heaved mightily. Titch scrambled to stay out of his way and to keep Gray moving in the direction he wanted, not by misunderstanding deeper into the bog. Gray dragged his hooves free for an instant and squealed when they sank once more. Titch hauled, cajoled, pleaded, called on any god that might be tarrying within earshot.

By the time they had turned about, the distance to solid ground had been halved, and Gray's flanks were heaving like a shaggy bellows. The mud came solidly up to his forearms and gaskins, was splashed even higher. Titch wiped sweat from his eyes, leaving mud in its place, and shifted to Gray's other shoulder. The horse was better used to being led from the left side, and looked for Titch to be there, not elsewhere. He patted Gray's wet shoulder, feeling the heat of exertion under the matted hair. He was streaming sweat himself, despite the cold air. "Once more," he panted. "You can do it. You *can!*"

Gray tried. He truly did. His quarters bunched, striving to lift his whole body free of the muck. He slipped, slithered, plunged, and lurched and gained another couple of yards. The pile of tack might as well have been on the horizon, it looked so far away when Titch took a bearing on it.

"Once more! You *can*, Gray!" Titch got behind him and tried to push, but that was no use—he couldn't get purchase himself, and Gray didn't want to move forward at all, much less without his master by his side. Titch struggled forward again, took up the reins. Gray's head was drooping. He didn't have that dull look in his eyes yet, but that dangerous stage wasn't far off. If he didn't make it to solid ground this time, he might not have strength enough for another try. Might lack the will to fight on.

Titch put his arms around the sweat-soaked neck, rubbed his face into the rough mane. "You're all I've got," he whispered. "I'm all *you've* got. It can't end here. Let's try again." Warm breath gusted down his back. Titch hugged the horse again. He could imagine how weary Gray was. He didn't actually have to imagine at all—he was falling-down weary himself. But he owed his old friend something—everything! It wasn't just that he didn't fancy a long walk in the snow on his own two legs—

"*Up!* Now, Gray! *Up!*" Titch backed away, holding tight to the reins and pulling for all he was worth. Gray's head stretched out, then his neck, as he resisted. The bit might cut his mouth—a small price to pay, if it saved his life. Merciless, Titch hauled harder, feeling his boots slipping. The reins were braided bullhide, made so as not to be easily cut in battle. They'd tear his hands off ere they broke. And he'd let them, ere he turned loose and let the bog have his Gray.

Gray heaved himself forward. His forehand lifted, came back to rest in the mud a pace nearer to safety. Titch whooped encouragement. Gray's hindquarters bunched for a final desperate effort, and Titch hauled with all his strength on the reins, trying to drag the horse free. And Gray was succeeding, pulling free of the muck with a loud

sucking sound, his hindquarters lifting him out with a valiant heave.

Titch's own feet were in deeper than they'd been yet—
the cold mud reached almost to his hips. Yet still his boots
were slipping as he realized that Gray was going to make
it *this* time, not the next. Danger shaded relief as he tried
to get clear of the horse so Gray wouldn't be forced to stop
for him, wouldn't get stuck all over again trying to avoid
trampling him. But the mud betrayed him, held him fast for
all he wanted to be moving frantically. It was like running
in place backward—and then Gray's upthrusting left knee
slammed solidly into his jaw. A shower of sparks filled
Titch's vision, then winked out into the night one by one.

The blow stunned him, flung him backward into the
muck, and he might easily have drowned as he lay there—
only, semiconscious and absolutely unstruggling, Titch simply floated limp on the mud's embracing surface, doing
nothing to sink himself. And when his wits began to come
slowly back, he did by instinct the only thing he could
manage at that point, which also chanced to be the *right*
tactic for such a situation—he crawled to safety. Had he
been able, and tried, to stand, he'd have been mired himself, maybe even sucked under as in cold quicksand. But
Titch was too dazed to think of seeking his feet, could at
best wriggle on his belly, like a snake. With his weight
spread out over the entire front of his body rather than the
narrow base of his two feet, he didn't sink more than a couple of inches. Titch got a generous mouthful of mud, but he
didn't drown. By the time his head had finally cleared a trifle, he was grasping the stems and roots of grass that his
fingers had found under the snow, and Gray's mud-crusted
legs were in his line of blurred sight.

Titch sighed, then pushed himself up onto his knees. After another moment, he lurched to his feet and made his
wobble-kneed way to Gray's side. "Not your fault," he said
huskily, taking the old horse's drooping head into his arms.
"I tried to get out of your way. Not your fault I couldn't do
it." His jaw hurt, and he carefully spat grit from his mouth.
The swamp tasted much the same way he'd have expected

a swamp to taste, if he'd ever had cause to think about it. Titch leaned down, using Gray's side for support, and began carefully examining the horse's legs.

Not a sign of the foreleg's supporting wrapping, of course. The bog had claimed that. Lucky that was all, they were. The leg felt hot—but most of Gray felt exactly the same way, from exertion. The heat of muscle strains wouldn't be distinguishable till later. Just now, all he could check for was blood, and with the mud plastering both of them, that was difficult enough to do. Still, near as Titch could tell, Gray seemed not to have sliced a leg on one of his own metal shoes or some bog-hidden root or stone. Titch whispered a heartfelt prayer to whatever god might be responsible for the miracle.

Gray was soaked all over, sweat and mud alike. So was his master. They'd both be stiff on the morrow. Therefore, they needed to be moving now, no matter how exhausted they were. It was cruel, but only sense. When the winter sun went down the chill temperature would drop yet further, and there was no sign of any shelter near. Also, Titch wanted to find his way around the bog's edge while there was light for doing so. He could lead Gray, that would be prudent, but he'd have to put the gear back on him first, because otherwise he'd be muddled enough to leave something behind. Unless he concentrated diligently, his head still spun enough to disconcert him, and he didn't entirely trust himself.

He was struggling with the mud-caked girths when the ground began to tremble, as much as its puddinglike consistency let it. And just as Gray let out a feeble whinny of challenge and greeting, six mounted men popped up on the white horizon. A banner the hue of fresh-spilled blood sported in the air above them, and light glinted sharply from metal caps and shirts of mail, not to mention spear points and shield bosses and sword hilts. Their faces were grim.

Had Titch been very quick, he could have been ahorse before they came up to him. But there was no point to that—even had Gray been recovered enough to run his best, there was nowhere to go. The bog and the pond lay at their backs, and the mounted men controlled all other directions, with their numbers. There was no escape.

And why would he be seeking escape? Titch asked himself. To run was to be chased. He was only a hapless traveler, Titch decided, nothing to these men. If he swore he had no knowledge of the person they surely sought, they could not prove otherwise. He had nothing of Gerein's save a promise.

The men drew rein a few paces distant. Two rode forward a little in advance, the others spread out to either side. Every eye was watchful, as if the place was well sited for an ambush instead of being wide-open marshland where nothing save bogs could be hidden.

"Told you Gerein wasn't stupid enough to ride so openly," a heavy-jawed man said conversationally. His nearest companion lifted a hand to silence him. The horses stamped and blew restlessly. They began to steam and snorted clouds of smoke from their nostrils, as well. Hard-ridden.

"Wish you'd come along earlier," Titch said into the silence. "I could have used some help. That's a bog," he went on helpfully, if unnecessarily, gesturing behind Gray's muddy tail at the churned mess of black mud and milk-white snow.

"Your companion should have been here to aid you," the leader suggested, a firm hand on the reins of his sweat-damp chestnut courser.

Titch frowned, glancing about. "Sir, I am alone here. And lost, to tell you the plain truth. If you could point me toward a road or a steading, I'd be most truly indebted . . ." He was beginning to sweat, because it had just occurred to him that one of the horsemen must be the one he'd left tied up in the inn's stable. Which of them? And had the man somehow got a look at him? Or heard enough of his voice to recognize it now?

The lead rider had slanting eyes, which were narrow with what could only be suspicion. A silver-pale beard managed to conceal most of the rest of his expression, at least to someone who didn't know him well. He looked angry,

Titch thought. Probably he was. His horse picked up on its rider's temper and refused to stand calmly.

"Where did you part company with Gerein?"

"Sir?" Titch strove to keep his voice empty of guilt, full of bafflement. He still felt dizzy, which was worrisome—he needed all his wits about him for this business.

"Gerein of Kendillin." The neat beard did not hide the pursing of the lips, which were wind-chapped. "He has done murder, and I am charged with taking him back to my duke so that justice may be carried out."

"What's that to me?" Titch asked, suitably baffled.

A flash of white in the pale beard. "You were seen with him at Faircam. You left the tower in his company rather hastily. And I am certain that our trailing *you* here instead of Gerein himself was no accident. Now, where is he bound?"

If he gave the knight up, he'd never get the black horse. "Sir, I don't know who you—"

One of the riders to the rear had the face of an angel. He also had a crossbow. There was a sharp twanging sound, and at what seemed to be the same instant something struck Titch in the left arm, so hard that he staggered back two steps and bumped into Gray's shoulder. He stared at his arm, wondering how he'd been struck, and saw the short bolt poking out front and back, midway between his shoulder and his elbow. It made absolutely no sense to him. Then pain caught up with surprise. Bleeding started, a hot trickle down the inside of his arm, under his leather sleeve and a couple of layers of wool and linen.

Before it had begun to drip off his fingertips to the snow, the leader had swung about in his saddle to glare at the crossbowman. "Olvan was my friend," the angel said, unrepentant. "And this wretch needs to think twice about lying to us."

It wasn't supposed to happen this way, Titch protested numbly to himself. *He said they wouldn't risk anything like this—*

Well, where was the risk, for them? a saner part of himself answered patiently. They were six to his one, and there was no one to stop them doing whatever they liked with him. He knew it was a mistake, but Titch whirled about and lunged for his stirrup. Ahorse, he'd at least have a chance—

Something smote him in the left hip and knocked him down. Gray squealed and plunged away from him as he fell. *Not into the bog again!* Titch tried to leap to his feet, but something slammed him flat to the snow again.

This time it must have been a boot that hit him, because there was a man attached to it. "Where is Gerein?" a voice barked into his left ear, which was uppermost.

They were dismounting one by one. Titch saw a lot of heavy boots cross his field of vision. One that didn't dealt him a vicious kick in his wounded leg, and he decided he'd be wise to tell them something. *Anything.* "He just hired me to show him the way to Faircam," he gasped. "I didn't know his name! I haven't seen him since we rode out of there—"

"He sent you this way to lead us on a false track!" the voice corrected him. "Where was he going?"

"He didn't say—" Titch gasped as another hard kick jarred his leg. His whole field of vision went scarlet. Was the bolt lodged in the bone, to hurt him so?

"Maybe not, but you can't have helped seeing which way he went. He used that river, didn't he? To hide his trail? Where does it go?"

"I don't know!" Titch tensed, awaiting another kick. "I'm a stranger here, I don't know where it goes," he gasped, wishing there was any chance they'd believe that simple truth.

"Did he go upstream or down?"

"Down," Titch answered resignedly, hoping that if he gave the information up with reluctance, it would be believed.

"He's got to be lying, Cullum!" the angel cried. "Downstream would mean—"

"Oh, he's lying, all right," the leader agreed, straightening. "Gerein will have known he could lose himself in the forest. And us."

Titch could see a lot of scarlet soaking into the churned snow. That would be his blood, so he preferred not to look at it—he fixed his eyes on the early evening sky as best he could. The wind unfurled the scarlet banner against clouds stained nearly the same hue. There was a device on the cloth—a black horse, running fast. This had all started with a black horse, Titch thought. How appropriate that it should finish with one as well.

"He's tricked us, misled us! It wasn't any accident, Cullum, except that we caught him! He should pay for his part."

"I don't want his death on my head, Harn. Nor should you. Leave him here. The gods can decide whether they want him in the afterlife or not. That's fair."

It took Titch awhile to sort that out, to realize that the discussion meant they'd leave him there to bleed to death, or freeze. And be a long way off themselves ere either happened, in case his ghost was vengeful, in case he proved more powerful dead than alive. He heard the creakings of stirrup leathers stretching as the men remounted their tired horses, the jingling of bits, then the pounding of hooves. *So all he had to do was lay low for a bit*—hope flared bright. He doubted he was hurt too badly to gain safety, blood loss or not—

All at once, snow showered over him, and there were hooves nearer than Titch felt was safe. Alarmed, he tried to crawl out of their path, though there was no safety if the rider *intended* to trample him, only the briefest of postponements, because Titch couldn't dodge all that well, crawling on his belly. Something swung down at him. He thought 'twas a sword after all, but the length was impossible, so he knew it had to be a spear. *Dodge the thrust, grab the pole*—maybe he could yank the horseman right out of his saddle . . .

The spear's butt-end swung easily past his outstretched fingers and fetched Titch a solid blow just over his left ear. No sparks now. Only darkness, crashing down on him.

A Winter for Icicles

WALKING IN DEEP snow was easier if you could walk in footprints, easiest of all if you could walk your very own tracks, which were comfortably spaced for your own stride and no one else's.

Wren's most recent trail had been covered by the past night's snowfall, showing only as small gray dimplings in the gently rolling whiteness. She found her way into them, all the same—the walk to the spring for fresh water was a regular event, even in the depths of winter. She had more than one set of tracks to choose from. Only she had to take care, lest she stumble into the tracks her master, Galvin, had made on one of his rambles—*his* legs were very much longer than Wren's, and fitting herself into his tracks would leave her strained and winded. It was much the same with magic, Wren thought, pensive a moment. Galvin could cut his old garments down to fit her, but he could not shape all of his spells to her measure.

Overhead, Alinor was gliding effortlessly through a sky of endless, impossible blue. The peregrine falcon would have been hard to see, a mere speck aloft in the blue, but Wren did not need her eyes to know where her familiar hunted. The falcon had mounted high, plotting to surprise a heedless duck, which would never detect her as she stooped upon it. If Alinor did take a duck, that was meat enough for them all—and the falcon might manage it. The sun was unobscured and warm, the waterfowl would be astir, seeking open water and their own food, taking wing and perchance grown careless or desperate with the weather.

Sunshine promised icicles. Wren ran her tongue across her lips with anticipation. She loved the treat of licking those crystal wands to quench her thirst. It had been a month of magnificent icicles. There'd been plentiful snow, to lie on thatch and pine branch, then bright sun upon it, to form fantastic glittering downspikes like unicorn's horns—and burning cold of a night, to preserve what had accumulated by day so that it might continue growing next dawn. Sometimes the sun was too powerful and loosened them—then there would be a fall, a sliding and crashing as if a cheval glass had been smashed with a cymbal—but mostly the icicles waited Wren's pleasure, and she could pluck spears as long as her whole arm or as slender as her smallest finger, depending upon her mood.

Somewhere deep in her head and behind her eyes was the spot where Alinor's wild-hearted presence dwelt. Now it was registering startlement, something baffling to the peregrine. Dragging Wren out of her reverie. She shaded her eyes with one hand, sought the falcon with eye and mind.

"Alinor? What's the matter?" Wren asked, missing a footprint and stumbling to a halt in untracked snow.

Much too big to eat came the cryptic reply, a wind-tattered bit of a thought.

Had she found a heron? It was far too early, the big birds only returned with the spring. And had one remained behind in the autumn, like the half score of confused ducks, they'd have seen it long since, surely. What would a heron find to eat, with all the frogs sleeping the winter away deep in the mud, with all the fish sealed beneath ice and snow? That was why herons flew off to warmer climes . . .

Long legs, but too many of them. Come see, Alinor invited.

Wren squinted at the sky. Alinor might not be far off, as flight went, but for one on the ground, one who must contend with snow and in any case would not want to cross the unreliably frozen pond and its surrounding marsh, distances differed. Then she realized that Alinor was not far from the spot where the spring of sweet water fed the pond. She had been flying a wider course, but whatever she had seen with her keen dark eyes had set the falcon circling back. Wren settled the bucket yoke more comfortably on her narrow shoulders and quickened her pace, though still keeping to her tracks for ease.

Wren had no idea whether Alinor had ever seen a horse before, but she was certainly seeing one that morning. As Wren drew closer herself, she could see that the beast was old, and weary and maybe injured, from the way it stood with head adroop, resting one hind leg. It bore a high-cantled saddle and a set of leather panniers for baggage, a brace of spears and a big horseman's shield.

Alinor had been waiting on, circling high over her mistress' head as if expecting game to be flushed. Now Wren lifted her left arm, and the falcon spiraled down to land lightly upon her gloved fist. The beating of her wings startled the horse awake—it flung its big head up in fright, then calmed as it saw only the girl and the hunting bird confronting it. It snorted softly.

"Poor thing," Wren said soothingly. "Whyever are you out here all alone?"

He isn't, Alinor observed, cocking her head and hissing like a teakettle.

Wren had been looking at the trampled snow, trying to read its tale. She knew what it meant when rabbit tracks ceased at a windswept spot, with the marks of wing feathers at its edges. Alinor told her that story often enough. So did Alinor's wild kin. Sometimes the tale was rabbit sign mixed with fox tracks—and then only the fox pawprints, trotting casually away. Here were the tangled tracks of many horses—too many tracks to have been made by this one lone horse, Wren could tell that with a glance. She was thinking of walking out from the edge so she could discover where a single set went, or where it had come from, when she saw the body lying behind the horse. Alinor was right. The creature wasn't alone.

She shrugged off the yoke and went forward carefully. The white of the snow was dyed crimson as a sunset. Wren's heart hammered, pounded in her throat. She could only catch details, could not take in the whole, not all at once. So she saw one bit and then another, there and here— the short wicked crossbow quarrels poking up from the man's hip and upper arm, the way frost had left its kiss upon cloth and leather, and where that same leather plainly showed the print of a shod hoof. Trembling, she stooped for a closer look . . .

Her shadow shifted, and sunlight gleamed on metal—a dented helmet lying to one side, the link-mail sewn onto the long quilted coat the man wore. Wren tried to gasp, but no air came. The winter world slipped away, carried on a rush of black water. It slid endlessly by, and she had no idea what it signified—she was desperately afraid, but not of the water, Wren thought. The water was her friend, her ally. Always. It was her essence, according to her master's lore. The trouble was something else, something more, some evil that would not allow her to draw a single breath, that set her poor heart racing fit to burst itself. Armed men. An armored man, like the Swords in her master's precious pack of cards . . .

She couldn't see the man, or his armor. Just the roil of night-dark water, with a single star reflected in it. Were her eyes open? Closed? Had she gone mad? Been bespelled? Her terror was swelling like the flooded river, threatening to spill over its banks . . .

"Alinor!" Wren cried.

She felt the sharp comfort of her familiar's talons instantly, gripping her fist. The tips pricked through her heavy gauntlet, a tiny pain to pierce through fear. *Here,* the peregrine said, competent, reassuring, never having encountered anything she was not equal to.

Wren opened her eyes. The river was gone. Night was gone. The man still lay before her, on the red snow. Probably he was dead, nothing she need fear, merely a curiosity—

The moan made Wren stumble back, fear-frozen no more. Alinor took wing, *hek*king with alarm as she found her battle station, but her mistress held her ground after the one step. Wren dropped to her knees in the disturbed snow and stretched out a hand.

The man's face felt cold as snow, but when she slipped her ungloved fingers beneath the leather collar and found the angle of his jawbone, there was a contrasting warmth, and a pulse beating in the neck vein, just below the signpost of the bone. Now that she was so near and no longer consumed by her own fright, Wren could hear a faint whistling as air went in and out through his parted blue lips. "Alinor," she called urgently. "Fetch Galvin."

Alinor winged back to announce her mission fulfilled, but Wren would have known, anyway—the only rise of the white ground that could hide a man of Galvin's height from her view lay very near their cottage, and so he had come into sight already, a tall black heron-shape against the white, long-legged and picking a careful way.

"The cards have shown little but Swords these past two days," her master panted, halting beside her. "Today, nine blades for suffering and desolation, then ten of the same just after: ruin and disaster and a plea for charity to those in trouble." His long nose was red with cold, and the wrinkles about his dark eyes seemed deeper than usual.

"This wasn't swords," Wren pointed out. "Those are arrows."

"Swords signify strife," her master corrected her too-literal reading. He cherished his pack of cards as she did Alinor, kept them swaddled in a silken cloth and safe in a carven box with a lid only he could open, whenever they were not sliding through his hands like drops of water, laid down in the endless patterns that Galvin read as easily as Wren did rabbit tracks in the fresh snow.

"Who is he?"

"The cards can't give names," Galvin admonished.

Wren bowed her head. She knew that—Galvin had tried often enough to discover her own true name, her own lost past.

"They did warn me to expect him. I didn't understand, but I see it now—hindsight's a wonderful thing! The readings were all plain as smoke against a clear sky. I knew some change was coming—Swords are change, besides being weapons. Fool that I am, I thought 'twould be a winter storm, never a man. He's lain in the cold too long. If I'd been keeping a watch for him, he might have lived."

"Will he die?"

He didn't meet her eye, which told Wren more than her master thought it did.

"I'll know that better when we have him sheltered and warm," Galvin said. "Help me—"

They put the wounded man over his horse, the better to convey him the little distance through the snow. Wren was then entrusted with the horse's care, and by the time she had figured out how to unsaddle the creature, fed him and done everything else she could devise to make him comfortable, Galvin had done much the same for their other guest. He had stripped the man, for Wren had to detour round a puddle of melted snow and a heap of leather, metal, woolen cloth, and tall boots to get to the fireside. The crossbow bolts lay neatly on the hearthstone, near a bowl of pinkish water and some stained cloths.

The wounded man was arranged on his right side, propped so that his weight should not press on either wound. He lay motionless, and his color was no better than it had been, despite the near warmth of the fire and the ruddy light it washed him with. Galvin crouched beside him with a little pot of salve, exploring the man's matted hair with his long fingers, parting it this way and that as if he divided his cards for a reading.

"I hope you have had better fortune with the horse," Wren's master said, not needing to look up to know she was there. No magic about it—the cold air curling over the floor when she opened the door had alerted him, sure as ever a spread of his cards would have.

"Won't he get well?" Wren asked, shocked to her marrow at what she guessed to be his meaning. She could smell the powerful medicinal herbs steeping, could see the remains of bandage-making. And she had never supposed that her master could fail at any healing short of raising the dead. Well, an orphan field mouse might die, but not a *man*, who had come still living into his care.

"Neither wound ought to be taken for mortal," Galvin agreed abstractedly. "The bolt in the arm even missed the bone, for a particular wonder! The one in his rump might have kept him out of the saddle for his comfort's sake, no more than that. Yet whoever did this left him to die of it, no mistake. If he didn't quite bleed to death, then he'd freeze—"

"But he didn't!" Wren protested.

"No." Galvin's fingers hesitated, then stopped. "Ah. See this? This wouldn't be fatal, either, but it would surely immobilize. Whoever did *this* wanted to be sure this fellow wouldn't be able to get himself to any help for the other wounds." Wren's master guided her fingers to the bruised lump just above the man's ear. "Hit him on the head and then left him. Wonder why they hated him so much they couldn't just stab him through the heart and have done with it?" Galvin frowned fiercely. "Freezing's a slow death and not always a certain one. They didn't smash his skull, either—just stunned him and left him for the cold to finish."

"But you've tended him—"

"With every skill I may command," Galvin agreed. "None of these hurts by itself is even close to fatal, but taken together . . . perhaps in Kôvelir itself, he'd stand a chance, even now. I rather think not." He gave Wren a weary smile. "That's not vanity, child. Just simple reality. His life-force is all ebbed away."

Wren digested that information, dismissed it. Galvin was capable of any miracle but was self-effacing. "Who is he, master?" She peered at the bruised face. A kinsman wouldn't have recognized him without much effort. If he had kin.

"Some wandering soldier, by the look of it," Galvin judged. "With an enemy or two, evidently. He carried no messages. He doesn't seem to have been robbed. If I had to guess, I'd say whoever did this was after *him*, not his silver. Of course, all he had on him was a copper."

"Your wards keep bandits away!" Wren reminded him, alarmed that he should suggest robbers were even a faint possibility. It was an affront to his powers, and she did not allow such.

Galvin smiled again, sadly. "The *marsh* keeps such miscreants away, just as it does honest folk. The wards assist, of course, but the isolation and the insects really do the trick. It's why I settled here." He frowned. "I wonder if this incident means that someone's stupid enough to be shifting armies about in the dead of winter?"

"Alinor would see," Wren said, about to offer her familiar for an immediate reconnaissance. "She saw *him*, and he's only one man. Armies would be easier." From her high perch, Alinor agreed with a shrill cry.

"A falcon's long sight is useful, to be sure." Galvin scrubbed at his own eyes, then whispered a spell for directing the fire's smoke more surely up the chimney. "There's no danger. The cards would show an army, if one was near. I think this fellow's a stray."

"I'll fix supper now, sir," Wren offered, aware she was a stray herself. The short winter day was coming to an early end—clouds had swept in, and more snow had been falling as she came back from settling the horse in the byre that shared a wall with their living quarters. She regretted that Alinor had had no time for hunting—her master sounded troubled and sad, and duck stew would have been a most welcome treat in the cold evening. Instead there would be plain barley pudding, and roasted potatoes, perhaps a bit of bacon—the flitch was keeping well, so they ate the preserved meat sparingly rather than being forced to consume it at once ere it was lost to spoilage. Fresh meat would have been a pleasant change.

Galvin nodded absently and fetched down his thick-bound grimoire from its place on the overmantel. There might be an overlooked healing spell therein that would serve better than the chants and herbs he had plied already as he tended the man's immediate crisis. He brought a small fancywork box to the fireside, as well, and gently lifted out a silk-swaddled block—his divining cards.

What *was* to be done for a man—the stranger was barely that, Galvin reminded himself, as his beard was so far less of a discoloration on his jaw than the bruise that companioned it—who'd had most of his blood let out of him? Woundwort had done its task, staunched the fresh flow of blood from both breaches in his skin, but there was nothing to replace what this hapless fellow had lost before Wren found him. The cold of the previous night might perversely have kept him from bleeding to death quickly, but that was merely a postponement. The case was yet desperate.

Galvin's long fingers riffled through the bright cards, stroking as much as shuffling. The cards fluttered and sighed, reformed into a pack once more. He laid them down in a two-part pattern—first an even-armed cross, then a narrow wand standing alongside it. The instant the final card had been laid down, he lifted the first, to reveal its face.

'Twas Swords—of course. Five of them, odd numbers always betokening imbalance. The painted sky behind the blades was lurid with storm and fire. The wounded man's immediate past was just what Galvin would have expected—disaster. Was there some countering force? A cure to seek? He twitched over the next card, the one that was by custom laid out athwart the first, which countered it for good or ill.

It was a High Card, most unusually. There were far fewer of those, just one over twenty. Each of the four Houses alone had nearly that many under its command. But there it was—a starry sky with a white-clad maiden kneeling under it to draw water from a still pool, pouring it out freely at the same time from a ewer in her other hand. The card could betoken hope. Sometimes it meant health. Galvin flipped more cards, to see what else lay in proximity, what would shade the meaning of the reading.

It was all Swords. The fellow was a warrior, no question of that. Not a single Coin for merchant temperament, no Staves to indicate a bent for some occupation other than destruction. No Cups for a priestly calling.

But he read into the cards as much as he read *from* them, surely. That was the art and the danger. Whenever he read for Wren, he saw Swords in abundance there, and knew by them that the past she could not speak of had been composed of danger and betrayal, destruction and disaster. The Nine came up frequently, the card of inconsolable weeping. The Six, which showed a woman ferried over water to an uncertain destination, from a tempestuous past. Swords and water, Wren's readings always were.

The spread cards said the man was dying. Over and over, they repeated it, a handspan of barely differing ways. And the grimoire offered Galvin no flash of medicinal inspiration. He'd done considerable. There was no more to do, unfortunately, save to watch the tale's last moments.

Wren had discovered the horseman's sword among the man's gear. "You be careful with that," Galvin advised, glancing up. "Iron and magic mix uneasily. I knew a mage in Kôvelir couldn't so much as touch the stuff without being blistered—though most of us are fortunate enough to lack such high-bred sensitivity."

Wren laid down the sword obediently and came to his side. "That's why our cooking pots are all soft bronze?" She looked sidelong at the cards as he gathered them in, trying to see what he'd seen before he hid them from her gaze.

"*That's* so our firelighting spells don't scorch the food black, child. The knives are all brass so we won't cut off a hand trying to slice bread. Brass and bronze mend themselves at a wizard's word, which saves waiting for a tinker to wander by."

Wren went to the other side of the hearth and bent to the cooking, stirring a bronze pot thrice with a wooden spoon and whispering politely to the pudding within all the while. She fetched out the flat skillet and whistled softly to Alinor. There wasn't really room in the cottage for a falcon to spread her wings in flight, but a nimble bird could leave her roost, cross the room with a single beat of her long pinions, wheel on a wingtip and seize the hanging flitch of bacon as she turned, fetching the smoked meat to her mistress, dropping it into waiting hands as she returned to her lofty perch. Like all birds of prey, Alinor hated walking, since 'twould dull her weapons, the sharp talons on her front toes and the great hooked claw at the back. She was a creature of the air, and did her best service in that element.

Galvin delved into the spellbook again. He had begun the grimoire under his own master's tutelage. Perchance there was an early spell of healing hidden there, overlooked because he'd never yet had need for it. Not a need as dire as the one his patient now faced. He tried not to despair. The card had said hope. Therefore, hope existed.

He found nothing within the carved leather covers.

It seemed reprehensible to fail to keep a watch on the dying man, to deny his soul any last comfort either one of them might be able to give if he woke at the end. At least they might learn his name, which would aid in laying his ghost, should the fellow prove more powerful after his death than he had been in life. Galvin wanted to spare Wren the doleful chore—it was hardly meet duty for a girl of perhaps sixteen years. Yet Wren was a witch in the making, not some mercer's daughter with proprieties to be observed and a reputation to guard. She asked for a turn at watching, and he would not use false morality to deny her. Still, Galvin would have preferred to spare her the pain of watching this chance-come stranger die—when Wren rescued some small creature, whether fledgling swallow or infant hedgehog, she was pained if for any reason it did not thrive. And Galvin hated to witness her dry-eyed grieving, which to his mind was worse than any storm of tears.

He gave her the mid-of-night watch, reasoning that the wounded man would be most likely to yield up his spirit just before dawn, the hour when every creature on the earth seemed to be at its lowest ebb—though most were fortunate enough to be fast asleep and oblivious to their state. *He* intended to be awake by then and to have sent his apprentice to her bed. Galvin set her a task while she sat watch—to read and commit to heart a long section of his grimoire. Simply sitting in the near dark and staring at a dying man was a most unhealthy way to pass even part of a night.

Titch lay dreaming. At first all about him was featureless blackness, and he wondered tremblingly whether 'twas the gloom of night or the narrow dark of the grave. Then the darkness sprang back away from him, and he saw that what had filled his sight was the glossy hide of a black horse standing close before him. As he stared, swaying, the horse began to gallop and took his heart running with it, with a wrench too sweet to be pain.

There was nothing Titch wanted so much in all the world as to follow that horse—to catch it up, climb onto its back, make its speed his, let their wills be one. The dark hooves lifted and flashed like black diamonds, the mane and tail floated on the wind as lightly as the down of sable thistles. No cold marble could take the polish of its ebony hide. No wind was half so swift.

Titch chased the horse over unseen hills, pursued it across unglimpsed plains. But though the thunder of the horse's hooves echoed through him louder than his own heartbeat, he never could draw any nearer. Scheme as he might, yearn and labor and struggle, he never could achieve the horse.

Wren shifted her gaze from the close-written page. Her master was silent in his bed—it had not been Galvin's familiar breathing that distracted her from her studies. Feathers whisper-stirred across the room from the fireside as Alinor resettled her plumage. Firelight winked back from her eyes—aware that her mistress was troubled, Alinor stayed wakeful as well upon the broad shelf over the door, though her thoughts tasted of what she called the sleep-sky.

The man lying before the fire's warmth might have been Alinor's kin, by the beak of a nose dividing his face. It seemed to Wren that it jutted out even more sharply than it had—as if the rest of his face was drawing back from it, sharpening all the angles in the process. The skin was already pale as the bone beneath it, a little translucent.

Her master had ordered her to wake him instantly if the man took a turn for the worse, but Wren had no idea what a man would look like, dying. Save for Galvin, she never saw anyone alive. There were drawings in some of her master's many books displaying the signs by which certain diseases and distempers might be known, but those were only lines of ink on mellow ivory parchment, not living flesh but only representations. Smudges of colored chalk offered her nothing by which she could judge this stranger before their fire. His breathing was louder, and he was struggling to get each rasping breath, Wren thought. His lips looked dry, and she wet a cloth in cool water and wiped them carefully, though it did not seem to ease him.

The sight of him did not bring back that dark rushing now. She had no idea why, but suspected that either she was used to the man, or his warlike garb and weapons had been the real trouble. Even now, if she called to mind the instant she'd found him, a faint taste of that black panic wafted back, like a drop of cherry juice curling through a cup of clear water. Something in her obscured past had taught her that armed and armored men were dangerous. She didn't know what it was, though she could guess in a general sort of way. But this man was neither armed nor armored now, and she no longer feared him. Wren studied him, rather, intrigued almost exactly as she had been by his horse.

What she knew of men was her master, and this one was nothing like Galvin—even with him lying unconscious, Wren could tell that much. He was very much shorter, broader and thicker in his limbs. The difference was not an idle life—Galvin was lean and hard from days spent striding through the marsh, from chopping wood into hearth-handy chunks after he'd dragged a log half a league to the chopping block. His long arms felt hard as wood, nearly, and the stranger's felt just the same to Wren's curious fingers, solid as Alinor was beneath her deceiving coat of soft-looking feathers. The man's skin was pale from blood loss where it wasn't black from bruising, but he had not lost the muscles hard practice at something—swinging a sword?—had given him.

His pallor did conceal scars. It was her fingers found those, a ridged line on a forearm, the bump where a broken rib had knit. She hadn't discovered those on her own—Galvin had commented often as he labored over the man—but Wren understood what he'd meant, that the scars were the sort of things warriors got by way of their trade, the way a falcon's flight feathers were tattered, while a chicken's would not be.

Alinor's slate-blue feathers whispered once more, and she shuffled from one foot to the other. *Storm-grounded,* she said. *Or stupid enough to go after an eagle's meat.*

"Even crows can give a falcon a hard time, if they gang up on her," Wren admonished. "This wasn't a fair fight."

The man's eyelids twitched, like a sleeping dog. Wren rested a cautious hand on his forehead. She would have expected to find him warm, so near to the fire, but his skin was chill. Wren thought sickly of the new-hatched swallow she'd discovered wind-tumbled from its nest, the summer past. Still living, but just so cold to the touch. And though she had lapped it about with cattail down and shed feathers from their laying hens, the little bird had gone steadily colder and finally had stiffened. All at once, Wren knew beyond doubting hope that her master was right, that this stranger would go just the same way the swallow chick had, because too much of his life had leaked out of him in the cold of the previous night. His rescue had come, but too late. Whatever his story had been, he would never tell it to her.

Wren's raindrop-clear eyes clouded, taking into themselves the colors of wavecrests with the sun shining through. Alinor gave a rusty squeak of consternation. Unheeding, her mistress gazed down into the stranger's still white face and a single tear fell from each of her brimming eyes, to splash gently onto his swollen cheek.

Titch dreamed of rain.

At first 'twas only a fat drop or two, then a spatter, all at once a deluge. For an instant it seemed to him that there was no air at all to be breathed, but only water, and he thought he would certainly drown. He began struggling, but the most he could do was to shut his eyes against the water. He could still hear the rain pounding all around him, could feel it striking his exposed skin, trickling down beneath his clothing. It tickled, then itched. He squirmed, tried to turn his head. His eyes opened, and he saw her.

She had eyes the color of the sea and hair that made Titch think of smoke, though it was neither white nor gray, but some dark color he had no more precise name for. Her face was broad at the forehead and pointed at the chin, like a cat's, all the features very delicate. And she was weeping as if her heart had been shattered within her, ceaseless drops falling from those lovely eyes. That was what he'd taken for rain, then, her tears . . .

Titch reached out to her, wanting to offer comfort, to beg her not to despair, not to grieve—but a white fog swept his senses away, spinning helplessly.

Wren's mind was empty of any image save the gentle spreading of wind-ripples on the surface of a still pond. She heard Alinor utter a high-pitched, dismayed cry and turned her head automatically to see what the trouble was—she moved as one in a dream, stately, without the least haste.

Her gaze traveled even more slowly and drifted across the dying man.

His eyes were open.

Between the lashes, they were the color of sycamore bark in the rain, mottled green and brown. He blinked, and stared, and reached out one hand to her—awkward, the way he lay. Wren sat back, in confusion, and easily evaded his touch. The remarkable eyes closed, and he sighed, deep as if 'twas the last breath he ever hoped to draw.

Galvin woke just at dawn, furious at not being able to lay a spell of waking upon himself with anything like accuracy. When he saw Wren sitting staring sightlessly at the dead man, he cursed himself more roundly and scrambled to her side.

He touched her hand, and she startled awake with a little cry, her pale eyes going wide as Alinor's sky. "*Oh!* Master, I'm sorry, I didn't mean to sleep! Is he—"

Galvin found it fortuitous she had dozed, though it did not expiate his own guilt. He put his arms about Wren, blocking the man from her sight with his shoulder. He hadn't needed his cards to see this outcome. "Child, I told you there was no more we could do . . ." He fell silent. Behind him, someone was coughing weakly.

Incredulous, Galvin turned his head toward the hearth. The coughing fit intensified, and then the wounded man opened his left eye. He perhaps opened the right eye, as well, but Galvin could not determine that, since the fellow still lay prone, hiding the whole right side of his face.

It was rather obvious that their rescued guest was alive, at any rate. Wren was delighted. She hugged her master, then went shy of the stranger she'd been staring at for hours, and dodged behind Galvin to begin preparing food and brewing herbal tisanes. The man stared at her, as well, as if her existence mystified him.

"A dream," he whispered, as Galvin began to examine him. Difficult to understand his speech—his lips were dry as winter leaves.

"A dream?" Galvin loosened the bandage about the man's arm, took a peek beneath it. "I shouldn't wonder.

You were gravely hurt, and knocked on the head into the bargain. The mind will play all sorts of tricks, and nothing's what it seems—"

He broke off midsentence, his own mind too plainly playing tricks upon *him*. The wound the linen covered was no longer bleeding, which was an excellent outlook. More confoundingly, it was no longer *there*, save for some pink and plainly very newly grown skin. Galvin turned the blankets back and lifted the pad of cloth he had bound to the wound on the man's hip. He had a hard time figuring out just where the wound had been. That whitish circle. *Maybe*. Or that slight dimple in the skin.

The wizard settled the blankets back and stroked his bearded chin thoughtfully. He knew some useful healing spells, but not a one of them could answer for this cure. Wren joined him, cradling a steaming bowl.

"Master? Can he have some broth, since he's awake?"

"I don't see why he shouldn't," Galvin said, glad of the distraction. "Let's prop him first—no need for him to lie on his face now, and hard to get the spoon into his mouth with anything still on it."

While they shifted the man carefully about, the wizard continued his examination. The patient still had the shadow of a bruise over his ear, but the lump that had been under it was gone, vanished without a trace. Healed like the other hurts—however that had been. The discoloration on his jaw had gone entirely. He needed to shave, but otherwise his sharp features were unmarked.

Titch nodded off midway through his breakfast, after three or four delicious spoonfuls of the warm broth. He slept through the midday meal entirely, but by evening he was recovered enough to sit up, to ask and answer questions, to hold a spoon and feed himself.

"So, you were not acquainted with the men who attacked you?" The question came to the accompaniment of cards being dealt out, faint whispering slaps, soft rustles.

"No." Titch swallowed another spoonful of porridge. He couldn't see the patterns the cards made, but for a game it went curiously, with a new one commencing the instant the old pattern was completed.

"I've no way to be certain, of course, but it didn't appear to me that they'd robbed you." Galvin cocked an eyebrow at him, cards poised in his long fingers.

Titch was sure the wizard wanted an explanation. And being what he was, could doubtless get one even if Titch proved reluctant to give it. Courtesy wouldn't stand in the way of curiosity—or security. The man would be concerned to know of a danger near his home, which might be a danger to him as well as to his guest. "They didn't rob me," Titch volunteered willingly. "They weren't bandits. They were seeking a man I had been traveling with, and when I couldn't tell them where to find him, they were ... displeased."

"Displeased enough to shoot you in the back. *Twice*. These unknown men are most serious about their work." The wizard was regarding his cards, as if they told him what he could just as easily have read from Titch's circumstances.

"That's why I didn't tell them where the man was bound." Titch used a finger to pursue a last trace of honey-sweetened porridge around the rim of the bowl. "I didn't really expect them to shoot *me*, though," he admitted. It had been a serious misjudgment.

"Didn't think you were that involved?" Galvin chuckled, wrapping his cards in a cloth and laying them aside, then lighting a pipe with a neat little gesture and a flicker of flame. Seemingly right out of his bare fingertips.

"You're concerned you've gotten yourself involved by rescuing me?" Titch asked, frowning, trying not to be rattled by that flame trick. It could have been some sort of illusion. "You said they left me to die, and they'll be after—" Names had power, to wizards, so he hesitated, unwilling to give up Gerein's unless compelled. "That is, they won't still be anywhere around here," he finished, hoping his hesitation would be overlooked.

"I am relieved." Galvin sent three puffs of fragrant smoke toward the ceiling, regarded them lazily. "You'd seem to be correct—I see no horsemen for a dozen leagues."

Titch's eyes widened as he recognized the rings of smoke for what they actually were—a scrying device, granting the wizard far-sight without leaving the warmth of his fireside. He'd been right not to risk having his own truth teased out of him, Titch thought, nervous all the same. He knew of sorcerers only from tales and ballads, but there always seemed to be dangers involved in dealing with such folk, risks to dance wide of—and here he was, very much beholden to an obvious sorcerer, even if he'd had no choice in the matter. He'd been rescued, and healed—and what sort of a price was going to be asked of him, in return for all of that?

The wizard's brown eyes seemed to read every thought in his worried head, with a single amused glance. "You may be easy, Titch," he said, his tone merry, as well. "You are a guest here. You've nothing to fear."

Titch flushed. "I don't mean to be ungrateful, sir." And just how did one hide his thoughts from a wizard? Were his still being read, like those cards?

The wizard smiled—which could mean anything, if it couldn't be taken at face value. "But you've never had dealings with a wizard before?"

Titch shook his head. No harm to admit that—at least none he knew of.

"The rules for guests are no different than you'd find elsewhere." The smile spread to the brown eyes. Maybe it was genuine.

"But if the guest transgresses them, a sorcerer can change him into a toad," Titch said, still wary. This was a bog to him, just like the one outside.

Galvin laughed aloud. Crinkles of skin made his eyes vanish, like a conjuror's trick. "Wren, tell the lad! Does he need to fear being shape-shifted into a toad? Have I ever done such a thing to a guest of mine?"

"We've never had a guest before," Wren said, gathering crockery.

"And come summer, there are toads and frogs aplenty.

Couldn't really use more of them. So if I wanted to change him, 'twould need to be something else."

"You changed *me* from an otter, though," Wren offered, putting the supper dishes into a pan of soapy water and beginning to scrub at them.

Titch had taken his bowl to her, trying out his legs, which seemed quite as they ought to be, the left only a little sore from the arrow's going in and being taken out. When she spoke, his mouth dropped wide open, even though he tried to stop it for courtesy's sake.

"He pulled me out of his fish garth, actually," Wren elaborated. "Well, he pulled out an otter, but when he laid it on the bank, it turned into a girl. Me."

"So, you're—" The precise definition failed him. Titch decided all must not be right with his head yet. Wren plucked the bowl from his suddenly nerveless fingers. She looked so human, Titch thought. There was nothing of the beast about her, not even so charming and graceful a beast as an otter. Her eyes were palest gray, clear as rain, her teeth were tiny and not the least pointed, or suitable for the catching of river fish. She had no fur, only waving dark hair on her head, hanging down her back. She was nimble, certainly, but not quite the way an otter was in a stream . . .

"I'm Galvin's apprentice," she said, taking pity. "That's all I know. I don't remember anything from before then."

"I think you may have been an otter for rather a long time," her master said gently. "But you certainly didn't begin as one. Some danger threatened you, and you shape-shifted, possibly for the first time. It was probably occasioned by a great shock, and 'twas a greater shock yet that it happened at all, so of course you don't recall how you accomplished it. The trauma has hidden it, that's all. Don't fret, it's an easy skill to relearn. You've proved apt to all the rest of wizardry."

The girl didn't look as if she fretted. She finished with the crockery and refused his help at drying the bowls, stowing them safely away. Titch felt rather dazed and disoriented still. He had no idea whether the weakness stemmed from his barely healed injuries, the sorcerous healing process they must have used to make him well, or simply the confusion occasioned by chatting with folk who could call fire out of their fingertips, yet washed dishes with soapsuds in a homey basin before a flickering fire such as any cottager would have had.

Titch realized that he'd sat himself down quite near to the wizard, who, having taken up his cards once again, laid out more of the seemingly endless patterns and spoke companionably.

"All the cards tell of disaster and turmoil—what I already guess of Wren's past," the man said with a shrug, a finger tap upon an ivory wafer painted with the image of many swords. Nearly every card showed a blade, Titch noticed, before the cards were swept away into a pile and the pattern vanished like one of the smoke rings. "Swords and water. Your own was nearly as bad, but your situation was more obvious. Wren, whatever she was before she came here, was certainly no warrior."

The only water Titch saw at the moment was in the basin Wren set by the door. Removing the slops on a winter's night would admit far too much cold air for even wizard folk to tolerate, he supposed.

"Is she your . . ." Titch cast about, chose the option least likely to give instant offense. "Your wife?"

The wizard guffawed. "Perhaps I'd have done best to take an otter to wife at that! I'm sure one or two of my old friends in Kôvelir would say so! She's not my daughter, either, lad, but she's closer than that, and you should be more wary of what she's learned from me than of any husband's or father's wrath. Wren is my sole apprentice in the Arts Magical, and an apt pupil who betimes surpasses her master."

"Sir, I meant no offense—" Titch had to retreat verbally, there was no way of doing it physically. He wasn't up to a conversation with such serious potential, and cursed himself silently for starting it.

Wren knelt by her master. "Turn him into a frog, it's quicker and kinder than scaring him to death by inches." She grinned.

"All the frogs are frozen in the mud, this time of year," Galvin objected, mock-serious.

"Will you read for me, again?" Wren put her hand onto the wrapped cards. "Please? Maybe something's changed. We thought he'd die, and he didn't. That's a change. Maybe—"

The wizard was frowning, jovial no more. "Child, your hopes are raised so readily."

"Please." She ducked her head respectfully but persisted.

"A stranger's being here changes nothing," Galvin said sternly. "Except maybe for the stranger."

The stranger held his breath and strove to stay out of it. *"Please."*

The wizard sighed. "I cannot deny you. There's no reason to, 'twill cause you no harm. But it hurts, not to be able to help you more. I wish you'd show mercy." He shook his head. "All right. Put your hand on the pack, then cut it three times."

"Left hand, and widdershins," Wren added, and did as bidden, making three piles to the left. Her eyes were closed, her lips moving with silent words. A spell? A plea? A question for the cards?

Titch made to withdraw discreetly, making no more sound than a mouse, he thought.

"Stay," the wizard bade him courteously. "This season, the only warm spot in the room is by the hearth. You aren't in the way."

Titch sank back, his eyes troubled, rimmed with white like a scared horse's. Healed by its agency or not, he wasn't anxious to be so close to magic working. Whatever was said, he felt very much in the way, especially when the nearest line of cards all but touched his bare foot. He tucked his legs tighter and told himself 'twas for warmth.

The even-armed cross, with a long line to its right. And then the cards went over, one after another, revealing their painted faces.

"Surrounded by disaster," Galvin interrupted. "The past we guessed. Countered by the Wheel, which turns for us all and promises hope. I see loss, and a queen who was not a queen. A journey by water—perhaps that would be the otter. Child, you ought to look, too—one reads the cards as much with the heart as with the head, and you may take meaning from a clue that means naught to me."

Wren opened her eyes and stared fixedly at the bright pattern, full of blades and foreboding. "I know Swords mean change that has been or will be. But I only see bits—I can't make a story out of it all as you do."

"I cannot make a story out of this one, either." Galvin gathered the cards in tenderly. "No more than I could the first time I tried it for you. These are nearly the very same cards as in that first reading, Wren. Almost nothing has altered, and the cards that have changed have similar meanings. It's as I told you then—another's disaster brought you here, like a leaf carried on the current. One day, you may recall the tree you fell from, but the cards don't show it now. Not yet. Maybe just not."

Wren bent her head, accepting. Titch wondered if she might be weeping, but the face she lifted up a moment later was dry, composed.

Ill at ease, Titch decided to stretch his legs. He wandered across the cottage, careful to touch nothing, either by design or mischance. There wasn't much in the way of furniture, save one long table and the rolled sleeping pallets, but there were shelves aplenty nailed to the log walls, and those were close-crammed with jars and bulgy sacks and abandoned birds' nests and books. Titch could read—his mother had owned two volumes of chronicles and had taught him his letters as befitted the station she'd hoped he'd attain. He longed to open a volume, just to test his rusty skills, but books were precious things, and he would not venture to touch these unless invited. If girls had been otters and smoke rings mirrored the future, what might a spellbook do to him?

The mantelpiece supported more books, a horn of ink, a pot of dead rosemary, a crock of sourdough for baking. All of the windows were shuttered inside as well as out for a double barrier against the persistent cold. The shelf over the door—where it was colder—held two chunks of white rock crystal, a deer's fine-boned skull, and a stuffed falcon. A peregrine, by the dark feathers that made the head look as if it wore a helm with cheekpieces.

As Titch put his hand out to examine it, the stuffed bird's yellow-rimmed dark eyes snapped open, and it clashed its hooked beak at him. Titch jumped back and upset a three-legged stool, almost fell to the floor himself. He took another hasty heedless step as the peregrine beat the air with her wings and screamed, ready to launch herself at him.

"Manners, Alinor," Wren admonished, glancing up without much alarm.

Manners let him keep his poking fingers, the bird replied, unrepentant, and hissed like a serpent at Titch, since he could not follow the exchange save on Wren's side. With her wings extended, she seemed to fill the whole room.

Titch stepped farther away yet, bumping the wall, spreading his hands to protest his innocence of intent, or to ward her off from his face as he realized his retreat was cut off. "I'm sorry," he said earnestly. "I didn't mean to disturb her. I thought—" Titch broke off, not wanting to say he hadn't known she was alive, and Wren laughed at his confusion and the falcon's prank.

"Alinor is my familiar," Wren said. She lifted her bare fist, whistled softly, and the falcon soared across the room. Titch winced, but the talons on the large feet only dented the girl's skin, did not pierce it. Wren began to soothe the bird, stroking the feathers of the falcon's breast with a forefinger. Alinor's mien softened, her expression grew mild. The bird wore no leash, no jesses, nothing to help a falconer keep control of her, but Wren seemed not to know she needed any such things.

His eyes felt saucer-sized, but Titch strove to feign composure by displaying curiosity. "A wren is a falcon's mistress? How so?" he asked. He glanced uncertainly at Galvin as the peregrine gave herself a head-to-tail shake, then fanned her train, mewing softly at Wren all the while.

"*I* did not name Wren," the wizard protested mildly. "She named herself. When she came here, 'twas all she could tell me. Certainly the name is not descriptive of my apprentice—neither her shape nor her ability."

Titch nodded gravely. And just then, the wall at his back shivered with the unmistakable sound of a hoof striking wood. Titch's head jerked up. He stared at the logs, thinking that the wizard folk probably had a cow or two, while his heart pounded his ribs. "That's not—" His voice faltered, refused to shape his hope.

"That is your horse, I believe," Galvin supplied. "The lean-to's cramped, but it gets him out of the wind."

"You found him!"

"First, in fact," Wren said. "Alinor saw him, then you."

Titch sought for another door, his senses swimming with amazed relief. He'd supposed that Gray had followed instinct and the other horses, leaving him when his assailants did—he couldn't spy another door, so he tried the only one he'd seen, undaunted by cold, by the discourtesy of letting it in, by the small drift of snow that spilled over his bare feet as he tugged the panel open.

The dark confounded him, however. The snow was light enough, and there were stars pricking the blackness above it, but Titch had lost his bearings and he stood swaying till Wren and a hastily snatched blanket appeared at his side.

"He's over here," Wren said, draping the blanket over him. She led the way into the beast-shelter, which Gray shared with a dozen hens. The girl still had her falcon on her fist—the hens on their roosts blinked sleepily at the lantern light, then tucked heads hastily back under wings and hoped for the best, while Alinor glared scornfully at them, far beneath her huntress' dignity save in extremest need.

Titch paid no heed to either sort of bird. He had his arms about the gray gelding's neck, his face pressed into Gray's rough mane. Gray dribbled half-chewed oats down his back—Titch cared not. A knight without a horse wasn't a knight at all—just a foot soldier with airs—but Titch's relief ranged beyond that cynical measure. Tears sprang to his eyes, soaked into the tangled white mane. Gray was all that stood between an orphan and an utterly empty world.

"There's not much for him to eat, but I gave him a little grain," Wren said. "There's no hay—we don't have a cow, and the hens took most of the straw for their nests."

"He's fine," Titch assured her, wiping his face, struggling for his lost composure. "It's just . . . that's twice I've thought I'd lost him. He got mired in the bog."

"I know. I saw the tracks when I found you. And the mud on both of you."

There was still mud on Gray's belly, coating his legs save where it had flaked off from its own dried weight. "Oh, Gray," Titch said, and looked about for brushes, began with his fingers when he saw there was nothing else to hand. There could be cuts under that mud, festering, or the swelling of a bowed tendon—Gray rubbed his big head against Titch's back as he stooped, picking mud away.

"Aren't *your* feet cold?" Wren asked, laughing.

"No," Titch answered distractedly, still examining Gray's near foreleg.

"I mean, he's used to going barefoot in the snow. But *your* toes are turning blue."

Titch glanced down. "Oh." He was probably in danger of Gray's stepping on him, too, even if by accident. He might be too numb to feel it, but that would be a temporary blessing. "A knight must accustom himself to privation. Silken pavilions turn out to be few and far between outside of the ballads."

"You are a knight?" For some reason Wren shivered, and Alinor tightened her feathers with shared apprehension as she adjusted her balance, and squeezed with her talons to offer reassurance.

"Not yet," Titch confessed. "But I will be, one day. I have sworn it, on my father's sword and my own honor."

Wren mastered the shiver, trying not to remember how he'd looked and how she'd felt looking at him, when this stranger had been clad in odds and ends of metal plate, links of joined metal. There was no reason to be afraid of him now, as he stood shivering beside the sleeping hens, wrapped in a blanket she had mended with her own fingers. No reason to be afraid at all—was there? Why should she think there was?

"I'll be a knight," Titch said again. "I'll have lands to call my own, in return for the service I will do my liege." He sighed with relief—the foreleg was the diameter it ought to be, no hidden swelling from the tendon. He was past lucky—to be alive, to still have Gray, and to have him sound into the bargain, after his misadventure. "It's like a great ladder. Knights owe service to the lords and barons, the lords owe service to their king. All I have to do is catch the bottom rung and pull myself up."

Ought to put his boots on first, Alinor observed wickedly, and rattled her feathers.

Next morning, Titch companioned Wren on the trip to the spring, since four buckets of water fetched in a single trip meant the chance to do laundry as well as the cooking—a rare event at the mid of the winter. A service he could do her, Wren said cheekily, mimicking what he'd told her of knighthood. Titch was mildly surprised that Wren couldn't simply wish the clothes clean, but she informed him that so much magic was more bother than hauling water through the snow. Knowing less than little of wizard folk, Titch accepted her explanation and willingly shouldered a yoke of wooden buckets.

Wren's clothes, dirty or not, had an odd look to them—partly 'twas the utility of keeping warm by adding many layers of garments, each atop the last—but mostly he suspected that an otter might have arrived without clothing, and what Wren now wore were cut-down bits of her master's spare garments, most of them still rather too large for her delicate-looking frame. She was as much a creature of patches and parts as he was, Titch thought. Evidently magicking clothing to measure was more trouble than 'twas worth, too.

Alinor darted through the white edges of clouds far above them, mounted up and began to soar—or so Wren said. Titch couldn't make out the speck that the bird would be, and he had already noted the peregrine's utter lack of the usual falconry accouterments—bells and jesses to help the falconer locate and control a tamed bird of prey. Wren did not appear to carry any sort of lure to induce her keen-eyed bird to return to her fist from a sojourn upon the wind. Nor had Alinor been hooded as they set out, to keep her from launching too soon at prey. She was carried or allowed to fly free just as she chose, evidently. Titch had never seen the like.

"She's not belled," he finally observed, with an eye on

the apparently empty sky over the absolutely empty marsh-land, weary of being perplexed. "How do you know where she is?"

Wren regarded him with mild amazement. "I *know* where Alinor is. Always." As if, perhaps, she had better eyes than he.

"Well, but suppose she rakes off after a tiercel," Titch objected practically. "Or a stiff wind takes her too far away for her to hear you whistle her back. What will you do? You'll lose her." A tragedy that would be, to lose such a fine bird. Wren might not suspect that such happened to every falconer.

"I *know* where Alinor is," Wren answered patiently, not even glancing skyward as she spoke. "She's no manned hawk, that needs to be kept leashed or tied to a block when it's not being flown. Alinor's my familiar, Titch. Our hearts are joined. I can hear her. She can hear me. Distance doesn't matter."

"Oh," Titch said stupidly. "Magic, you mean?" Of course. Apparently keeping a falcon by magic *wasn't* too much trouble. He felt his face coloring.

Rabbit, Alinor interjected, pleased, somewhere very far away. Wren turned to look, then pointed so Titch could see. *"There!"*

Titch squinted, following the line of the girl's gloved finger. A dark speck was coming down out of the clouds like a falling star, scimitar wings folded. The height Alinor had reached made Titch's stomach clench. He had seen falcons hunt before, both tamed birds and wild, so he expected the high-speed stoop, the vertical dive that would slay the chosen prey in midair and send it tumbling earthward amid a scatter of feathers knocked loose by the impact. Only *this* falcon struck nothing, but continued diving earthward, faster and faster yet. Titch sucked in his breath. The bird could never be landing, not at that speed, and if he could see Alinor, he ought to be able to see her target. He couldn't.

At what must surely have been the final instant she could still imaginably do so, Alinor pulled out of her dive at last and skimmed just above the blinding snow. She hit the unsuspecting rabbit so hard that it went end over end, while the falcon rose sharply once more, then wheeled on a wingtip and returned to land delicately upon the still-twitching corpse.

Wren walked leisurely toward her, Titch trailing behind. Tufts of brown fur already littered the snow, and Alinor was plucking more loose with tugs of her wicked beak, pausing to wipe her weapon clean upon the crisp snow. She mantled possessively over her kill when she spied Titch, spreading her wings wide and then leaning back on her tail so that her sharp talons were completely free to threaten him. Titch, chastened, squatted down as Wren did and looked at her sidelong. No bird of prey liked humans standing over it, or staring—especially strangers.

Mine, the falcon said, unmollified, eyes deadly.

"Hush, Alinor," Wren coaxed. "He's not going to steal it. We'll let her eat a bit," she said aside to Titch. "She doesn't care much for rabbit, but she didn't find anything the last time she was out except you, and she's hungry."

Too hard to pluck, Alinor retorted scathingly, still glaring at Titch as she leaned over the rabbit once more.

Wren laughed, then shook her head as Titch looked a question at her. "She just said you weren't worth eating, never mind. She'll be in a better mood when she's fed, and there'll be plenty left to stew for the rest of us."

"I've never seen a long-wing falcon take prey on the ground," Titch said, still awed by the speed and control of that dive. Success and disaster had been separated by a hairsbreadth. "Goshawks, of course. It's what they're best at, but I thought falcons like this only killed in the air."

"Alinor will hunt anything." Wren used a little silver bodkin to slit open the carcass, and Alinor did not object. The task was a little beyond even her formidable beak, and her progress was too slow to suit her.

Wherever I choose, the falcon agreed smugly. She tore into the rabbit's body cavity and swallowed the organs down as fast as she could pull them out of the steaming rabbit, tipping her head back to let a kidney slide down her throat, then a long shred of liver. She paused, roused her feathers, then looked at her mistress with a touching mildness as she wiped her beak once more.

"Is that enough, dear?" Wren lifted the bird to her left fist and held the half-gutted rabbit out for Titch to take. As there was nothing at all to keep Alinor in her place on Wren's fist, he hesitated nervously, thinking of talons in his face. Wren shook her head, tossed the rabbit to him instead, and began to tickle Alinor's cheek feathers with a forefinger. The falcon closed her eyes, making soft mewing sounds to indicate her pleasure.

She looked docile as a pet canary, seen so. If one chose to ignore the sharp-hooked beak, the puissant talons with their needle-points stained crimson with rabbit's lifeblood. Talons that could pierce to the bone if Alinor chose, rather than balancing tenderly upon her mistress' wrist. Daylight brought out a subtle bloom of blue-gray on the slate-color feathers of her back and head, revealed a faint tinge of rose to the barred pale feathers of her breast. Every flight feather lay in its place, perfect, ready to take her to the air in an eyeblink, but Alinor sat relaxed, not wasting herself on nerves as some high-strung falcons did. Partly she'd just fed and was satisfied, but Titch suspected more to the tale. She was easy in human company, lacking the air of being only a wing-beat away from returning to the wild. He sensed Wren was right, that she needed no crude controls over a creature that was where it chose to be.

"How did you come by her?" he asked Wren. Had she been a tamed falcon blown downwind and lost to the falconer who'd so expertly manned her, rescued by Wren as he himself had been saved? He couldn't imagine Wren scaling a cliff to take down an eyass still in the down—no cliffs near anyway, that he could see. Haggards, wild-caught, never got this tame. Or was the bird some hapless human ensorcelled into falcon form? That would explain her intelligence—

"There was a storm, and next morning she was on the roof, watching the chickens," Wren said, fingers still pleasuring the falcon. "It was an awful storm. Alinor can't remember anything more of where she came from than *I* can. Just flying, she says, flying with the wind because she couldn't escape it. Flying in the dark for a long, long time, with no idea where she was."

"How did you tame her?" He'd never known the business done without hooding and constant forced contact with the falconer, carrying the bird everywhere for days, all places and all weathers, not allowing it sleep until it relented and fed from the man's hand. And still one had an excitable creature, flapping and screaming at the least upset, apt to fly away in a fury if it missed its prey.

Alinor opened an eye dark as the bottom of a well at midnight, within a ring of featherless skin yellow as butter. *Tame me?* She slowly flexed those talons, seemed to measure the distance to Titch's face.

"She's not exactly *tame*," Wren confessed, joggling the bird to distract her from her too-obvious plans, or at least spoil her aim. "Alinor is free, and here by her own choice."

I am not a horse or a stupid dog, to be leashed and mastered, Alinor declared. There might have been more, but just then a brace of ducks rose from the marsh, and the falcon bobbed her head once, then took wing in pursuit of a dinner she relished better than rabbit.

The rabbit met its destiny as stew. Titch skinned and cleaned it while Wren set water seething in a small bronze cauldron. When he brought her the readied chunks of meat, she was already busy chopping an onion. Potatoes and a few wrinkled carrots lay waiting their turn, alongside a handful of turnips already chopped. Winters were hard and food got scarce toward the end—Titch could see what an asset Alinor must be, since she was able to bring in fresh meat with her hunting. All the foundlings ought to contribute likewise, he thought.

Gray was outside, pawing diligently through the snow in quest of a buried grass, but his saddle still sat in the shed where Wren put the horse at night. Titch rummaged in the saddlebags until he located the journeybread he had carried away with him from Katlin's inn. The stuff was baked to last—though it had suffered a trifle from the traveling it had done with him. It wasn't moldy, though, so he offered it as his contribution to the evening meal.

The fumes from the onions stung Titch's eyes, but Wren chopped doggedly on, her own eyes dry. Some spell, Titch guessed, remembering Katlin's face running wet as she did that part of the cooking, and his own eyes streaming, too, when he lent his hand to it. Not so bad a thing, to be a wizard's apprentice. Surely there would be many a tiny, smoothing spell to ease one's way, even if the laundry still had to be done in the usual way.

He was asking Wren's master about routes deeper into Josten, stitching up the arrow holes in his jazerant, which had not healed like his flesh, when Wren's knife slipped on a carrot and sliced bone-deep into her left forefinger. Titch heard her gasp just as Alinor screamed, and they all sprang to her aid. The bleeding was quickly staunched with pressure, the wound was salved and a healing spell was said over it while the wizard wrapped it tight with a bit of linen. And though she was white-faced the whole while, Wren remained as dry-eyed as when she'd been peeling and chopping the pungent onion.

"She never weeps," Galvin said, when Titch hesitantly probed. "Not in the three years since she came to me. She knows sorrow, she feels pain—as you see—but she never sheds a tear, no more than Alinor does. It's nothing I've taught her, no." *Slap-slap* went the cards, but Galvin said nothing of whatever they revealed to his practiced eye.

Titch's dream rose up again before his eyes. Wren weeping, her eyes that bright green tinged with blue. It had merely been a dream, of course. Wren's eyes—red-rimmed just now, and shadowed under—were plain gray, though almost too pale to be called any color. And if she couldn't weep for her own finger, whyever should she have been crying over him, a stranger? Her dream-tears had turned into rain, which wasn't possible, either, no matter what he thought he remembered.

No, it had been a dream. And by their nature, most dreams made no sense by daylight. No more did this one. Best he wake, and be on his way.

Combat-at-Large

TITCH TOOK HIS leave of the wizard and his baffling apprentice the following morning. Galvin sketched him a map in the wind-smoothed snow, pointing out nearby boggy areas best avoided, a consideration for which Titch was grateful.

Other than that, he could pretty much follow his not-inconsiderable nose into Josten. He wasn't so much seeking a particular place as a particular person—and there was no way of knowing just where Gerein had actually gone, whatever the knight had said he'd intended. He might have found a need to adjust his plans.

Gerein wouldn't dispute the debt and the payment he owed Titch—but Titch was certain he'd have to find the knight to collect his due. Not likely the man would come searching for *him*, the incomparable black stallion's reins in his outstretched hand—he wouldn't expect the knight to ride back into danger just to repay a debt. There'd been an understanding that they'd meet once the pursuit had been given the slip, but the location had been left imprecise, in case that pursuit proved troublesome and persistant. The trouble Titch had found had delayed him overlong, and he thought Gerein of Kendillin might not be expecting to see Titch of Nowhere again.

Wren watched the young man riding away on his white horse, visible for a long way against the pure white snow and the pale morning sky. Her heart was troubled—more so than when one of the foundling swallows she rescued each summer essayed its first wobbly flight.

For one thing, the stranger had donned his gear first

thing, after spending the evening previous garnering advice on travel from her master. Unlike a just-fledged swallow, he seemed quite capable of looking after himself, and there was something about the way the metal-studded coat draped over those wide shoulders of his, the way the glittering steel cap changed the shape of his face beneath, that made him seem a complete stranger once more, as if he put on the person he had once been with the martial garb and masked entirely the rather gentle soul they had been learning to know by the firelight, over the evening meals. Wren went quite shy of him as he accoutered himself and could not force one word past her lips when he finally departed.

She could not leave off watching him, either, even when he'd gone too far for her sight of him to be clear, into Alinor's distance.

I could ask Alinor to watch him, Wren thought gladly. *She'd be able to follow him for leagues.*

But to what purpose? the falcon would want to know. And what would her mistress answer? That he frightened her? Then good that he was gone. That he troubled her heart, that something stirred in her breast when she looked at him, like a seed sprouting beneath the deep fall of snow, waiting for the spring sunlight? Would Alinor understand that? Wren didn't understand it herself.

It was a false feeling, anyway. It had its genesis in that Titch was a stranger, someone other than her master. She'd seen no other in the three years she could command memory of. He was unfamiliar and thereby fascinating. Having diagnosed that, Wren decided she could be free of the disquiet, discard the hopes she knew were foolish, merest drops of water falling from the tip of an icicle, vanished by sunfall, far less by springtide.

Why would he want me? she thought, watching a speck grow smaller yet. *What could I be to him? I don't even know who I am myself.*

Just at day's end, Titch and Gray came into a village. Titch asked after Wystan and was met with blank stares and head-scratchings, which did not very much surprise him. Wystan's holdings and his tournaments were doubtless a long distance off. Next day, as he overtook another traveler, he simply stated he was bound for a tourney, asked whether he'd far to go, and got very decent directions and a sense that he was far from the only warrior passing through with such an intent.

The roads got worse—heavy traffic had churned snow-covered earth into a pudding of thick mud. The road appeared to widen, as well—Titch was not the first horseman to try to pick himself a less quaggy way along one verge or the other. Titch was heartily thankful that he was not a carter, struggling to haul a heavy load through the muck. He saw some few of those, and acquired new oaths to add to his own small but choice store of profanity.

Clandaran fortresses taken over by Eral overlords tended to be located near the coast or upstream on navigable rivers, and built of local stone. Strongholds erected by the Eral themselves were newer, and most commonly were wooden buildings upon great mounds of packed earth, surrounded by ditches and bristling with palisades of timber. They looked crude and unlovely, but they were admirably defensible, from all Titch had heard and seen. They were certainly designed to be, and included all the most innovative designs in fortifications.

Stone walls were of course the ultimate objective, once a lord could afford them. Titch was not at all surprised to see the scaffolded gray walls crowning the eminence of the man-made earth mountain that rose up out of a straggle of huts, lean-tos, and tents ahead of him. Mud did not cease as one neared the fortress, though some effort had been made to subdue it with quantities of straw and sawdust. Gray plodded doggedly along, perhaps sensing that the scents and sounds of many horses meant they'd be stopping and he'd get a meal.

Titch hoped they both would. He had a few coins, funds enough for Gray's fodder and some sort of lodging for himself. He sighed inwardly at the sight of the tents—he'd won himself a canvas pavilion once and had needed soon to sell it. It would have been pleasant to have his own shelter, without need to spend scarce coin to get a roof over his head. Come to that, it would have been delightful to have a servant, someone to hold his horse and cook his food and arrange his lodging for him, but he might as well set his heart on the moon's rolling down out of the sky so that he might bear it for a shield.

The lord who'd begun the castle had made astute use of a bend of the river, letting its water enclose two sides of his domain with a natural moat, in addition to supplying his stronghold's drinking needs. Not that the river was to any degree unfordable—Titch could see horse-lines on the far side of it, and when he rode Gray through, the icy water did not rise more than halfway to the gelding's knees. But water in any form made siege and assault chancy things. Even a dry moat or a simple ditch had its uses.

The picketed horses turned out not to be from the castle at all, but rather they belonged to fighters come like him, for the tourney. Titch spied one or two black horses along the lines as he bargained for Gray's keep and parted with his coin, but not the particular one he sought. He sighed and left Gray contentedly munching, while he wandered the place empty-bellied to see whether he knew anyone there, to learn when the main combat-at-large would be held, what smaller contests were springing up beforehand, what would be worth his going after.

No formal fighting was taking place, since the hour was late and the light was going. Most of the men weren't even armed, and were either occupied with cooking their evening meal or were drinking idly while their servants fetched them their food. Titch strolled on through the enclave, and every face turned his way was a stranger's, though in a sense he knew them all by their shared occupation. As they knew him, newcomer though he was. Their speech was his—Eral with a liberal sprinkling of Clandaran terms, altering even as the name of the land had, Clandara into an Eral Calandra.

Then, unexpectedly, there was one face he *could* put a name to. The black stallion might or might not be thereabouts, but Gerein of Kendillin undeniably was.

The knight was sitting at his ease behind a cookfire, large as life, a mug clasped in his right hand, leaving the left free for the occasional descriptive gesture to punctuate his words. His small audience was in good humor, attending closely and lifting their own cups frequently. Somebody flung down a cloak and got out fat wooden dice. As the sun sank into the horizon, someone else started to sing. Titch judged the moment, then sidled close to Gerein.

"You have the most interesting friends," he said conversationally. "I hope this lot aren't so hasty as the last."

Gerein's head whipped toward him. The knight's right hand groped reflexively toward his dagger, sloshing his ale before it steadied. Annoyance the firelight hadn't quite masked shifted to possibly unfeigned delight. "*Titch!* I didn't expect to see you here—"

"Why not?" Titch raised an eyebrow inquiringly. "You said your friends wouldn't give me any trouble, not so far from their home country."

"*Did* they?" Gerein asked, apprehension showing through courtesy.

"They put two arrows into me," Titch answered flatly. "Lucky for you I couldn't tell them what they wanted to know: where they'd find *you*."

Gerein paled with shock, despite the ruddy firelight. "They *shot* you?" He glanced warily into the gathering darkness behind Titch's back, expecting treachery.

"They aren't done looking for you," Titch agreed. "But don't fret, I doubt they followed me here. They didn't expect, when they left me, that I'd be traveling anywhere except to the afterlife."

Gerein tugged at him, offering and unsubtly insisting that Titch join him on the log he was using for a seat, so their conversation could be a shade more private. Titch let himself be guided. With a broad grin, Gerein introduced him to his fireside companions. Someone gave Titch a cup of ale. Titch sipped, making a face and thinking that sour as it was, it was still better than anything he'd gotten from the last friends of Gerein's he'd met, while the knight spoke into his ear.

"You seem pretty hale for someone who claims to have been left for dead. Maybe you misunderstood."

"I was lucky enough to get to shelter," Titch disagreed, and forged ahead. "Where's my horse, Gerein?"

"Let's talk about that later, shall we?" Gerein refilled both their cups.

"I'd rather settle up now," Titch insisted pleasantly, holding the brimming cup untasted. Winter travel didn't leave one *that* thirsty. Gerein would have reasons other than friendship to want to see him drinking deep. "I've done a lot more on this business than either of us bargained for, and by the look of it, this is going to be a choice tourney. I could use a really good horse for it—"

"That's just the thing of it." Gerein tried unsuccessfully to top his cup again. "If I give him over to you now, you'll have Cullum on your track again the minute you ride out of here. It's far easier for him to track that horse than me. People remember seeing a stallion like that."

"And without a horse, you'd be stuck with foot combats at the tourney," Titch guessed shrewdly. "Lesser prizes."

"There's that, yes. I can do very well here, Titch. There are men here have no business going against such quality. Rich, and ripe for the plucking as fruit on the tree. I'll pay you what you've earned, just as soon as I've got the coin in my hand. Tomorrow, or next day for certain."

"I'd rather have the horse," Titch persisted.

Gerein's expression was irritated, till a hasty glance assured the knight they hadn't been overheard. "Look, I *never* said I'd give you my horse! I didn't swear, and I didn't give you my hand on it."

Titch sucked a breath in sharply. "What about your *word*? You said you knew what I wanted—"

"Well, you want a lot of things, don't you?" A white-toothed grin as he ticked off fingers before Titch's shocked gaze. "You want to make yourself a name. You want to be a landed knight—"

"None of that's in your gift, and you know it!" Titch tried to jump to his feet, and his fingers were aiming for his sword hilt.

Gerein held him down, though it meant spilling the overlooked cup of ale. "I can help you get it," he said matter-of-factly. "Why else did you tag along with me? Did you really think I'd offer to give you that horse the first time I got into a little trouble? I'm not that much a fool, and neither are you. I can set you up with combats you can win, and I can make sure Melcia's captains know your name. Better than a horse, even that stallion, believe you me."

"Melcia?" Titch stared at him, uncomprehending.

"She's the regent for this kingdom, till her son comes of age. Her father took Josten by the strength of his arm in proper Eral fashion, and the lady hasn't lost an arrow's-length of ground since it came to her. Formidable woman—you'd never believe the tales they tell. She's building herself a strong force of cavalry, and her captains are looking for good men, especially right now."

Titch shook his head. "Hiring an army's not military tenure. I'm not selling my sword for a couple of pieces of silver! I won't get what I want that way—nobody's knighting mercenaries out of the ranks!"

Gerein snorted. "You'd be surprised. And no one's saying you have to sell anything. That's up to you. But I'm in a position to help you, and you're in a position to need it, boy! Be sensible. And don't try holding me to something I didn't agree to. I'm grateful for your assistance, but there's no way I'm giving you my horse. I don't even know that Cullum ever saw you."

Titch swallowed his outrage, smiled, and began to describe each of the six riders in turn. He ticked the names he'd heard off one by one, the devices he'd seen painted on their shields, the colors of the horses they rode. He'd have done a herald proud. Then he recited what they'd pledged to do when they caught Gerein. "And all of them under a red banner, with a black horse running on it. Sound familiar at all?"

Gerein appeared to flush, but that might have been the firelight as much as shame. "All right! There is a debt. I admit to it. But I can't very well settle it now, unless you expect me to ride that ancient beast of yours into the fighting here."

Titch felt a chill. *That* had never been a part of the bargain, but there was probably no way he could stop Gerein if he took the old horse. And for Gray, that sort of bargain promised nothing good. Gerein would have small cause to care whether he lamed the faithful horse, used him up, or even got him killed outright. And Gray deserved better from his lifelong master than to be tossed away to that kind of fate. There were those who could do such things without the slightest qualm. Titch decided he wasn't one of them. He yielded the point, and Gerein grinned with relief when he saw it sketched on his face, illuminated in his slumped shoulders.

"Thank the gods, sense at last! You won't regret it, either." He clapped Titch hard on the shoulder. "I'll win enough to buy you any horse here. And you'll not do badly, either. We'll talk specifics later. Now, the combat-at-large falls day after next, but there'll be some sparring about tomorrow. Private stuff, wagers and forfeits. Let me advise you . . ."

Titch fought three sword bouts for forfeits of coin, afoot so as to spare Gray for the morrow, and won himself silver enough to cover his and his horse's expenses, with extra for the unforseen, though no wise sufficient for purchasing a destrier. Another match yielded him a pelerine-style gorget of interlocking mail, which he donned at once over his leather throat protector, and a pair of too-small gauntlets, which he sold on the spot. Gerein's advice had mostly been on matters Titch already understood well—that until he owned something they would want, none of the better fighters would bother contesting with him. No insult was meant—he simply wasn't worth their trouble. He had to wager his sword the first time, but after that he'd coin to risk instead, and Gerein's canny assessment of that first opponent had bolstered his own opinion, made Titch a shade less uneasy about risking his father's blade on the outcome. The knight was, to that extent, truly helpful to him.

Titch studied Gerein's sword bouts, wondering whether he'd misjudged the man's intentions, uncharitably wronged him in his heart. Gerein fought like an avenging angel yet always tendered the utmost courtesy toward his opponents. All his actions were chivalrous, his manners absolutely beyond reproach. He was, after all, being pursued by vengeful men on a spurious charge, and surely wishing to retain a horse whose fleetness could save him was not unreasonable, given the circumstances. And the man had never said—Titch had to admit that was true—had never said in exactly so many words that the black stallion would be the price of Titch's eager help. Titch had been deluded by his own desires, that was what had happened—nothing he'd done for Gerein equaled the horse's value, whatever he'd hoped.

Which no wise meant that Titch had ceased to covet the horse in question. Gerein had the stallion staked out well away from the other destriers, its hobbees linked to an iron chain that allowed it to graze whatever grass the persistent wind had uncovered, without straying. When the day's combats were ended, Titch went with the knight to take it additional fodder. Just looking at the stallion's topline without the masking of a saddle, seeing clear the strength of his loin-coupling was enough to take away what little breath Titch had left after the long trek beneath an armload of prickly hay. Imagining how a horse so made could collect itself, coiling those powerful loins to tuck its hindquarters well beneath itself; contemplating the power that would place in a mounted warrior's hands made his heartbeat erratic as the throbbing that carried faintly from the distant camp, where even the musicians were drunk. The stallion wasn't his. It might never be. But if there was any way, any way at all that it ever could be, Titch would not let himself shrink from it. It might be an unknightly thought. He didn't care. He wanted that horse.

The camp was astir ere the sun arose, as men armed themselves and readied weapons and steeds. In that way, the tourney was precisely the same as a war—if aught went amiss with equipment, there was nothing to be done about it save curse. One did what one could, one practiced diligently and prepared stringently—and then flung it all into the laps of the gods. The great combat was intended to be for sport, but the swords and spears used had sharp edges, and if deaths were uncommon, serious wounds were not. The affair would be rough, for all that no kingdom stood at risk.

Lots were drawn to choose up the sides. Titch had heard

of blood feuds carried out at tourneys, and he suspected the lots could be rigged, but fairness was the aim—or at least randomness. He drew a wood chip from the bowl when his turn came—it had a smear of red paint on its underside, like a splotch of blood. Hopefully not an omen. He stroked Gray's neck, then mounted.

The place of the combat-at-large was a broad river meadow, flat ground and not too soft owing to the chill weather. A sort of loge had been thrown up on one side, where the local gentry could watch in safety and such comfort as open-air seats afforded on a winter's day. Many a knight paraded himself up and down before the spectators, beneath wind-flaunted silk. Most of the horses were responding to bit and spur by producing the desired displays—prancing, rearing, tossing heads, and squealing in martial fury. The air was choked with banners and pennons. Trumpets called brassily to one another, echoing the stallions.

A sleek black head appeared to the left of Gray's, carried on a neck that arched like a drawn bow. Silken tassels danced from his bridle, jigging gaily in the wind. Gerein was as resplendent as his steed. He had won himself a new cloak the day before when his second opponent yielded to him, and the clear scarlet suited both the man and the horse that bore him.

"Which side did you get?" Titch asked, tugging at the strap which secured his helmet. He wished he'd had coin or time enough to see a smith about getting the dents set to rights—they were beyond his skill, and the nasal was pushed enough out of line to chafe him.

"The side of the right, of course," Gerein answered expansively. He opened his hand, and showed a scarlet-stained shaving of wood. "How could it be otherwise? Will you ride beside me? We will make a formidable team, and look out one for the other."

Titch shrugged agreement. It was every man for himself in a combat-at-large, but private alliances were not forbidden, no more than in a true war.

"Picked out your ransom yet?"

That was a worthy goal—to capture a man rich enough

to pay dear for his release. Titch scanned the opposing side as the marshals guided the combatants into two facing lines. Of course, he could simply spy out a man of approximately his own size and hope to get his gear, but a lot of the participants were wealthy enough to provide coin atop the spoils. A bad day at a tourney could bankrupt a small landholder, and often did, but the risk seldom kept them away from a good fight. Tourneying came second only to the hunt in the life of a warrior. A resource to exploit, for itinerant and perceptive jousters.

Titch had made his choice as soon as he saw how the mass of men had been divided, but he wasn't about to tempt fate by saying so. Gerein grinned at his silence, mistaking it for caution.

"You could take anyone here—save me. I've had my eyes open."

So had Titch. It was an extra weapon in one's hand, to observe wisely. So was keeping one's own counsel. "There are plenty of good fighters here," he said modestly.

The crowd of onlookers stirred as a figure garbed in scarlet ascended into the loge. There was another raucous blast from the trumpets, repeated thrice. The personage announced must be of some importance, Titch guessed.

"That's no less than Melcia, the queen regent," Gerein supplied. "She ought to take the field herself—I've heard tell she used to. They call her the Red Queen." He fingered his new cloak, which might gain him royal notice.

"*She* fought?" Eral women did that sometimes, and Melcia was the only child of a famed warrior. Titch had heard ballads to that effect just the evening past.

"They say her sword arm was the equal of any man's in her Guard. And that when the king she was wed to played her false and sported in another's bed, Melcia made war on him, defeated him in single combat—and then cut his head off."

They hadn't sung about *that*. Possibly it would have been considered impolite. Titch squinted at the red-clad figure. He was too far off to see much beyond that the lady seemed tall. She was lifting up a silver baton. At the signal, the marshal began shouting rules and instructions. Horses, held tight by rein and leg, flung up their heads or pawed violently at the frosty turf. The two lines of armed men began to look at one another with more than casual interest, picking out first opponents, laying plans, scheming schemes for thus and such an action. All at once, the marshals went silent, and the silver wand flashed downward like a falling star.

The trumpets' brisk clarion was drowned in the thunder of hoofbeats. Spears leveled, dropping into line as if every gauntleted hand shared a single brain.

Titch crouched low behind his shield and held the butt of his couched spear tight against his leather-padded ribs. He had no need to urge Gray for speed—the old horse knew this work better than he knew his own stable. Gray sprang forward eagerly, like a wave leaping at the shore. The black stallion kept even with him on the near side. With his speed, he could have been the first to meet the enemy, but there was no advantage to that, and Gerein held him in check.

It was unlikely that many would be unhorsed in this first engagement. Mistakes came later, when men and horses grew weary and careless, when the less chivalrous chose the advantage of deliberate impact and let one horse career into another. Titch took true aim, but his spearpoint was deflected by the other rider's carefully angled shield—while Titch's own shield did the selfsame service for him. There was a small shock of impact, and then the two lines of horses were passing through one another, wheeling and regrouping. Gerein and his black stallion kept their pace easily. The knight was laughing.

They'd only stay in their formal lines for one more run, perhaps two. Then the massed charge would dissolve naturally into single combats, or one small group besetting another such. Titch stayed at Gerein's side awhile, to avoid being overwhelmed by half a dozen men still riding as a tight unit, but by the time he'd unseated a tall narrow man on a skewbald horse, tossed his shattered spear away, and drawn his father's sword, the fighting had finally swirled them apart. He gave a mental shrug, for the separation didn't matter to him in the least.

Gaining favorable notice meant staying in the thick of the fighting, where the marshals could see you and remember your deeds. The faint-hearted got—and deserved—no recognition. Titch was resolved not to be one of those unfortunates, and plunged in boldly. Back and forth the battle raged, across the now-churned meadow. Men went out of saddles, and sometimes horses went down, as well, to add squealing confusion to combat, crushing to the other dangers.

Titch and Gray did not hold back, but neither did they squander their strength in indiscriminate galloping about. Titch had picked out his best target long before, and he went after him single-minded as a sheepdog cutting a wether from its wooly flock. The warrior was older, plainly experienced, and his gear was sparingly adorned but very well made. If he wasn't worth a ransom, no one on the muddly field was. Titch stalked him first, sparring with others just as his quarry did. And then at last they were face to face, with nothing to impede either one of them save the other.

The man might be old enough to have sired him—the club of hair behind his helm was iron-gray, and his beard was silver—but two exchanges of sword blows told Titch of his strength. He thought he might still have the edge on stamina, but the older man could and did outreach him. That unassailable reality required that Titch close to a distance that favored him and stay there, come what might, an awkward target inside the other's long reach.

Every stroke he made was countered or blocked. Titch did as well in his own defense—the swords danced brightly with each other, conversed crisply. The old man's chestnut horse backed away a step, but Gray, obedient to Titch's leg and well schooled to battle, went right with him and did not permit him to slip away. Both Titch's arms ached—the right from dealing blows and the left from deflecting them with his shield. His throat was raw, his breath coming harsh. Despite the winter cold, he was streaming sweat. Hot trickles ran down his ribs, along his spine. His eyes burned with salt.

He disengaged suddenly into a cutover, and got around

both shield and opposing blade with the attack. It was a flat hit, bruising more than cutting, but his opponent grunted, first sign he'd given of mortality. Titch swung again to press his advantage, but Gray slipped in the muddy footing and could not quite keep him close enough. It didn't matter, Titch thought. He had the man on the run. He could see his adversary trying to retreat, struggling to haul the chestnut horse back out of range. He wasn't begging for quarter, though, and Titch gave him none.

The hacked shield splintered right through its bright-painted design of crossed axes, and the man flung the broken device away, defending himself with his blade alone. The horses continued slowly circling while their masters pounded away at one another.

They were locked blade to blade, held by strength of arm and deadly resolve. Titch kept the pressure on, holding Gray steady with his legs, pushing him into the other horse. He felt the opposing sword yield slightly against his and suspected an attack to another line the instant the contact broke. Titch drew his own blade back to slip past first—and got smashed in the face with mailed gauntlet and sword hilt. His helmet's nasal bar gave way into his nose, his bottom lip split, the sword's pommel cracked against his chin, snapping his head back.

The world went white, as if Titch were staring into the sun. The cantle of his saddle slammed into the middle of his back, hurting but holding him in his place as it was meant to do. Titch shook his head frantically, trying to clear his sight.

The first thing he saw when vision returned was that gray-bearded face coming at him, eyes hot and white teeth bared. The man's blade was even closer, but somehow Titch interposed his own sword at the last instant. The blades scraped along one another until their hilts met, and Titch gave a mighty shove, his whole weight behind his arm. Gray screamed and bit at the chestnut's neck, making it plunge. The combination had an effect. The chestnut's rider began to lose the battle for his balance. Struggling to recover, he dropped his sword arm, and Titch's shield caught him in the ribs, quick as thought.

A fine mail shirt protected the older man from wounds, but the bruising blow toppled him the rest of the way out of his saddle. His horse plunged nimbly away from him as he crashed into the mud.

Titch tried to dismount, to leap to the ground with dagger ready to press to his adversary's throat, claiming a ransom. But for an endless instant he was too dizzy to fumble his right foot out of the stirrup, and when he dismounted he staggered, overreaching the dagger's hilt, fingers coming up to guard, but empty. He found the weapon, finally, and lurched toward his prisoner.

The graybeard had gained his feet by then, brought his sword to guard, no wise ready to yield the day. Titch tasted blood in his mouth, tripped as he stepped forward, and the point of his long shield snagged the ground. It was more handicap than protection now—he tossed what was left of it aside, out from underfoot. He strove to push his helmet back into place, but it stayed stubbornly askew, blocking his vision a trifle as he attempted to press his attack.

His intended prisoner wasn't minded to wait to be captured. He set upon Titch fiercely, rained blow after blow so that Titch was too busy defending himself to launch any sort of offensive on his own behalf. *Fine,* Titch thought. *Let him tire himself. I can wait—*

And sure enough, a dozen strokes later the man was winded, his blows appreciably weaker. Titch could get a stroke of his own in. Not as hard as he'd have chosen—he *wanted* to do better, but his legs and arm refused to accommodate him fully. His attack was parried, he barely slipped away from the old man's counter. Air burned like fire as he gasped it in, lifting his sword suddenly felt like trying to lift Gray.

Careful. Tired fighters make mistakes. Let him do it, instead of you. He'd had good teachers, some inadvertently, all of them battlewise. *Wait for him, exploit whatever he does.*

A sweeping parry, to beat the other sword down. No, the man would have none of that—he pulled back, out of reach. Titch pursued, careful not to be lured a step too far. The ground was treacherous, he kept stumbling. And afoot there was ever the danger of being trampled by someone's horse—

One of the many wandered-in mercenaries who'd given an orphan stableboy a few generous words of advice had told Titch that defense was twice as wearing as offense—one needed to save oneself and then make some sort of attack come out of that defensive move. To purely defend was to be defeated, in the long run. Better to strike out, lead the dance of the blades. Titch saw that desperate truth in his enemy's white face, in the narrow gap between helm edge and cheek guards. And all he had to do was keep pressing what was already his advantage, stroke after stroke.

He was still countered, but more weakly, less surely each time. Another dozen such, and the man would have to yield, and Titch was going to ask for the largest ransom he could imagine, out of spite. He beat the other sword smartly, shoved it out of line so he could get in a stinging blow on the sword arm. It had the effect he wanted—the man's grip loosened, and his sword fell from temporarily nerveless fingers.

Now. "Yield," Titch tried to demand. Only all that came out of his lips was a croak. He coughed and spat blood out of his mouth, tried to get enough air in through his smashed nose for a shout. He might not be able to, so he decided to level his sword at his opponent's unprotected throat, to make the demand visual. The man staggered back a step on legs obviously limp as porridge, then sat down heavily. Titch followed him, his own legs not much more nimble.

"Yield," he finally managed to get out, and all at once the edges of his sight darkened and drew in, till there was only a tiny point of brightness left at the center. Titch fought the faintness, stayed doggedly on his feet, and pushed his sword-point another half foot closer to his prisoner. There was a roaring in his ears, but he ignored it steadfastly.

"Hold!" Someone grabbed at his arm, and Titch noticed distantly that all about him the clamor of fighting was dying away. He blinked, trying to understand. Had his relentless pursuit drawn all eyes, stopped all other combats?

Was his adversary more important than he looked? He tried to pull free of the restraining arm. He wasn't so far gone as to want to kill his foe—not quite. Did they suppose he was? All he wanted was his ransom—

Against a blood-red sunfall sky, the chief marshal was holding a white baton aloft. The day's fighting was ended.

"Sorry," a voice said in Titch's ear. The hand released him. " 'Tis ended, and all honorably."

Titch numbly watched his erstwhile prisoner getting to his feet, being helped away by his concerned friends. He could do that freely—he wasn't anyone's prisoner, since the combat had been declared ended before Titch could claim anything of him. By chance of heartbeats, he was free to go his way. Free as the air.

Titch sat down in the mud—or hazily discovered he already had. He didn't remember sitting. His head was spinning, and he could feel the wet crawling of blood running down his chin. The disaster was trying to sink in, but having a hard time of it. He still couldn't breathe properly, even when his lungs settled down and stopped demanding air so urgently. People came and went, horses were led up or away. Night descended, chill and dark and surprising.

"Here." The voice was Gerein's, though it had an odd echo to it. Something hard and cool was forced against Titch's lips, and his head was tipped back. The movement increased his misery. Fire ran down his throat, exploded in his belly. He started to choke, and a second draft of flame coursed after the first. He felt himself being hauled to his feet, but his legs no longer seemed to be his own. Titch wished he could say the same for his whirling, aching head and his broken nose.

The ground looked incredibly far away. It was the first time his trouble with heights had ever afflicted him when he was merely atop his own short legs, Titch thought curiously. And then he thought of nothing at all.

The Queen's Guard

"PUT HIM ON one of those," the cloaked officer directed, gesturing and keeping himself well clear. "Take the other one for your own."

"My thanks," Gerein grunted, with a sidelong glance at the rest of the barracks, and flopped Titch down onto the low cot. Dust puffed, and a spider scurried hastily away. Titch's only response to the change of position was a snuffle or two, till Gerein turned his head for him so that he might breathe through his open mouth. He was still noisy after that, but no longer sounded as if he might be strangling.

The officer regarded him with distaste. "You can leave him here to sleep it off. There's your pay." He offered a pouch. "A crown apiece, as agreed. And you might tell your friend—when he's in shape to hear you—that I won't tolerate drunkenness on my watch again. A lot of men can drink as hard as they fight. The Guard's not so short of likely men as to welcome them in."

Gerein grinned and made sure his cloak was covering his own flask of potent mead. "I'll mention it."

Titch sprawled on the narrow cot, snoring like a pig. More swooning than slumbering, he was quite unaware of the noise or that some testy soul had thrown three heavy cloaks over him in a vain attempt to muffle the racket. He was content, dreaming of the black horse again, of flying on its back as if it were a soaring falcon and he himself was blissfully untroubled by lofty places. Then all at once the horse dove earthward like a salmon seeking a pool bottom, and he woke himself up, trying to scream and choking instead, smothering under a weight of woven wool.

"Feeling better?" Gerein asked with sympathy.

Titch regarded him without the least interest and only slightly more tolerance. His head felt as if it had been stuffed with wool and thistles. It hurt cruelly, he couldn't breathe through his wrecked nose at all, and he couldn't get his eyes to focus together save by the most supreme effort of his will, which hurt his head yet again. His most recent clear memory was of Gerein forcing strong drink down his throat, so he judged the knight responsible for at least a measure of his misery.

"Just as well you're awake," Gerein said cheerfully. "I'm charged to get you on your feet so you can report. The captain was willing enough to let you sleep off a drunk, but after two solid days—" Gerein shook his head at the sheer magnitude of the indiscretion. *Two* Gereins, till Titch looked harder. The conversation, halved, still made no sense to him.

"What captain would that be?" he asked thickly. Titch fingered his nose and flinched. He could feel a cut across it, but couldn't tell whether the blow had shoved it sideways as well as breaking it, or only flattened it across his face. It hurt too much to investigate. It was swollen closed. Small wonder his mouth was dry as ashes and tasted worse—he must have had it wide open for hours, breathing, else he'd have smothered. What had happened? He had a cut on his chin, too, because Titch could feel caked blood that hadn't just run down from his smashed nose, and besides, touching it hurt—though nothing like the nose did. Had he been kicked by a horse?

"The captain of Queen Melcia's Guard. We're ordered to report for duty at sun-high." Gerein lifted up a leather jazerant, dyed black with oak galls, studded with small plates of dark steel, with little strips of link-mail sewn over the shoulders. "Not much by way of selection, but I think I found one that might fit you in the shoulders. And the cloak dresses it up a bit, even if the color's dull."

"What are you gabbling about?" Titch asked crossly. He

didn't really desire an answer. He'd have heartily preferred that Gerein leave him alone to die in peace, though he lacked the energy to say so.

"Your livery." Gerein tapped his own murrey-draped chest with one finger. He wore a dark jazerant, also, under the reddish cloak. "Just the jack and the cloak—you can use your own trews and boots, they'll do. Want to duck your head under the pump first? Clean up a bit?" He seemed dismayed at the scope of the task before him, as he took a better look at it. For all he'd managed to sit on the edge of his cot, Titch had a boneless look that suggested he wasn't going any farther.

"What do I want livery for?" Titch's brow furrowed. It was the only part of his face that didn't hurt him when he moved it, so he frowned again. Memory was a roil of shattered images, like a smashed mirror in a bag.

Gerein chuckled, swept the cloak back to better reveal his own polished black apparel. "All the Guard wear it. What did you think—they expected you to buy your own? You don't even need to furnish your own horse, though they like it fine if you do."

"But I'm not joining any Guard," Titch said thickly, with what he felt was extreme forebearance. "I told you before, I'm not here to sell my sword. I'll never get a land grant that way—" He ran out of air and had to stop to recover.

Gerein looked disconcerted. "Titch, don't you . . . you got smashed a good one in the face. That old man's a bastard of a fighter, I think I warned you about him. But I didn't think he'd done you any harm beyond a bloodied nose. Nothing a few sips of brandy and a night's sleep couldn't put right. When the captain invited us to sign on for the Guard, you seemed happy enough about it—you agreed before *I* did! I thought—"

"I can't remember." Titch put his head into his hands, trying to dodge the foreboding. He couldn't. It was as unavoidable as his nose, as inevitable as breathing. "Are you telling me I signed on?" That dreadful falling sensation swooped back, and he thought he was going to be ill.

"Well, you made your mark on the Roll. A bit shaky, perhaps, but I witnessed it for you—"

"Gerein, I can *write* my name!" Titch raised a white face, eyes burning amid swollen bruises.

Gerein held his ground. "Well, I didn't know that. Neither did the captain, and the mark's binding enough with even him for a witness. He gave me your pay—" The knight fumbled in a pouch. "I held onto it for you, didn't want you being robbed while you slept. Here 'tis—half a crown. That's pretty decent wages. With maybe a bonus later for good service—"

Titch dropped his swollen face back into his hands. He groaned once, then was suddenly very sick, all over his cracked boots and the splintery floor of the barracks. His eyes watered, and his nose wanted to run, which it couldn't do, so it settled for making him miserable instead.

Hands seized his shoulders in an iron grip. "*On your feet!* Like it or not, whether you knew what you were doing or not, you signed on. You've got to report now, or they'll flog you. Want that?"

Titch wobbled, speechless. Shaking his head only made his dizziness worse, which he'd previously supposed impossible.

"I didn't think so," Gerein said, relieved. "It'd probably kill you. Look, boy, it's only a year. Then you're free to do what you like. A year's nothing! And you and that horse of yours get fed meantime and have somewhere to sleep. There's worse fates than that, the gods know! It's lots better than being pressed into Melcia's standing army with the rest too dim-witted or drunk to dodge the officers. At least the Guard gets to ride."

The knight began marching Titch bodily toward the back door of the barracks, holding him upright no matter how he stumbled. Muttering to himself, Gerein hauled Titch to the rain barrel and thrust his head briefly under the cold water. While Titch coughed and sputtered and was sick again, Gerein propped him against the nearest wall and kept him upright, peeling away his fouled garments till he came to the last layers, the linen sark and leather breeches.

Titch still refused to stand without support, which made dressing him impossible. Gerein cursed. "Got to get your legs under you somehow," he said under his breath. "Here.

One swallow. Don't want you drunk again, but you're not going to make it *this* way."

Something banged against Titch's front teeth, assaulting his torn and swollen lips. A fiery liquid slopped down his throat again, despite his feeble protests. On an emptied stomach, the mead seemed to bypass digestion and go directly into his blood, blazing a bright trail along even the smallest vessels. The process cleared his head enough that Titch was aware of the pain in his nose once more. He moaned, then swallowed hard, feeling sick again.

"Right," Gerein said approvingly, grabbing clothing, tugging and strapping and buckling. "Now stand up, straight as you can manage. Don't speak to anyone unless you absolutely have to—I'll try to do all the talking for us both for a bit. No sense the officer thinking you're a habitual drunk. Try not to breathe in his face, won't you?" Gerein wrestled the leather coat around Titch, did up the laces, and threw the cloak over the top. He settled a steel cap onto Titch's head and grinned at the result. "Good job for you there's no nasal on any of the queen's nice shiny helms—I doubt we could get one over that beak of yours even if it *wasn't* broken and swollen like a sausage." The knight made a brief inspection and a few swift adjustments, gave Titch his weapons, and watched while Titch slowly stowed them in sheath and scabbard. "Not too bad, but you look like the underside of a frog, boy. Going to be sick again?" Gerein looked ready to step back, out of the danger zone.

Titch shook his head—carefully. He intended to survive the next few minutes. That was all the energy he could spare for planning his future. He couldn't bear to look the disaster over any more closely than that.

There was arms practice, and riding endless patrols—but castle sentry duty was the undoubted worst: They put him up atop a new-built wall and expected Titch to stand there, looking down. Since it was most unlikely that any enemy could penetrate the ramshackle town and the outer defenses and proceed undetected, Titch decided that sort of torture was quite unnecessary. If the Lady Melcia liked to see her new stone walls manned by sentries in her dreary chosen colors, he could oblige—but with his eyes tight shut as his nose, unless his ears warned him of an officer's approaching boots.

His first off-duty hours were a dim fog—Titch slept every minute he wasn't at some post, for half a week. His stomach settled down, and his headache became bearable, though his nose still refused to admit a single breath of air to his lungs, forcing him to keep panting through his mouth like some village idiot. Peering into the distorted mirror of his polished helm, Titch noted that both his eyes were still thoroughly blackened. The nose between them was unrecognizable. Titch didn't know whether he could weep any more than Wren had, but the first night that he actually lay wakeful on his cot rather than sinking into a swoon, reflecting upon what fate and mischance had done to his hopes and his future, he felt something hot spilling across his cheeks, and salt stung his cut lips. His nose began to ache, uselessly and miserably. In a way, it was a pity he could still shed those tears, Titch realized—saltwater was no cure for the situation he found himself in. Time itself might not be much of a remedy.

A year. An entire year, bound as a common sword-for-hire, and maybe *never* seen as anything more than that! Unless fate intervened and offered him some spectacular way of distinguishing himself ... which was not something he could depend upon, or work at. Being a member of a supposedly elite cadre was in practice only a tiny degree better than the lot of an ordinary foot soldier, so far as a rosy future went. Riding instead of walking, as Gerein had said.

Gerein. He'd have avoided the man like a plague town, only the close quarters of the barracks made such an endeavor impossible. Depending on their watches, they might only pass one another occasionally, but they slept scarcely a yard apart, off duty. Worst of all, the black stallion was stabled next to Gray, so that Titch could not avoid him, either, though every glimpse was like vinegar poured into a wound.

Gerein seemed unaware that he was being shunned, for he made pleasant conversation every time he and Titch crossed paths over the evening meal, as if nothing whatever

was amiss between them. Finally, Titch was forced to con-
clude that it was he, himself, who was being unreasonable.
What offense had Gerein committed, after all, save by
shielding him from a few of the consequences of his own
foolish actions? Titch couldn't rightly hold the man responsible for the ruin he'd brought on himself. As well blame
the oak for the lightning that strikes the beech tree. Gerein
hadn't lost him his ransom, nor drunkenly signed him into
a year's servitude. Titch finally swallowed his pride with
his supper one evening and asked a pardon, which the
knight graciously gave.

"What about *your* lord, though?" Titch inquired curiously, as he carefully picked through a bowl of stew, hoping for some bits tender enough for his still-sore mouth.
"You hold lands of him, you owe him battle service. How
does that work when you're in the Lady Melcia's pay? And
what does he owe *you*?" The knight shouldn't have had to
flee, to hide himself in a foreign court till he could get justice. His lord should have dispensed it.

"My duke's been deceived by Cullum and his friends,"
Gerein explained sadly. "Certainly I ought to be able to expect open-handed dealing of him, but this is the real
world—justice can be bought and sold like a milch cow.
Cullum has influence at Keverne. I do not. I fear my lord
no longer desires my service." He sipped ale. "I took
Josten's livery to throw Cullum off my track—one day I
will be able to return to Esdragon and hope to clear my
name. Just now, I'd not reach my duke alive, to put my
case to him."

Titch nodded. They'd freshened his helm-cut with a ra-
zor, and the lower portions of his scalp were now blue stubble with red scrapes running through them. He noticed
every draft, every chilly shift of air as if it had been a foreboding.

It was a very great injustice for a knight to be falsely accused, to have to run and keep on running rather than being
allowed to honorably prove his innocence. Titch didn't
doubt that one day there'd be a ballad sung about Gerein's
tragedy and how nobly he'd borne it. His own troubles

wouldn't merit a whistle, and it felt churlish to lament them to one demonstrably more fate-cursed.

Get your horse and make ready, the officer had ordered. The seneschal had doled out what looked to be a sizable load of supplies, though it was spread between the Guardsmen and a sumpter mule. Titch had yet to hear what this new duty was to involve, but at least he didn't need to anticipate being sent up another one of the stone towers that were rising uncomfortably high above the intervening walls. That was something to be grateful for. He scratched Gray's jaw, knowing the gelding relished such attention to a spot he couldn't reach for himself, and waited for further details. He wasn't alone. The bailey was thick with Guards and their mounts, all doing the same thing as he was.

Gray whickered, and Titch glanced to his left to see Gerein leading his stallion toward them. "Heard anything?" the knight asked. Gray and the black touched nostrils, blew politely at one another, doubtless asking the same question.

Titch shook his head. Chatting in the ranks wasn't much favored. There were ten murrey-clad Guards holding horses in the courtyard, but there were a score of horses waiting. It looked to Titch as if they'd be escorting someone somewhere, but Gerein could pretty easily deduce that for himself. He heard the sound of a salute being given, spear butts rapping sharply on paving stones. "Someone's coming."

The stair leading down from the second story of the keep would be dressed stone one day, faced with ashlar blocks like the rest of the new building, but just now it was still planks in a framework. Five people were being marched down them by half a dozen ordinary guards wearing Melcia's mulberry-colored cloaks over black surcoats rather than the sable jazerants of the Guards. The civilians weren't shackled in the manner of prisoners, but they didn't look to be at their ease, as guests ought. Nor were they dressed the way a queen's guests would be, Titch decided. Common rough homespun and leather, save for one man who was garbed in a long mantle of wool dyed to what was self-evidently a very costly deep cobalt, ornamented with embroideries in scarlet and green.

"Listen up!" the officer rasped. Titch gave the man his instant attention, curiosity and self-preservation dovetailing. "We're ordered on escort duty, conducting these folk while they go about some business for the queen."

There was a murmur, though Titch couldn't make out the precise words better than one in ten. The officer scowled, more anticipating than understanding.

"Aye, they're wizard folk! You're not to fret about that— you all wear and bear iron, don't you? It's a known fact that iron bites magic, turns it back, same as a wall does an enemy assault. Don't fret about witchery! You're safe from them, and it's your job to keep *them* safe. They're seeking after something, and we're to see they get to it and that no one bothers them. Also, none of them leaves. Got that?" The officer glared about, anticipating again. "Yes, they'll try. This wasn't much their idea, but our lady requires their service, and she shall have it! Treat 'em politely, but see they stick to their work. Keep them safe, but keep them close. Mount up!" He put a boot into his stirrup and swung up onto a flaxen-maned chestnut with a bald face and one weird blue eye, which rolled as if it, too, feared wizardry.

Titch was pretty sure there was more to the situation than they were hearing. He mounted, gathered Gray's reins, moved easily into his place in the file of riders. As he passed, one of the escorted folk lifted his head. The man had a bony face, with large features and sad eyes—a familiar face, Titch abruptly realized. *Galvin.*

Wren was too frightened to recognize anyone. A rushing of dark water veiled her actual surroundings from her sight much of the time. Each glimpse of weapons and armor, every sight of stonework rising against the white sky only drove her back under the sheltering flood again. It had been so ever since the armed men had dragged her and her master from their hut, shouting orders she had only half heard.

Her master had done nothing to hinder them. Or perchance the magicks he had worked had been ineffective against men clad in cold iron, as his wards had been unable to turn those same men away. Wren remembered seizing an icicle and stabbing out with it, her fear lending frantic strength to her arm—but her weapon had been shattered into diamond chips against the endless iron links of a coat of chain mail rather than piercing and freezing a soldier's heart.

She would nonetheless have struggled till they killed her, only she had Alinor to think of, and trying to shield the falcon from harm had constrained her till her master could get close to her and whisper his reassurances. Then somehow they were on horses, and though she had been hard-put to know how to care for Titch's steed, yet she felt—her body *told* her—that she had been astride a horse beforetime, somewhere in her lost, drowned past. She rode without much incident, and was thus conveyed to the present place of horrors, thick with iron and soldiers and toothed walls that froze her blood in her veins if she gazed at any of them. Voices came and went, there were intervals of light and dark, of indoors and outdoors, and then she was on a horse once more, jogging at her master's side. His face was taut with concern for her—he recovered a trifle as he saw her draw in a breath she was less likely to let out in a scream. They were out from the walls then, at last, and in the open country, where all would be well, if only they were not so close-hemmed with armed and armored soldiers. Alinor, high overhead, numbered them for her mistress, and told her that though all was as well as it could be in disaster, there was still no space for escape.

It was possible to adapt to anything. After a few days Wren could look at those same men with only sensible respect and dread instead of outright panic. And then she saw a face she recognized and knew who had betrayed them.

Titch's place in the line of march was well to the rear, so he couldn't see much of the prisoners—he could think of them as nothing else, whatsoever the officer said—and they were all muffled against the cold of the late-winter days, further confounding his inspection. Still, he could scarcely mistake the falcon soaring dizzyingly high overhead, dogging them. Galvin was here, and Alinor. Certainly one of the other four prisoners was Wren. What was going on? What help could a mere girl render a queen she'd probably

never heard of? Why had she and her master been dragged
here? The distance from their cottage was considerable—he
knew, he'd ridden it. He hadn't even realized the frozen
marsh was in Melcia's territory.

The sun sank at their backs as the officers ordered them
to make camp. There were tents for sleeping in, but Titch
was set on guard duty till the midpoint of the night and had
no chance for a good look at anyone by the light of the
cooking fires. His duty was to challenge anyone who ap-
proached, but no one did, till his relief came hours later. By
then he was worn out, and cold to his bones, and wooing
sleep was an effortless thing.

He didn't come near her, gloating over his treachery.
Maybe that was guilt, Wren thought—or else she had been
mistaken. Surely she remembered his nose thinner, though
still with that raptor's hook to it. Yet she knew Titch by his
walk, even when she couldn't see his face. She knew him
by his shoulders, so much wider from arms practice than
from nature. She knew the solidity of him, that she'd foolishly taken for faithfulness, for trustworthiness ... she'd
known not to trust a man by his face alone, and why should
shoulders lie less than eyes did? Wren asked herself angrily.

Whatever was going to become of them, she'd work to
do, and could not sink any longer into her fears. There was
Galvin to care for—it was her duty to see that her master
got the best food that might be had, that he'd a dry place
to sleep, that his clothes were looked after. She was a wizard's apprentice, and it was her place to serve her master,
not cower in his shadow. Away from the castle, the armed
men did not paralyze her with terror—she grew accustomed
to the sight of them, though Titch's face always woke a
flame of outrage, a lust to pay him back in his own false
coin. But she could go among the other guards, gathering
firewood or pine boughs to soften a sleeping spot, and
ignore her captors as if they were so many trees.

One or two of those black-clad men would have forgotten their orders and hindered her in the ways that men
hindered young girls—ways having nothing to do with sorcery. *Real* trouble Alinor could have dealt with, but the

minor harassments, the fumblings and beggings for kisses, Wren tended herself by the simple expedient of casting a minor glamor over a peeled twig. Cast in front of an annoying Guardsman, it seemed to be a living snake, a water moccasin unlikely come early out of its winterlong sleep. Unlikely, but it put the man to flight all the same when she flung it at him. After another, similar incident, Wren went unmolested.

Whatever quest they were bent upon, its object was evidently fairly distant. They rode to sunward for three gloomy winter days, not halting save for resting the horses or camping through the dark nights. The country was not utterly empty, but they passed through no villages, paused to lodge at no fortified holdings. They just rode on, at the steady pace the officers dictated. Some of the prisoners were not experienced horsemen and soon complained, but the pace only slowed a trifle in response to protests, and vast tracts of snowy ground were covered each day. At some point they would surely pass from Melcia's territory.

Titch had no idea what lay beyond it, whose land it was, whether they could cross it without trouble. He stayed alert, without being so bidden. The guard detail still had its stated dual purpose—he and his companions kept the wizard folk from running off, but they also kept them safe, should danger threaten them and their quest.

And a Guard carried water when the need arose, though Wren protested to the officer who commanded him that she could be suffered to walk a hundred paces to the fast-running stream, bravely waving a pail at him for emphasis. She would not vanish into the empty woods, especially not before dinner. Titch, just arrived with a gleaning of firewood, was curtly detailed to escort her. The officers heard all complaints but acted upon rather few.

It was the first time Titch had been close to Wren, been certain she wasn't some unknown wizard boy muffled in cut-down garments. He didn't think Wren had recognized him yet—all the Guards were perhaps featureless lumps of implacable authority to her—but he felt her eyes on him, and when he turned his own eyes to meet her gaze, he saw accusing recognition, plain as a spear thrust.

"This is a hard way to earn your bread," Wren said coldly. "I didn't know you, at first."

She probably didn't refer to his livery, or his task. His blackened eyes had returned to normal, but Titch's swollen nose and chin were still discolored, the cuts across them scabbed and looking even worse than they felt, as his streamside reflection assured him. His own mother would have had to look hard at him to be sure of his identity.

"You ought to go on as if you still don't," Titch advised softly, a trifle confused by her icy anger. "If the captain thinks we're acquainted, he'll just order me to keep away. We aren't to speak to any of you."

"I just wanted some water," Wren said in a tiny voice. Alinor was trailing them, ghosting from tree to tree like a goshawk. "I didn't ask for you. I want to make tea for my master."

Titch's heart misgave him. She must be half out of her wits with terror over this inexplicable abduction, and now she thought him cruel on top of it. "If you don't turn toward me, they won't know we're talking," he said, trying to make amends. "What happened, Wren? Where are we taking you? They haven't told us anything, except to watch you."

She looked sidelong at him, probably assessing the idea of trusting him. "A lot of men dressed just the same as you rode up two days after you'd left us and told us we had to go with them," Wren said coldly. "You didn't know anything about that, I suppose?"

Titch shook his head, astonished at the accusation in her voice. "I came to Josten for Melcia's tourney. Joining her Guard was an accident." He lifted a hand toward his face. "As you see."

"My master said it was just a coincidence." She hadn't believed Galvin. She still didn't. "He said you weren't the sort to repay kindness with betrayal."

"I'm *not*, Wren!" Titch forgot his own advice and turned toward her, but there was no one to see.

Those eyes could lie to her, be false in as many ways as

they had colors in them, Wren thought. She must remember that. "What did you get hit *with*?" For justice's sake, she hoped that it had hurt.

"A fist." He misread her expression, thought it was incredulity. "Well, it had a sword in it, at the time." Titch bent to dip the pail into the stream, trying to get the bucket into the water without doing the same to his boots. "Combats-at-large can get rough. I was after a ransom, he didn't want to pay one. So, they brought you to Melcia? Why?"

Wren stood staring into the flowing water. She'd been thinking of shoving him in, since he hadn't the sense to be wary of her and had turned his back so conveniently—but there'd be consequences whether she drowned him or only scared him. And she'd been at such pains to save him once, even if there'd been only disaster come from that folly, Wren couldn't quite make herself hurt him.

The streamside was stark—black water, gray ice covering much of it, white snow on the banks to either side. She was afraid of what the water might show her, and tried not to look too intently, but Titch seemed untroubled. To him it was just water, filling a pail.

"She wants us to find her son, the prince," Wren's voice whispered, remembering what she'd heard, standing frozen at Galvin's side, confronted with a terror greater than fanged castles or armored men, a terror so great that her mind refused to hold onto its physical shape, would not show it to her even at the safe remove of memory.

Titch remembered Gerein saying Melcia was regent for a son. Otherwise, he couldn't recall a single mention of the youth, not even in those lurid tales of how the lady had dealt with her deceitful consort.

"They say he rode out with his friends in the summer. They met a girl, and ... and the prince took his pleasure with her, and because of who he was, she couldn't say him nay. But he didn't know she was a witch, and when he would have left her without a by-your-leave, she spitefully transformed him from a human youth into a wild swan. The prince's friends slew the witch for what she'd done, but the spell didn't break with her death, and the swan flew away from them, too fast to follow."

Wren watched the water, thinking of witches being killed. Titch stared at her till she spoke once more and gave the rest of the tale.

"When spring comes, the swans will return from their wintering grounds. So the Red Queen has gathered together every mage, every wisewoman in her domain. We're to search the prince out from among the swans and restore him to human shape. Or we'll be killed."

She turned her gray gaze full at him, and it was like being run through the heart with a blade of ice, even before she spoke. "We saved your life. And this is what you did to us in return. I hope you're proud of it."

Attack by Night

A KNIGHT, TITCH thought, would have rescued Wren and her master, snatched them away to safety whatever it cost him. It would have been the chivalrous thing to do, a way of repaying them for succoring him in his own time of direst need. But he was no knight yet, whatever his private and heartfelt ambitions, and there was nothing a common soldier could do for any of the wizards at present. To attempt an escape was certain suicide—the officers had their orders from their queen. A Guard could guess what his fate would be. Sorcerers who would not do Melcia's bidding would die on the spot, even if 'twas not so much a matter of would not as *could* not.

None of the sorcerers showed particular enthusiasm or aptitude for their enforced mission. One of the men sat staring fixedly into empty air much of the time, and the lone woman—other than Wren, who dressed like a stripling boy and was probably safer so among soldiers—passed the hours by complaining loudly that she was only an herbalist, with no knowledge of dark magicks or the habits of birds, and so carried along by grievous error. The remaining mage spent much time in discussion with Galvin, but Wren confided that her master did not agree with the fellow's schemes or theories.

Why had the prince's mother allowed so much time to elapse before attempting his rescue? Or had she? Titch wondered. Wren had said *all* the wizard folk had been gathered in, garnered like ripe ears of corn, but he wasn't greatly impressed with the harvest. Granted he was no expert, but was he seeing the whole of it? Four sorcerers—if you gave the herbalist more credit than she gave herself—

and one apprentice. Surely there were more? Or there *had* been. If the queen slew all who failed her—

As if to push that point home—that failure would not be excused away—the captain led the fireside talk onto the bloody ground of Melcia's history that very night. It was a little like the songs, only less glitteringly embroidered, and told by one who'd been on hand for part of it.

Two Eral lords had sailed as sword-brothers to Clandara and hewed out kingdoms for themselves and their kin. One had several sons to pick his heir from among, while the other's wife bore him but a single child—a daughter. Melcia was the equal of any man for courage and was well trained in arms by her father. The Clandaran nobility might look askance, but the Eral valued pride and courage in a woman, and they did not scorn skill, either. They thought it no shame to permit their daughters to go to war if they so chose. The young Melcia possessed a fine sword's terrible beauty, the captain said fondly. And when Kenric of Crogen rose to the kingship out of the pack of his brothers and half brothers, he agreed with his councillors that Melcia of Josten would make him a suitable wife and queen. They were pledged to one another, handfasted across a sword's naked blade in the Eral way.

Yet ere they were wed, Kenric betrayed his proud bride. His attention fell upon a woman who stood among prisoners taken in a border raid, a woman fair to his eye as the first bright star of the evening. Kenric took her to himself, got her with child, and kept her far from Melcia's sight.

At length, Melcia learned of his perfidy, and her fury was the stuff of legends. Taking her young son with her, she stormed from Kenric's lands and returned to her own kingdom—and when next she faced her husband, it was at the head of the army that had been laying waste to his domain. They met before their massed hosts, each armored, each astride a great warhorse. The quarrel was between the two of them alone, Melcia declared. Kenric had grievously wronged her, but if he would meet her in single combat, that would be an end to it—she would wreak no further hardships upon his blameless people. Without enthusiasm— for truly he *had* wronged her—Kenric agreed to her terms.

They had met in the council hall, they had met in the marriage bed—now, for a last time, they met in war. And Melcia, her strength and training bolstered by love turned to hate, distilled by savaged pride and righteous anger, prevailed. When Kenric lay helpless before her, she struck off his head with her bloody sword.

That done, she kissed his dead face, tied his head to her stirrup by its long hair, and set off in pursuit of her rival. She came upon the hapless woman and her young daughter beside a rain-swollen river and ordered them both drowned in the swift water.

The tale's moral was too plain to need stating. There was no mercy to be expected, not of the queen, not of the queen's men.

Galvin's sparrow-brown mount had picked up a stone in her near forehoof. Titch was working at it with the point of his dagger, struggling to pry it out. Trouble was, the stone was jammed tight against the iron shoe, and the grateful horse had a tendency to lean on him as if he had become her fourth leg. The blade slid; Titch slipped in the muddy snow and hissed an oath under his breath. Sleet was falling out of a leaden sky.

"Have a care of your fingers," Galvin advised.

"Thank you," Titch said, digging away once more. He didn't want to cut the horse, either. Nor break the tip off his knife. "What use is magic, anyway? How are you going to rescue this prince if you can't shift a pebble?"

"The mare wears iron shoes," Galvin observed mildly. "If I were to use magic on her foot, I'd lame her."

"I might save you the trouble—" Titch grunted, as the flint finally popped free. He flung the stone away and then inspected the hoof for damage. One of the stone's edges had seemed sharp.

"Is she hurt?"

"No." Titch set the mare's foot down with some relief and gave her shoulder a relieved pat. He glanced about. Neither officer was anywhere near, and the captain generally rode far to the front. "*Can* you find the prince?" he asked Galvin, pulling his hood up to thwart the icy rain that had begun to fall.

"I would not have offered to undertake this quest, no," the wizard answered wryly, wiping a drop of water from the tip of his nose. "I understand you are not exactly here by free choice either."

"More of a misfortune," Titch agreed ruefully. "Sir, believe me, if there'd been anything—or if there *is* anything I can do to help you—"

"I tried to tell the soldiers Wren was only my servant, nothing they'd want. I hoped to spare her this. But they saw how the falcon did her bidding, so it was no use. And the queen cares not and spares no one." Galvin sighed. "Your heart is true. Not much use in this situation, but it does you credit."

"I don't think Wren would agree." Titch made a show of checking the mare's other three legs, as an excuse for lingering near, should anyone be glancing in their direction. "What are you planning, sir? I can't help but notice that we've seen no birds." Indeed, they were lodged in a thick belt of forest, had been for the past two days. Titch had seen plentiful signs of deer and fox and quite possibly bear, but no bird larger than a thrush, and he did not expect to do so. True, rain did keep birds under cover. Alinor looked miserable as only a wet falcon could contrive, and probably hated him no less than her mistress did.

"The swans winter far from here, perchance even across the Great Sea," Galvin said helpfully. "They are dauntless fliers. Beyond this forest—*well* beyond it—lie their nesting grounds. They return to its lakes each spring. We are attempting to reach that country before they do. We aren't guiding you by any magic; your captain knows the way."

"That's the whole plan?" Titch felt a sinking in the pit of his stomach, an awful presentiment. He'd hoped for better, for schemes and spells and he-knew-not-what—these folk were supposed to be experts, even if most of them disclaimed it. "How will you know which swan used to be the prince?" They'd have to, surely?

"The swan we seek will bear a collar of golden feathers about its throat," the wizard answered serenely.

In the manner of the Eral nobility, who all collared themselves with precious metals cleverly worked. It made sense, but it didn't answer all the questions. "How will you catch this swan alive?" It would need to be alive. Otherwise, they would have sent a company of archers. Whatever befell the swan befell the Prince Evin, just alike.

"Master Insny advises nets and is likely correct," Galvin said with a nod toward the rest of their party, where the well-clothed man rode. "And there is always Alinor."

"*Alinor!*" Titch forgot to pretend to be looking after the horse.

"A would-be knight ought to be better versed in falconry." Galvin tisked. "A trained peregrine can bring down a great heron. A swan is no bigger."

"They're lots bigger," Titch corrected sternly, his brows lowered. "Strong fliers. And if she needs to bring him down unhurt—"

"True, it won't be easy," Galvin agreed. "There's no one in Kôvelir could manage it, even if the Red Queen's reach stretched so far . . . but the cards offer no choice. Give me a leg up now, someone's coming."

That prediction evidenced no impressive occult knowledge—Titch could feel the approaching hoofbeats through the soles of his boots as easily as Galvin could. He cupped his hands for the wizard's foot and boosted the man into his saddle.

"What's wrong with the horse?" Gerein asked, drawing alongside. The black stallion nickered softly at the mare and was carefully curbed by his rider.

"Stone," Titch replied. "I've fixed it."

"You're rearguard now," Gerein informed him pleasantly, "when we move out. Keep a sharp watch—I thought I saw something."

Titch came alert and moved well out of Galvin's earshot. "You tell the captain?" he asked.

"It's not something I want to discuss with the captain," Gerein said firmly. "It's old business."

Titch felt a coldness again in the pit of his stomach, a certainty of onrushing disaster. He could guess how Gerein felt.

"How can they still be following you?" He wanted to believe it impossible, but couldn't, quite. And Gerein was no help.

"Cullum won't quit till the earth melts and the sea boils away," he said. "I should have realized."

"Maybe you're seeing shadows," Titch offered hopefully.

Gerein shook his head. "This snow makes tracking us too easy."

"There's no way they could know you're here." Titch knew already that Gerein was serving Melcia incognito, having given her captain a partly false name when he signed on. And this time there was no green-hearted lady to betray the knight to Cullum's dogged pursuit.

Gerein jiggled his reins, and the black stallion tossed his head, making the harness fittings ring like bells. "Oh, they'd know."

"If it's the horse they're following, then you should have given him to me after all," Titch said slyly.

"It's probably nothing," Gerein said smoothly, disregarding the issue. "An old habit, knowing they're behind me. Just ride wary. You know he's got archers."

Titch rode wary. The thing was, he became utterly convinced, despite his better judgment, that they *were* being stalked, trailed by someone just out of sight but always *there*.

There was never anything he could put a name to. He never had the least sight of any strangers, mounted or otherwise. Whoever 'twas, he was most careful never to silhouette himself against the pale winter sky, even between the trees. Titch watched over his shoulder till his neck ached with the constant craning, but there was nothing he'd have chosen to report to his captain—or even to a more sympathetic Gerein. Yet he had a persistent itch between his shoulder blades, as if the skin there expected an arrow aimed at him. It wasn't evidence, but he'd been followed before. And it had felt just like that.

Riding rearguard was unpleasant. Riding any other position was torture, because Titch was miserably certain that no one else save Gerein was really keeping an adequate lookout in that direction. And on they rode, through a forest that allowed no distant horizon, no long—and safe—lines of sight to scan.

One of the officers developed a sniffle, which spread to most of the Guard like fire touching dry straw. With all the wizard folk about, a cure shouldn't have been hard to come by, but even the herbalist was disinclined to be helpful. When the captain pleaded, she declared she'd been dragged from her home and hearth without the slightest consideration or the opportunity to collect her medicines, and thereby had nothing to offer to the sick men. Moreover, the horse she'd been given made her back and her head both ache with its rough gaits. No, she'd not dose them for the complaint. They could sneeze their heads off, for all she cared.

The winter snows had transmuted to icy rain in an eyeblink, one pewter-colored afternoon. Stuffed noses escalated to racking coughs, and a few nasty-smelling tisanes were grudgingly produced and shared round. Titch wouldn't have touched any of the herb woman's brews on a bet, though he observed that *she* never ailed, however cruelly the rest of them might suffer. He didn't care to risk belly cramps atop the fever and the agony of his muscle aches, so he drank only a plain tea brewed from dried mint leaves, laced with a little honey to nurse his raw throat. He coughed a little, but mostly his head cold settled into his ears, muting the sounds around him and producing an unbelievable pain beyond the reach of physic, where nothing short of beheading was likely to quell it. Titch stopped fretting about unseen pursuit. No use anyway—their party could have been tracked through the deepening mud by a blind man, solely by the sounds of men hacking. One or two of the horses even caught the cough, though Gray stayed healthy despite the relentless damp and chill.

Titch was standing watch one murky evening—which is to say that he was leaning against a rain-soaked tree in such a way that the officers would *think* he was standing should they glance his way—when a cloak-muffled wraith appeared at his side. His plugged ears made her approach silent and all the more ghostlike.

"Drink this," Wren's moving lips ordered.

Titch stared at the cup she thrust into his hands. The liq-

uid was black, but in the dimness anything save milk would
have looked exactly so. He couldn't smell well enough to
guess what it might be. He would have been glad enough
to warm his hands, but the cup was cold as the wet earth.

"It's better hot, but I wouldn't have been able to bring
it." Her words gave nothing away, and he couldn't tell a
thing from a tone he couldn't hear.

"We're all sick, aren't we?" Titch asked her, his voice
thick from coughing. He had a foggy echo in his head, he
discovered. "All but you sorcerers. Did you do this to us?"

Wren's pinched face gave away no more than the cup
did. "No, we *didn't*," her thin lips vowed. "Someone was
probably sickening with it when we set out, and now we're
passing it hand to hand. It's not only you—some of us are
sick, too. This rain makes it worse," she added reluctantly.
"My master thought you might like to stop yours short of
lung fever."

"Tell your master my lungs are fine, it's my ears that
hurt," Titch said warily. "And thank him for me, but I don't
dare drink this on duty—if I fall asleep they'll give me a
punishment to make me forget my earache."

The cup was snatched from his fingers, and Wren was
gone, without a further word. At least, without one Titch
could hear.

One had a choice of cold and damp or smoky and wet—
there was no way to heat their little tents, and the trees
above offered no real shelter from rain and sleet. The fire
made you pay dear for its scant warming, with stinging
eyes and choked breath, but Wren chose the smoke, since
it might help to keep lice away. Alinor seemed to think it
would, and lifted her feathers to admit the pungent air to
her skin, a winter version of anting. Wren spread her cloak
so that it kept a portion of the rain off them both and stared
angrily into the sullen yellow flames.

How dare that traitorous wretch mistrust her? She could
hear coughing—there was rarely a moment, day or night,
when one could not. Wren wasn't sure which of them it
was, though. The captain's cough was distinctive, a very
deep bark, and Mistress Agatha's hacks always ended with

a sniffle. One of the Guardsmen produced a high-pitched whine as he struggled to get his breath back, which was very likely what had made her master fear lung fever, but Titch's cough was just one of many, anonymous as any of the raindrops dripping from the trees.

She ought to be glad he was suffering—being ill in such weather was far less than he deserved for what he had brought them to. Whatever Titch claimed, Wren needed no more evidence than she had from her own experience—he had come and so, shortly afterward, had the soldiers. Nothing her master said could convince her of his innocence—she did not even consider it.

Alinor lifted up a twig with one strong foot, twirled it, then used her beak to strip and discard its bark. *Hate this rain,* she declared unnecessarily.

"I know." Wren took the offered twig, held it out for her familiar to snatch at, the talons missing her fingers by a hairsbreadth, like a cat after a dangled string. In summer, Alinor would do the same with daisies, practicing her strike and her grip. "You can't hunt."

Too many trees anyway. No sky. She damned the country in the worst way she knew.

Falcons weren't woodland creatures by choice. There was no room for their style of flight in goshawk country. Free as she was, Alinor was every bit as much a prisoner as her mistress, and every bit as melancholy.

The damp wood smoked fiercely as the rain fell onto it. Soon the flames would yield the contest. Wren coughed, waved a hand before her face to no avail, then stretched the hand out decisively to Alinor, who hopped onto it with a glad cry, spreading her wings and fanning her tail. Better the chill of the tent, where Galvin's cards whispered softly as he read them over and over. The familiar sound would soothe her, lull her, so she'd forget the mistrust in lying eyes.

Galvin didn't openly offer his potions to anyone else. Titch wondered whether the idea of escaping had occurred to the wizards. If it had, the sicker the Guardsmen got, the better they'd like it. Even if they hadn't caused the sickness, they could exploit it. Except they seemed to be recovering, one by one, day by day. Tempers remained perilously short, but the illness was passing, despite the chilly, incessant rain. Coughing diminished. No one was ever too ill to ride.

Titch's ears unclogged. The right drained, which disgusted him. The left did not—the pain migrated down his jaw instead and settled smolderingly in one of his molars. Titch began to chew on the other side of his mouth and pondered who'd be most trustworthy as a tooth-drawer when need made him risk it. Gerein, likely, though he was positive Galvin would hurt him less. He postponed the matter for several miserable days, hoping for a spontaneous cure he knew to be unlikely.

The pain in his jaw swelled to a pounding. He'd never have been able to sleep, except his fever came back, and lying down was as good as being drugged with poppy juice, setting him adrift into a stupor.

Titch woke up with a start, realizing hazily that while the throbbing pain was real enough, the pounding came from the ground he'd been sleeping upon, not the inside of his mouth. He disentangled himself from his bedroll, came dizzily to his feet in the darkness of the tent, bumping its ridgepole and making it list crazily. All about him, other Guards were also rising. Questions were called, orders shouted. The muddy earth was shuddering to the hooves of what seemed to be an amazing number of galloping horses. The first of them burst among the collapsing tents.

At first, Titch supposed the picket line had come down, that their own horses had stampeded and were escaping. Then all at once he recognized the long flash of a sword striking down, and his astonished eyes made out the bulk of riders on some of the horses. Armed riders—*they were under attack!* He yelled a warning, snatched at his sword.

His legs felt like someone else's, and that someone didn't know what he wanted. Titch managed two stumbling steps, then snagged a foot and fell onto his face. Something large went over him. He felt a hoof brush him, hard, and then he was scrambling up again, running for their horse lines. A man afoot stood no chance against a mounted charge. That was why knights were so useful in battle, especially against footsoldiers. He had to get to Gray.

Not every horse careening about carried a rider. Titch reached the spot where the horses had been picketed but found nothing there save the long rope their mounts had been tethered to, lying like a dead snake between the trees, slashed in three places. He cursed furiously. His chances of catching one of the loosed horses without being cut down were nil. At least he'd be able to spot Gray, and maybe the gelding would come to his call—but there was no white horse shining in the darkness. If nobody'd stopped him, Gray could have run half a league already. Titch went from tree to tree, needing the support and the shelter, trying to survive.

Then, blacker than black against the gloomy forest, a horse appeared as if conjured. It was plunging wildly, but it was plainly anchored to something, for it stayed pretty much in one spot as it struggled—and Titch remembered in a flash that Gerein never left his incomparable stallion picketed with the others, but by custom staked it out alone, with an iron chain that let it graze a ten-foot circle, enough forage for a single night and less trouble.

The horse was before him, but there was no sign of Gerein. The mayhem seemed mostly headed in the opposite direction, a running fight dwindling away. Screams ripped the darkness. The stallion reared, fighting the chain, slashing the air with his deadly forehooves.

Titch hesitated no longer. He ran to the stallion's head, caught hold of the bridle as it came to earth once more, and found the reins with one hand and the catch at the chain's end with the other. It yielded to his fingers, and he flung the chain away, keeping the reins. A stirrup hit his ribs as the horse pivoted. Titch was astonished that Gerein had left the horse saddled as well as bridled, boon though it was. Planning for a quick escape, had he been? The knight didn't seem to be managing it. There were more screams in the night. Titch found the stirrup again, hopping, keeping a tight grip on the reins. Just as his boot went home, the stallion finally bolted, but Titch let its plunge forward throw him into the saddle, using its momentum to his gain, thankful the stallion hadn't reared back from him before it began to run. He was used to hard riding, but Gray never fought him. No matter. He was safely up, a leg on either side, even if he couldn't find the offside stirrup, and even if the stallion ignored the bit and ran away with him, no one was going to catch him now—certainly not ride over him. He was on a horse, where he belonged.

Trees whipped past. Some were too near to miss, and Titch crouched low over the stallion's neck. It might be trying to scrape him off—his right knee took one very solid whack, but fortunately the tree that gave it to him was a mere sapling and he slipped past it without losing his seat or breaking his kneecap. He shortened his reins, trying to establish contact with the stallion's mouth. It might calm the creature. It might enrage it, for all Titch knew, but he could only try. He'd wanted this horse. Now he needed it, as well, with an equal desperation. His life might depend—

They plunged into a maelstrom where the camp had been. Glowing embers marked campfires scattered by hooves, revealed patches of carnage and confusion. The officers were trying to rally the Guards, shouting orders. Titch was the only one mounted that he could see. He hauled on the reins, swinging the stallion about, reaching for his sword with his right hand. He could scarcely distinguish their attackers, except by their horses, and he couldn't discern their identity from their dress or their weapons, not in the muddled snatches he got. He didn't see any banners bearing black horses ...

The black horse bearing *him* took Titch straight into the low branches of a fir tree. His sword was nearly torn from his hand. Needles sliced his skin and did nothing to cushion the impact of a branch on his jaw. Titch reeled back in the saddle, then was unexpectedly thrown forward onto the stallion's neck as the ground seemed to fall away under them. He saved himself from falling by well-schooled instinct, thankful that for an instant the horse was too busy with its own footing to think further of shedding him. If that branch had been an oak's, he'd have been on the ground with a split head. Had the horse not been agile as a salmon, it would have gone down and crushed him under it, or hurled him into a tree trunk. He was still with the stallion when it got its balance back, which seemed a miracle in heart-pounding retrospect. He'd thought himself *safe* on this horse?

The ground continued to drop away toward the river. Such terrain might seem to offer safety, but there was fighting there, as well. As Titch sat up in Gerein's saddle again, he saw Wren and Galvin on the bank, their backs to the water. The wizard did something that produced a flash of light and a howl of pain from the horseman swinging an axe at him—and using the instant of respite he'd gained, Galvin whirled and flung Wren headlong into the water.

There was a scream, and a huge splash. Galvin turned back to the fight for his own life without a glance.

Titch raised his sword, amazed he still had hold of it, and wrenched the stallion's head around with all his strength. He clapped his heels to its sides, hard behind the girth to urge it forward. Of course, if it was still intent on fighting him, he'd be going over its handsome head in a moment—

The horse leapt into a gallop, in harmony with him at last, if only for an instant. Titch's blade slashed out, by chance as much as skill caught the other horseman's bridle hand. He either cut the reins or the hand—Titch couldn't tell, but the other horse plunged away from him as if its rider had no control over it. Titch swung back toward the wizard, managed to halt the stallion without running Galvin down.

"Wren!" Galvin was running along the streamside, stumbling on rocks.

"Where is she?" Titch yelled, watching sharp for other horsemen. The one he'd hit hadn't turned about yet. He must have gotten the rein after all.

Galvin turned, raising a hand to do the gods knew what to him, then recognized Titch. "I thought she would find the otter-form again if the risk was great enough, but I don't see her! *Wren!*"

"You threw her in?" Titch was appalled. "Can she swim?" The river was rain-swollen, pale with mud and running high. Its surface looked empty except for the too-frequent floating logs.

"She can if she's an otter!"

But if she wasn't? The girl might have gone down like a stone. She might have been swept away.

Wings beat the dark air. Titch saw the barred white of a falcon's underside, meant to confuse her shape to her prey, but nicely visible against the benighted forest, when daybirds didn't hunt. *Alinor!*

"I'll find her!" Titch shouted, and spun the stallion to follow the falcon's flight.

No Matter What Guise

PERCHANCE IT TOOK a demon-bred horse to outrun a falcon on the wing, a river in spate. Titch didn't know, couldn't spare time to think. He urged the stallion on, struggling to keep Alinor in view. If Wren knew where the falcon was, always, then surely the bird could find her mistress by the same means? And her sight was keener than any human's even by night, when falcons didn't customarily hunt.

The bird hadn't mounted up into the sky, as she would when seeking prey by day. Her powerful wings beat hard and fast as a pigeon's, carrying her only a few yards above the water, and she stayed over the middle of the stream. Titch was hard-pressed to follow her. The streamside ground was broken and boggy—once they had to leap over a small stream feeding the greater one, its gravelly banks crumbled half away, and Titch was certain they were undone, sure he'd be thrown to his death. The stallion leapt hugely and landed running. Titch tried to find his breath, his wits. He held onto the long mane as much as the reins, amazed that he no longer needed to guide the horse, that it seemed to know they followed a bird, which followed a river otter.

Had Wren changed herself to an otter? Would Alinor know her mistress in that guise? There wasn't time to question, to falter.

The falcon screamed. The thin sound cut like a dagger of ice. Titch tried to rein in, but the stallion was already sliding to a halt, and he was flung out of the saddle as much as he dismounted of his own volition. He slid down the steep bank, boots momentarily in contact with nothing, then splashing into the rushing water. He stopped just short of plunging in. *"Where?"* he screamed, throwing his head back—as if the falcon would answer him.

Then he saw the snag of a fallen tree, caught a little on the mud of the far bank. It hadn't been there long, not much had been snared against it yet—and not much would, for the current was tugging at the branches already, and it wasn't firmly caught. Alinor swooped low over it, almost hovered, calling anxiously.

Titch tore off his sword belt and flung his weapons back to safety on the bank. No time for pulling off his boots or even his cloak. He waded straight into the flood.

The current nearly took him on his second step. The water barely reached his waist, but that was plenty deep enough. It was bone-numbing cold, fast as a running deer. Rocks shifted treacherously beneath his boots, trying to throw him or trap him by an ankle. The cold possessed him in a heartbeat. Cloak and jazerant weighed him down, but not enough to anchor him. He floundered on, to reach the streamswept tree with the water up to his armpits.

The branches showed buds that would never open with spring, now that the flood had dislodged the tree forever from its roothold upon the bank. But those same branches had snared a tangle of wet cloth as the current swirled it by, caught a thread or two and then held the whole snarl fast in a twiggy grip.

There was something twisting inside the cloth. An eye rolled, white teeth flashed. An otter caught in human clothing could not swim a stroke, and the beast was half drowned from the element it should have been most at home in.

At least it was alive. Titch, teeth achatter, took a grip on the branches with one hand—his frozen toes could not give him a reliable feel of the rocky bottom by then—and began to unwind the cloth. The soggy wool caught and caught again, either on the otter's webbed paws or on submerged branches. Maybe he could cut it loose—but with what? His weapons were on the far bank, Titch recalled with sinking heart. The otter, terrified, bit at his hands whenever it could reach him. He couldn't feel the teeth except as blows, but he shifted his grip to hold it more securely by the scruff of its neck, as a mother cat carried her kits.

The otter heaved frenziedly, and of a sudden, 'twas a brown duck Titch grasped—and could not grip firmly at that, since it no longer had loose furry skin but *did* have wings to pummel his face with, blinding him with feathers and tears. Titch stumbled, lost his footing, but the current held him against the branches and he was able to get a sort of balance, finally pinning the wings to the duck's sides.

A duck could swim as well as an otter. Better, it could fly. But she was still snared in heavy cloth, try as Titch might to remedy the situation. If he let her go, she'd go under, maybe snag again, worse, out of sight and underwater. A duck still breathed air, so it could obviously drown. He dared not let her go—

Her blunt bill stabbed thrice at his face, and then all at once she shifted again—the feathers vanished and he felt smooth scales instead, the change obvious even to fingers numbed by cold. The salmon he gripped humped and heaved, wriggling free of the last of the clothing. Its tail slapped Titch's face, and its fat smooth body weighed him down like a millstone.

Staggering, struggling to hold it, he lost contact with the bottom again. This time his head went under—water burned up his nose, filled his open mouth. Titch felt the branches tearing at his back, the rocks rolling under his boots. He tried to stand, but he couldn't with his arms full of the salmon. Titch felt panic in his belly, colder than the water outside it. If he didn't release the fish, it was going to drown him. The tail clouted him again, to emphasize the point, and he went under once more, but this time his boot touched a rock too big to shift, and he shoved himself upright with its help. He shook water from his eyes.

The fish was free of everything save his grip. All he had to do was release it, Titch realized. Fish could swim even better than otters, Wren would be safe . . .

But if he let her go, how could Wren find her own shape once more? Last time it seemed to have happened only because the wizard took her from the water. If Titch let her go now, would they ever be able to find one single fish in a whole river? Even by magic? The tail slapped his face again, stinging. What should he do?

Throw it ashore, Titch thought in flash of inspiration, remembering Galvin's dealings with the otter. Touching dry land had broken the spell last time.

Not this shore, however. Too high, too uncertain a bank. He'd have to get them back across to the other side, somehow. And if he stumbled, the fish would slip away from him . . . Titch reached back for the tangle of wet cloth with one hand, tugged till he feared he'd bring the barely snagged tree crashing down on him. All at once something gave, and he had wet cloth to wrap about his burden, to bind the salmon to him as it had been bound to the tree.

It was not a docile burden. Parted from water, the salmon was anxious about air. The fish thrashed and snapped in a perfect frenzy, and over Titch's head the falcon was diving and screaming, her wings striking him as often as the fish did. The current fought him, the bottom deceived his numbed feet. Just at the edge, Titch stumbled into a hole and knew that he was falling—with the last of his strength, he hurled the salmon onto the bank as he toppled forward.

Scales flashed silver in the starlight. Titch couldn't see anything more—he hit the shallow stony bottom with a splash and nearly stunning force, having been too busy salmon-flinging to spare much attention to saving himself. It was a moment before he could get up even to his knees or crawl up the slippery bank. He was so cold—bone or flesh, it was all one, and might as well have been wood.

He had left his purloined horse free to desert him, but it was contrarily still on the bank, staring down at him. It started back when Alinor alighted on the ground beside its hooves, squealing angrily. Titch paid neither creature any heed. The white shape sprawled close to the water was too big to be a salmon, and it was not. Titch put his good ear against Wren's chest, then her icy lips. He thought he could detect a heartbeat, but he couldn't hear or feel breath. Wren was cold as the mud she lay on, and her eyes showed white between half-open lids. The air bit like steel with cold, so Titch flung the sodden cloth over her—better than nothing.

239

Class No.	Author			Publisher		Price	Reason
		Title			Edition		Year
L.C.							
W.							

Her eyes were closed now, her lips would probably show blue in better light.

Wren didn't respond as Titch rolled her onto her face. Desperate, he put his hands on her back and pushed down, hard. He did that three times, and all at once muddy water gushed out of her open mouth, trickled from her nose. Suddenly Wren gasped in a huge breath and coughed it out. Titch whooped, raised her up, and doubled her over his shoulder, where she continued coughing and spitting up water. Alinor began making a great racket and beating her wings, and Titch hadn't the slightest clue whether she was rejoicing or berating him for manhandling her mistress.

Wren's pale eyes were probably the only dry portion of her. Titch finally managed to kindle a fire, striking sparks from his sword hilt with bit of flint he dug out of the streambank. He hoped he might be able to dry them out before they died of the cold or were asphyxiated by the thick smoke curling from the wet wood. He dragged his boots off, dumped water and gravel out of them. He squeezed their clothing as best he could and was trying to do the same for Wren's hair when she began to whimper. It was the first sound she had made, and Titch was slow to realize he was hurting her. The thin daylight showed him a purple lump on her scalp, which Titch thought explained her erratic shape-shifting about as well as anything else he was prepared to think of. If she'd hit her head when Galvin threw her into the water, she might have been stunned, unable to help herself, save by raw instinct.

Suddenly she looked at him with recognition and hit him as hard as she could with a balled fist. She was weak—the blow was more insulting than painful. When she drew back to try again, Titch caught her wrist easily.

"Stop that!"

"Let me go!" She thrashed, and he thought that if he kept hold of her wrist, she might dislocate it trying to twist free. It was no wise different from the salmon, or the otter, whose teeth had marked both his hands with little red holes. His face ached where the duck's bill had struck him and the salmon's tail had slapped. Wren leaned forward suddenly,

and Titch realized she was trying to bite at him again—or else chew her own hand off, like a trapped fox. He decided to grab hold of her other arm, to keep her still, and safe, both for her sake and his.

"I'm just trying to—" He saw Alinor coming at him and threw himself flat, reckoning the falcon's weapons far more dangerous than Wren's. He covered his head with his hands, felt talons strike leather, missing skin by inches and mere chance. Alinor shrieked her disappointment and wheeled about with a rush of wings that promised a return.

She couldn't do much damage to his back. It would be his face she wanted. Titch braced himself for the counter-strike, his nose pressed the muddy gravel. He'd offer her no target save studded leather, till she got tired of going at him. He heard scrambling as he dodged the falcon, then a cry as Wren was tripped onto her face by the tangle of her ruined clothing. Alinor sailed distractedly close to the stallion, which reared and struck at her, making her wheel widely and hastily.

"*Let me go, let me go, let—*" Wren screamed—then realized that nothing more than wet cloth was constraining her and collapsed to the ground, whimpering. After a moment—and with a wary eye for Alinor's certain return—Titch crept to her, putting a hand on her shoulder. Wren flinched, but she didn't try to hit him again. She was sobbing, shaking with it, but not one tear fell from her lids.

"Wren, it's me. Titch. I wouldn't hurt you," he said, alarmed at her distress.

"*You lie!* You betrayed us to the soldiers, and now they're killing us!" She pulled away from him, as much as she could.

"It's not the soldiers. They were getting killed, too, from what I saw. It's someone else." He looked over at the stallion, standing on all four of his legs now, but with his head upraised alertly and his nostrils flared. If the *horse* was what the attack had been about, then just how safe were they, even away from the others? Titch wondered. No one seemed to have pursued him, but Cullum seemed a rather unyielding sort, not to be lightly turned away or easily deflected from his business. If he was on their track . . .

A shadow passed silently over the gravel, and Titch flinched, prepared to dive for cover again. The falcon was wise enough to wait for a decent target, so he wanted to be *very* sure he didn't offer her one, while he spoke to Wren.

"If you'll think about it, you'd *know* I didn't send the soldiers after you," he said gently. "There wasn't *time*, between my leaving and their coming for you. They'd already taken you by the time I was having my brains rattled in that tourney."

She stared at him. Alinor's shadow crossed them again.

"You think I got myself stuck in a bog, then shot and left for dead, just to flush out any wizards hiding in the area? *Think,* Wren!"

Her blue lips shook. "You didn't do it," she whispered. "You didn't lie."

"No, I didn't," Titch said, relieved. Then his heart misgave him, as he realized that his sworn duty was to return this girl straight back to her captivity, now that he'd nearly won her trust. He would be careful not to speak of it with the falcon still at large, though. That was only sense.

"You rescued me." Wren poked at her mangled clothing, pulling some of it closer about her. "From the river."

If Titch hadn't been so cold, he might have blushed. He shrugged, instead. "Your master threw you in, to save you from a horseman with an axe. I suppose he thought you'd change to an otter again, but you got swept away, and he didn't know if you'd shifted or drowned."

"Did I change?" She looked at him blank-eyed.

Could she not remember what befell her, while she was out of her proper shape? What use was that? Titch wondered. Still, it wasn't as if it was a magic she was expected to be good at. It didn't seem to be something she'd been practicing. And there was the bump on the head, enough to confuse anyone. Wren's lower lip was trembling again. She bit it, so hard that blood flowed.

"I suspect your master didn't think about your clothes," Titch said. "They nearly drowned you. But yes, you changed. You were an otter most of the time, but there was a duck, too, and a salmon." He touched a fresh bruise on his cheek. "A very big salmon."

Wren dropped her face into her hands. "What *am* I, then?" she whispered, and there was nothing Titch could do to comfort her, but to try to keep the fire going, for what small good the smoky warmth and dryness could offer either of them.

There wasn't much dry wood to be found, and in the end the fire sputtered out long before either one of them was even close to dry. Titch helped a still-shivering Wren up onto the surprisingly patient horse, then climbed up behind her. Finding the Guards' camp shouldn't be difficult—all he needed to do was follow the course of the river back to it. And maybe Wren wouldn't realize at once what he was up to, if fortune was on his side.

"Titch, where's my master?"

Last he'd seen, Galvin had been alive. "He's all right," Titch answered with certainty he prayed was justified.

"They killed Mistress Agatha. And Master Insny. I saw, before we ran." Wren's voice was tinged with horror.

Titch steadied the horse as he tried to spy out a path avoiding the worst of the streamside obstacles. "He was all right when I left him to go after you, Wren. I swear it." He couldn't quite puzzle that out—he'd seen few Guards being killed outright, but the supposedly powerful wizards evidently had been, and deliberately. Why? Who exactly *were* their attackers? Not Gerein's enemies, surely. They'd have kept on the track of the horse, which he hadn't been troubling to hide. Someone else? Possibly going straight back wasn't such a good idea after all. But what other choice was there? Titch's bad tooth shot a jet of flame through his head, making it difficult to think clearly. He regretted no longer being frozen half insensible.

Wren glanced skyward. Titch looked up, too, and watched Alinor sweep out of the circle she'd been tracing above their heads. She winged upstream, swift and direct as only a determined falcon could fly.

"He threw me in to save me," Wren said, miserable with guilt. "Because I couldn't help him, or even myself."

"He thought you'd take the otter shape if you had to," Titch excused. "He only wanted you safe."

"I *told* him I didn't know how to do it." Wren made a choking sound, but no tears came. Titch had a clear view of her pale cheek.

"You did shift, and you're safe, just as Galvin wanted. And he *was* alive," Titch insisted stoutly.

Wren's dry eyes were fixed on the gray sky.

"Why would they be killing wizards?" Titch wondered. "You're just trying to rescue Melcia's son. Who's against that?" *Know your enemy.* Couldn't guard yourself if you didn't.

Wren trembled, possibly from cold. She'd lost her boots from an otter's tiny paws, and they'd wrapped her feet in rags, which couldn't be terribly warm. Titch tried to keep his woolen cloak draped around them both, to take the teeth out of the wind. He had only marginal success. And Wren still hadn't answered him.

"You think the prince has enemies?" he guessed. "That tale about how he got changed into a swan, does that make any sense to a witch?" It didn't to a common soldier, but he was no expert. "Wren?"

She didn't answer. She probably didn't hear him. The distance to the wrecked camp wasn't great as the falcon flew. Alinor was returning. Titch waited, time's passage marked by a speck drawing nearer and nearer and the pain throbbing in his jaw.

"They took him back under guard," Wren said, her eyes never leaving the slim form beating toward them, listening to Alinor's report. "He was the only one left alive of us. They're riding back to the Red Queen's castle."

"I *told* you he was alive," Titch said happily. He gathered up the reins. They had a hard ride ahead of them, but they'd manage. He knew exactly where the retreating party of Guardsmen had to be, and once he'd found them, they'd have food and a real fire and warm clothing. Not to mention protection.

"But for how long?" Wren wailed, sitting up against Titch and smashing her head against his jaw, so that he gasped with pain. She hadn't hurt him half that badly when she'd been *trying* to. He barely heard her words. "He failed. We *all* failed. The Red Queen kills sorcerers who fail her."

"It's not your fault," Titch insisted reasonably, his eyes tearing. "Or your master's. When the captain reports what happened, she'll just send him out again, with more Guards."

Wren rejected his comfort. "He still failed. Will it matter why, to *her*? You didn't see her, Titch. You didn't have to stand in front of her! I think she's crazy. Her eyes . . . it hurt to look into them." It was only then that Wren could make herself remember doing so. She shook like a leaf about to fall to winter winds.

Melcia would be frantic in the matter of her missing son, Titch agreed. Royalty set store by their heirs, and the prince was her only child, so maybe she'd be deranged, maybe just not caring, in the manner of aristocrats, about those who could serve her no further—those who failed to achieve a queen's ends. Titch acknowledged that it was his duty to return Wren to her master and to the task they'd been set to by his liege-lady. But if that duty was only sending her to the executioner alongside Galvin . . .

Knights protected women. They didn't drag them to the block.

Alinor arrived, backwinged hard, and alighted on Wren's upraised wrist. That put the falcon barely a cubit distant from Titch's nose, and her dark eye fixed balefully upon him, calculating, measuring the help he had been to her mistress against the trouble he could be. She snapped her beak twice, a signal he could not mistake.

"There's only one thing to do," Wren said, after a moment's private conference with her familiar. "*I'll* have to do it. I know as much about it as any of the rest of them did, even if that's not much! I'll have to find the swan myself and take it to the Red Queen. My master can change it back to the prince. All I have to do is find it for him."

Titch would have agreed—if he'd been asked—that the only possible motive for the night attack had been to ensure the failure of the sorcerers' mission. He had seen enough of the affray to know that the opposing force had been at least as disciplined as the Guards—certainly they had not been outlawed bandits. Had it been any sort of a territorial squabble, there'd have been an open challenge, not a mid-of-night attack. And if the men had been Cullum's, they'd have had no way to distinguish the sorcerers from among a large group of strangers. They'd only have wanted Gerein and, faced with equal numbers, would likely have demanded he be given over to their justice, rather than trying to snatch him from the middle of an ambush.

So, who wanted their mission to fail? It would need a better grasp of Josten's politics than Titch could claim, to answer that. He couldn't hope to solve such a riddle, any more than Wren could.

Melcia had nothing to gain by slaughtering Galvin the instant he was taken before her, he thought. She might have a use for him still; surely she hadn't so many wizards handy as to slay them *all*, unless she was mad past all reason. If she truly wanted her lost son restored to her, she'd keep Galvin alive—for a while. They could depend on that, little as it was.

One wild swan, out of thousands of migratory waterfowl. Could the girl do it? She could pick the proper bird out easily enough, Titch was sure. *He* might even be able to do that, if 'twas marked as Galvin had said. But catch it alive, unharmed? Could even Alinor do that, as Galvin had hinted? Should he be letting her try? Did his duty lie with Wren's self-chosen mission, or the orders he'd been given? And weren't those one and the same?

The first order of business must be to get to the swans' nesting grounds, before the great birds themselves returned. Titch turned the stallion's head sunward at Wren's direction. They were already beyond the forest. He struggled to recall what else Galvin had told him about their eventual destination, as the stallion picked up an easy canter. What lay after the forest? Grassland, his eyes said, but what more?

It occurred to Titch, as the leagues rolled away behind them, that he was probably a hunted man. He was astride an undeniably twice-stolen horse, and he had from his captain's viewpoint deserted his post and his companions.

Had he? As a Guard, he had been charged with keeping the wizard folk safe, with seeing they got on with their quest unmolested. He was doing that, wasn't he? What was right—go on or go back? Did it vary, depending on who was asked? It was hard to decide, hard even to think. He could not follow a trail of logic, nor of morality. His aching jaw kept distracting him. He'd chosen the right, surely. He believed that, at least half the time.

Were his choices his own? Or was Wren bespelling him, bewitching him to ride in *her* chosen direction, to do *her* bidding and never guess the truth? Was she sternly resolved, or suspiciously content? How could he tell? In the end, it was easier to keep riding along the path the sun had laid out before them, letting his doubts and his worries straggle behind as they would.

The stallion had paces as silken as anything Titch had dreamed of, but lying upon a foot-thick featherbed would have tortured him by then. He felt every beat of his heart, every breath he drew in his teeth, like blows. By day's end he was in agony, each soft step the horse took translating into throbbing flame as it worked its way up his spine and down along his jawbone. He rifled Gerein's saddlebags in search of a flask, but there was nothing to be found—no mead, no potent brandy, not even the thin sour comfort of ale. The cold wind made him shiver helplessly, but Titch couldn't collect his wits sufficiently to locate wood for a fire. He'd try by the river, he thought, there'd be driftwood there, storm-wrack . . . only he couldn't remember exactly where the water was, or if there *was* water . . . surely he hadn't camped where there was no water? He knew better than that? It was all changeable as smoke, or a shapeshifter.

"What's the matter?" It was Wren speaking, peering at him through the dusk. He seemed to have sat down, Titch discovered with surprise. And she was human, which also surprised him for some reason he couldn't put a mental finger on.

Admitting to trouble so commonplace as a toothache seemed impossibly unknightly. However, his cheek was so hugely swollen that Wren saw the source of his misery at once, without need for further questions to get past his evasions and disclaimers. She laid a hand on Titch's chin, her touch soft as cobwebs, coaxed him to open his mouth for her.

It was hard to see, but Wren scarcely needed her eyes for a diagnosis—she could feel the source of his trouble from the heat under her palm. The last molar on the left side, sitting like a bottle cork over a pocket of blazing infection. The thing to do was drain it, before it found a way into his blood and killed him, but the tooth was in the way, a formidable obstacle.

What would her master do? There were many remedies for toothache, but this was beyond most of those already, and it would only grow worse as time passed. A spell of sympathy? That seemed best, something to reach by magic where fingers and medicines could not quite go ...

"You were wrong about Mistress Agatha not cursing us," Titch whispered when the examination was concluded. He struggled to speak without hurting himself, which meant moving his lips but nothing else, so some of the words were slurred or impossible to distinguish, others strangely accented by his still-swollen nose.

"Hush," Wren commanded. "She didn't do this to you. And she's dead, poor thing. Let her lie." She wracked her brain for what she'd need, considered what she'd be likely to find at this early season.

"Can you draw a tooth?" He hated to think what that was going to feel like, especially if endured without the numbing solace of strong drink. Maybe he could inhale smoke till he was overcome—that reminded Titch that he hadn't yet built a fire, and his thoughts wandered full circle, a snake swallowing its own tail.

There was no answer to his question. Wren was nowhere to be seen, though Alinor sat glaring at him, leaning forward as if deciding which of his eyes she wanted to pluck out first. Too bad *she* couldn't draw out a bad tooth, for she'd be willing—unfortunately, probably willing to take his tongue out first.

* * *

Leave him for the crows. You don't need him.

"I can't do that!" Wren cried. "Alinor, he saved me. I'd have drowned, and never even known—"

The falcon tilted her head. *Misplaced compassion. You had already saved his life once. You were only even. Now you tip the balance.*

Wren sought thin edges of snow, where light would have penetrated the icy cover. It was spring's light already, the pale sun now vanished. The land knew. Very early, only a whisper, but the life was there, leaping from the thawing earth. That was the good of training as she had, that she was able to identify a plant at any season of the year, even when 'twas naught to the casual eye but last season's dried stems and leaves . . . Galvin had made sure she knew that.

All you need is the horse, Alinor observed. *So you can keep up with me.*

"If I leave him, he'll die." Being back by the river's edge brought back snatches of memory to her, of scenes viewed through other eyes. Nothing came clear, except the feel of arms about her—arms that had refused to let loose of her, no matter the punishment she'd inflicted with her frantic struggles. "I'd still be a salmon, if he hadn't held onto me. Or an otter. For the gods know how long. I can't help Galvin if I'm trapped in another shape. And I'm all there is to help him."

And if this broken-beaked wretch betrays you again?

Wren tried desperately not to hear, not to let the doubt be sown. But what could she be sure of, after all? How could she tell truth from lie, right from wrong, when she did not even know her own true name?

After a few moments Wren reappeared, her hands barely full of green leaves. She smiled, to reassure Titch as he sat nursing his jaw with a hand held to it to keep away the chill air. "I found some things that will help." Her fingers selected a root from the bundle, brushed dirt carefully away from it, followed that with a rinse of water. "Plantain root. Chew on it, while I heat some water."

Titch blearily regarded the knobby root. The prospect of

chewing anything at all was not appealing. The root looked tough, woody, unwholesome. Chewing it would hurt.

Wren guessed his reluctance. "Start on the other side and then shift it over when it softens," she suggested.

"What's it do? Make me sleep?" He was hazily concerned. If Wren still felt he'd betrayed her master, she might well be poisoning him. Titch decided that death couldn't hurt much more than his mouth did. But he still shied from inducing fresh agony.

"No. I couldn't find anything to do that. But it cuts the pain, for a while."

Titch wondered what she intended to use to pry the bad tooth out of its socket. Maybe Gerein's pack held some implement that would serve, though he didn't remember seeing anything like that during his hasty search of it. He'd lost most of his own gear during the ambush, and all Wren had was a little leather bag tied to her belt, which had survived her near drowning. She pulled a battered cup from it, while Titch hoped they wouldn't be forced to use a stick, with a rock for a mallet. Maybe he'd be lucky enough to faint at once . . .

There was water somewhere nearby—the silver cup was brimming and shedding drops when Wren returned to his view. A few woody stems soon made a neat little blaze at a flicker of her fingers—she made fire just the way Galvin did. Titch doggedly chewed at his root, hoping it was only pain made his senses reel drunkenly and sweat pour out of his skin. *Knights endure,* he admonished himself. Tooth-drawing was probably another thing that was too much trouble to do by magic. Alinor was watching him inscrutably.

"Balm," Wren whispered, dropping tiny green leaves into the cup, where the water now gently seethed. "Pennyroyal. Both of them hiding new shoots under last year's dead stems. Winter's done already, for them, if you know where to look. Mullein leaves would make a fine poultice if 'twere later in the year. Now I have to put a whole baby plant in, to equal one leaf. You have an abscess," she informed Titch matter-of-factly, out of the middle of her botanical recitation. "The poison from your ear got trapped under one of your back teeth." She continued to speak, but it was a crooning to the brewing liquid, nothing meant for his dimmed ears.

The plantain root hadn't tamed the pain, but it had put a curb bit into its mouth, at least. Titch found that if he held his head still, his jaw didn't throb quite so violently. "Can you take the tooth out?" he asked carefully, around pain and chewed plantain root.

"I don't need to." Wren scooped hot leaves out of the cup with two fingers, poked a wad of them into Titch's open mouth. She swiftly plastered another palmful onto the outside of his jaw. The heat stirred the pain, then gentled it a trifle, like a beehive smoked docile so the beekeeper could work. Titch's senses spun in a lazy circle, like Alinor catching an updraft. Wren eased him back, till he lay flat on the brown grass, turned his head to the right.

Reaching out, she selected a small stone from a pile waiting beside the cup. Wren cupped her choice carefully in her palm, stared intently at it, then pressed it very lightly to the swollen side of Titch's face. She began to sing softly, no words he knew. Magic, he supposed, or something to lull him further. He didn't know what to expect, when it came to spellcraft. He watched Wren's face, trying to antic- ipate. No tears for him this time, Titch saw. Of course. She never wept, whatever he'd imagined. He'd seen that proved.

He shut his own eyes, struggled to concentrate on the mint taste of the pennyroyal in his mouth rather than tens- ing for the butchery of the extraction. The root had been bitter. The herbs were more pleasant. Till she made him open his mouth wide, there was no point to stiffening every limb against the coming agony—

Wren's hand left his face. Bereft of that tiny comfort, the air icy on his skin, Titch opened his eyes. He was just in time to see Wren hefting a much larger stone over his head. No magic to it after all—she intended to dig after the tooth, after first stunning him! Only a rock that size would do more than stun. It would smash his skull in—

"Don't!" Titch tried to fling himself aside, his trust yield- ing to self-preservation. His flesh was slower to respond

even than his hazed wits, and he could not stir, only push the right side of his face harder against the frozen ground.

The herbs in his mouth muffled his shout, nearly choked him, too, as he started to inhale them. Still chanting, Wren slammed the cobble down—upon the smaller stone, which lay waiting on a flat rock, like a horseshoe upon an anvil. There was a resounding impact.

The small stone vanished, became no more than shattered fragments and grains of sand. The pain in Titch's jaw ceased the selfsame instant, even as he rolled onto his face and wrapped his arms about his head. He yelled from fright, nonetheless, and gagged again on the healing herbs.

Wren patted him on the back a few times, then coaxed him to swallow the liquid remaining in the tarnished silver cup. There was a lot of it, as if the cup were somehow larger inside than out. "I have been a good pupil," she said, while Titch ran his fingers wonderingly along his jaw. Already the swelling was disappearing. "I can find the queen's son, too, because I must." She looked weary, but her voice barely faltered. "I *can* do this thing. And I swear that I will."

Choose the Right

IF SHE SAID it boldly, it would come true: She could save her master. She must, Wren thought, admit no doubt of that. She was a nameless wretch, but she was all Galvin had to rely upon. If her plan was hazy—find the swan, bring it back to Josten—it was no worse a scheme than more seasoned wizards had concocted between them. She'd sat by the fire enough nights, listening to them debate and wrangle. Master Insny said thus and so, and Mistress Agatha disputed it, in whole or in part. Her master let his cards speak for him, even if he did not always volunteer the information they imparted to him. They talked theory and logic, and concluded nothing at all, save their fear of the Red Queen.

Maybe the ambush had been unnecessary. Maybe they'd have failed anyway. Wren dared not think so, for to admit such thoughts made her heart beat awry, her breath come so thick that she felt she was smothering. One instant she wanted to hide herself from the huge eye of the sky—the next, she felt that sky had drawn down to crush the life from her. The sky was Alinor's world—she dreamed of it when she slept, head tucked beneath her wing—but her mistress feared that boundless expanse all at once and missed the sheltering forest. The rainfall ceased when the wind carried the clouds away, and that night the whole expanse of the heavens burned with stars, countless glittering eyes to judge the unworthy.

I can do this, Wren insisted, but the stars remained unconvinced.

Sunfall showed Titch a flat landscape, glinted crimson from numberless pools of standing water. The tiny lakes

146

were snowmelt, not spring-fed or permanent, but they must remain a long while on the poorly drained ground—most were still fringed darkly with the spiky remnants of the past season's growth of reeds. Fresh green shoots were poking out, and the occasional whine of an insect suggested what was to come when the season reliably warmed and the population of mosquitoes rebounded. His shadow stretched far away from him over the scarlet-dyed ground. The stallion's did likewise.

Titch had rope for a tether, and a stake to fasten the rope to. New shoots and old grass alike made decent horse fodder, and he'd selected the least-boggy spot within a reasonable distance, to spare the stallion's feet from the hazards of constantly standing in water. A little mud helped keep a hoof flexible; too much led to foot rot.

Titch pulled a handful of the coarse dry grasses and diligently rubbed the saddlemarks out of the black coat. Shed hair drifted on the light breeze. The days were lengthening as winter wore away, and the stallion's short summer coat was already pushing out the longer winter hair. Gray always looked as if he'd been shorn, once Titch got to work with the curry brush.

He hoped with a pang that Gray was all right. No reason the old gelding shouldn't be—the ambushers had probably just loosed all the horses so their intended victims couldn't catch them and gain mobility. There'd been no reason to hurt them, nor time. Assuming no one had caught him, Gray was likely nibbling his way from one end of the forest to the other, happy as he could be. Once he reached the grassland, the old horse would think himself in heaven.

Titch would have thought the stallion would be just as eager to graze, but it didn't even put its head down after he tethered it. It stood gazing out over the darkening landscape—and then it turned its handsome head so that its left eye gazed full into Titch's.

Straight into his soul, it felt like, the impact almost a physical blow. The eye was large, as horse's eyes always were, and dark—but darker than most. The color wasn't brown, but indigo, or a purple even deeper than that, the color of midnight. The long pupil couldn't be seen against it at all, but there were glints from the last edge of the sun sinking behind Titch—tiny sparks of ruby and citrine, brief flashes of peridot. The horse's expression was sad beyond hope.

Titch thought he knew why that was. He couldn't see, but he had felt the dark crusts at the corners of the stallion's mouth, where the iron bit had rubbed and rubbed till hair and skin wore away. He'd been careful to keep a light hand on the reins as they rode—and the horse had never given him cause to do otherwise—but all Titch's care could not undo what wearing a bit every hour of the day and night did to a horse's mouth. Titch hated to think what the inside must be like. Bruises for sure, maybe cuts and sores. But if he dared not take the bit out, then he dared not go poking his fingers into the stallion's mouth, either.

"I'm sorry," he said softly. "I'd take it out if I could. But if Gerein was telling the truth, you'll kill me for my trouble." He ran a hand up the stallion's crest, scratching the roots of the mane. The horse sighed and put his muzzle into Titch's other palm. It might be a pledge, a plea. *Or a trick.*

"All right, I don't really believe you'd hurt me." Titch slid one finger under the headstall, scratching gently. "But if the iron's all that controls you, then you'll run if I take the bit out. And I can't risk that. I can't lose you."

It occurred to Titch that he had unexpectedly acquired almost every one of the things he'd dreamed of for so long a hopeless while. This amazing horse, for a start. And his own freedom, because he was a long way clear of Melcia's reach, if he wanted to desert. He could go anywhere he chose, offer his sword to some worthy lord, and with this black horse under him, he'd do such wonders in combat that he'd surely be granted the lands he sought, the position he deserved. His fortune was made. It had all come about as he'd desired, whether he found the swan or not.

Then why should his heart be as heavy as an iron bar? Every horse wore a bit; the one the stallion carried wasn't even especially severe. It wasn't paining him, even if he was weary of it—the matter of his own tooth had granted Titch some sympathy, but he knew the discomforts were not of the same degree. Not even close. He'd treat the horse well, and it would be no more his prisoner than Gray had ever been. It would be his partner, just as Gray had been.

So, why couldn't he bear to see his own tiny self mirrored within that great dark eye? Why did he half flinch from the horse's gaze? Taking the bit out would be madness anyway—if he let the horse get away, how could they ever track the swans on foot? And Wren depended on him, for her master's life. He couldn't cast that away on a whim. His wits were still disarranged by his illness, that was all, loose and accepting of wild fancies.

The stallion still watched him, no matter how he dodged the contact. Titch felt a lump rise in his throat. He'd been through so much with the horse as his obsessive goal—how could he yield that up *now*, with the object of his quest his at last? It was nonsense to consider such a course, and pointless—horses weren't sad or happy, either, except of the moment, depending on food, or weather, or—

The beyond-black eye gazed unblinkingly into his heart. There weren't any lights in it anymore. As if there were no light inside his own soul, Titch thought with sick dread, because he could not pity a horse, could not show it compassion, or mercy. That eye was judging him, mirroring him.

"I'll treat you well," Titch whispered, pleading. The eye still regarded him. Then, finally, the stallion turned his head away in apparent resignation.

Titch's throat ached. His eyes prickled. *It's only a horse,* he told himself sternly. *He doesn't think like a man, or feel like one. You can't make him promises. He can't judge your heart and find it wanting—*

He'd been tangled up in too much magic of late, that was his trouble. Reality was seeming boggy as the thawing ground. Well, under that shifty muck had to be the rock of common sense. He wanted this horse, and now that it was his, he wasn't giving it up, not for anything.

A knight wasn't a knight without a horse. Bedrock truth, granite bones of his world. His birth had granted him little else in a hard world, but he had that much—the right not to have to fight on foot, but to be heads above the common soldiers, to be ten feet tall and command a strength and scope beyond his own. Release this hard-won horse? Not likely!

The wind sighed softly in his ears. It blew the stallion's mane forward, and the somber eyes looked down the wind, as if longing to go whither it blew. *Nonsense again!* Horses cared for grazing and grain, for rest when they were weary. For a considerate rider with hands and seat that did not punish unduly or unthinkingly. Brave they could be, and loyal, but they were dumb beasts, and this one was only watching the dark landscape, maybe scenting a fox on the roving breeze. It wasn't pining for a freedom it wouldn't know what to do with, and as it grew accustomed to him treating it well, it would reward him with loyalty the equal of any dog's.

It looked at him again. Only looked, but all the sorrow and loss in the world brimmed in those great eyes, and all at once Titch knew that somehow *this* horse was different, that it *was* a prisoner, that it knew it was, and cared, and even grieved. The wind blew, and the horse could not follow. Its sorrow was as dry-eyed as Wren's, and no less terrible to behold.

It was so long between beats, Titch thought his heart had stopped, that time itself had ceased to be, while he teetered on the edge of right.

Horses don't—but this one did.

The sores at the corners of its mouth accused him. *It's in pain,* Titch thought. And the more fool he, to continue Gerein's abuse. He could take the chafing bit out of the horse's ruined mouth—he could do it very easily, for he had a tether rope in his two hands. All he needed to do was to make a loop in one end with a nonsliding knot, and he'd have a neck rope. He wouldn't need anything else—the stallion was so docile in hand, a neck rope would be enough to restrain it.

He threw the cord over the stallion's high-crested neck, caught the free end of it and set swiftly to work. "You'll like this much better," he assured the horse, making the loop snug enough that it wouldn't slide off over its ears when the horse put its head down to graze. "Nowhere near your mouth. Easier to eat, too." The ears flicked, as if to attend his words.

Done. He'd get the bridle off first, then tie the rope's other end to the stake. His fingers went to the buckle that fastened the throatlatch. The tongue resisted, then yielded to him. The horse held very still during the struggle, but its neck felt hard as rock where Titch's knuckles brushed it. Titch reached up behind the pricked black ears, grabbed the headstall and pulled it over and down with one fluid motion. There was a hot puff of breath on his other hand, and the iron bit fell into it.

The stallion flung his head up—and his whole forehand rose after it, as the head-toss became a rear against the dark sky. The rope went taut in Titch's hands. He shouted, surprised, and tugged hard to bring the horse down. It obeyed, only to rear again at once. Its forelegs flailed out, forcing Titch to keep his distance, to stay at the rope's end.

"*Stop it!* You'll hurt yourself—" The flashing hooves raked the sky.

He got a better grip on the rope, wrapping it about his hands. That was stupid—the stallion reared again and lifted him off his feet. Titch hung grimly on until it touched earth again. Then, as it bolted past him, he dug his heels in, hoping a sharp jerk on the rope might at least make it alter its course, but it was no use. The horse paid him no heed, simply towed him behind it as if he were no more than a knot at the rope's end.

The first few yards, he was dragged upright, skidding on his bootsoles. Then one of his toes snagged a heather root and the rest of his body knifed forward. Titch still refused to let go, and was hauled on his belly for a hundred paces, till the rope finally slid burning through his hands.

The clods of earth and turf that had been flying back into his face ceased to pelt him. The horse still tore them from the grassland, but it was farther away now, apparently running straight for the horizon like a sable comet—just as Gerein had predicted. Titch lay prone in the cold grass, regret bitter in his mouth, the useless bridle still looped over his shoulder.

The horse was gone. It hadn't spat chimera-flame—not

that he'd seen—but it had abandoned him, swift as thought, sure as night falling at the end of day.

Titch dragged himself upright after many long moments, then let the bridle fall back to the ground. He felt bruised over every inch of his body, as if he'd fought in a melee. His hands were a bloody mess. None of it was any worse than he deserved. He didn't relish telling Wren he'd let the horse go—it was her master's life he'd just lost with his stupidity, as well as his own glorious future.

Putting off telling her wouldn't ease matters. Alinor, hunting, might even have seen the horse flee, though falcons hadn't an owl's night sight and the bird probably wouldn't care. Titch rubbed a scraped knuckle over his left eye, sure that whatever else she might do, at least Wren wouldn't weep—if only because she couldn't.

How could he have been such a fool? Why hadn't he believed Gerein? Understood what the horse was? It was free, that was what it was, under no man's hand. As it probably should have been all along, but that was rather hard on the mere mortals who'd tangled with it. The horse was gloriously free, and he—his future didn't bear thinking upon. Better he go find Wren, have the last of the worst over with. Maybe she'd curse him with something fatal. Titch bent, picking up the bridle out of habit and tidiness.

Warm air gusted down the back of his neck. It didn't feel dangerous, but it wasn't a wing-gust from Alinor. Fresh out of guesses, Titch decided 'twas his imagination, giving warmth to a swirling breeze.

Something brushed his close-shorn hair, tickling.

Titch whirled, and the world was full of horse, no less black than the wide night sky. Those star-filled eyes captured his, effortlessly.

I am named Valadan. One or two of the star-sparks winked a pretty purple-blue color.

"Gerein said you were demon-bred," Titch whispered stupidly. He just hadn't believed.

I am magic-bred, the stallion corrected. *And I am in your debt.* The slender head, so broad between the liquid eyes, so narrow at the delicate muzzle, dipped a foot toward the grass. *I was born to serve the dukes of Esdragon. Gerein compelled me with Cold Iron, because he had not the right by other means.*

"Why did you come back?" Titch asked, his knees shaking. His guilt smote him—he had been perfectly content to extend the bondage Gerein had begun.

Debts must be paid, especially debts of honor.

Would it make him pay for Gerein's crime as well as his own? Titch's heart beat hard enough to choke him, but it was no less than he deserved.

I pledge you service, the horse said, astonishingly, incredibly, into his head.

"You shouldn't," Titch admitted in a tiny voice, knowing every word of it true. "I don't deserve such a gift. I deserve—" He couldn't think of a punishment suitably severe for what he'd been a party to. Those eyes, full of swirling sparks, seemed to draw his soul out of his body. If there'd been a hole handy, he'd have crawled in, to hide himself where this glorious creature of wind and night could never see him.

You chose the right. So shall I. The horse extended its head toward him, nostrils fluttering, taking in his scent.

Titch held his hand out, felt the velvet muzzle and the warm tongue that soothed the rope burns on his palm. The liquid eyes filled with flickers of gold, tiny pricks of adamant and emeraude. The sense of welcome and acceptance where he had expected wrath and punishment was enough to make his head swim. Titch shivered, tangled his fingers desperately in the long mane so he could be sure he'd stay upright. He shut his eyes, felt a gentle puff of air as the stallion blew into his face. Its breath smelled like summer, hay and flowers. Not a whiff of smoke, or flame. All his lost dreams were under his fingers, tangled into the silken hair of the black stallion's mane.

"Valadan," Titch breathed, accepting.

At least it didn't prove difficult explaining to Wren about the horse—not that Valadan was magic, not that Titch could receive silent messages from the horse inside his head just as she did from her own familiar. Magic-trained, Wren ac-

cepted the news measurably better than Titch did himself.
She helped Titch detach the foul iron bit from the leather
headstall and bury it deep in an abandoned rabbit hole.
Then she met Valadan formally and offered herbs to tend
the sores at the corners of the stallion's mouth. In serving
Titch, the stallion would be serving Wren, as well, till the
swan was found and Galvin was rescued.

What astounded Titch most—beyond waking and seeing
the stallion grazing peacefully and unrestrained nearby at
dawn—no longer a figment of a fever-dream—was the
change he felt when he sat upon Valadan's back once more.
It was the impossible-to-express difference between a cut
log and a living tree with its roots thrust in the ground and
its branches sporting in the wind. It was the ineffable contrast between a cup of still water poured from a pitcher and
a deep draft from a free-flowing stream. Now that he felt it,
Titch could scarce believe that he hadn't missed its lack
while it was absent. All that from the removal of a bit? It
passed belief. It smote his heart.

"Cold iron," Wren explained patiently. "Iron poisons
magic. Didn't your officers tell you your iron weapons and
armor would protect you from our sorcery?"

"Frankly, I thought they were lying to make us feel
braver," Titch said. "You mean you really *can't* work a
spell on someone wearing iron?" Had she stripped him before she set to work on his tooth? Titch couldn't remember.

"I can't work magic if *I'm* touching cold iron." Wren
frowned, reasoning the theory out. "And spells bounce off
it, so you need to be careful of that. Sometimes they throw
sparks, same as a flint does. It makes the magic dangerous
for the bespeller as well as the bespelled."

"So, we were safe from you?" He ran a hand over his
jaw, still suspicious of the late Mistress Agatha.

"None of us escaped, did we?" Wren poked a stick
fiercely into the fire.

"*You* did." Only even as he said the words, Titch knew
they weren't true. Wren hadn't escaped, or even attempted
to. She was alive, where certain others were dead, but that
was Galvin's doing more than her own. And she certainly
wasn't free of the probably impossible quest after the ensor-

celled swan-prince. If anything she was more firmly tethered to it, since Galvin's life all too certainly depended on
her success. Her clear eyes went dark with sorrow, and
Titch put a hand on her thin shoulder. "I'm sorry. I didn't
mean it that way."

"He's all I have, Titch, except for Alinor. Don't you have
family?" It seemed impossible to make him understand how
little she possessed, how desperately she'd cling to it.

"Not now. My father died when I was small, and my
mother a little after. That's all. If there'd been anyone else,
they'd have told me. I was raised by the innkeeper's wife."
His turn to stare into the dancing flames. "We'll save him,
Wren. The queen can't afford to kill every sorcerer, she's
got to know she'll need one to restore her son! And we'll
get the swan—"

As if to a music master's cue, a sharp cry echoed far
overhead. The sun had gone down, but the sky was still
light—between mauve islands of clouds, a skein of birds
flew. Alinor stirred restlessly from her perch on the saddle-
bow. Her shoulders rose, her knees bent slightly as if she
was about to take wing, but she only jerked her beak upward once or twice as she stared.

Titch could see that the birds flew in a vee behind a
leader, but they were too high for him to count reliably or
distinguish precisely. Their cries faded, like wails of wandering ghosts. Titch looked sadly at Wren. "I always paid
more attention to battle skills than hunting, except rabbits
for the pot—"

Gray geese, Alinor observed scathingly, folding her
wings, using her beak to make fine adjustments to her
feathers. Wren reached out to soothe her.

"Swans are strong fliers, by day and night," she told
Titch. "They cover lots of distance. I don't know just where
we are, but we probably have a long way to go."

He nodded and glanced at Valadan. "We'll be in time,
Wren. I can feel it—he was fast before, but now—"

The wind sired me, Valadan whispered gently into his
tumbling thoughts. *I am well acquainted with its speed.*

Waiting On

THEY WENT WITH the wind as their playfellow. Alinor explored it currents above them, but she could no longer outdistance them as she had in earlier days, such was Valadan's now-effortless speed. To glance at nearby landmarks was not possible—those rushed past in a blur. To fix one's gaze farther afield still unsettled, for the most distant points leaped nearer with dizzying haste. Well acquainted with the wind's speed, indeed. Valadan *was* the wind.

Alinor customarily hunted for her own food, and as they'd lost their supplies to the ambush, Titch and Wren relied on the falcon's skill to feed them, as well, or at least help their meager store of dried food to stretch for more days. That was no hardship for the bird—when Alinor had made a kill, she'd pluck its feathers deftly away and pull out the kidneys, which she especially relished. She would then allow Wren to claim the rest of the carcass, and if she had fed especially well, Titch might even lay his hands on the half-plucked remains, so long as Wren had touched them first. Game was plentiful, and Alinor killed consistently, but she relished flight for its own sake and would constantly stoop at birds she had not the slightest intention of striking, purely for the joy of the hunt, the thrill of the hurtling ambush from the clouds.

Yet Titch thought she didn't fly enough, and risked saying so. "You expect her to take a swan," he explained patiently to an indignant Wren. "She's never gone after anything that big, has she?"

"That teal drake was huge!" Wren protested, recalling the previous day's dinner.

"Delicious, too," Titch agreed. "But nowhere near the

size of a swan. And mostly Alinor takes pigeons, or gulls. Nothing wrong with that, and I don't say she *can't* bring down a bigger bird—but she needs to learn how to manage it. Swans aren't her natural prey. She'd never go after one on her own. We've got to teach her."

"How?" Wren asked tightly, watching Alinor, perhaps listening to her.

"Like any other hunting bird. She's got to practice. Single out one bird in a flock and make her go after it. Trained hawks will take heron, but you'll never see a wild one even think about it! They have to be taught. And they are, by falconers who don't have any control over their birds but a lure and a whistle. You and Alinor can do much better."

Wren stared up at Alinor, soaring in pointed silence through silver edges of clouds. It was past sun-high, when falconers vowed hawks flew best. The peregrine had cast well that morning, relieving herself of the indigestible parts of the previous day's meals, fur and feathers and a tiny bone or two. She was in good temper, not yet sharp-set with hunger, eager for play. "But if she doesn't kill, she'll be upset," Wren fretted uncertainly.

Titch patted the saddlebag. "There's a bit of that magpie left." Magpie wasn't very good eating for humans, but it might content Alinor. "And I don't know that we want her to kill—just get used to dealing with something bigger than she is. If we ride over that way, I think we'll scare up some geese." He nudged Valadan gently, a shift of weight and knee and an instant alteration of course. Even burdened with a rider and passenger, Valadan was nimble as any roving breeze.

Wren carefully explained the plan to Alinor. "Do you really care *which* one she goes for?" she asked Titch plaintively, half her attention still on her familiar. Evidently, the falcon was unhappy with his meddling.

"We're going to eventually," Titch pointed out sensibly. Letting Alinor call the tune would be a bad beginning, he thought. "Tell her the second one to go up."

The geese stubbornly stayed put as they trotted close, refusing to take to the air. They might have noticed the falcon overhead and made the determination that they were safer afloat. Titch finally aimed Valadan straight at the water, and they went splashing in at a canter, throwing up a sheet of water. Startled geese took wing in honking confusion. Wren squealed.

Alinor was invisible against the sun. Titch circled the stallion back toward dry ground, one eye on the scattered geese. Where was the falcon? The geese were wheeling, too, heading nervously back toward the water. One or two landed at once, honking and hissing with irritation. The remaining fowl began to swing about in ragged formation, trying to align themselves with the breeze for a smooth landing. Would he have to put them up a second time? Where was Alinor? Sulking, refusing instruction altogether?

A slate-color thunderbolt shot through the file of geese, wind whistling shrill music through her feathers. She struck with her talons, missed a young gander by a handsbreadth, was forced to pull out of her dive before she ran out of sky. The gander made an awkward landing on the water and thrashed into the safety of some tall rushes. Alinor shrieked her displeasure and threw up steeply once more, *hek*king furiously.

"That wasn't so bad," Titch said encouragingly. "Tell her it's a game, and she'll enjoy it more, the better she gets."

"She's really upset," Wren said, her brows knit, her head tilted back as she scanned the sky.

"I can tell." Titch grinned. "Mention that I said she's too fine a falcon to content herself with easy prey."

Wren gazed mildly up toward Alinor—then went wide-eyed.

"What?" Titch asked, feeling her stiffen against his back like a horse about to shy.

"You don't want to know," Wren whispered, shocked. "I didn't know she *knew* words like that."

"I hated my first swordmaster sometimes, too," Titch said, still grinning. "I think lots better of him in hindsight." He halted the stallion, considered options. "Have her wait on. I'll flush her something else." He dismounted and began to walk through the tall grass, still brown but showing green around the roots. The water was shallow, the pondlet was small. No room for every goose to find safety in the middle. Some would have hidden out on the fringes, instead—

"Titch, watch out!"

Valadan screamed the same warning.

Titch ducked, stumbling on the uneven and unreliable ground, and Alinor's talons missed his right ear by an inch. Her downsweeping pinions brushed his hair. Since Titch couldn't fly to evade her, Alinor didn't need to climb to come back at him. All she had to do was wheel smartly about, turning on a wingtip. Titch dove flat into the grass. A brown mallard, its nerve well broken, clapped into the air and straight into Alinor's path. There was a *thump* overhead, and a few feathers flew free on the wind. The duck was stone-dead in midair, plummeting to the muddy earth. Alinor followed it down, snatched the carcass and bore it back to her mistress' feet, then commenced tearing at it with her scimitar of a beak, scattering more feathers.

Titch lay for another moment with his arms wrapped about his head, then slowly arose.

"Alinor says 'thank you,' " Wren dutifully reported, as Titch cautiously rejoined them.

Alinor detested being told how to fly, especially by a wretch who was without wings himself. Titch struggled to put the point across that he merely wanted to offer her prey worthy of her undeniably superior skill. There was more to hunting than eating. In that, luckily, Alinor was disposed to agree with him. Such agreement did not translate into agreeability, or alter her opinion of him. Titch still kept a wary eye on the sky whenever the falcon wasn't on Wren's fist. Better safe than ambushed and sorry.

Alinor could, all on her own, execute amazing feats of strategy. She'd mount high, then allow potential prey to fly out of sight behind a rise of ground before ever giving earnest chase. Most such birds never had the least idea they were in peril, but at other times the falcon would openly spook a fowl for the pleasure of darting at it repeatedly, panicking it with near misses until it flew blind with terror. As often as not, she'd then let it go free.

The flat land was good hunting country for a falcon, without obstacles or hindrances. It was inevitable that they would see wild raptors sooner or later.

"Careful," Titch advised Wren, meddling again. The circling bird was a tiny speck riding a distant updraft, but Alinor was keenly aware of it. She tightened her feathers, bobbed her head eagerly. "It's spring. They're looking for mates." No way to tell at such a distance whether the strange bird was a tiercel.

"She won't leave me," Wren said—but she sounded uncertain. Then, with relief, she relayed: "That's a gyrfalcon."

There were probably eagles in the area, as well. They'd need to worry about Alinor becoming prey herself, should she fly unwarily. Not that Alinor ever did so—she was mistress of the air, uncontested, faster than the bigger birds, more maneuverable on the wing, the best diver of any of them.

"Ask her to stay closer. If she sees another peregrine and rakes off after it, she may not listen to you," Titch cautioned.

Wren nodded. Alinor circled nearer. "What's that white over there?"

Titch squinted, shook his head. "Have to ask Alinor. She can outsee me. Might be snow geese." The birds were untroubled by Alinor's overflying them, as well they could afford to be. Peregrines didn't normally take prey from the ground, nor on the water. He heard honking, though. Something was coming in, aiming at one of the tiny snowmelt lakes but still airborne.

Alinor wheeled smoothly toward the sound. She let Wren choose for her, without protest, and settled to business.

It was like watching a good sheepdog work a flock. Alinor's pitch was twice as high above the skein of geese as the geese were above the marshy ground, and her unexpected arrival among them when she finally stooped threw them into confusion. She let them all go save one, which she stayed on relentlessly, not so much cutting the bird from its flock as refusing to allow it to join with its scattered kin again. Wren's face was white with strain, as she watched the duel through falcon's eyes as well as her own.

"Alive," Titch whispered. Alinor had brought down two graylag geese thus far. She crushed the skull of the first with her deadly beak. Next time Wren had restrained her better, but the terrified goose had flown straight into the ground and broken its silly neck. They dared not risk that with the swan. The idea was to rescue the prince *alive*, and as close to unhurt as they possibly could.

Alinor struck a feint at the goose, which went into a tumbling sideslip. It landed hard, but broke the fall in the last inches with outspread wings. Titch sent Valadan leaping toward it as Alinor pounced and disappeared into the rank grass.

They came up to find the falcon crouching triumphantly over the white goose. The downed bird's beady eyes were swollen huge with fear, but at least they were not glazing over in death. Alinor mantled protectively over her prey, sitting back on her tail so that her sharp talons were free for use. Titch took the hint and kept well back while Wren called her off, tempted her with a bit of rabbit's kidney. When 'twas safe, he went to the panting goose, inspected it critically with eyes and hands. He partly expected to have to grant it a merciful dispatch, but was pleasantly confounded.

"A few broken feathers, but I think it can still fly!" Titch exulted. "Good work, Alinor!"

She hissed at him from Wren's fist, and he suspected she was wondering what *his* kidneys would taste like.

The sky was so vast, the soaring falcon so tiny against it. Wren, overwhelmed with the sharp taste of limitless range, lost all sense of the distance Alinor had flown. Mind to mind, it was always as if Alinor was but arm's length away, within her touch. She felt the icy wind aloft as if it blew through her own tangled hair. The sky's colors—lavender, apricot, pale teal, rose—might have been before her own eyes. It wasn't till Titch squeezed her shoulder that Wren came back to her earthbound self, blinking as if all the light had gone out of the world.

"There's a storm on the way," Titch said urgently. "Look at the clouds!"

Wren looked, with her own gray human eyes. The clouds looked to be the same fantastic piles they had been all that day, flying fast, their great shadows ghosting swiftly across land and water beneath them, unimpeded. The cloud castles were too white to look at for long in the low-angled light of the falling sun, their edges picked out in an emperor's treasury-worth of purest gold. The vast towers were even prettier where Alinor was, flying between them. Wren's eyes lost focus as she watched once more through a falcon's keen eyes.

"Wren!" Titch shouted, jerking at her shoulder for emphasis. "Call her back! Can't you feel the wind?"

There'd been wind all the day long, bending the grasses, snarling her hair. But was it a bit colder, a touch swifter? More predatory? Wren stared with nervous awareness at the castles and towers, soaring right up to the top of the heavens. Their bottoms were flat now, and dark as iron. And they were *vast*, only seeming small because there was so much sky surrounding them, so much land flat as a bedsheet beneath. As she stared, lightning forked through the base of one mighty tower. The storm was far off, but it traveled fast as the enchantment-bred horse. It would very soon be upon them. Already she could hear the thunder. Wren cringed, not liking the sound.

Alinor! Her familiar could not survive among the storm's powerful winds. She would be hurled to the ground on a downdraft, or swept helplessly ahead of the storm, carried a hundred battering leagues away and lost. Where was she?

Alinor was not the least concerned about the storm. She did not come winging back to Wren's urgent call—she did not even alter her course. She soared on, through a golden sky, borne on the wind's strong back.

"Alinor!" There was nowhere on the endless plain for a bird to take shelter. There wasn't a tree for a thousand leagues, a cliff for twice that distance. No other birds were flying. Anything with sense had grounded itself. Wren said so, urgently. There was nothing to hunt but destruction. But if Alinor heard, she still did not heed.

"Which way did she go?" Titch asked. "We'll ride to her."

He was right, Wren realized, half sick. Alinor would not fly *into* the storm, to return to them. They'd have to go to her.

"I don't know where she is!" Wren realized, disconcerted. The sky was too big, the brown plain too featureless. There were no landmarks. The loss of contact panicked her more than the ominous thunder, the too-dark sky. Why didn't Alinor answer?

"She won't have gone *toward* the storm! Keep calling her!" Titch swung Valadan about, sent him racing along the wind's course. The stallion was surely fleet as any storm wind, but the sky overhead was already dark as a bruise. Lightning flashed, again and again. Between one cloud and another, then from the clouds to the ground, like the stab of a heron's beak after a frog. The storm was outflanking them, no matter how swiftly they sped. Wren clung to Titch, arms about his waist, her face raised toward a sky that seemed crowded but was empty of all that mattered.

"Can you ward off lightning?" Titch called out worriedly, over rushing air and pounding hooves.

Wren had never put much stock in the sprig of lightningwort Galvin had kept nailed over the cottage doorway. She'd just stayed snug indoors when storms came, under a roof and safe behind her master's other wards ... wards that had not kept out armed men. Wren tangled her fingers in Titch's cloak and shook her head. She felt as if her brains would rattle. The air was shaking.

We should seek low ground. The storm could not be outpaced, not given the vastness of the area it crossed. Filling the whole sky, it could not be evaded. Only mountains or forest could halt or deflect it, and there was none of either nearby. Valadan raised his head high, to spy out the roll of the land as he galloped. *I could outrun this wind, but I do not know where we would find ourselves, then.*

"We can't take shelter!" Titch shouted. "We have to find the falcon!"

Wren put her whole heart into another desperate call to Alinor. Somewhere, far off, she thought she felt the falcon wheel about, angling her long wings. But she could see nothing, and the touch was no more than the merest brush of a feather, gone before she could examine it.

She had always been mistress of the air, but now that air was an enemy, keeping her from her goal, hurling her back, buffeting her, threatening to dash her to the unforgiving earth. No more safe, friendly sky where she reigned supreme. Safety lay behind a gloved fist, a perch upon which no harm could befall. Alinor aimed herself at that refuge, but it was impossible to see so tiny a quarry at so great a distance, even with her eyes. She heard her mistress call— but the summons was faint against the storm's din.

She knew where it was. She longed to reach it, but the storm conspired to thwart her—

We are cresting a hill.

"We are?" Titch struggled to see through the wind-whipped dust. He felt the stallion's weight shifting the other way and he leaned back to help balance their descent. That lasted only a moment—it wasn't much of a hill. The wind could howl right over it, and did.

But at least they were no longer such a tempting target for lightning. If they dismounted, they'd no longer be the tallest things in all the broad windswept landscape. Titch swung Wren to the ground, despite her sudden struggles and protests.

"*Titch, she can't see us!* She can't come to me if she can't see me!"

That was probably true—the hill would hide them, screen them from eyes as well as wind. "Tell her to come to your call," he suggested.

"She can barely hear me in this wind," Wren wailed. "If she can't see something to aim herself at—" Lightning smote the earth a thousand paces off. Thunder cracked almost instantaneously in answer.

"You stay down here!" Titch ordered her fiercely. He legged Valadan back up the little hill, poised the stallion snorting atop it. A nice big target for a homing falcon to glimpse—or for the lightning. "Keep calling her!" he yelled back to Wren. He raised his left fist, to give Alinor an easy perch. The sky was absolutely black; he didn't suppose he'd see her coming, even though her breast feathers were light in color. Falcons were very hard to detect in the air if they were flying straight at you. Their underfeathers were patterned to confuse, even without a storm's assistance.

The rain arrived first, great slashing sheets of it, a thousand tiny blows melded into one huge slap across his head and shoulders, all down his back. Titch hunched forward as much as he could, while still keeping his hand raised for the incoming bird. Surely she would choose the known safety of a gloved fist rather than veering past him into the storm's teeth. It wouldn't have mattered if her mistress had belled her—he'd never have heard tiny silver bells over the long rolls of thunder, the lashing of rain.

Flash and crash. They were still separate, but not by more than half a heartbeat. Valadan stood steady, unpanicked, which was more than Titch could say for himself. Thunderbolts were the gods' arrows, and he felt as if one of them were taking deliberate aim at him now. His back itched, the skin between his shoulders burned. All of his hair was standing on end except that on his head, which was plastered flat to his skull. The force of the rain seemed to double and redouble—flashes of stark white light showed him hailstones bouncing into the grass.

The sky and the earth were rumbling as one, as if they'd been swallowed by some hungry beast. Titch quivered where he sat as the vibration came up Valadan's legs, was transmitted to his own spine. His teeth chattered together, though he did not feel cold. Lightning blinded him, and his upraised arm weighed like molten lead—painful and too heavy to keep aloft much longer. He could hear Wren calling the bird aloud now—Titch wondered whether that had any better chance of success. How well did birds hear? The thunder had deafened him—

There was a great flash of light, a clap of sound like a harpy's wings. Titch heard Valadan scream. And then nothing except darkness, and falling.

* * *

"Alinor!"

Titch realized he had grass in his mouth. He spat it out, raised his head groggily. That involved pushing himself up with his hands, since he discovered he had unaccountably come to rest upon his face on the bumpy turf. He felt the hard pebbles of hailstones burning cold under his fingers. "Is she all right?" he asked Wren dazedly. "Did the lightning hit her, too?"

"She's fine." Wren's voice sounded strange. His ears were ringing, Titch realized—not surprisingly.

Valadan nuzzled his shoulder. *The lightning did not hit her,* the stallion corrected him gently. *It did not hit you—the falcon did that.*

Titch managed to hitch himself onto his knees. Thunder cracked again, and he flinched, almost diving flat. When he jerked, his head throbbed sharply, and a wave of dizziness washed over him, leaving him colder than before, feeling as if he were about to be sick. He waited for the sensation to pass, grateful when it did. His ears still buzzed.

Grounded and alive. And he's much bigger than any swan, the falcon reported gleefully.

"Shame on you!" Wren cried. "He was trying to help me keep you safe. You've hurt him!" Wren would have gone to Titch, but that would have forced her to carry Alinor into striking range of him, and she did not dare.

Titch put a hand to his head, to steady it as he arose. Something hot was trickling through his hair, over his fingers. Rain still pelted him, but that wetness was icy cold. Titch decided he was bleeding. Something had sliced his scalp, just above the stubble of his helm-cut. He tried to explore the injury, ignoring the swimming of his senses.

Alinor ruffled her feathers, shedding rain, fuming. Wren draped her cloak as best she could to keep the rain off her unsettled charge.

Valadan's side did a little of the same for Titch, as he used the stirrup to climb the rest of the way to his feet. Lightning didn't seem to be a significant risk any longer— the thunder was receding, swept on the wind into the dimness ahead, and of all the storm's trappings, only the rain remained with them. Titch looked uncertainly at Wren—

wet as when he'd pulled her from the flooded stream. She
wasn't looking back—there was a silent, nonetheless furious exchange taking place between witch and familiar.

Don't you ever do that again! Wren's eyes caught the last
of the lightning.

Addled like an untended egg, Alinor hissed. *Sitting there
waiting for the lightning to stoop on him.*

He was waiting for you! I didn't think you could find me.

I knew where you were. Alinor raised the feathers on her
head and neck, belying her tone of unconcern. Rain made
the dark feathers stand up in spikes, and she shook them
down irritably.

You didn't come back. I was afraid, Wren confessed.

You trusted him but not me? The falcon cocked her head,
and the grip on Wren's wrist tightened.

What would I do if I lost you? Wren pleaded.

The falcon shook off her concern, with another vigorous
feather-settling. *There is only what is. A foul sky.*

Wren pushed wet hair out of her own eyes. The falcon's
feet were still gripping her wrist tightly, meant as a reassurance to her, like a handclasp. Perhaps Alinor had been
frightened—she would never in this life admit it. Perhaps
the strike on Titch had been partly accidental. *Don't you
hurt him like that again,* Wren ordered sternly.

Alinor looked totally unrepentant, but after a moment she
turned her head away, and Wren considered the battle won.

"Tell Alinor . . ." Titch fingered his scalp gingerly. There
was a painful lump on the left side of his head, where talons had struck a glancing blow to his skull. Falcons
scarcely needed to *catch* their prey. If they got anywhere
near it, they left it in no shape to escape them. He looked
at Wren and smiled lopsidedly. "Tell her I said she doesn't
need any more practice."

The falcon preened herself placidly, as if she understood
him very well.

Seeking the Swan

THE STORM GIFTED the land with a thousand new tiny ponds. Every hoofprint Valadan left behind him sparkled within seconds. The swan-seekers rode through a kingdom's ransom of gems each morning, though the effect vanished by sun-high as the gems' moisture was given to the air—which did not very much require the addition. Under the sun's full heat, it felt thick as soup.

'Twas alive, as well. Some of the ever-present sound came from the frogs hatching in every wet spot. There was a constant whir of dragonfly wings. And, their numbers seemingly increasing tenfold each minute, mosquitoes and midges. The frogs and the dragonflies preyed on them. Plainly, there were too few of either to put even the tiniest dent in the buzzing hordes of bloodsuckers.

Titch slapped his jaw, then stared at bloody fingers and the remains of three insects. He'd thought he'd been in time, and hadn't. Valadan tossed his head, as well, but to little avail. The insects were very well adapted to feeding from moving creatures. Their numbers went a long way toward explaining the lack of large grazing animals across the landscape.

"This is going to be a problem," Titch said, slapping again. Already he itched. He expected matters would only get worse.

"No, it isn't," Wren answered placidly. She had kindled a modest fire and set her cup over it, brimming with readily available water.

"I'll grant, it's not quite so bad when we're on the move. There's not a mosquito hatched that Valadan can't outrun. But we have to rest sometimes. And whenever we do, we get bled white. All except maybe Alinor. Don't they like feathers?"

The falcon gave him a pointed glare and snapped her beak at him.

"Titch, I live on the edge of a marsh." Wren gave her cup a stir, then sprinkled in powders of various shades of green and brown. Her fingers made strange stirring motions over the bubbling liquid without touching it. "One of the first charms my master taught me was this salve for keeping biting insects away. And he expected we might need it before this matter was done, so I have the herbs I need."

Titch watched an especially husky mosquito make a stealthy landing on the back of his right hand. He moved deliberately into the drifting smoke of the fire, but fumes failed to bother the insect. He slapped it into oblivion just as two more jabbed him in the left cheek. Valadan snorted and moved about restlessly at the center of his own small cloud of midges, tossing his head. Titch glanced back at his arm—the sleeve was crawling with insects trying to bite through the leather to his skin. A loud whine in his ear suggested something was hunting for an easier target. He pulled his cloak over his head, to shut out the high-pitched whines as much as to save himself bites and stings.

"Does it really work?" he asked, muffled.

Wren, concentrating on whispering over the cup, didn't answer. Alinor favored him with another glare, then snapped her beak at a passing dragonfly.

Wren's biting-insect salve had to be rubbed into all exposed skin and combed through the hair. It didn't keep the midges away from one's nose and mouth very well, Titch noticed as he rubbed Valadan all over with Wren's second batch, which she had brewed extra-strength for the horse. He learned to breathe through his nose as best he could, and that carefully, taking whatever advantage he could of any strong breeze. The alternative was a mouthful of midges. Valadan rolled his head far to one side, letting Titch salve his ears liberally. A pair of horses could stand head to tail and defend one another from pests, but on his own Valadan had only his own tail for insect-chasing, and that did not reach so far to the front as his ears. It flicked across Titch's back as he worked—most of the insects had gone in search of less difficult meals, but a single buzz was enough to trigger instinct, and swishing. Titch appreciated the stallion's willingness to help him.

"Where are the swans, anyway?" he asked Valadan, stroking fragrant lotion into the hollows above the stallion's eyes, under the edge of his jaw. Thin skin was irresistible to the insect pests.

They had far to come.

Titch stopped his stroking. "They're here already?" he asked, shocked.

I heard them in the night. Swans navigate by the stars. Ahead there is a great lake that empties into the sea.

All the waterfowl they'd seen on these seasonal puddles had been various sorts of ducks, a crane or two. Swans needed more in the way of water for breeding and nesting, Titch supposed. "How far to this lake?"

Tomorrow we will see the nearest edge. But the water is large, Valadan amended.

Finding the lake, and swans, was far from the end of their quest. They needed a particular swan, and the birds would nest along leagues of shoreline if it was available to them. Titch passed on the news to Wren, uncertain whether he gave hope or despair.

Swans weren't the only birds selecting mates and nesting. There were falcons soaring the broad sky, some of them seeking partners, Alinor said coyly. She affected disdain for birds forced by geography to nest upon the bare ground rather than proper lofty cliffs, but she could not disguise her interest in the tiercels. Wren had controlled her through storm and over distance, but would the bond hold fast against the pull of a potential mate? Titch wondered. Each strange falcon was a danger of one sort or another— either it would lure Alinor off after it, or it would dispute her free passage through its home territory. A battle that injured a flight feather could compromise her when it came time to capture the swan.

Valadan brought them to the edge of the lake at sunfall,

but night hid its size from them. Morning revealed it, despite mist and sun, dazzling their eyes. The cries of a mighty multitude of birds rose into the air, with the thunderous beat of many wings for a counterpoint.

There were long-necked geese, at least half a dozen sorts by their varied colors. Ducks were easy to identify in the air by their flying style, which looked awkward and frantic compared to any of the geese. Herons, trailing long legs and with equally long necks recurved so as not to impede flight, were among the most impressive fliers. There were shorebirds past numbering, and white-throated kildeer that went nowhere near the shore, but ran crying across the grassland. There were many gulls, a few pelicans, a loon or two.

And swans, at long last. Titch saw one paddling effortlessly upon the lake like a drifting cloud, and pointed it out with an eager arm. Wren looked, and on her fist Alinor bobbed her head excitedly, tightening her feathers in readiness for flight. Farther out, other white shapes were visible. Titch searched the shoreline nearby, guessing that there would be nests among the reeds. He spotted one at last, and the snow-white pen swan sitting close on her early clutch of eggs.

"We're lucky, they'll be near enough to the shore for a good look," he said. "With their mates on the nests, the cobs will all be swimming sentry duty."

Wren pondered sending Alinor aloft. The falcon was desperately eager.

"I wouldn't," Titch advised soberly. "She'll only upset them. Till we find the bird we're after, she probably shouldn't even hunt by the water."

Alinor took the news badly, which was ill news for Titch, as well—Wren carrying the bird left the frustrated huntress rather too close to him. His left ear was easily in range of beak or talons. Titch had to fight against uselessly tensing that shoulder, knowing Alinor was just behind it. It wasn't as if he could stop her, but the temptation to try was continual.

"This is why falconers hood their hawks," he pointed out as Alinor fidgeted and fussed. She looked murder at him, yellow-rimmed dark eyes surrounded by their own hood of slate gray feathers. "They don't let them see anything they aren't to be set on." He touched his left leg to Valadan, and they proceeded along the lakeshore. Motion might keep Alinor content, or at least out of trouble.

Bright dragonflies dove and stooped upon prey, like bejeweled miniature falcons. A kingfisher flashed after something unseen. Titch spotted a blood-red fox secretively crossing their way, and many scurrying voles and lemmings, the fox's prey. Doubtless it had itself a meal of stolen eggs now and again.

So great a concentration of nests attracted egg thieves of every sort. Some, like the gulls, had nests of their own in the area. Others—the ravens, for sure—did not. Those birds flew in, watched their chance to seize an egg or a just-hatched chick, then departed with their loot despite squawks of protest. A horseman was not seen as a threat per se, but any intrusion bothered at least some of the nesting birds. More than one challenged Valadan with great bravado and fair success, sending him into snorting retreat.

Eventually, the sheer size of the lake forced a change of plans upon them—they had to let Alinor fly to search out swans. Riding slowly about the fringy boundaries of the lake and examining every inch of shore would have taken an impossibly long while. They'd still have been at it come autumn, when the swans departed for their winter homes. Alinor sprang up so eagerly that she was a mere speck against the sky in half a dozen heartbeats, but she settled equably enough when Wren asked her and began to ride the updrafts above the water, scouting in lazy, nonalarming spirals.

Wren was enchanted by the lake. She had never to her knowledge beheld the sea, had never before watched the play of colors across a vast expanse of wind-whipped water. She had not thought there were half so many shades of blue and green in all the world, and the deep lavenders were absolutely unexpected. The lake waters had as many colors in them as Titch's eyes did, or even more, and all endlessly changing. So much water made its own weather, as the sea did—there was nearly always a breeze off the water or off the land, depending on the time of day. It kept the sun's heat at bay, welcome since there was little shade available for anything so tall as a person or a horse.

Wildflowers bloomed everywhere, some in varieties Wren knew from her home marsh, others strange to her. "Forget-me-nots," Titch named some minute blue blossoms, which were pink in the bud, like lungwort's. If she made a tea of them, Wren wondered, could she hope for even a crumb of her past to be given back to her? Or had she spent her whole early life exactly as she feared betimes—as an otter, and no human girl at all? They ate fish at every meal; suppose that some morning she woke to find herself covered once more with sleek brown fur?

Nonsense. When she had *needed* to change to an otter, she had barely been able to do so. She had nearly drowned; *would* have, had Titch not rescued her. She glanced covertly at him, that falcon's face now burned brown by sun and wind, his hair grown down over his ears, his once berry-colored cloak stained and snagged and beginning to fade. He kept all his gear well polished, though. Not a spot of green on the brass, or red rust on the iron and steel. That was how knights were, though true knights had squires to do for them, as she'd done for her master . . .

Wren tried very hard not to think of her master. If Galvin was still alive, he was depending utterly upon her. If he wasn't—it was hard to think of such a grief when one could not shed a single tear in its service. Wren did not think she could bear it, to lose Galvin without being able to weep.

The lake was far longer than it was wide, Alinor informed her mistress. A river fed it with snowmelt, winding across the great flat plain from the distant mountains like a silver ribbon. Wren could not see those mountains, even in the clear air of early morning—Alinor said they were so far off that even her keen falcon's eyes saw only the infrequent sparkle of sunlight on glacial snows.

The lake owed its existence to an earthshake that had long ago opened a rift in the plain, deep and narrow as a plowed furrow. There was no real outlet for the waters that collected—at the far end of the rift the lake became extensive marshes, some of which finally touched the sea. It was perfect nesting country for waterfowl. Half the birds in the world seemed to be spread out among the wilderness of reeds—the sky was crowded with wings, large and small. Wren's ointment proved happily efficacious, and the bloodsuckers and midges left them in relative peace.

Alinor soared over the wet land for hours at a stretch, with Wren constantly reminding her familiar of what she sought. Swans, yes, but a swan different from the others. The tale of a collar of golden feathers might be true—Eral lords wore torques of precious metals about their necks, where Clandarans had favored crowns and coronets—but even if it was not, there must surely be some mark to distinguish the changeling prince from the true swans.

Had *she* looked different from an ordinary otter? Wren wondered. Her master had never mentioned it—he had never suspected he was hauling anything ashore beyond a fish-thief unluckily caught along with the fish in his trap. She had not been revealed till her feet touched dry land ... swans were creatures of so many elements: air, water, and land. Fire was all they seemed to lack an affinity for. Might flame or smoke show the prince to them? Wren listened to thwarted insects humming in the darkness, trying to use her schooling to discover an answer.

Iron broke magic. A spell would shift or fail when it touched cold iron. Only not always—a witch could be slain with an iron sword, and her curse would still hold the prince she had caught. You couldn't cast a spell *at* iron, but fire-sparks could be called from a flint with a bit of steel, even by the most unmagical of folk. A magic-made horse could be held prisoner by an iron bit, but she could herself lay a hand on Titch's sword and take no hurt from the contact. There was so much her master had not explained to her, so much she had not thought to ask of him. He had intended to take her to Kôvelir, the city the wizards had built for themselves. Maybe someone there could have told her about herself, unlocked her secrets, and unsealed her tearless eyes. There was no chance of that now.

* * *

While Alinor flew, Wren and Titch rode slowly through the drier fringes of the marsh, eyes always busy. Swans resented intrusion near their nests and generally announced themselves in spectacular fashion, the cobs making hissing charges at Valadan if he inadvertently ventured too near to a nest. Swans didn't back off as readily as did geese, either. The stallion's splashing, snorting retreat from beating wings became routine.

All the swans looked much the same—if one could get a good look through their furious approaches. Feathers white as milk in moonlight, tiny black masks about their eyes. There was little variation. How could they even hope to discover which bird-shape held the ensorcelled prince?

The swans fed on underwater plants, dipping their heads beneath the blue water or upending to reach even deeper with those long graceful necks. Some came out onto land to feed on the fresh shoots of the marsh grasses, waddling along by day and returning to the safety of the water at night. Noticing that, Wren made it a point to have Alinor aloft at such times, when many birds could be seen at once. Not every bird had paired yet, nor all pairs begun to nest. Some, too young, would not mate at all this season. Would the prince be as youthful in swan-shape as in human? It seemed a likely thing. Checking *only* nests could be a mistake. But how to check every bird?

Sometimes the swans emerged from feeding with water weed draped round their long necks. But that was a collar of green, never of gold. Wren half despaired of ever seeing that circlet of golden feathers. Had it been a lie told to the queen? Had they seen every swan on the great lake yet? It seemed possible that Alinor at least might actually accomplish that. Her eyes were keener than any other creature's, and she knew what she was looking for.

Hah! the falcon cried, and executed a rolling turn, fanning her tail and sweeping back over the lake, high above the blue water.

Wren came to attention. Alinor glided silently, making no further comment. Valadan walked on, knee deep in a channel of water. Wren tugged at Titch's right arm.

"That way?" he asked, glancing back at her, then searching the sky for the falcon.

"Along the shore. She sees something."

The wind made music in reeds and rushes. A few irises bloomed, their petals even brighter than the flashing colors of the dragonflies. A reach of deeper water opened before them, and Valadan halted.

Ahead, two swans glided toward one another, scarcely a ripple behind either bird, so stately was their progress. They halted breast to breast, necks raised, beaks tipped down toward the water. The sleek short feathers on their necks rose up like cats' fur, as they did when the birds warned off intruders, but there was no hissing, no flapping of wings to indicate that they saw Valadan or the watchers on his back, and they would have no fear of Alinor above. Both birds lifted their wings slightly, but they then wheeled together, so that they swam side by side.

One cloud-white bird dipped its masked head beneath the water, then began to preen itself. The other bird dipped its head, also. This the pair did several times, till at last they were dipping at precisely the same instant, raising their heads as one and holding them close together on erect necks. And still they swam as one creature, effortless turn and turn about, like a measured dance on the mirror of the lakewater. The female lowered her wings, trailing them into the water, and drew a little ahead. The cob mounted her gently, grasping her neck feathers tenderly in his bill. As he slipped away from her, both birds gave a soft, trumpeting call, an announcement of triumph. Then they rose up out of the water together, breast to breast again, neck to neck, rubbing their bills against one another. They bathed and preened, then swam off slowly, still side by side.

"Did you see?" Wren whispered, awed.

Titch flushed to the roots of his hair and had a difficult time finding his voice to answer her. He stared fixedly at the departing swans.

"He's found a mate," Wren said.

True. Titch flushed again. Then he saw what Alinor had—the narrow golden ring of feathers encircling the cob's long neck.

* * *

"We can't go after him out on the water—he'd drown Alinor, or even us." Titch hadn't gauged the depth fully, but he knew the lake was too deep for wading out, net in hand. The swan could escape by flying or swimming, either one. "And once they start nesting, he's going to stay in the water by that nest just like all the other males do. They're defending the nests from each other, not us, but that's no help—we need to have him over land, flying, so Alinor can catch him. We need to keep him out of the lake." They'd camped well back from the water so as not to disturb the birds, but the move would have been necessary anyway, to find a spot dry enough for minimal comfort.

"Some of them *do* come out to feed," Wren observed. The birds looked smaller on dry land, and lost a large measure of their grace.

"Not the ones nesting. And he's been pulling reeds and passing them to her all day." Titch was no expert on swans, but he'd seen plenty of them about the lake, enough to recognize the obvious. Nesting was the seal set on the bond between mates.

The prince's pen was happily constructing the customary mound of piled vegetation. She didn't trouble about concealing it—as the largest birds in the landscape, the swans mostly feared only one another, and threats and posturings would deflect interlopers and encroachments. Camouflage was unnecessary.

"How do we get him to come out, then?" Wren inquired reasonably.

"We're going to have to hope he gets hungry," Titch decided, reluctantly admitting he couldn't think of anything else that would lure the bird.

"They feed in the water."

"Yes, but he might come ashore a bit, before she starts to lay eggs and he settles down to guarding them. Keep Alinor well away—they don't seem to be bothered by her, but he won't be so likely to come out if he thinks there's danger, to him or to his lady. Meanwhile, we'll do well to start making a net. We've got to hope we'll need it."

Some of the past season's dry grasses were yet strong

enough to twist into a cord of sorts. They gathered those from among the new green shoots and set to work as industriously as the swans at their nest. Wren's fingers flew, her lips and fingers both cast spells of binding, weaving the makeshift cords into the broad web of a net. Titch judged they'd need all the help magic could lend them, and more—they were neither of them skilled fiber craftsmen. He was best at gathering, come to that. The grasses broke in his hands when he tried to knot them. Wren was a trifle more patient, thereby slightly more successful. But the spellcraft was vital.

Nor were the newly paired swans expert, by appearances. They'd work for an hour at the nest, then destroy it in a moment, evidently deliberately, but for no reason Titch could detect. The ring-necked cob swam farther and farther off in quest of materials, and Titch wagered the net would be done ere the nest.

Wren looked up from the grass stems, her eyes gone out of focus. "A *glamor* would work," she breathed, very much to herself.

"What's a glamor?" Titch rashly intruded, but got no answer. Wren's face was tipped to the sky, evidently to facilitate asking a question of her airborne familiar.

"What could I use for a mirror?"

Titch shivered, though he knew there was no reason for unease. Wasn't he used to magic yet? Didn't he ride a horse made by it? So why did he feel that someone had just brushed an icicle down his spine? "My sword blade's mirror bright," he said helpfully. "You could use that."

"It's iron." Wren frowned, not looking at him.

Steel, but the same thing where magic was concerned. Titch was abashed. "I'm sorry. I didn't mean to meddle." He fought the urge to duck his head for safety, unable to believe that Alinor was safely far away and would not swiftly punish his intrusion.

"We've nothing," Wren muttered. "And nothing white, either. I almost wish you still had the other horse—*he* was white as a swan, at least."

Titch was completely baffled. Mirrors. Whiteness. What

had either to do with the other? Or with what Wren wanted to attempt?

Snow is white.

Titch looked toward the stallion. The observation about snow made no sense to him, though of course it was incontrovertably true. Snow certainly *was* white.

Valadan pawed the grass deliberately. *There was snow here a week ago. It is still a long while till high summer. There will be drifts lying about yet in sheltered places.*

Titch stared into the stallion's eyes. He understood the suggestion, if nothing beyond it. "Get ready," he bade Wren. "We're going to fetch you some snow."

Valadan all but put the stirrup on his foot, he stood so near and so still. But the instant Titch's leather trews touched the saddle, the stallion was away at a sweeping gallop, and the wind roared past Titch's ears, cooled and then burned his cheeks. He turned his head to glance back at Wren, and she wasn't even in sight. Titch wobbled an instant.

You must hold on better than that, Valadan advised, amused.

He shouldn't be able to ride the wind, Titch thought. There was nowhere to put a saddle . . . you couldn't bridle the wild wind, either.

I am not wind. A storm wind sired me. Titch nodded dumbly. *My back carries a saddle and a rider as well as any other horse's.*

Titch nodded again and tried not to be alarmed at the way the landscape rushed past him. It ought to be easy enough to ignore—there was nothing but moor and sky, one bit looking just like another. They couldn't possibly be going as fast as it felt they were.

You need not fear.

No. He could trust. But he might need to shut his eyes. An amused whicker answered his thought, inside his head because the wind was too much for mere mortal ears, and he would never have heard so soft a sound.

Snowfields.

Titch raised his face, and the wind of their passage made his eyes tear fiercely. There was a white blur ahead: snow, or a bank of sunlit fog, a white cliff. No way he could tell, he must take Valadan's word for it. He felt the stallion slacken stride. Titch dismounted as Valadan came to a halt—and nearly pitched onto his face when his knees misjudged what they needed to do about holding him up. That even a magic-bred horse could run like that made his senses swim. It was a moment before he could bend to the snow without falling into it.

The topmost layer was icy—the sun had been at the drift, though it had not vanquished it. Titch broke through, used his hands to scoop a great quantity of the cold stuff into the center of his hastily doffed cloak. He should have thought to bring a sack of some sort—but when had he had time to think?

"This isn't going to last long," he warned the stallion.

She will not need for it to last. Valadan snorted.

He must understand what Wren intended. "Do I have enough?" He probably had all he could manage to carry, Titch thought.

The stallion's head nodded, and he turned his side for emphasis, to encourage Titch to mount swiftly. Already the cloak was wet, as the outermost snow turned to water.

Well, that wasn't from the warmth of his hands. They felt like ice themselves, and Titch had to loop the reins over his elbows, because even if his hands had been free, he doubted they'd have been reliable. If the horse intended to go that fast again . . .

You don't use the reins to stay on, idiot! Titch told himself angrily. That's what the gods gave you balance for. The way he runs, you couldn't hold tight enough to stay aboard if he didn't want you there!

Perceptive, Valadan said approvingly, and his handgallop all at once extended into that other, tempestlike pace. *What brought you to your senses?*

"I've just remembered that I don't fall off horses unless someone pushes me off with a lance." Titch laughed. "Sometimes not even then."

You may trust me.

"Just warn me if you see Alinor coming."

Valadan snorted. Evidently her attack had disconcerted

him as much as his rider—he had a habit of flinching now when the falcon came in for her landings. Titch didn't blame him one bit.

The melting snow was soaking through the cloak. How far had they needed to come to find it? Would it last till they reached Wren's side once more? Titch felt the gallop dwindle to a gentle canter, between one heartbeat and the next. He had never ridden a horse with transitions so smooth under saddle. Titch sat up a little and saw Wren standing in the rank grass just ahead. The finished net lay beside her. She stared as he got down out of the saddle and thrust the cloak at her. It dripped profusely, but in the center, well shielded—

"Snow," Titch announced. "Lovely white snow." He peeled the dark-red wool back to show her.

Wren's mouth opened with surprise, but she mastered herself and took the soggy cloak in a protective grasp. She lowered it to the grass, and her hands began at once to work on the lump of icy whiteness.

What do I do now? Titch wondered. He cleared his throat, loath to interrupt her but even more reluctant to fail out of a lack of understanding.

"Pick up the net," Wren said. The snow was taking a swan-shape, crude but obvious enough.

A rush of air announced Alinor's arrival. Those swans feeding out on the grassland took no heed of her, no more than they did of the humans. Hunters must be very few indeed, Titch thought—though he knew that without Wren's insect ointment most folk would be too occupied swatting and scratching to be any real threat to the birds. He wasn't truly surprised at the lack of human predators in the marshland, and the swans were too big and powerful to be bothered by a lone falcon. He'd been overcautious about Alinor.

The sun stood high in the sky. The nights were dwindling, and one day the sun would nearly always be above the watery horizon. The snow under Wren's hands was melting rapidly. Titch watched a swan swallow down a toad. Not a usual meal, but the birds needed bountiful food reserves for successful breeding and rearing of their young. Plenty of space, too, since the larger, older birds defended territories with ferocity. The prince, being young, and new to being a swan as well, would have his work cut out for him in his first try at it.

Wren's small hands were making passes in the air above the snow-swan. She commenced a singsong chanting, soft as the wind sighing in the grass.

Titch blinked. All at once, the biggest, whitest swan he'd ever seen stood before Wren's raggedy figure, though it was facing the lake and the other swans. It raised its long neck high and trumpeted a challenge, the feathers on its neck bristling up like an angry cat's fur.

The effect on the real swans was astonishing. Each cob took the insult personally. Hissing filled the air. As one, a baker's dozen of male swans rose up with beating wings and fairly ran upon the water as they hurled themselves ashore, bent on repelling the invader, the threat to their mates and their nests.

The swan-prince did not shirk the duty. He came with the rest of the hissing flock, neck snaking, wings beating.

"The net!" Wren reminded Titch.

He spread it wide, was ready to leap and enfold the golden-necked bird. But as he sprang, an older cob chose to switch its attack from the false swan to the nearest moving object, and hurled itself at Titch's legs. He didn't even see it coming, just tripped hard and went down, the net short of the prince by an ell. He tried to get back up as the swans converged on Wren's bit of sorcery—pummeling wings pinned him down for long seconds, and all the while the snow was melting.

The glamor shattered apart the moment the first swan's bill hit it, became just flying gobs of ice and snow. Wren gave up trying to hold it, grabbed for the nearest edge of the net. It was full of swan—the *wrong* swan—and it began to rip as she struggled.

Their enemy vanished, the swans began to notice the other commotion. Such big birds could not take to the air without a running start, so they were effectively grounded. Still, one or two chose the safety of the lake, which they could run to as quickly as they might launch themselves into the air.

Titch felt a flutter of panic in his belly. "I *can't.*"

Valadan tossed his head. *Hold my rein. Let that be your anchor.*

"I still can't." He could hold his eyes open, but his knees were water. It was all he could do to stand, even clinging to the horse. And no one so unsteady on his feet should go near such a danger.

You must. Quickly. Look at me!

Titch looked, unwary, and was caught by that great dark eye, full of unexplainable colors once more. Bright flares of citrine and pricks of ruby transfixed him. The horse was trying to infuse him with the courage he lacked. Titch felt the stallion take a step forward. The rein tried to tug him along; it pulled him off his balance, though he pulled back with all his strength.

Titch's heart beat as if the blood pumped through it had gone thick as curds. He couldn't breathe, and the edges of his sight were darkening. Or was that the horse's color, shading the rest of the world?

Look at me, the shining eye said. *Nothing else.*

Titch could do that. He did. Something tugged him one step forward, then another. He stared into color-shot depths, afraid to blink.

And all at once, he stood beside Wren. She was speaking, and pointing, and tugging his arm to make him look over the edge. Titch didn't want to do that. He nodded politely, but he kept a death grip on the rein in his hand and his mind on Valadan's eye. He wouldn't look. He couldn't. He'd see where he was, he wouldn't be able to deny it, no matter what the horse told him. He might be mad enough to think a horse spoke to him, but he wasn't deranged enough for *this*!

Wren cried his name again, urgently. Titch managed to turn his head toward her, but he couldn't see her face except as a flesh-colored blur. He still couldn't breathe. The rein jerked in his hand as Valadan tossed his head, struggling to remind him of safety. Titch's skin was dewed with sweat. His mouth was dry as ashes. Slowly, slowly he brought Wren's face and words into focus. The world became something more than the suffocating pounding of his own heart.

"Down there!"

He winced at the "down," but Titch made his eyes follow Wren's jabbing finger.

At first, all he could see was the sparkle of the sea, dizzyingly far below, blue and green and white, swirling in patterns he couldn't read. Then he made out the thin black ledge a third of the way down the sheer cliff. It was broad enough to support some green growth and to hold the gold-necked swan. Alinor was sitting on the big bird's back, clutching at it, staring up at them across a hundred paces of cliff face. Titch stared back, helpless.

"Is he alive?" he asked finally. Whether the prince was dead or not, this was a disaster past reckoning.

Wren cocked her head and leaned out over till Titch thought he'd faint if he watched any longer. "Alinor says he's stunned, but stirring. She can hold him, for now." Wren grabbed at the net, began unknotting and retying. "Do we have any rope?"

Titch shook his head dully, answering without really understanding. It seemed a nonsensical question, nothing to do with present troubles. Alinor couldn't lift the swan an inch, much less back to the clifftop. Nor dared she release the bird to save himself. If he flew at all, it would be to the sea, and they'd never recover him if he survived the drop.

Wren had pulled the saddlebags down from Valadan's back, upended them onto the ground for easier rummaging, heedless of the sheer drop so near, which Titch could not forget for the space of two breaths. She extracted a length of thin line meant for fishing, a bundle of spare laces, held them up and sang a phrase at them. She spun, grabbed the front of Titch's padded jazerant, and dragged the laces out of that, as well, to add to her materials.

Quick as spun thread on a whirling spindle, a rope was taking shape under Wren's deft hands, to the counterpoint of rapidly chanted magic. It was wrought of grass stems and leather laces and hasty spellcraft, and it looked impossibly thin, as it stretched longer and longer still. Wren gave her creation a last pull, found it passed inspection, handed an end to Titch.

"Here. Be quick. I don't think she can hold him much longer. She says he's awake now, and frightened." Her fingers were still moving like quicksilver, bent in places where they ought not to have joints to bend, as Wren sought to bolster the spell on the rope. "You've got to climb down and get him."

Titch looked toward the cliff edge with dread. His head swam, even though he couldn't see the drop from where he stood. Didn't matter. He *knew* it was there. He was on solid ground—only the ground had betrayed him by being farther up in the air than the loftiest castle wall ever built by Eral or Clandaran. He shut his eyes, shook his buzzing head slowly. "I can't," Titch whispered.

Empty Air

"I CAN'T," TITCH whispered hoarsely, shamed to his bones, but helpless, hapless. His knees were wobbling, and he couldn't stop them. Sweat beaded his forehead, his upper lip. His skin prickled. "It—it's too high—" he stammered, staggering backward into Valadan.

"It will reach!" Wren insisted, waving the rope at him. "Titch, you've *got* to—they'll both go over if he wakes up enough to fight her!" She looked back toward the birds, desperately afraid, frantic over each second wasted in argument.

"There's nothing to tie the rope to!" He was stalling, but it was perfectly true. They hadn't seen a tree in days. There were no bushes. There wasn't a heather root stout enough to see, much less support a man's weight. Titch felt a stab of guilty relief, unable to get past that to the greater disaster, the loss of the swan.

Loop the line around me, Valadan suggested to Titch's complete horror. His startled glance went to the horse—and Wren followed his gaze, leaping to carry the rope's end around the stallion's chest, knotting it to itself behind his tail.

"You don't understand," Titch said carefully. "I *can't.* I can barely stand here. I can't *look* down, much less *go* down there."

Wren stared into his white face, some understanding of his confession beginning to pierce her fear for Alinor. "You can't?" she repeated doubtfully.

"If it's much taller than a horse, I can't get near it," Titch explained, hanging his head. Knightly pride wasn't worth venturing near that edge. "I just can't do it. I—" He tried, despite himself, to take a step in that direction, but his legs wouldn't obey him. He felt cold all over, and dizzy, as if he'd eaten tainted food, or taken a wound.

"Then I must," Wren said, her expression resolute. They both of them knew she couldn't hope to succeed. Next to Titch's arms, Wren's arms mere sticks, twigs. She might not be able to climb all the way down, far less return burdened by the heavy swan. No knight would stand by and allow her to attempt so unlikely a quest.

"I'm sorry," Titch murmured abjectly, shutting his eyes tight. He was dishonored, but he knew he would rather fall on his sword than face that drop.

Keep them closed, Valadan ordered. *Does what you do not see still frighten you?*

Titch thought about it, frowning. "Yes. But not so much." At least it became easier to breathe. "But—" He tried to look at the stallion.

Keep them closed. Remember, you will never be far from the earth—it will be just beyond the tip of your nose.

Titch felt Wren passing the makeshift rope beneath his armpits. Panicked, he started to open his eyes again. Wren hastily put her fingers over them, keeping him blind. "He's right! A horse will walk through fire if you cover its eyes first, and a hawk will stay quiet through anything if it's hoodwinked." A scrap of rough cloth replaced the fingers. Titch fought the urge to tear it away. The rope in his hands felt odd, sticky. "There's a hold-fast spell on it," Wren explained. "You won't fall. It won't let you."

Every muscle in Titch's body disbelieved her. He'd seen the rope. He knew what it was made of. If the magic on it was as piecemeal as its fibers, there was no way it would support him.

Your accouterments came from many men and many combats, yet all serve you, Valadan said.

Piecemeal rope for a patchwork knight? Titch shuddered. A hand tapped his shoulder, and the grass bumped against his knees. Wren secured the knots, tugging and testing as he knelt. She guided him toward the edge he could not see. "Lie down. On your belly."

He could certainly do that, Titch thought. That much

wasn't so awful. It felt better than standing, considering where he found himself. He stretched himself along the ground. Soft heather pressed against his face, tickling his nose. He felt about and got the rope between his hands, held it tightly. It seemed to grip him back, the hold-fast magic functioning.

"Start crawling backward." Wren put tension on the rope, so that Titch needed to pull against it to make any movement. He crept backward as she ordered, one inch after another, wanting with all his heart to be going the opposite way but trapped by a lack of alternatives, bespelled like the rope, for all he knew.

Suddenly his boots weren't touching anything. Panicked, Titch tried to scramble forward again, but the sea-pink on the verge tore away under his toes, he lost his balance and his legs slid over. The rope dug hard into his sides. He clung to it for dear life with both hands, afraid he'd slip out of the loop, trying not to realize he'd just swung himself over the lip of the cliff. Terror sealed his eyelids, all but stopped his heart.

"Put your feet against the cliff. It's right there, Titch! Just reach for it." Wren's voice was only inches away, calm and reassuring.

He felt for the vertical face, found it with his boots and his elbows. That was better. He could almost breathe. He could smell the wet stone. He had the rope, and the solid bones of the earth were close by, even if they weren't arranged so he could stand on them. That was something. Enough, if he could empty his mind of everything else.

"Walk down it now. Lean back a little. We'll let the rope out very slowly, as you need it."

For an instant, Titch remembered where he was again, and he could not make himself move. He could feel the rope stretching, giving to his weight. He wasn't standing. He was hanging, from a very dubious support. A stiff breeze shoved at him, threatening to set him aspin over a yawning abyss he could not lose awareness of.

You cannot fall came a cool promise he could not mistrust. *I anchor you. You are safe.*

The cloth across his eyes itched, and Titch realized as he

blinked against it that it was not cloth at all, but a couple of dry brown mullein leaves tied on with a twist of grass. He tried to center his attention upon that roughness, on the hard rock under his boots. Yes, he'd climb down, the rope being paid out just as he needed it. There'd be nothing abrupt, no falling to the rope's end, no jolting. If Wren did her part very well, he'd never suspect he wasn't simply lying on solid ground, pressed against it. The seabirds crying in his ears were only an illusion. The smell of the sea was a fantasy. He was too high for spray to reach . . .

Too high. He shouldn't have thought of that, as he tried to entrance himself. His carefully held illusion cracked right across.

"You're nearly there!" Wren's voice sounded much too far away. "Careful, there's not much room on the ledge."

He'd want to take care not to step on the birds, she must mean. He couldn't fall, no matter how narrow the ledge— they'd promised the rope would hold him, and Valadan held the rope. Titch could almost feel the way the stallion's legs were planted on the earth. Best not to think of what the lifeline between them had been made of, though.

A rope of cobwebs would bear you up, with the right spell upon it, the stallion said, amused.

A magic-bred horse would consider itself an authority on things magical. Trusting, Titch inched his way down the cliff, the scent of sea-wet rock sharp in his nostrils. *Remember, you're not that far from the ground. It's right there, close as the end of your nose.* His left boot bumped something. He could, he supposed, still fall *off* the ledge, even if not much farther. He minded his feet, and did a lurch and a stagger onto the ledge, balanced precariously on his boots and the tethering rope.

Alinor *hek*ked at him fiercely, scolding the way falcons did when enemies came close to their nests. Not that Titch would ever have robbed a cliff nest of chicks or eggs, either one. No, Titch assured her, he would never in his life be guilty of that crime. He was there to help. She wanted him there. As he groped about, Alinor struck him hard on the hand, but Titch thought she was really after the swan, which he could feel stirring strongly. He needed to subdue its wings, so it wouldn't thrash away from them both, but he couldn't decide what part of the bird he was touching. He tried to take the direction of feather growth for a clue, but that wasn't working, between his awkwardness and Alinor's striking at him—

No help for it, his itchy blindfold would have to come off. He turned his head and scraped his face against his shoulder till the leaves slipped away. If he didn't look down, except at the birds, all ought to be well—

Only to reach the swan Titch had to lean over—and thereby see beyond any hope of self-deception that the ledge he perched upon was no wider than the length of his foot, toe to heel. And he stood at the very widest point.

The ledge was scarcely as broad as the span of the swan's outspread wings. It was dark rock—all else about was blue seawater and evening-blue air. They were all of them poised in midsky, but he was the only one of the three lacking wings for flying to safety. Titch felt a desperate urge to become one with the rock, to embrace the cliff and press himself into it. The falcon gave a high-pitched cry.

"Alinor says to hurry!"

Titch hardly needed Wren's translation. The swan had begun to thrash its wings, its pinions slapping sharply against his left ankle. Alinor still stood upon its back, but swans carried their own young there without hindrance while they swam, and she was only a trifle larger than a well-grown cygnet. The swan might not contrive to take to the air with Alinor clinging there, but he could certainly spill both of them off of the ledge. He'd hardly care about dying—he must think Alinor meant to kill him anyway. The swan's little black eye had a despairing look in it, an expression of utter hopelessness.

Titch reached, but came up inches short. Alinor screamed at him again.

"I need more rope! I can't reach him!" He couldn't believe what he was asking for.

Without the rope's taut support, he could easily topple off the ledge. And if Valadan needed to back to the very brink to give him slack line, he might easily pull the horse over, too, with an unexpected fall. But if a tight rope held him erect, he couldn't bend to get his hands around the bird. He'd keep one hand on the rope, if he could. He'd feel safer that way.

Titch's stomach clenched. His head wanted to whirl. The line loosened terrifyingly as Valadan let him have the slack he'd asked for. Titch leaned down carefully to his left, keeping as much of his body's weight close to the cliff as he could manage. He could do this feat. Could he not ride a horse at full gallop and scoop a brass ring from the ground? In full armor? Therefore he could do this thing, as well. There was nothing the matter with his balance. Never had been.

All he had to do was forget where he was.

The swan had certainly been stunned by its precipitous arrival on the ledge. It let Titch refold its great wings, then lift it and clutch it to his chest before it began to struggle again, as if it took a moment for sensation to reach its brain. He swaddled the bottom part of his cloak about it as best he could, hoping to keep it subdued. The bird was paddling at him, and those webbed feet *did* have claws—Titch could feel them through the woolen cloth. He captured the head once his left hand was free and struggled to tuck it under the swan's own wing, with a vague recollection of having seen geese carried to market so. The stratagem didn't calm the bird so much as Titch had hoped, but it was so muffled by the cloak and its constricted position that it was rendered nearly helpless. Alinor launched herself from the ledge and reclaimed the air with a scream of triumph.

"Have you got him?" The rope tightened a degree, to Titch's relief. He realized he'd been holding his breath, wondered if that was really what made him so dizzy.

"Bring me up!"

His ascension was ever so much easier than the blind descent. No reason to look down, and between the bird in his arms and the cliff's face so close to his own, there was nothing frightening for Titch to see. If he'd been able to hold the swan and the rope with both hands, as well, Titch would have been a happy man. If he could have forgotten what the rope that his life dangled from had been made out of, he'd have been able to draw a free breath. If he'd been anchored to something more substantial than a horse, however magical—

You are safe, Valadan assured him, again and yet again.

He could see dirty roots, then green leaves of the sea-pinks. Wren was leaning carelessly out beyond them, hands reaching for the swan. Titch handed the bird over with relief—he couldn't think how he was going to get over the lip of the cliff one-handed.

The instant he got both hands on the thin cord, the question was answered. Valadan leapt away from the precipice, and Titch was hauled up over the rim like a boat being dragged up on a shingle beach. He went on bumping over the grass tussocks for a dozen bruising yards, and then the ensorcelled rope disintegrated into grass and old leather laces and spiderwebs once more. If it had happened an instant earlier—Titch had no leisure to brood upon that. The instant he stopped moving forward, Alinor came slicing out of the air at him, screaming like winter storm-wind. Titch threw himself flat just as Valadan whirled to stand protectively over him.

To the Red Queen

"So ... WHAT DO we do about changing him back?"
Titch asked, nodding toward the swan.

The swan, wings securely trussed to the sides of his
body, glared at them in the firelight. His neck free, he could
still snake his head and did so, hissing. He had lost more
than a few feathers but had regained his temper. Alinor regarded him with distaste.

Wren stared, alarmed. "I don't have any idea."

"Well, what did that gaggle of wizards chat about of an
evening, while I was standing sentry duty?" Titch prodded.
"Not the likelihood of a bumper crop of oats this year,
surely?" He was trying to tease a laugh out of her. Surely
their success entitled them to merriment? Galvin would
have laughed, he thought.

Wren frowned, instead. "They argued all the time. My
master said they reminded him of all the reasons he left the
Wizards' City. That more than two wizards together is un-
natural and probably someone else's idea."

Titch was baffled by her reluctance. "Can't you at least
try?"

"It's too big a magic for me!" Wren exclaimed, half panicked, half frustrated. "I don't dare. If I hurt him—"

"The queen will kill your master," Titch finished. He
chewed at his thumbnail.

"She may be ready to. Titch, we've got to make haste!
My master could be in danger, right now—"

Titch had been hoping to make supper and let a night's
sleep begin to soothe bruises and rope burns. He sighed.
"Maybe the queen will think more kindly of your master if
he restores her son to her, right under her eyes? Is that it?"

"Titch, I truly don't know *how* to change him back!"

She could craft a snow-swan real enough to fool a dozen live swans. Spin a rope like a spider. Cure a toothache—well, perhaps she *was* telling the truth. How was a poor soldier to know? He was just lucky to have come out of it with most of his skin. Titch picked at his right palm, which had the lion's share of the blisters.

He felt a gentle touch on his shoulder and warm breath down the back of his neck. Titch reached back to stroke the soft side of Valadan's muzzle. "I suppose it's simpler to take him back in this shape anyway—you can probably carry the weight of three and never notice it, but we'd never all fit, would we?" He took up the saddlebags and began switching the odds and ends of Gerein's gear to the off-side bag, to balance the swan's weight in the near side, as well as make room for the bird. "And there's no real reason to wait for morning, is there? The wind blows day *and* night."

It does indeed. Valadan pawed the turf.

They were on their way ere the stars had finished coming out. There was half a moon, but it seemed to stand still in the sky rather than proceeding on its nightly course. At first Titch felt uneasy about galloping headlong through the darkness, even with the night's great lamp lighting their way, but Valadan's own confidence soon put his objections to the shame they deserved. The stallion ran freely and happily, and Titch relaxed and let the wind sweep past him. If there was one thing Valadan knew how to do, it was run. And when he wearied at last and slowed to a saner gait, they would have put a lot of country behind them.

Titch had no idea just how much. Grassland and forest blurred past—Titch recognized that they could never have come to any trees so soon, but Valadan, amused, assured him that they were not lost. He ran onward so smoothly that his riders might almost have been lulled to sleep, rocked in the cradle between his alert ears and his bannered tail, dreaming of forests and rivers.

Titch lifted his chin from his chest, blinking sleepily. His eyelids were gritty, the skin of his cheeks taut from the continual rush of cool air past it. There were walls rising ahead of him, sunlight glinting from the courses of new-laid stone. Was the whole world suddenly fascinated with improving fortifications? Or was he still snared in a dream?

Valadan snorted and tossed his head. His mane was wind-twisted into elflocks. Titch gave the warm black neck a pat. The hair beneath his hand wasn't even damp, and had they merely *walked* all night, it still certainly should have been. And they'd been galloping. He might have slept, he might have dreamed, but not about that. It seemed quite impossible, but Titch suddenly knew beyond doubt that when they reached the gatehouse, the livery on the guards there would be a match for his own. He was learning fast to accept the impossible.

"Open in Melcia's name!" he shouted, and knew without question that they would.

"I have my orders," Titch insisted stoutly. "The Lady Melcia *only*. No one else. She was most particular about that."

He could feel Wren staring holes in him. Of course he had been nowhere near Melcia when the sorcerers had received their orders. But the swan was the only bargaining piece they had—he would not yield up that advantage, not until there was proven no other choice. He was in fact keeping that advantage well out of sight, though careful that the swan could breathe, stuffed into a bulging saddlebag and concealed by his cloak over the top of it.

"It's hardly past dawn. If you enjoy having your head attached to your shoulders, you'll answer *my* questions before you get yourself into more trouble," the stern-faced man declared.

The officer wore Melcia's usual gloomy colors, but he wasn't of the Guards, for his cloak was black-sheep gray. Titch wondered again how many besides the sorcerers had died in the ambush. He hadn't yet seen a face he recognized. Alinor, having no interest in the Guards, had taken note of no one's presence save Galvin's when she scouted the retreating force. There'd been survivors, but Titch couldn't depend on their support. He must stand his ground, with no idea whether reinforcements were available. It should be easy—he was part of the elite, the Guards, chosen to wear her bloody colors by her captains, and he could deal with lesser servants of the queen from a position of pride and strength.

"The trouble's not mine if she finds you kept her waiting. Sir," Titch added, just late enough to make his point. He was not truly answerable to this watch commander. "She charged us to make all haste, and we certainly did that. I've just ridden all night, because those were my orders. Along with reporting to the lady *at once*."

"You didn't get those orders from *me*," the officer blustered, hand to sword hilt. Possibly, Titch thought, it was helpful to have been one of the elite long enough to be recognized as such.

"He had them from *me*."

The voice came from behind his back, beyond the tail of his sight, but Titch guessed the speaker by the expression on the officer's face as the man hastily knelt. Very slowly Titch turned to face the Red Queen.

Torchlight was unkind to the lady at close range. It mercilessly delineated each line in her face, particularly the forked ones flanking her deep-set eyes. *It hurt to look into her eyes,* Wren had said. Titch was surprised to find that the hysterical statement was literally true. Rich cloth and costly jewels did nothing to cloak Melcia's torments. Those eyes, still the dark blue of priceless gems—as her bards had sung of them, in her youth—stared out as from deep caverns, the expression in them bleak as midwinter rain. Once the lady must surely have been incomparable, overflowing with life-joy. Melcia was a warrior's true daughter beyond doubt—big-boned and tall as most men, carrying herself spear-straight and proud. Youth would have added a pretty gloss of health and vitality to the raw power. Her silvergilt hair would have been gold as ripe corn then, and brushed till it shone before being done up in intricate braids. Those big hands still looked capable of wielding a sword and a shield, of fighting as her own champion when she was wronged, slaying her enemies without hesitation or mercy.

* * *

It was as if she had been struck blind, but in a most curious way, for Wren found she could still see the stone walls to either side, the flaring torches, the guards and their wicked iron weapons. It was only the Red Queen that her eyes could not catch hold of. Where Melcia stood was a woman-size void—not empty, but too dangerous to look at, as if a dark glamor cloaked her, turned the gaze back and shot the heart through with such fear as was near enough to stop its beating. Wren fought a desire to crumple to the floor, to fold her arms about her head and creep on her belly to the most remote corner of the castle, to the most distant part of the realm—or of the world.

Weight shifted on her wrist—Alinor, bobbing her head with keen interest. The pupils of her dark eyes contracted. She saw something. Did the glamor not affect birds?

There is no glamor, the falcon said firmly, tightening her foot-grip.

Then why can't I see her? Water rushed before Wren's eyes. Dark water, with a solitary star's reflection dancing upon it. *Is she still there, Alinor?*

She is. Look into my eyes.

Wren stared into the dark eye that seemed all the darker for the rim of pure yellow skin about it. The torches made highlights on its surface, little dazzles of reflection. Something else reflected there, as well ... the waters began to rise about Wren once more. Trembling, the girl looked past them, into the falcon's eye.

Another shape was reflected there, besides the torches. A woman of hard middle years, garbed in a blood-red gown—and all at once Melcia was in the sight of her own eyes, also, and time seemed to proceed once more. The torches flickered, the guards made unobtrusive shifts of their weapons. Wren drew in a welcome breath, to find that her lungs were aching as if she'd been trying to stay underwater. The Red Queen spoke; Titch answered her.

"*Well?*" the royal lady asked impatiently. All the hair on Titch's head lifted, making his scalp itch. For the first time, he felt the lack of the helm he'd left behind in the confusion of the ambush. He started to reach for the saddlebag, to undo the thongs that latched it closed.

Wren stepped forward half a pace, going beyond him. "First, Lady, where is my master?" she asked bravely. "I believe your men brought him back here to you, after we were set upon in the dark of night. Galvin is his name. Is he safe?"

"He is of no concern to me." Melcia glared at Titch, hardly sparing a glance for the inconsequential girl. She had fallen in with his falsehood to speed his report to her— perchance she was regretting that.

"He is of concern to *me*!" Wren objected, undeterred. "And he should be to you, also, Lady. You have need of him."

"Do I?" A flicker of something sparked within those deep-set eyes. Hope? One big-knuckled hand gestured abruptly to her captain. "Fetch the wizard here, at once."

"Thank you," Wren said, gravely polite. The order was confirmation that Galvin still lived, and she plainly had not been quite sure about that. Titch saw her relief. What she had intended if things had been otherwise, he could not guess. He had been amazed to hear her speak, knowing how frightened she was of the queen. Evidently, fear for her master had cast out apprehension for her own safety.

"If this is a trick, he will die before your eyes, and you will follow him," Melcia said, her voice emotionless as she stared at Wren.

"No trick, Lady," Titch interrupted, trying to draw her attention away, as he would have a stalking lioness from an unwary otter. He shifted the folds of his cloak so that the queen could have a glimpse of the burden it slightly concealed. "Wren has brought you what the sorcerers were sent forth to fetch."

He had her attention back and wasn't sure he wanted it. Her gaze was deadly as a sword, as eager to draw his blood. "And you, Guardsman?" She didn't know him. She had no reason to. But now she would never forget his face, for good or ill. It could mean honors; it could mean his death just as readily—less than a coin toss of difference. "What were *you* doing?"

"My duty, Lady." Titch met her stare, unflinching. "My captain ordered that we were to keep the wizards safe. Our camp was attacked by night, there was confusion and death. I made sure there was no more of that, while this one went about the task you set her."

"Commendable. You serve me well." Again, no vestige of emotion. "You have my gratitude."

Once a queen's gratitude would have delighted Titch's heart, been the sum of his dreams. Now the words made his blood run cold in his veins. Titch gave the queen half a bow, and hoped most earnestly that the tale of the swan had been true as they'd heard it, that they had not simply chanced on an oddly marked but otherwise quite ordinary bird. He judged that Melcia would be a creative executioner, but not a quick one.

Guards were dispatched to stations at the chamber's entrances. Almost at once the first pair issued a challenge, and immediately afterward a brace of others entered, holding Wren's master upright between them.

Galvin looked as if he had not seen an instant's sunlight since they'd forcibly parted company. Sleep might also have been a stranger, and he certainly limped, but his face shed a score of years when he spotted Wren. He kept his delight in careful check, with a sidelong glance at the queen. Titch couldn't quite tell whether his escort was holding him on his feet, or just flanking him.

"We found the bird!" Wren cried, heedless of danger. "We brought him back—"

Hands were already seeking to relieve Titch of the overfull saddlebag. He suffered them to do so—there was no objective to be gained from fighting them now, though his heart misgave him with every beat. The bird wasn't a hostage, and he was delivering it, not giving up his only safety—however much otherwise it felt. The leather thongs were undone, the disheveled swan was extracted and placed upon its webbed feet among the dirty floor rushes. It hunkered down at once and panted at them through a partly opened bill, making no attempt to fight its wing bonds—having had plenty of opportunities to learn the uselessness of that activity.

The queen stared fixedly at the distressed creature, no doubt searching for some vestige of her only child within the bird-shape. The bird regarded her with the same dulled panic he did all the rest of them—suffered her to touch him because with bound wings he had no other choice. Titch felt cold to the marrow of his bones—if this bird was by cruel chance *not* enchanted, it would be gracing the lady's dinner table that evening. Whereas he—

Melcia traced her fingers down the long white neck and paused at the ring of golden feathers. They were iridescent under the torchlight, showing fleeting colors just as insects' wings might. She smoothed the feathers with a finger, then touched them lightly with a metal key she wore upon a long chain at her belt.

Titch sucked in his breath, unsure what to expect. The key might be something other than iron, but it very likely was not, iron's protection against sorcery being a given. Key touched feathers, and there was a startling spark—a very tiny one, the sort one got on dry winter days when polishing armor or brushing a horse. Melcia whirled to glare at Galvin.

"Not so easy as that, Lady," the wizard said with a smile nearly bitter. "Iron troubles magic, twists it, wards it off. You have heard all of this, and it is true. However, iron will not necessarily break a strongly crafted spell—no more than running water will, or the death of the sorcerer." He nodded toward the bird. "But you have confirmed one thing: That is no ordinary swan."

"And you have work before you, wizard! Restore my son!"

"If I can, the captive will be set free." Galvin swept the room with a red-eyed glance. "That will require time and privacy. I do not object to being guarded, but there's no need for so many goggling eyes and wagging tongues. Your men can watch as well from the outer side of the doorways."

The queen stared at him, taking his measure. Galvin, fresh from her dungeon, starved and bone-weary, looked placidly back, as if unconcerned.

"You'll have what you ask for, wizard. Just don't try my patience with foolish tricks," Melcia snapped.

"I would not presume to," Galvin replied hoarsely.

The swan reposed within a stout wickerwork cage, upon a bedding of fresh green rushes. It looked desperately unhappy despite the comforts, and it refused the bread Wren offered it, turning its masked head away with orange bill stubbornly held closed.

"Master? *Can* we change him back? He won't eat." Birds could starve to death in a surprisingly short span of time, and Alinor was concerned for the fasting swan, if rather disparagingly.

Galvin looked up from his cards. "I changed you from an otter, didn't I?" He smiled at her distress. "Child, I don't know. There are ways; we'll try them, all of them. I'm not sure I ever thought we'd find him—and see, you did it. It's a world of surprises. There may be more to come."

"But if those ways don't work, either? He's touched land, he's touched iron, he's been carried over running water—"

"You know more sorcery than the Eral queen does," her master said disapprovingly. "You know there's more to it than that, or every man would be a sorcerer."

"I remember a story about an enchanted horse that asked its master to chop off its head, to restore it to human shape." Wren looked nervously at the swan.

"Let's hope it doesn't come to that," Galvin said severely. "There's no going back from that kind of cure."

Treachery

IN THE RED Queen's stable, another enchanted horse—not the one Wren spoke of—contentedly munched a generous measure of barley laced with honey. Titch stood watching, evidently lost in his thoughts or weariness, but did not startle at the hand that settled upon his shoulder. His nose still told him nothing, but his ears were sharp.

"You brought him back," Gerein said, wonderment shading his voice. "I thought you had him, I *hoped* you did, when I couldn't find him with the other strayed horses—"

"He isn't yours, Gerein," Titch cut in dispassionately, through the rush of inconsequential words.

"Look, I promised you payment for your . . . assistance," Gerein blustered. "But I never agreed—"

"That 'assistance' almost cost me my life. And he never was yours, was he?" Titch turned to face the knight, recognizing an anger that had nothing to do with the way the knight had treated *him*. "You stole him, used that bit you said couldn't be taken out to keep him with you against his will."

"*Most* horses would rather graze in a meadow than be ridden to war," Gerein said with the same sort of false patience one would employ with the feebleminded.

"You know what I mean. You know what he is. You told me Valadan was demon-bred. He's not. And he's not wearing that bit now." Titch looked into the knight's face and had the pleasure of watching Gerein try to evade eye contact.

"So, you're stealing my horse?" Gerein switched his tactics from lying to bullying.

"I can't steal what was never yours." Titch swept a fleck

206

of dust from Valadan's rump and thought idly that if he was Gerein, he'd never stand so close to the stallion. The stall door was only oak, no match for determined hooves and righteous anger.

"Think you're high in the queen's favor now, because you brought back one of her tame witches and a wild bird?" Gerein snapped. "You're getting everything you wanted, aren't you? Just heaped around you, no end to it?"

"Where's Gray?" Titch asked, ignoring the assault.

"Was I supposed to look after him for you, while you were off stealing *my* horse?" Gerein asked, his face flushed scarlet.

"No." Titch smiled without humor. "I just can't imagine you walking all the way back here, and Gray's easy to catch. He probably strolled up and put his reins into your hand." He felt the stallion quivering under his palm and silently wished him quiet. "Where is he, Gerein?"

"Out on grass," Gerein conceded wearily. "Most times, they keep all the horses out except a few for couriers and emergencies. Saves on stable-mucking. You know he's got a leg swells up like a sausage? I kept it wrapped till we got back here."

"Thank you. I was worried about him." He had been. What he shared with Valadan didn't wipe out what Gray had always been to him. And there was Gerein. Shifty as he could be, Titch wouldn't have wished him dead. "And I'm happy you're here yourself—I didn't get much of a look at the enemy that night. I was afraid some of them might have been your old friends."

"Sorry to disappoint you." Gerein's eyes were still hard. "I have no idea who that lot might have been—I was too well occupied ducking their arrows. The captain caught one in the throat. Drowned in his own blood. Thought something like that had happened to you, when you didn't regroup with us."

"Sorry to disappoint you," Titch aped him, unsmiling.

Gerein stared, then unexpectedly laughed. "All right! You're welcome to the horse. I've no real choice but to be gracious about it, have I? Just remember your friends when they make you an officer."

It was Titch's turn to go wide-eyed.

"You're high in favor," Gerein explained. "No one missed that. Also, the Guard's down two underofficers and a captain, courtesy of that little debacle in the woods. Don't look so shocked—it's meant to be good news."

Of course it was. It was probably an honor. And only incidentally another chain, as well, binding him to a future he'd been tricked into in the first place, Titch reminded himself.

The officers of Melcia's elite Guard knew a degree of comfort. They had privacy, if a nearly airless cell at the far end of a barracks could count for such. Common soldiers slept on the ground, wrapped in cloaks or bedrolls. The men of the Guard each had a pallet stuffed with old hay or grain stalks, or whatsoever else was handy to an Eral stronghold. Their officers had the further luxury of their own chambers to contain pallets that were exactly the same. There wasn't room for anything more in a place where the right-hand and the left-hand walls could both be touched at once without any real stretch of the arms—except the fleas, which were admirably impartial and fed upon every man, whatever his station. Titch captured one especially bold pest, cracked it between his thumbnails, and hoped to achieve sleep before another flea sought a meal from him. Feeling something crawling across the nape of his neck, he doubted his prospects for success.

He'd slept more peacefully on cold, muddy earth, wreathed in woodsmoke from a campfire that gave off little light and even less heat, with a scattering of stars for his roof. Now he was every bit as weary as he'd been then, but sleep's oblivion wouldn't come to him. His back felt cold without Wren curled against it, and whenever he shut his eyes he saw her sitting in the yellow firelight, cupping her chin in her palm, her fingertips pushing the skin of her cheek askew. It was as close as she came to changing her shape in normal times.

Normal times. Wren was still in danger, so long as the swan remained a swan and not Melcia's son, but she was with her master, which was certainly where she belonged.

She doesn't need you to protect her anymore, Titch told himself sternly.

His back still felt cold. And there was definitely a flea creeping through the stubble at the back of his neck.

Too many interruptions of nosy folk, till her master swore oaths such as Wren had never heard him use and insisted they be kept away. None of it mattered to Wren—the only person she'd have been happy to see in the doorway was the very one who never appeared.

He doesn't need me anymore, she thought, a lump in her throat. That was as far as sorrow could get, though. Pain, fear, sadness—not even the wind could bring tears to her barren eyes. *No wonder he doesn't come back. Human women weep. And you don't, whatever you are. You were a duty. Don't confuse that with being a knight's lady. Whatever you are, you aren't that, and never will be.*

As an officer of the Guard, it was one of Titch's many tasks to post sentries, to oversee their diligence, and take their reports.

"Sir, the witch is asking leave to go outside the walls, to fetch fresh herbs." The tone was distasteful—the man either disliked the request or his superior officer.

Titch swallowed a sigh. There were plenty of ways for a man to plague an officer he resented for being jumped up over him. Refusing to use his own good sense, clinging to the precise wording of orders given, served very well. Passing along a problem he was perfectly well equipped to solve was another. Perfectly correct, exceedingly tiresome.

"I'll escort her myself," Titch said, refusing to give the fellow satisfaction. "And next time, send word. Whatever they need that can be fetched, they're to have."

"Nobody in or out. Those was the orders. *Sir.*" The title was added tardily enough to be either an afterthought or a calculated insult. Not only a jumped-up officer, but somehow connected to witchery, by uneasy rumor. Beneath the contempt of honest soldiers.

"They're to be given whatever they need," Titch rejoined

irritably, out of patience. "*My* orders." He unbarred the door and went through.

"*Watch where you step!*"

The floor was covered with an intricate pattern of lines in colored chalk. Titch balanced precariously in midstep, wondering what would happen if he teetered onto a symbol, or smudged one. Some of the scribbles appeared to be writing, but he couldn't make out the words. What retribution—

"Oh, it's you." Galvin, the hem of his robe chalk-smudged, crossed the room. Wren was bent over a mortar, grinding busily with the pestle. "Come in, never mind the lines. The real ones are over here anyway. Those are just to hold back nosy guards."

"The sentry said you wanted some things," Titch said, stepping carefully into the room, studiously avoiding lines despite the wizard's assurances. "I'm sorry he didn't fetch them for you. I don't think it'll happen again." He tried to catch Wren's eye, but all he achieved was a glare from Alinor. Alinor's mistress stayed bent over her work.

"The herbs were a deliberate excuse to let Wren have a breath of fresh air," Galvin confessed. "I'm still trying to pick the spell apart, and there's not much I need for *that*. Removing it will be another matter entirely. You're an officer now?" He glanced at the brass badge pinning back the left side of Titch's new cloak.

Titch grimaced. "It's not an unmixed blessing, but I'll help you however I can, from my exalted position. How's it going?"

"Most strangely." Galvin gestured at the swan in its stout cage. The big bird was on its webbed feet, watching them with glittering eyes. "I think we've been lied to."

"That's not the prince?" Titch hastily tallied the number of gates between them and open country.

"Oh, it's him." Galvin smiled at his discomfort. "No, I meant as to what befell young Evin. The tale as told is one of hasty revenge, but the spell is far too complex to be any such creature. This was a most deliberate ensorcellment, carefully planned and flawlessly executed. No more random than the 'chance' attack that nearly kept us from finding him."

"The story is we were set on by bandits," Titch said carefully. "It's lawless country out there. Not so civilized as Josten."

"Full of displaced Clandarans?" Galvin raised a brow. "Is that how you see it?"

Titch shook his head, smiled a bitter smile. "No one who was there would put any stock in that fable. Whatever those men were, they were only after one thing—killing wizards."

"Someone didn't want the prince found," Galvin suggested. "That someone may not want him restored, either."

Titch's back prickled. He had to resist the impulse to turn around, because he knew there was nothing actual behind him and he didn't want to look a fool—but it was a hard thing.

Galvin rubbed his eyes, then looked down at the spread pattern of his cards. "If they but knew—I've done all I can think of, and he's still a swan. Will you take Wren out of here for a while?" he asked abruptly.

"Certainly." Titch nodded politely. The request was well within his authority to grant. "Why, sir?" Wren still hadn't looked at him.

"Alinor needs to hunt, for all our sanities." Galvin dropped his voice to a murmur. "And there's Melcia's daily appearance. The queen comes each evening before she retires, to wail over her son and threaten me with what she'll do if I cannot make him as he once was. Yestereve she decreed we'd have another three days, no more. It's most upsetting for Wren. She'll sit and shake for an hour, after."

"Why?" Titch stole a glance, but Wren was still carefully absorbed by mortar and pestle.

"I've no idea," Galvin said. "Granted, there's the sense of fearing Melcia and her power, but this runs far deeper, right into the bone. She can't even look at the woman—I wonder if mothers threaten disobedient children with Melcia's name?"

"It would work," Titch agreed soberly.

"I wish I had been wise enough to take Wren safe away to Kôvelir a year ago." Galvin closed his spellbook gently.

"I am certain there are those there who could assist her in recovering her past. They couldn't be worse at it than I've been. And she shouldn't die not knowing so much as her own true name."

"Sir, I'll keep her safe with my own life!" It sounded like an empty boast, and Titch's face went hot, but he did not try to call the words back.

"Even that may not suffice, if we cannot do Melcia's royal will," Galvin observed mildly. "But I see your heart is true, and I thank you, Titch. I'm as much of a father as Wren has, I suppose—and she is certainly all the child I shall ever have." He pitched his voice to carry across the wide chamber. "Wren, bring Alinor! Now that our friend has been made an officer, he can at least offer her a chance to catch herself some dinner."

If he mistakes me for an owl, Alinor said huffily, bobbing her head, *I'll have my dinner out of his hide.* Wren took her up, clucking at her and scratching the falcon's cheek feathers to distract her wrath.

"Hush, love. *I'll* be flying you. But he must go, too, or we won't either of us be allowed out. Don't be unpleasant, he can't help it."

The door closed, and Galvin returned to his cards. He removed those he had hastily thrown down as a screen when he heard Titch at the door and surveyed the true pattern that lay beneath. It was scarcely altered from previous arrangements—the cards would vary slightly from reading to reading, expanding, amplifying, differing ways of delivering what was always the same message. In the main, the same cards were there each time, rocks in an ever-changing river of fortune.

Swords fenced the present, which was only to be expected. Cards of bondage, trouble and looming destruction. There was the card of journeys, flanked by the Tower, falling. A dangerous journey, then. And the card of the Lady, the Moon. He could not decide what that meant, in its context. It was a card of secrets, of unfolding and revealing. It could mean Wren's long-sought past—or hidden enemies.

Many High Cards, that was troubling. He was too insignificant a person to merit so many such. He had, this final time, allowed himself to use the Sorceror to represent himself—but he had reversed it in a moment of black humor, to stand for the weakness of will, the indecision that had so long ago sent him dissatisfied from Kôvelir. If only he could remake himself as easily as he could right the card, be the sort of master who could guide Wren truly to her potential, restore a prince to his heritage almost as an afterthought—

He could not. It was too late to change his whole life. It was plain too late. The final card, the Card of Outcome, was not the Queen of Swords, which would have meant Melcia. It was only the Five, the symbol of failure and defeat. A small card at the last, for a rather small man.

The river meadow where the castle's horses grazed seemed a likely spot for small game. It was the hour of the evening meal, but night had not quite fallen once one got away from cloaking walls. Titch managed to flush a dove after a reasonably brief search, and Alinor did not need an owl's sight to capture it. She was hungry, and disinterested in sport. While the falcon fed, Wren roved off on a quest of her own after certain herbs.

"Sunwort changes you, but only if you tread on it on Midsummer's Eve," she muttered to herself. "Mandrake's just dangerous to gather. Nightshade—"

Titch was walking among the grazing horses, seeking out the pale ones. There were a good number of those, out of the threescore beasts kept on the meadow. He gave a low whistle. More than one head came up, but most went back to the greening grass fairly soon. One did not. Titch strolled toward Gray.

To his eye, the bad leg looked swollen, but Titch's fingers found no heat or puffiness, and Gray walked sound enough. True, walking sound wasn't *riding* sound, but still Titch permitted himself to feel a measure of relief. Gray seemed none the worse for his experiences during and after the ambush. Given that he'd been ridden in a desperate retreat, that was a wonder. Gerein would have had no reason to take special care of the old horse—had Titch been there himself, he might not have managed it. But Gray was well, to Titch's delight and peace of mind. He had no reason to expect Valadan's further aid, he reminded himself, now that Wren's quest had been accomplished and the swan returned to Josten. He would not be surprised to find the stallion vanished out of the stable like a puff of dark smoke. Gray, common-bred though he was, was mortal and unmagical and *there*.

Titch realized he'd lost sight of Wren. Not that there was any urgency attached to that—she wouldn't be trying to escape by deserting her master. But he should be keeping his eye on her, all the same. Galvin had said they'd been lied to about what had been done to the prince ... nothing in Josten was quite to be trusted. The meadow wasn't dark yet, but the hour was later than it had been when they crossed the water, and the light was failing. Falcons didn't fly much at night, maybe they didn't see so well—he wanted to have his own eye on Wren.

There was a sudden whir of wings, the abrupt clasp of talons on his shoulder. Titch started, and the claws dug deeper as Alinor pretended to need to keep her balance, coming near to piercing the padded leather. Gray shied and snorted, and Titch swore. Alinor gave her beak a vigorous wipe against his mail gorget, leaving pale dove feathers behind. Dove down drifted across Titch's nose, and he started to swipe it away, then decided he'd lose a finger or have his shoulder pierced through if the falcon mistook his motion, or thought 'twas aimed at her.

"Where's your mistress?" he asked with a sidelong glare into the murderous dark eyes. "*One* of us ought to be watching her."

She clouted him on the head with her wings as she departed instead of answering, but Titch watched where the falcon went, and followed. Wren was kneeling beside the stream, one hand in the flowing water, her eyes fixed on the rising moon above, its crescent thin and old.

"Nothing transforms like water," she whispered, as if reciting a lesson committed to heart. "Water will even dissolve stone if you give it time enough." She turned her head. "Titch, I don't know what to do! We've tried everything to change the swan back, and nothing's worked, and if we fail, the Red Queen will kill us!" She lurched to her feet, came into his arms in a desperate rush.

Titch held her close, trying to soothe, hoping Alinor wouldn't take the action violently amiss. The falcon had flown to a nearby tree limb, 'twould be nothing at all for her to launch herself from that vantage. Against his chest, Wren's heart beat fast as any bird's. Her dark head was tucked just under his chin, she would feel the reassurances he spoke, as much as hear them.

Once before he'd held her so, come what might, no matter what shape she took upon herself. He'd held fast till she was safe. Holding couldn't save her this time, at least he didn't see how it could. Maybe he ought to rescue her another way, toss her up ahead of him on Gray this instant, then just ride away to safety. Even if he went back for his gear first, he could manage it, Titch thought crazily. Maybe that was what Galvin had intended him to do, all along. Clever wizard, to save what he could out of this mess . . .

Break your oath to Melcia, and ride away? That assumed there'd *been* an oath—Titch had no memory of much of anything that had transpired during those first days after the disastrous tourney, and he already knew—being an officer and responsible for paying wages—that Gerein had cheated him in the matter of his pay. No reason to think an amoral man—as Gerein had relentlessly proven himself to be—would have balked at forging a mark on a contract of arms-service, when all he'd have needed to do was put his own fingers around Titch's on the ink-dipped quill. Just helping a friend temporarily incapacitated, a kindness . . . No, probably there'd been no oath. Not spoken, or written. Only assumed, acted upon.

Titch had been taught that a knight's honor lived within him, was more than the bits that showed on the surface, though one was expected to be a worthy man in public view as well as private. He'd never knelt to Melcia of Josten, never pledged his sword or himself—but to ride away now would be to split that hair too finely. One could still be foresworn without having first sworn to a lord or a lady. Titch did not doubt it. The heart was straiter than a law court.

He owed a life-debt to Galvin. He could hardly reconcile *that* with his service to Melcia, if the queen intended to kill Galvin and his apprentice. It would have been a cruel dilemma—if he'd believed that Melcia actually intended to go through with her threats.

"The queen can't afford to kill you—if you're dead, how will Melcia get her son back?" Titch asked, stroking Wren's dark hair. It was curling and limp both at once, like water weed in the current. He liked the way it felt under his fingers. "Think she wants to crown a swan as her heir? Way I've heard it, she's hauled in every wizard and wisewoman she could put her hands on, and they're all either useless or dead. She's running out of choices, and you proved *your* worth when you brought the swan back to her. You and Galvin are precious to the Red Queen now."

"*I'm* not," Wren whispered, shuddering like a wind-rippled pond. "I can't fix the prince—"

She sounded so *lost*, as if she thought she'd no value to any soul living—all Titch could think to do was to hold her closer yet. She pressed her face into his shoulder, clenched her fingers on the folds of his cloak, and trembled like springwater after a stone's dropped in.

"She won't harm you, Wren," Titch insisted. "Would your master help her, if she did that? You know he wouldn't! The queen may threaten, but they're empty threats—"

"No," Wren whispered into his cloak. "They never are. Never."

She spoke with uncanny certainty. Her tone made the fresh-shaved hair on the back of Titch's neck try to rise. If he looked into her dry eyes now, they'd be blank and empty, like a sleepwalker's . . . "Wren? How do you know that?"

She lifted her face toward his, and he saw her come back to the present moment, from wherever she'd been. "I don't know." She looked, at that moment, bereft of every hope in the world. Titch's heart turned over inside the cage of his ribs, full of crazy schemes. He wanted to shed the tears

Wren could not. He wanted to gather her up, to keep her safe for all of time, so she'd never need to have that look on her face again.

He couldn't tell her that with pretty speeches—words were empty things. He was a warrior, not a clerk or a courtier, skilled with such weapons. And as he stood there in the quiet night, with Wren shuddering in his arms, no words came anyway. Titch put his lips over hers, continued to hold her close, reassuring her in the only way he knew. Her lips parted under his, he felt the warmth of her breath, where the rest of her seemed colder than springwater.

There was a noise of rushing water in his ears, the roar of a river in flood-spate, tearing its banks in a ceaseless quest for freedom. It died away. Titch heard the patter of raindrops on leaves, the musical plunking of water dripping into a still pool, the ripples spreading out from the center, wider and wider yet till at last they touched the shore, the shores that were the edges of the world . . .

He opened his eyes and was still gazing into calm water—no, that was Wren's left eye, the clear gray hue of a raindrop in the spring, hanging from a branch tip. But he was *standing* in water, his boots abruptly informed him. Somehow he'd blundered into the stream. Titch cursed softly and lifted Wren to drier ground, and tried to wring the water from the hems of her clothing as best he could. Wren giggled at his consternation, and held onto him for balance, nearly sending them both back into the water headlong.

"Too cold for this foolishness—this is a high-summer game. The air may be warming, but the water's not," Titch grumbled, his teeth beginning to knock against one another. He helped Wren farther from the water, smelled mint they were trampling underfoot. The scent recalled to him the herbs Wren had been bent on gathering. The sun had gone to its bed, but the moon was silvering the meadow. Some herbs were even better gathered by moonlight—at least so he'd heard.

Wren's hand was fast in his, warmer now, trusting as a little bird.

"You wanted some herbs?" Titch asked thickly. He was

struggling against a discovery—he wanted to feel her lips under his again. He wanted to bury his face in her cloud-soft hair—he felt like a drowning man, water closing over his head, and he didn't want to fight his fate. He wanted to let the water have him, for all of time. This would *not* be why Galvin had sent him out into the evening with his young apprentice.

"The herbs were only . . . I couldn't just sit and do nothing, thinking of what will happen to us if we fail," Wren said. "It's the way Alinor gets during a rainy winter. Makes you crazy to watch her. My master doesn't need the herbs—there aren't any here we haven't thought of—but he couldn't just tell me to go out. He needed a reason." She sighed, very quietly. "We should go back now."

"You're sure?" He had his arms around her again—because the air was cool, Titch told himself. Nothing to do with the empty way he discovered he felt when she was only *beside* him. "We could gather some mint anyway. Freshen the rushes. They could use it." His breath was coming short, as if he'd been running. He felt dizzy, ever so slightly and not at all unpleasantly.

Another clap of wings, and Alinor was on his shoulder again, a better chaperone than any jealous father could ever have contrived. "Time we went back," Titch agreed, and released Wren save for her left hand. She smiled as she shook her head wonderingly at her familiar.

For a few moments, the river meadow had seemed a thousand leagues removed from Josten. Yet they had crossed it, and the stone walls were rising before them, and their wet clothing had yet to cease its dripping. The outermost pairs of sentries passed them through. Titch kept a sharp ear cocked for snickers, but Wren's mind was already back to darker troubles.

"Three days," she whispered to herself, but Titch heard her.

"She won't hold Galvin to that," he insisted. "It's not as if he's not trying. Your master told me he thinks someone had the prince enchanted purposely. When he tells the queen that—"

Wren stopped in her tracks. "Had him enchanted? Why should someone do such a thing?"

Titch shrugged. He could think of many motives in the abstract, but had no way to guess which might apply. "No idea. But if she's wise, the queen will turn her attention from threatening you to finding out who her son's enemies are. And she'll guard you like gold, because *her* enemies won't be *your* friends—"

He realized what he'd just said. Wren wasn't far behind him.

"Titch, we left Galvin alone!"

They were, Titch thought, too prone to scaring one another. But that spot on his back was itching again, trying to warn him, and he trusted it. "Galvin's all right," he said, struggling to convince himself along with Wren. "He's a wizard, with the Sight, and his cards. He's in a guarded room. He's fine." But he wasn't convincing even to his own ears, and as he began to hurry along after Wren, Titch was loosening his sword in its scabbard.

Yet when he saw the posted guard was gone from the door, Titch was more angry than alarmed. How dared the sentry flout his express orders? Then it struck him—desertion of post *far* outweighed any gain to be realized from embarrassing a disliked officer. And the air held a faint scent of burning, different from the charcoal in a brazier, or pungent magical herbs being used for incense.

His sword was drawn before he even set his hand to the bar that held the door. *"Stay back!"* Titch ordered Wren, who was crowding close enough to hamper his arm.

Smoke billowed forth as Titch yanked the door open. Wren cried her master's name, gasped a lungful of bad air, and began to cough. Alinor flapped her wings but did not launch herself into flight. The first thing Titch saw with his stinging eyes was the swan's wicker cage upended on the hearth, flames tonguing it. He ran forward and snatched at it, then realized—as he was trying to get the point of his sword through the frame to lift it out of the flames—that it was empty. A draft swirled the fire up around his hands as he backed away. Confused, he looked for the source of the fresh air. Galvin's cards lay in a scatter across the floor, like impossibly bright autumn leaves.

Beyond them, the chamber's second door stood open. Titch had never seen that so before—it gave onto one of the areas of new building, so no one could readily enter or exit that way. It *had* been barred on both sides and guarded on the outer. Now the stout wooden bar lay partly blocking the dark opening. So did Galvin.

Wren had run at once to her master's side. Titch joined her, coughing. The smoke was thinning. The chalk-smudged floor slates were further blotched with patches of soot that looked as if flaming pitch had been hurled there. Magic cascading off of iron weapons? Enchantments foiled? He recalled the spark when the queen had touched her key to the swan. Galvin would have been trying to defend himself with the weapons at his command. Presumably those were more than just sparks of light. They'd kept him alive.

"What happened to the guards?" Titch asked, kneeling.

Bright-red blood trickled from the corner of the wizard's mouth. "It *was* the guards," Galvin said, enunciating carefully. "You must—" He began to cough, and pink bubbles ominously followed the blood Wren was wiping away. She supported him as best she could through the spasm, fear in her eyes.

There was a dagger hilt sprouting like an iron flower from the center of the wizard's chest. Galvin saw Titch's eyes go to the weapon and gave a barely perceptible shake of his head. There was nothing to be done. They both had experience enough with wounds and weapons to know that when the blade was pulled out, his lifeblood would gush after it. Leave the knife in place plugging the hole it had made, Galvin had perhaps a few minutes still to live, ere his lungs filled with slowly seeping blood. Take the blade out, he died at once. Leave it alone, and no magic could help him, but time gained him nothing, either—the wound was well beyond any surgeon's skill. 'Twas a wonder he had not died the instant he was struck. That his heart could still pump was a marvel.

"You must retrieve the bird," Galvin continued gravely,

staring at Titch, eyes burning like coals, attention firmly fixed. "There's time. I held them as best I could."

Galvin had sacrificed himself to do that. The gesture must not be allowed to come to naught. Titch sprang to his feet, leaping past Wren, over the dying wizard. A trail of white feathers gave him his direction, even in the darkness.

He hurtled through a second doorway, and then he was in a gallery between the new shell of stone courses and the old wall of wood. His boots scattered debris—chips of stone, crumbs of mortar, tools left ready for the next day's work before Melcia ordered the wizards' work area off limits to her masons. Titch tried to move quietly—the traitors might not be expecting pursuit so soon, and he could come at them with surprise as his friend if he didn't make a clatter at the outset. He ran softfooted down the empty passage.

At the last instant, he realized he was about to go headlong down a short unfinished flight of stairs. The air yawned empty ahead of him, black as a nightmare. He came at it too late to stop and realize the height of it, too late even to yell—his momentum took away the option of horror. Titch leapt wildly to clear the half-seen mess of stone and timber—a sharp sting in the soles of both his feet told him he'd landed, a jolt traveled up his spine till his skull stopped it. He had no time to realize what had almost happened, to rejoice at his safety. One of his ankles throbbed alarmingly, but the pain didn't slow him down a whit. Titch burst out into the open air of the bailey, dodging awkwardly around a heap of ashlar stone, trying to use it for concealment.

Where would the false guards aim, making their escape? The stables first? Supposing they slowed their pace and acted as if nothing were untoward, they could easily walk out the town gate as if they were bound for a wineshop. They must be intending to release the swan—if they'd meant to kill the bird, they could have done so on the spot and let Galvin take the blame for it. So all they might want was to get the bird to open air—

Or atop a wall.

* * *

Galvin's eyes held no pain—only the same gentle amusement that always lurked there, deep inside the brown, in the nests of fine wrinkles and lines.

"The cards foretold this," Wren accused. "That's why you sent me away."

"The cards said you would be safe," her master whispered. "And you are. It was all I could think of, spur of the moment. Your young knight would lay down his life to keep you from harm, and he's much more effective at that sort of thing than I could ever be."

"Tell me what to do," Wren begged, staring at the knife hilt, which jerked with his chest's constrained rise and fall. Cold iron, bane of all magics! "What herbs—"

"Myrrh makes a pleasant incense."

Wren shuddered, shook her head. "That's not a healing herb."

"No," Galvin softly agreed, his lips crooking into a smile. "Even so." He looked at Alinor. "Child of the wind, take care of your mistress."

"Master, no! You can't die!"

"We all of us do, Wren." He gasped for air, planning his speech, gathering reserves for it. "Magic is not immortality. Not even in Kôvelir, thank the merciful gods. Gather my cards, they've gotten themselves scattered, and they're lonely for one another—"

"Woundwort," Wren mumbled, her hands obediently seeking wafers of ivory, bright colors against gray stone, gathering them in almost blindly. "Heal-all—" Which had she seen, in the meadow by the water? How fast could she run? Could Alinor fetch them—

"Such determination, my little bird—" Galvin coughed, gasped, stifled another cough with a look of desperation. "Come close, child. There's no time left for soothing yourself with false hopes and busywork. Come here."

Wren collapsed forward onto her handful of cards, with a great dry sob, a tearing noise, as if she were being ripped asunder. "You can't die! You can't—"

"I had counted my life worthless . . . which it was, by Kôvelir's standards," Galvin confessed softly. He took the cards from Wren, enfolded the pack in one big hand. "Their purposes were not . . . mine, and so I left the city and the wizards, and told myself that I had failed. But had I stayed safe in the Wizards' City . . . who would have pulled a poor lost otter back to dry land, back to herself?" His eyes bored into hers. "Wren, you are my purpose. Because of you, I leave something behind me after all, and that's cause for content. I had been so afraid of dying an empty failure—"

"You were never a failure!"

"I couldn't find your past," Galvin reminded her sorrowfully.

"It doesn't matter!" Once it had been *all* that mattered to her. Tragedy offered another perspective.

"But I think you will find it. I gave you the skill, Wren. One day you'll use it. And . . . I know how the swan may be restored."

His words were coming fainter and fainter still, because deep breaths threatened to start the disastrous coughing again. Wren leaned very close, not because she cared about the swan, but because her beloved master beckoned her.

"Tears," Galvin said, with his final breath.

Titch lifted his head, like a hound trying to catch a scent. Just to his right, his eyes detected a blur of white in motion. He flinched back into the shadow of an archway, wondering if the men abducting the swan had seen him following them. They must be aiming for the reach of wall that followed the river. If they threw the bird from its height, the swan could either take flight or glide to the safety of the water. And once it got its wits about it, it would be off as fast as its powerful wings could take it—off the gods knew where.

When stone curtain walls entirely replaced the timber palisade, there would be proper stairs to let warriors mount swiftly up to the battlements. Just now, stout wooden ladders did that office, and they got moved from place to place as the construction proceeded. For Titch, they'd been the worst part of standing sentry on the walls—climbing higher and higher with nothing but a bit of slippery wood under his boots—

He went up the nearest ladder with his sword in his

hand, thinking that it was actually a little easier by night, that he really wasn't as nervous of something he couldn't see well . . . like a hoodwinked hawk. The walkway at the top was an armspan wide. It looked narrow as a bridge of swords, to Titch's eye. To his left ran the waist-high parapet made by the tops of the palisade logs, their tips axe-hewn into spikes like the teeth of dragons. To his right lay the drop back down into the bailey below. There was no rope railing there, just the drop. One misstep and a man would fall to his death, with just time enough for full awareness of what was happening to him. A swan's feather lay just at the brink, gleaming. A puff of breeze sent it skittering and then it fell from sight, drifting down lightly as a man would never do.

Titch ran along the walkway, up on his toes for quiet. A shadow among many other shadows warned him of a gap in the planking—he leapt it, landed in a noisy stumble on the abused ankle and recovered almost onto the point of a blade, held by one of Melcia's Guards.

"Don't get yourself any more involved, boy."

Maybe the man assumed confusion would stay his hand for a critical instant. But Titch had Galvin's warning—and he was an avenger pursuing traitors, not a sentry who'd heard a suspicious noise. He attacked rather than hesitating, and knocked his assailant sideways against the parapet with his first blow. The second stroke sent the man to his knees. Evidently dazed, he took a wrong turn getting back to his feet and went almost silently over the edge of the walkway. His shout was cut short as he hit something on the way down. Titch spared him no further attention—the man with the swan was still somewhere ahead of him, and they were very near to the river. He sprinted in pursuit, throwing away silence no longer an advantage.

The swan's wings were still strapped to its body, and the man had set it down to release those bonds—he spun to his feet with the task unfinished when he heard Titch running at him. His sword cleared the scabbard as he rose, but instead of bringing the long blade up to guard, he took a vicious swipe at Titch's ankles.

His boot's sturdy leather turned the blade, the keen edge

didn't penetrate. But the solid impact tripped him—Titch missed his footing and went headlong into the parapet. The logs knocked the breath out of him, and he had a dizzy glimpse of black water sparkling far below. Then he felt hands on him, ready to tip him the rest of the way over.

Titch kicked out, made flailing contact, and the grip on him loosened. He fell flat onto the walkway, trying to get his legs under him. A boot stamped at his sword hand, missed the fingers but held the blade down so he couldn't lift it. Something crashed down resoundingly on his helmet. Titch went flat again, as if he'd been stunned, but he tightened his hold on the sword. He rolled over, swinging the blade up as best he could, but a weight smashed into his arm and his sword went sailing down into the bailey. A kick tried to send him after it, just as he heard metal ring brightly on stone.

Titch wrapped his arms around the kicking leg. The guard lost his balance and fell backward. As he twisted wildly to keep from taking the fast way down into the bailey, Titch managed to scramble back to his own feet, his shoulders pressing against the logs of the parapet. He reached for his knife, wrapped both hands about its long hilt just under the crossguard, and brought it up to face the sword.

The Guard expected his sword stroke to smash right through the short dagger, but Titch was desperately determined to hold the parry at all costs. This was no fencing match! Metal screamed on metal, but neither blade nor cross-hilt snapped from the blow itself, and Titch put all the strength years of training had lent his arms and his back into the contest. It was a shoving match more than a blade duel, and the first man to yield would certainly see no second chance, no riposte or counterparry. Infighting was a matter of strength, not finesse.

They wrestled back and forth on the narrow way, progressing by grunting inches. The logs dug into Titch's back. Better that than the drop he couldn't see, he decided. He feared losing track of where that unguarded edge was.

His arms ached. Titch longed to shift his awkward grip. There wasn't really room for both his hands on the dagger's hilt; his fingers cramped and weren't able to detect the tiny shift of pressure that could warn of his adversary trying to break contact for a fresh attack. He must push back *hard* if he felt anything like that—if he let this man get loose of him for even a heartbeat, he was dead. He wouldn't be lucky enough to make so sound a parry the next time, or the blade might just break if it got hit hard again—it wasn't meant for this sort of work, and he wasn't sure he could rely on it much longer.

All at once, Titch got shoved back hard himself, his opponent trying to loosen their contact that way—Titch slipped and stumbled and found himself pivoting about, away from the pressure despite himself. He found he wasn't backed to the parapet any longer, that he and his enemy had exchanged positions, blades still locked as if welded together.

Suddenly Titch could no longer ignore his location. The moon was well up, aging and on the wane but looking so very *close* when one was up so high, so near to it. His senses swam. He forgot the reason for the fight, why he wanted to win it. All he wanted was to draw himself up into a ball. Instead, he found himself teetering precariously upon a very narrow strip of wood somewhere in the middle of the night sky, behind a blade that couldn't protect him, and his heart was beating so hard, it was going to explode right out of his chest—

No longer resisting the sword's push, Titch staggered back two steps and his left foot slipped off the edge of the boards. He screamed, losing his balance and his nerve. His adversary barked a laugh and took his left hand from his sword hilt to push Titch the rest of the way over.

It was a long way down.

Titch yelled again and hurled himself away from the danger, not caring what he went toward, digging his toes into the dry wood, striving to grip the splintery boards through the soles of his boots. He would have gone straight onto the sword's point and not minded, but somehow he slipped past it. He caught the swordsman off his own balance and thrust the big man back—against either of their expectations. As his back jarred against the parapet, the man was noisily close to the swan—the alarmed bird thrashed about in panic. The swordsman tried to reach for the bird, was caught pivoting just as Titch plowed into him. His boots came up into view. The low wall was at his back, but not high enough to stop him. He grabbed wildly at the sharpened logs, missed the grip, and went helplessly over. He screamed.

Titch fetched up against the logs, too, splitting his chin open on the nearest. Boneless with reaction, he stared down toward the far-off river as he slid down the rough-barked surface. His knees jolted against solid boards. Just as the logs cut off vision, he heard a splash, and Titch slipped the rest of the way down, to lie on his face upon the walkway.

He sobbed for breath, for self-control. The night breeze whispered over the palisade. The river made music over its rocks. In the end, Titch had to gather up the swan and *crawl* to the nearest ladder, because he could no longer force himself to stand erect upon the high walkway.

Melcia's Curse

A DOZEN MEN came rushing at Titch, across the bailey. His only avenue of retreat was back up to the parapet, and he would truly rather die than face it, Titch decided. He recovered his sword and turned to face the onrushers, the swan juggled clumsily under his left arm.

They were not necessarily his enemies, Titch reminded himself. Or only some of them might be, while others were innocent. But how could he hope to distinguish? Then he spotted familiar, noble features. They cloaked a less-than-noble nature, but Gerein, whatever other unknightly conduct he might be guilty of, was at least safe then it came to *this* treachery. He'd been on the wrong end of it whenever he'd been near it at all.

Titch yelled Gerein's name, made it an order by his tone. Then he sent the rest of the Guards to his left along the wall—just to see whether they'd do it—with a tale of assassins who shouldn't be allowed to escape. All of the men went with reassuring haste, but that wasn't saying one or more might not double back and come at him less obtrusively. Titch hastened for the keep's interior, motioning Gerein after him.

"What's going on?" Gerein asked conversationally, with a pointed glance at the swan. "Arms drill?"

Titch filled him in, short gasps of sentences, while the swan made a determined effort to split his head with its loosely bound wings. He took some heart from its struggles—at least the prince hadn't been mortally hurt by the scuffling—but he tugged the wingstrap tight again. His face was beginning to hurt as his heartbeat settled down.

"There's a dead Guard in the bailey," Gerein mentioned offhandedly.

"Unless he's a splendid swimmer—in his mail—there's another one in the river," Titch rejoined. They came under the light thrown by a smoking torch, and he started at the sight of crimson dapples of blood on white swan's feathers. Then, as more drops appeared, Titch realized that the blood was his own, falling down onto the bird. He swiped his free hand at his chin, winced. "Look, Gerein, I have no idea how many of the Guards are in this, or which. Far as I'm concerned, anyone trying to stop me gets my blade first and questions as to his intent later."

"Prudent," Gerein agreed. "Why are you trusting *me*?"

"This was going on before either one of us got to Josten. No reason you'd be part of it. And I was desperate," Titch admitted.

"You were that." Gerein smiled thinly. "Do I hear boots?"

Titch cursed.

"They're probably just wanting to escort us back to the queen," Gerein suggested uneasily.

"I don't care." Titch juggled the swan about and drew his sword. "I won't risk it. We're going right through them; make yourself useful."

Instead of taking up the defensive position Titch expected, Gerein jumped in front of him and hailed the foremost soldier. These wore black cloaks—common castle guards, not Melcia's superior horsemen. But Gerein had a knack for making friends wherever he went, and probably knew each man in the garrison by name. "About time you got here, Talf! Take us straight to her, no mucking about," he said, as if he'd been expecting support to arrive and was impatient with its tardiness.

One of the guards reached out for the swan, but Gerein interposed his blade, fast as a snake's tongue flicking out. "None of that, the creature's fine where it is."

"She sent us after it," a burly man persisted.

Gerein stared him down, along his blade. "Then let's not keep her waiting. *Move!*"

In a trice, Titch found himself at the center of a knot of armed men, marching briskly back up the corridor. Gerein fell in, just to his left, and grinned at him. "Going through them would have been messy. Better to use them—don't fret, moving feet means busy brains, with this lot."

Titch scowled at him, but he risked putting his right hand under the swan's breast once more. The bird must weigh two stone, and his left arm was aching from supporting it unassisted. If he needed his sword, it wasn't likely he'd be able to use it in the press of bodies anyway. He felt trapped more than safeguarded, but there was no help for it.

Their procession swung into a torchlit gallery, then clattered up a sweep of stairs. Another pack of henchmen bore down on them, then halted smartly to let them pass. A door banged open, and Titch recognized the chamber as they entered it. There were more torches than there had been, and more sentries, now that 'twas too late for either to do any good.

Someone had cleaned the blood from the floor, and much of the chalk in the process, but the char marks remained. So did Galvin's body, though he had been moved out of the doorway and laid out in more seemly fashion, his limbs straightened and his robes arranged neatly about him. Wren knelt at his side, her face a mask of pain, but dry as baked bread. There were half a dozen Guards standing by, besides the pack he and Gerein had entered with—Titch looked past them and their torches, to the queen. As was her custom, Melcia had arrayed herself in costly blood-scarlet, trimmed now in sable pelts against the evening chill.

Titch marched straight up to her, oblivious this time to the hands snatching at his feathered burden. "Not all of your Guardsmen are quite trustworthy, Lady," he said accusingly, not caring he was surrounded by them. His blood was well up—it had been an unsettling night so far.

"My son is heir to his father's kingdom as well as my own," Melcia observed with cold fury. "Evidently at least one of Kenric's cousins is not utterly lacking in ambition." The queen turned to her chief-captain. "Detain every man in my service whose loyalty you would call into question, guards and common swords-for-hire. And I care not if that is every last one of them."

Titch rather thought it might be, since that interpretation would best preserve the chief-captain's own life.

"They are to make answers. Those who cannot give plausible accountings will be executed at tomorrow's sun-high." She flicked a glance at Titch, then at Gerein. "These two are exempt. They have proved their character by their service."

How the captain would manage to arrest his entire command, Titch could not guess. Happily, it wasn't his worry. He watched impassively as the men filed out.

The swan wiggled against his side, jabbed his chest with its hard bill. Titch knelt awkwardly, trying to keep his already bruised face out of striking range, and set the bird on its webbed red feet. Poor creature—whether it knew it had been a prince or not, it had been very much abused in the course of the last few days, through no fault of its own. No reason to expect manners better than Alinor's from it, he told himself.

"They feared to take his life, as if such scruples could stay my avenging him! Oh, my sweet Evin! My son, they will pay for this outrage all the same—"

"If you had told my master the truth about what happened, he might have been able to restore your son to you," Wren said. She still knelt by Galvin's body, overlooked as a carpet on the floor. Why she had chosen to cast that safety away, Titch could not imagine. He knew how she feared the Red Queen, past all reason—though of course there was reason enough. And she laid her head on the block again. "This was no chance-cast spell of revenge. It was a deliberate working. And you had to have known that. My master told me so."

"Much good his sorcerous learning did him—he could not foresee his own death." Melcia swung round on the kneeling girl. "You had best hope he taught you better! The one who cast the spell for the traitors is dead—that much of the tale is true—and I therefore cannot compel her to undo her working. You will serve instead. I gave your master three days for the task—there are still two remaining. Restore my son to me, or you shall follow your master into death as dawn follows midnight."

Wren flinched as if at a blow, but rather than crumpling with despair, she got to her feet slowly, stiffly. She raised her chin, looked the Red Queen in the eye. "Then you should send me to him now. I cannot make your son as he was."

"Cannot, or *will* not?" Melcia asked with venom.

Titch recollected how the hailstones had felt beneath his fingers, so cold that they seemed burning hot on his skin. Just so, the queen's face, the echo deadly in her voice. What was Wren thinking, to challenge her so *now*? She still had two days left to her, two days to effect a cure or hope to escape—

"If I could do what you ask, I would, so as to be let go from this place," Wren said. "Why would I lie to you? I could not save my master, and he mattered more than life—how should I be able to help your son, whose fate means nothing at all to me?"

"I think you will help him, to save yourself," the queen suggested craftily.

"You are mistaken," Wren whispered. "I cannot do what you ask. I am only an apprentice. I do not have the skill."

"*Dissembler!*" Melcia's face was pale as a skull. Her eyes blazed like dragonfire, like the edges of a glassblower's flame. "By your blood, you are more than a half-taught student! You are a witch, and the true daughter of a witch!"

Wren's resignation shifted to horror. "*Lady—*"

"You thought I would not know you? You thought I could forget that face, that is as much *his* as *hers*? She was a witch, your mother, who took Kenric from me with her sorcery, stole my husband and shamed me before the world. When I ordered the death she deserved, she pleaded with me to spare you, his child!"

But the Red Queen had not shown that mercy, had she? Surely the tales he'd heard had ended with the king's leman and the child both drowned, Titch thought. Melcia's just revenge, offered up as an object lesson, song after song. There'd never been a variation in the theme.

"You think I do not know you?" the queen growled. "That I account you dead? *You should be!* I decreed you should be drowned, as your mother was—but you cozened my knights with your sorcery, and escaped my just sentence."

Drowned, Titch thought, with a lurch in his stomach. Like blind kittens in a sack—only river otters probably are hard to drown. And finally, leagues away, a wizard pulls such an otter from his fish-trap and gets a great surprise—

"Now you are come into my hands once more, and I must keep you there awhile, for my son's sake. You *will* restore him, witch! If you fail, you will die; but if you refuse even to try, then I have ways to make you long for the death I will finally give you—*Savrin!*"

This is my fault, Wren thought dully. *I let myself see her. And then she could see me:* the Law of Polarity, of things equal and opposite, standing in balance. It would shame her master, that she could not keep hold of so simple a Principle. He had tried so hard to teach her . . .

The door hadn't slammed when the Red Queen exited the chamber—Melcia's henchmen had closed it carefully behind her and dropped the bar into place on the far side of it—but Wren stood as if deafened by a clap of thunder all the same, staring blindly into space.

Savrin. That was her name. And with it, she had all the rest of her past. The fear, the dread of discovery, the years spent hiding herself from the eye that had finally, inevitably fallen upon her. *I even learned to hide myself* from *myself,* Wren thought. *How very clever. That way she'd never find me again . . .*

The Red Queen. Water rushed in Wren's ears, tugged at her legs, swirled around her, and dragged her under.

Titch saw by her face that she was fainting, and caught Wren as she went down, eased her gently to the floor. Bad enough to lose your identity, he thought—and surely it was worse yet to regain it in such a wretched fashion. Wren's pointed face was white as swan's down, and her fingers were chill as river water. Her eyelids fluttered as he put his folded cloak under her head for a pillow, first sign of her senses returning.

Motion caught his eye—the swan was trying vigorously to settle its feathers, frustrated by the strap restraining its wings. Titch thought about releasing it—it couldn't escape the room. But it could do itself harm trying, and a swan's wings could break a man's bones, too, if it got in a lucky hit. It wasn't right that a prince should be bound, but he was best left so, for the present moment.

That prince would be Wren's brother—half brother? They wouldn't have met while he was in human shape, but there might nonetheless be a bond between a brother and a sister, whichever side of the blanket they came from. An affinity that could help Wren restore him—

"I don't think I've expressed my gratitude for your involving me in this," Gerein said blandly. He'd been trying to stay out of sight in case Melcia's wrath should require a target—whether it had worked on the queen, Titch couldn't guess, but *he'd* forgotten the man was still in the room.

"You're overlooking the alternative," Titch said calmly, answering the censure. "I'll take being locked in here over the chief-captain's inquisition any day. Even if the pay's only half a crown a twelvemonth."

The whites of Gerein's eyes showed, just for an instant. "Look, that was a mistake. I meant to tell you—I was just holding onto it for you—"

"I never doubted your intentions," Titch said pointedly. "Or expressed my gratitude to you for getting me this post. Let's call it even. Would you mind watching the door?"

Gerein relaxed visibly. "Love to. Pity it's the *other* side's barred."

Titch turned back to Wren. Alinor was standing beside her, shifting from one yellow foot to the other, glaring—well, maybe he was wrong about the interpretation. What else could falcon eyes do, but glare? Still, Titch kept his fingers to himself, and off of Alinor's mistress, till Wren gave a faint whimper and Alinor answered with a creaking croon and an expression in her obsidian eyes that could only be called mild. She leaned forward the way birds must, like a person with hands behind back, and rubbed her beak against Wren's cheek. Wren's lids opened, blinked twice. Her eyes slowly found focus. Titch, with a sidelong glance to assure Alinor's permission, offered his hand so she could sit up.

"Wren—"

"No wonder I called myself that," she whispered, lips and voice dry as old leaves. "It must have been all of my name I could remember, or could say—"

Her hand was still water-cold. "Wren—"

"I've been afraid, ever since they brought us here, that her eye would fall on me. That was the worst thing that ever could happen, certain disaster. I didn't know *why*, but I always knew it." She tried to smile at him, though 'twas only a twitch of her lips. "Sense, you'd think, given the sort of person she is, the power she has, but I always knew it was worse than that. I was more afraid of her than my master was, because I'd learned to be, from the time I could learn anything. It was like knowing that it's air we breathe, not water—I knew the Red Queen must never find out about me, because if she did, I was dead. From the time I was a child, she was lurking there, the evil that must never see me. I don't think I wanted to know who I was, Titch. I wanted to *forget*. And I made Galvin look so hard with his cards—"

She shuddered, and Titch tightened his grip on her arm, trying to keep her with him. He didn't want to watch that emptiness rise in her eyes like black water again. "You don't have to fear her *now*." He glanced pointedly at the swan, which was sulking now, sitting quietly. "She needs you too much to be serious about killing you."

"You heard the songs the captain sang us. They were *true*, Titch! Melcia killed her own husband—my father—because he shamed her. She had my mother put to death. She wanted to kill me, too, and if I can't do what she wants, she finally will."

"Then do what she wants," Titch suggested practically.

Alinor *hek*ked at him, and Wren tried to pull away, looking upset and almost angry. "It's not that easy! My mother *wasn't* a witch! She didn't enchant my father—she was taken captive in a border skirmish, and he claimed her, and they fell in love. When he was dead, she had *nothing*. I know. I was there. I saw."

"You have something," Titch objected. "*Think*. Your master said so—*knew* so, or he'd hardly have been teaching you his magic, planning to take you to the Wizards' City. Wren, if you'd just been a foundling, he'd have set you to sweeping the floors, not conning spells! Believe me—I'm an orphan myself. What happened to you wasn't the normal run of affairs. I swept a lot of floors and mucked out a lot of stables. I'd much rather have been a wizard, but nobody ever offered to make me one." He gave her a crooked smile.

"You wouldn't want to be a wizard," Wren suggested gently. "Especially now." She glanced at Galvin's body.

"I *couldn't*," Titch corrected. "But you could. You *are*. And you can help the prince."

"Because he's my brother?" Wren said, reading his assumption in his eyes. "You think that matters?"

Because it absolutely didn't, her tone implied.

"If he was my brother, I'd do all I could to help him," Titch insisted.

"You think I *want* him to stay a swan forever, just because he's Melcia's son?" Wren looked horrified. "I'm not the Red Queen. I don't punish people just for being born who they are!"

Alinor jerked her beak at him, with obvious intent. Titch spread his hands—a protest of innocence even if he couldn't fend her off.

"I'm only saying *try*. Your master thought it could be done, didn't he?"

"Oh, yes," Wren said softly. "He told me, just before he—" Her voice choked off, she turned her face away.

Titch was astonished. "He told you? But why did you tell the queen you couldn't do it? What's the cure? A rooster's egg? Dragon's blood? A blade of grass from the end of the world? A flask of the Water of Life?"

"*Tears.*"

"Tears." So prosaic, so far from the arcane cures the folk in ballads were always questing after.

"Perfectly sound reasoning," Wren admitted. "I told you before, water transforms everything it touches—even just by itself, it has so many forms that seem unlike but are all part of the one—liquid, fog, snowflakes, ice. Tears are even more powerful. The sun weeps tears of gold, the moon of silver. Rain is crystal tears, from the gray clouds. You can make a river flood by weeping into it the right way. Tears can make a barren woman conceive a child. Heal poisoned wounds, restore sight to the blind, even if they were born that way. Tears can join souls. Some say the Otherworld lies behind a waterfall. And its water is tears, endlessly falling."

"Tears?" Then why didn't Wren seem happy? If not elated, at least relieved? "You have to bathe the swan in tears? But that's easy—the queen probably weeps a bucketful over him, every night! Just—"

"*My* tears, Titch."

He looked into her face. Wren's grief for Galvin was etched there, under the trauma of recapturing her own tragic past—but her eyes were dry as he'd always seen them, clear gray like still pools in the forest, with not even one single drop welling between the fringing lashes.

"I cannot weep," Wren said. "I have an affinity for water—I came to my master by it, we lived by a marsh, and all the shapes I can shift myself into are water creatures. Even Alinor—you know some falconers call peregrines duck hawks, because you often find them taking waterfowl? If I have any magic, then it's the magic of water. Galvin's cards always said so. But one part of water's power is denied me."

She looked toward her master's still form. "I thought . . . when I knew who I was, it would make me stronger. I'd claim all my magic . . . names are power, after all. If I knew my whole name, my true name, that would make all the difference. But it's not so. The day Melcia slew my parents and almost me, the springs of my eyes dried up. I have my name, but it doesn't matter. I have no tears, Titch."

Wren's Tears

TITCH HELD WREN'S head against his shoulder while she heaved dry sobs the more dreadful to hear because he knew they were her only release. After some while she grew quiet, then raised her face and made a husky request of him.

So Titch carried Galvin's body to the hearth, and watched as Wren placed the pack of cards between his cold hands. She stood with head bowed a long moment, then stepped back and spoke two sharp words. Her fingers moved in counterpoint, command. She wielded neither flint nor steel, but a smokeless yellow fire kindled all about the wizard's corpse. The bright-painted cards curled and blackened at the edges, and the flames grew brighter and brighter yet, till it was impossible to look into them. The heat they threw off was no more than summer sunshine.

The swan and Gerein both made startled noises. Titch watched mutely till the flames died, blinked as a tiny heap of ash was wind-whirled up the chimney, leaving the hearthstone bare. There was no further harm the Red Queen could work upon Galvin, but all the same Wren had chosen not to leave his body at the mercy of an enemy she regarded as evil beyond reason.

There'd be no one to do a similar last service for Wren herself. Titch shuddered, wondering if he'd be ordered to lead her to her pyre. Likely he'd be joining her on it, since the rescue he knew he'd attempt didn't offer all that much hope of success or escape.

Wren sat by the cold hearth, letting herself remember her childhood. Her mother's gentle face came back to her at last, and her father's booming laugh. She hugged the memories to her. She recalled lying snug abed on winter nights so cold that snow collected on the windowsills just the other side of her sleeping chamber and gave her a harvest of icicles come morning. She remembered soft rain falling outside that same casement in summer, when there was so much green that the very sky seemed tinged with the color, and the stone bones of the castle grew a thin fur of emerald moss over themselves.

She listened again to her mother's tale of an even moister land, Esdragon, and her father's stories of crossing the Great Sea in a boat that seemed no larger in memory than half a walnut shell.

She could have remembered tales of the Red Queen, also—but in her heart Wren had never forgotten any of those.

The hours crept by. Titch lifted his head, aware by the stiffness of his joints and his gritty eyes that he had yielded to sleep. He was not surprised that he and Wren were the only humans in the chamber—Gerein had gotten the guards to let him out and vanished without a word. Someone had brought them a tray of bread and cheese, a flagon of sweet cider. Gerein had eaten most of it, but Titch offered some of the scraps to Wren, not surprised when she did not respond to his entreaties. He settled back down at her side, because it was all he could think of to do, and ate a few bites of the food. The cut on his chin had finally scabbed over, and chewing hurt, but going too long without food made a man lightheaded and weak, neither of which he might be able to afford. Knights endured privation but did not seek it foolishly. Blunted weapons were no good to anyone.

Without windows to give a sight of the sky, there was no way he could judge the hour. There were candles lit, but they were such thick things that they burned down with glacial slowness, and as they had not been fresh when all the trouble started, they were no use for reckoning, either. They might have been lit days past, for all he could tell.

Finally it occurred to Titch that *he* wasn't the reason the chamber door was barred. He went to it, tapped to get the attention of the men outside, gave the password, and asked what the hour was. It being the first past sunfall, he sent for hot food and some grain—the swan had not eaten in a long while. It might not intend to, but he did not want it to starve through his neglect.

In a fit of perversity, he asked for Gerein by name, to fetch in the food. Titch told himself that it was mere prudence, that he knew none other of the men well enough to risk trusting one in even so minute a matter. He had no idea how the chief-captain's questioning was proceeding. But the plain truth was, he trusted Gerein even less, except in this one thing. It wasn't likely he'd manage to steal Valadan away again, but the risk wasn't worth it.

Gerein was predictably displeased with the duty.

"Fetch and carry, is it?" he asked as he slammed the tray down onto what had been Galvin's worktable. Stew slopped out of a crockery bowl, and even Wren jumped, though she did not look long in his direction, but slipped back into her reverie.

"She'll be high in the queen's favor when this magic's done," Titch said slyly, with a pointed glance at Wren. "Help me make sure no one bothers her, and you can bask in the royal gratitude, too."

"Thank you, no." Gerein shook his head. "That's still a swan over there, and my coin says it *stays* a swan. You'd do better to come with *me*."

"She's still got another day." Titch lowered his voice, not that he really thought Wren was listening. "Just help me out, Gerein. Watch the door—who's out there now? Anybody you'd trust?"

"Juril and Rik."

"I don't know either one." Titch frowned. Who'd been posted there before? Who'd let in Galvin's murderers? Had they known what they did, or only been lured from their post?

"The stuff they make officers out of these days!" Gerein clapped him on the back, grinning. "They're all right. Neither one's drunk or asleep, and you likely don't have to worry about bribes—the risk's too big now they've heard what the penalty is. Also, there's talk you might have done for all the traitors."

"There were only two of them?" Titch's frown deepened. That wasn't much of a conspiracy, two men.

"You'd have preferred four to one instead of two? Count your blessings, boy!"

"I'm not counting on rumor." Titch ignored the insult. "You're the only one I'm *sure* of."

Gerein smiled wickedly. "I can be bought."

Titch shook his head. "Too big a risk, just for money. No. You have your limits, but you're safe—in this."

"For tonight."

"That's all I need. And if you're right about the guards, it's an easy night's work for you." Titch picked up the tray of food and watched Gerein try to wriggle free of the hook he'd set himself on.

Neither the swan nor Wren was interested in the food. The swan was huddled with its long neck recurved and its masked head on its breast, looking at nothing Titch could see, and Wren was still sunk in her private thoughts. Was she in a trance, communing with her master's shade for advice about changing the swan back into a prince? Was she sifting through her reacquired memories of what must have been an awful childhood? Or was she simply waiting for the death Melcia had promised her? He sat just beside her, and might as well have been a thousand leagues away, for all the good he was to her.

All at once, Titch felt Wren's hand steal into his, like a blind kitten seeking the warmth and safety of its mother's side. Neither of them spoke. Fingers twined, they sat shoulder to shoulder, watching the dozing swan.

"I came to you by water, too," Titch said, because he had been trying to understand the connection.

"I went to fetch water, and fetched you instead," Wren recalled with a wan smile. She shivered slightly. "I was afraid, when I first saw you—I didn't understand then. It was the armor, I think, and the sword. The last men I saw with those things were the ones who caught us, before we could cross over the river to safety. Not that there really *was* any safety for us, once my father was dead. My mother knew that. After she saw his head hanging from Melcia's stirrup, all she did was weep, till they drowned her. We had loyal men with us, but she didn't ask them to help us."

"Did you cry then, too?" Titch asked curiously. Were those the last tears she'd shed?

"Tears were no use. Not by then."

"And you've never wept since then?"

Wren's head bumped his shoulder as she shook it. "Not for grief, or fear, or pain," she recited. "You know that's true, you've seen me through them all." A squeeze from her hand said she was grateful—and resigned to her fate at the Red Queen's hands.

"Wren, I—" Against all sense, Titch wanted to hold more than her hand, wanted to promise her he'd keep her safe. His ears were full of the sound of water lapping at a shore, flowing but calm, and he wanted to sink beneath that water, let it touch every inch of him—

"There isn't anything more you can do, Titch." Wren looked straight into his eyes. "If you'd any sense at all, you'd start acting like her liegeman instead of my friend, before you wind up dying with me."

"I'm not letting her kill you." Knights did not kill women, nor allow them to die. Titch glanced toward Gerein, who rather carefully avoided his eye. No help there, then. The one night he'd asked for was all he'd get. "You saved *my* life."

"No, I didn't." A line faint as spidersilk formed on her forehead, but a smile flickered on her lips at the same time. "You did that yourself. My master thought you'd die—I think he was trying to be sure I'd be asleep when it happened, in fact, so I wouldn't be upset. I was forever bringing home birds and animals too sick for even Galvin to fix, and he probably thought you'd be the same, only worse. He was amazed you were still breathing come morning. That was the turning point, that first night. Then you just got well . . ."

Except Titch discovered he had a rather different memory of events—he recalled lying helpless at death's door one moment and waking with his wounds healed and his health restored the next. How had that happened? There'd been something else . . . had he been out of his head, losing all track of time's passage? That seemed likely. Or dreaming? He thought he had been dreaming part of the time . . . some of it came back.

Rain. He had dreamed of rain, those crystal tears of the clouds. Raindrops, falling by ones and twos and then all at once a great deluge of them, a rain so thick he'd thought he might drown from breathing it in, except it put the life back into him instead, shored up his faltering heart and inflated his weary lungs till some unseen scale tipped and he was more alive than dead. And on the heels of that, the greatest wonder of all—realizing that those magic raindrops were the tears spilling from Wren's eyes as she leaned over him, distressed at his dying. Those gray eyes had filled with color as well as salt water—they'd been green as the sea, blue as a kingfisher's crest or a robin's new-laid egg.

Her parents' tragedy had stopped up the wells of Wren's eyes. But not entirely. The tears were still inside, and she could still shed them—Titch knew she could, he had proof. She'd shed them over *him*, out of compassion. She'd healed him. *Restored* him. Galvin was right about the power of her rare tears.

But if that was so, why hadn't she healed her master? She'd been grief-striken enough to weep a river, but her eyes had stayed dry as sand. The wizard was, as she'd said, her only family. She'd done harder things than weeping, trying to save him. Fear, grief, loss—none of those held the key to unlock the wellsprings of Wren's heart? She didn't cry for her own pain. But she'd wept for *him*, a total stranger fallen into misfortune. That was the riddle Galvin hadn't solved, maybe hadn't known of. Somehow Titch's plight had moved her—

Gerein gave a start, and the door beside him was thrust open. His hand went to his sword, but he did not draw the weapon. He wasn't going to throw himself on the pyre, was Gerein. No. If it was morning, if the Red Queen had changed her mind or lost her patience and it was time for Wren to die, then that was that. Just a new day's dawning for Gerein of Kendillin, knight.

Titch got to his feet hastily, putting Wren as much behind him as he could, in a useless gesture of protection.

To his astonishment, no guards entered. Only the Red Queen crossed the threshold, alone. The lantern she carried made a ghastly mask of her face. The light was far kinder to the collar of yellow gold about her neck than it was to her skin or her sharp features.

Why had she come unattended? The queen spoke no word, no order, no inquiry, passed them all without even the hint of a glance, the briefest acknowledgment of their existence. She went straight to the swan, which had retreated into a corner and now huddled there forlornly, not even sleeping, but merely drawing one breath after another. The feathers it had lost during its abduction gave it a moth-eaten look, and its back was dabbled with brown stains from Titch's blood. Its eyes were dull as stagnant water.

"*Evin,*" the queen said, and her harsh voice broke on the name, piteously.

The swan opened its red-black beak and hissed weakly, either a threat or a protest at being disturbed.

The queen took the sound for a greeting and went down on her knees, sobbing and reaching. "*My son—*"

Galvin had said she came each evening, to wail over her lost son. This must be the hour for it. Of course Melcia came alone—the Red Queen would not want her men-at-arms to see her on her knees, human size at last, weeping, ravaged in mind and body. She would not want her courtiers to know the extent of her distress. Kingdoms fell over less. Titch's skin crawled. It was dangerous to be an intruder on such a private moment, when the woman weeping was royal and notoriously vengeful and apt to notice inconvenient witnesses eventually. Prudence would make a man withdraw, but he could not, no more than Gerein could, who stood just by the still-open door.

"*Evin—*"

She was a woman to fright unruly children with, even if you weren't her husband's bastard, who must be kept from her sight on pain of death. Wren's weren't the only nightmares the Red Queen stalked, Titch was very sure. He listened with increasing discomfort to the sobbing, the words scattered through it like mercenaries at a tournament.

"My fault. My crime. I wanted her child dead, so I should never have to see Kenric's face *there*, mocking me, living proof that he loved another well enough to risk so much for her sake. I wanted her dead, and her child, too. I called it justice, because my arm was strongest, and no one contested my will, but the child was innocent, and now I am repaid. Now my own child is taken, as cruelly. *I* should be punished, not you! Not you! Oh, Evin—"

There was sort of rough justice to it, Titch silently agreed. Melcia had her son back, but he was a swan—and likely to remain so. All the Red Queen's tears could do *nothing* for her son, though she filled the room with them, though she made all of Josten a salty sea. She had crippled the one thing that could have helped the prince, and threats were even more useless.

"My fault, my fault, my fault! And my pride, when I learned Kenric had taken her to his bed before ever he wed me! I said it was my great love, that could not bear what he had done to me, but it was my shame that sent our armies against one another. *Love* would have let him live and go where he loved, but I could not bear it, the whispers and songs and sly glances. He was the only man I had ever loved, and if I could not have him, no other woman should! All I kept of him was you, Evin. It has all been for you. *You are my life!*"

The queen spoke freely, either not knowing or not caring that she was overheard. That boded no good, for eventually Melcia *would* know and *would* care. She would be shamed by what they had heard, and the Red Queen had but one way to deal with humiliation—being in that room was a death sentence for each of them, not Wren alone. Yet, listening to Evin's mother weeping hopelessly over her son, Titch discovered that 'twas hardly concern for his own life that made his throat ache. A man would need to be made of stone not to hear Melcia's grief for what it was—a mother wailing over a child gone forever beyond the reach of her love and protection, beyond the reach of her arms. Alive yet dead.

Not fear. Not pain. Not grief, or loss. Suddenly he knew what the key was, what unstopped the well.

"Wren!" He spun to face her, put a hand on either of her narrow shoulders, though Alinor screamed at him for the affrontery. "She's not the Red Queen now! She's only his mother!"

Wren's eyes were empty as raindrops. As if they looked elsewhere, did not see the room, or the swan, or Melcia, none of it. Titch locked onto her gaze and saw dark water sliding by, endlessly, overwhelming. He faltered, found his balance once more, tightened his grip on her, as if he expected Wren to take salmon-shape again and swim away from him for good and all.

"Don't you *hear* her? How can you listen to that and not be moved?"

The rushing waters seemed to divide around a rock, swirl him for a moment into a quieter eddy. "I have no compassion left," Wren said. "It's been burned out of me, like my tears. *She* did that. I don't weep," she declared stonily. "Not for pain, not for fear, not—" She looked at the empty hearth, as if she could see that much of the room, at least. "Not for grief."

All at once Titch found himself back in the main rush of the current, about to be dashed on the rocks. The thing to do, then, for once, was to yield rather than fight, to let the river have its will of him, wasting no precious energy in vain struggles—and to hold on to Wren, come what might.

"You don't weep for *your* pain, *your* grief. But you weep, Wren!"

She stared, not comprehending. The current rushed on.

"I was dying. And I dreamed of rain falling on me, healing me. I opened my eyes, and you were weeping over me. The rain I felt was *tears*—your tears."

She shook her head, like an otter trying to wriggle free of his clasp.

"It wasn't pain, or fear—it was *pity*. You still have that, Wren! You could shed those tears for me, a stranger dying by your fire. Can't you weep for a prince, stolen from his own shape and shoved into another's? Can't you shed a tear for his mother's pain? You let yourself see her—*now let yourself listen to her!*"

For one unguarded heartbeat, his feet seemed to touch the river's bottom, firm rock and stone beneath the flood. With all his strength, Titch tried to thrust Wren up onto the shore, where she'd be human again.

Listen to her? How could she not? The hoarse wailing would fill all the world if one let it. Where was the pride Melcia the Queen was so far-famed for, the pride that had made her slice off her own husband's head, drown a woman and a child? This woman kneeling on the rush-strewn floor, confessing past atrocities and claiming the guilt of them with abandon, could she be that same queen?

She was not. This was no longer the Queen of Nightmares, but only Evin's mother, weeping for her lost child. Each night she had come to him, long after the queen had retired for the evening, and knelt there sobbing and lamenting. Always she came alone—no one could share this pain, and Wren thought there was no one who'd choose to, either. Melcia's life had held only one, terrible love, and she had nothing beyond the fruit of that savage and twisted passion, a son huddled before her now in swan-shape, frightened half to death of her.

Melcia's head sank till her face pressed against the cold tiles. She was nearly silent now, spent, choked by her position, but her back still heaved with sobs. It was unthinkable that they should be allowed to see her like this, even if they were to die, but Melcia had at last passed beyond her pride. Wren took one tiny step toward her, then stared at her feet as if they'd turned traitor. She looked again at the crumpled figure in the fine scarlet robe, weeping her heart out so uselessly.

Her own eyes prickled. As if in a trance, she continued across the chamber and knelt down beside her lifelong enemy.

Titch released his hold but followed Wren, a little afraid she'd faint before she got anywhere near Melcia's side. Wren's face was white as a cloud, and her feet wavered as she set them down, as if she had no idea where the floor lay. A sleepwalker stepped more surely. He glanced toward the door—there was no sign now of Gerein. He'd seized the chance to bolt, then. Titch tried to swallow away the bitterness he felt at the desertion; it was hardly unexpected.

Wren sank down at Melcia's side and put one small hand tentatively on the queen's shoulder. She looked toward the enchanted swan. The gray of her eyes transmuted to pure aquamarine as her tears began to well up.

Titch hauled the swan roughly toward her. The bird gave a hoarse croak and struggled as best it was able, to no avail. He held it still and thrust it closer.

Drops trickled down Wren's pale cheeks. One splashed the slate tiles, and Titch hastily shoved the white bird closer yet. He couldn't see whether more tears were coming, dropping, and they wouldn't show well against the white feathers. If he'd been too late, if they'd missed curing the prince by an inch, by one drop of salt water falling amiss—

A drop beaded upon the thick white feathers, close by one of the many brown stains. A second joined it, catching the light like a drop of rock crystal. A third fell close by the first.

There was no flash of fire, no puff of sorcerous smoke, no reek of sulfur. Between one heartbeat and the next, two-stone's weight of swan in Titch's arms became the head and shoulders of a young man, naked save for a collar of bright gold about his pale neck. The rest of the prince didn't fit in Titch's lap, but sprawled across the tiles. Well made but limp, as if the transformation had made him swoon.

The youth's chest heaved. His dark eyes flew open, stared about in horror. He fluttered a hand into his line of sight, spread his fingers. His eyes went wider yet. His lips parted.

"What have you done?" the prince wailed, with a piercing cry very like the swan's had been.

A Prince Restored

THE PRINCE EVIN was still weeping and shrieking and flailing his arms about like his lost wings as his mother's chamberlain and a dozen burly ushers of the bedchamber bore him away to his own rooms, wrapping warm robes about him and trying to shove slippers onto his stumbling, kicking feet. In the end they wound up carrying him out bodily. Wren watched the struggling procession and the rejoicing in the manner of one who sleeps with open eyes, which she might even be doing, Titch supposed, all things considered. The evening's events had been no easier on her than they had been on the prince.

"I'm sure he'll be fine in a few days," he said uncertainly, staring at the emptied doorway, listening, whether he wanted to or not, to cries that sounded odd coming from a short human throat instead of a swan's. It was an unregal racket. "Think of all he's been through! Tonight alone—"

Wren turned and buried her face against his left shoulder. Titch put his arms around her, let his hands gentle her as he would have a frightened horse. He stroked her hair, touched and then traced the line of her cheekbone with one finger. The skin was dry now, and the eyes she raised to his were gray as raindrops once more.

"It must hurt, to be changed back after so long, even if it's changed back to your true self," Titch hazarded.

"I can't remember being an otter," Wren confessed, thinking he was questioning her. "Did it hurt when I wasn't one any more? I can't remember."

"It was a long time ago. In a week he probably won't remember," Titch suggested gently. "It will seem like a dream."

There was a discreet throat-clearing from the vicinity of the now-unguarded doorway. "Lady? May I show you to a sleeping chamber?"

Titch cast a cold eye on the servitor. He looked long and hard, but his suspicions appeared unwarranted. The man bore no weapons and only looked like what he certainly was—a servant who had been routed from his bed and given orders he barely comprehended. Titch let his sword hand relax back to his side. But after Wren had taken up Alinor, he stayed beside her and made it plain he would not permit her to be spirited off into the bowels of the castle alone. The gentleman usher seemed minded to protest but, when he looked more closely at Titch's mien, gave it up and led them off with no further ado.

"I'd rather just keep on going, out the gate," Wren whispered, holding on to Titch's arm as to life itself. "Aren't I free to go now? The prince is himself again. I just want to go home."

"When you've rested," Titch answered sensibly. She was white and stumbling as the prince had been, and though Titch would have conveyed her to the world's end if she'd asked it of him, he'd feel easier if she slept awhile beforehand. His own weariness and hurts didn't even enter into it. He'd endure what he must, but Wren seemed both fragile and precious, a freshwater pearl in the setting of the Red Queen's treasure-crammed gloomy halls.

"Surely she'll let me go now," Wren pleaded, hardly able to set one foot ahead of the other, whether on dressed stone or looted carpet.

Titch agreed. "No reason she shouldn't."

Except that Melcia did *not* release her prisoner. There was no harm in it, Titch thought—hoped. He'd been thickheaded from drowsing on his feet outside of Wren's chamber, but the tidings of a feast to celebrate the Prince Evin's recovery had sounded innocent enough to his ears when they'd reached them. Wren was a prisoner no longer but had transformed herself into an honored guest. She was appointed a hand-span of servants and sent fine gowns to array herself with. Musicians were ordered to play sweet airs while she napped, while she broke her fast with dainties gleaned from the queen's own table, while her hair was washed and combed and dressed with strands of tiny pearls.

The attention terrified Wren. Not the overwhelming luxury of it—she had been born a princess, if a secret one, and being clean and well dressed and tended by many hands was not utterly strange to her. But Wren trusted none of it, and regarded her situation as a gilded cage. The only demands she made—and the palace folk had been ordered to deny her nothing—were that Alinor should go with her everywhere and that Titch should escort her whenever she left her chamber. Alinor's perch of gilded wood, padded with purple-dyed leather, stood on Wren's left hand, and the falcon had an usher of her own, charged with feeding her scraps of fresh-killed duck as often as she desired them during the feasting. Titch stood ceremoniously behind Wren's tall-backed chair, garbed in clothing so new that it was scratching him raw and boots that fit so close to his measure that they made his toes ache out of novelty. He didn't have his own servant, but he had a good view of the queen's hall.

The prince was dressed richly as anyone there, and should have cut a fine figure. Evin was taller even than his mother, his features were pleasant—though his nose *did* have a bump at the top of it, like the knob on a cob's beak—and his freshly barbered hair was a shade between dark mahogany and ebony, which went well with the blue of his silk-velvet mantle. Only his comely face was still as death, and his dark eyes were pits of despair. Titch made the mistake of looking into them once; he was determined not to commit the error a second time.

The prince dined, and the prince drank. Titch thought that might be because the servant hovering at his elbow told him to do so, frequently. A discreet whisper, and a bite of some dainty was conveyed to the royal lips, often with a shaking hand. Between bites and sips, the prince watched the far distance, looking at the gods knew what—certainly *not* the entertainers celebrating his release from sorcerous captivity. It might be that no one noticed—the high table was a long way from the queen's guests. It might be that the distance was deliberate.

By contrast, Evin's mother glowed with joy and health. Her skin was the usual alabaster, but there was a flush of fine, unaccustomed color in her cheeks, upon her lips. She wore a broad collar of gold thick-set with carnelians, and there were balas rubies hanging pendant from her ears. Her hair had been intricately dressed, piled high, and held with jeweled pins. The gleam of happiness in her eyes outshone even the rubies. One hand lay stretched upon the table's damask cloth, long fingers within easy reach of her son's arm, so that a touch might instantly reassure her of his presence.

There were dancers and tumblers in the hall. Fire-eaters and minstrels made good use of the vast space. Rich foods appeared without ceasing, piglets cooked whole, their mouths stuffed with quinces, a peacock roasted and then reclad in its own feathers to make a gaudy show. Silver salmon, and porpoise caught in the sea and carried inland to Josten for roasting. Towers of spun sugar falling to siege engines wrought of marchpane. A swan baked of fine pastry, paddling in a sea of jellied wine.

That conceit went too far at last. Titch heard a stir and looked discreetly aside to see the prince's place empty, his royal mother dismayed but frozen in her place by pomp and protocol. All that night, weeping echoed through the gold-filled halls of the keep.

The nature of the Prince Evin's misfortune had been kept a strict secret; his recovery was not. Feasting and dancing were the order of the nights, while feats of arms were done in the prince's honor for each of seven days. After that first night the royal servants were more alert—there was no midnight weeping to be heard in the galleries and passages. Any commotion was kept behind enough doors to muffle it. But upon the seventh day, as Titch was waiting his turn at the lists, to ride a joust of honor for the prince against another of Melcia's Guards, a cry drew his and many another's attention skyward.

There was no mistaking that the bird was a swan—she

made a white cross against the blue sky as she soared just above Melcia's gaily fluttering pennons. Swans' cries always sounded mournful—some folk took that to mean that the birds presaged death, or carried souls away with them—but this bird's cries grieved and keened exactly as the prince's did. His swan-mate, Titch thought with a certainty he could not justify but could not dismiss either.

All day she circled the castle, calling. Probably the servants were wise enough to keep Evin well away from any windows, but they could not force him to attend the seventh banquet doubly celebrating his return to humanity and the betrothal his mother had just arranged for him.

His royal mother was trapped at the high table by her own pomp and show, by the twelve-score eyes of her guests, but Wren found no difficulty in slipping from her lowlier place, with Titch as ever at her velvet-shod heels. They left the hall discreetly, unremarked.

Every door that led outside or to high battlements was scrupulously guarded. Wren turned aside from such again and again, not out of fear, but using the guards as her compass, happy to have all the false ways ruled out for her ahead of time. After some while, she passed through an archway and exited into a tiny walled garden, enclosed on four sides by new stonework and on a fifth by the earth beneath it, but open to the black sky and the diamond stars on the upper side of the cube. A wind was blowing, sobbing through chinks in the stonework, whistling lightly and crying softly.

The Prince Evin stood in almost the exact center of the garth, beside a stone fountain. His head was tipped back, his eyes fixed on the spaces between the points of light above. It took a moment for Titch to realize that the sounds he had heard came not from the wind, but from Evin's throat—the prince was keening. And somewhere above, too high to be seen, the wild swan was answering.

Wren went to her brother and put her right hand upon his arm. It was the first time Titch had ever seen them touch. Evin turned toward her at once, but his eyes were wild and black as the sky above, and there was nothing of a man in them, save for the pain.

"Do you know what you have done?" he demanded of her harshly. "Bound me fast to this dead earth, nevermore to taste the wind beneath me—"

Wren flinched, remembering her tastes of Alinor's wild, free flight. "I only wanted to help you," she whispered. "You were stolen away from yourself by treachery and sorcery."

"However it happened, I was free," Evin corrected bitterly. "I could fly from earth's end to earth's end, finding my way by the moon and the stars. You have stolen me back. Now where am I? What have I?" He looked at the sky once more.

"Your mother loves you," Wren said.

"She has caged me!" A sharp cry echoed Evin's from among the high stars. "I took me a mate, and now she is lost to me—forever. And my mother has found for me a *human* bride." He shaped the word as if 'twas filth in his mouth.

"You're a man, not a swan," Titch said, trying to hold the boy to reality.

The prince spun toward him, like a cob repelling intruders from its nest area. *"I was a swan for a year and a day!* My wings have borne me to the wintering grounds and to the breeding place in the Summer Country. I achieved the quest and won my reward!" He threw back his head and screamed at the sky above. He was answered, but almost too faintly to hear. Evin looked back at Wren, his face awash with tears that glittered like frost in the starlight. "They say swans die singing the loveliest song that human ears can hear. Soon you shall know whether that is true. And I shall be free."

"I didn't mean you harm," she pleaded.

"I know that." Evin relented unexpectedly. "But dying is the only way I have to be free again." He looked longingly at the high walls he was not permitted to scale, then stole a casual glance at Titch's sword. Titch locked his fingers stubbornly on the hilt, warning the prince not to try.

I didn't mean to hurt him, Wren begged her own conscience. She'd thought of him as a swan, never her brother.

Melcia's son, not a human being with his own dreams, his own loves.

She couldn't remember being an otter, or a salmon. She hadn't regretted the loss of their shapes when she had her own back—they had been escapes for her, borrowed skins. If she'd held one for the magical year and a day, would it have been different for her? Would she have felt as Evin did? Or would she have known that the other shapes were always inside her, hers for the reaching? For him, that wasn't true.

How did he plan to die? The overt ways would surely be denied him, but he could still go the way birds often did, by willing it, ceasing to live long before plain starvation would have claimed them. He'd die of his grief, by his own choice. And it was her fault. She'd brought him to this, not the paid sorceress who'd changed him to a swan in the first place, Wren thought miserably.

Everyone said the prince was recovered, was his old self, or would be soon, any day. Their eyes refused the truth. Come some morning not too distant, they'd find him dead in his bed, and high, high above a lone swan would fly slowly into the sunrise with all that was left of him—his soul.

She sought her familiar's mind, that breath of fresh wind and freedom. *Alinor, what shall I do?*

All one sky, the falcon said judiciously. *Give him back to it.*

Wren lifted Alinor to the stone lip of the fountain, gently coaxed the falcon to step back onto it. The prince took no note of her movements. He was staring at the sky again, hopelessly, tears streaking his face. Wren watched him a long while, her own face still as a millpond. Then she stepped near and put her arms out to embrace him.

The dim light prevented Titch from instantly recognizing what she was about. He couldn't see the colors well up in her eyes, and by the time the starlight glistened on her tears, it was far too late—the first salt drops were already falling.

"Wren, no!"

He reached desperately for her, but even as he moved,

Titch saw he would be too late. Something confused his senses an instant, he misjudged the distance and stumbled helplessly, nowhere near her. By the time he recovered his balance, Wren's arms were burdened with a swan's weight, and the prince's rich velvet clothing was slipping down like shadows to lie at her feet.

The cob uttered a shrill cry, stretching its neck back. It was answered at once from above, and Wren began to walk carefully toward the center of the open space. The swan's wings were already thrashing the air, making her steps wobble.

Swans were such heavy birds that gaining flight required a running start. He'd have time enough to stop her, Titch thought, lunging. But Wren was throwing the swan upward as he jumped, and the huge wings were catching the night with a mighty effort, and the bird was aloft and out of his reach by a finger's length. Titch nearly went into the fountain headlong and touched not so much as a feather.

Joyful cries rang out overhead. And just after, a single anguished scream echoed from the stones of the garden walls. Wren turned slowly to face the Red Queen as the swans departed, flying wingtip to wingtip across a field of stars.

Forfeit

THERE WERE NO guards. Not that it mattered. They'd arrive soon enough. *"Why?"* Melcia sobbed, her mouth a black pit in a white face. "Why? *Revenge?"*

Titch wondered the same as he picked himself up. Certainly Melcia had earned it a dozen times over.

"Could I weep for *your* hurt and not for his?" Wren asked wretchedly. "He was in such pain—"

"You have stolen my son—as your mother stole my husband! He was *nothing* to you!" The queen shook her head, and the ruby eardrops danced like drops of blood flying from an axe-stroke.

"And nothing to you, either, if you could let him suffer so," Wren said, surprised and bold with it.

She'd know she'd forfeited the rewards and honors the queen had pledged her. She wouldn't care about those, Titch supposed. But did Wren realize she'd also earned herself a death sentence? He made a methodical, covert search for exits from the garth. It was intended for a very private spot, a personal retreat. There was only the one way into it, the way they—and the queen after them—had entered.

Melcia the Red Queen, the Queen of Nightmares, would have slain Wren on the spot, with her own sword. But fresh-come from a sumptuous banquet, Melcia bore no weapons beyond her hands and her voice. The voice was probably the greatest present threat—she could use it to summon her Guards, and their iron weapons. Titch looked hopelessly at the lone archway and loosened his sword in its sheath. He doubted he could save Wren, but he couldn't surrender her either—

"Thieving witch!" Melcia had chosen to waste speech upon a pointless attack. "Bring my son back!"

Wren's gaze darted skyward. Nothing there now save the impartial stars, scattered like daisies in a field. She smiled. "I cannot, Lady. And I would not, anyway."

"Then *die!*" Melcia shrieked, whirling. *"Seize her!"*

She was looking straight at him. *Gods,* Titch thought, dazed by realization. *I am the Guards!* The queen wasn't summoning others—she didn't think she needed to! Titch put his right hand on his sword hilt and his left hand on Wren's arm, to make a good show of obedience, and Alinor's outraged scream enhanced the effect. Melcia turned and swept through the archway, out of the garth.

Wren shrugged off Titch's hand and lifted up her arm so that Alinor alighted on her interposed fist rather than slashing his eyes out.

"You should go now, dear," she said softly. "Fly while there's open sky over you."

Talons clamped hard on her wrist—not so hard as to pierce the skin, but impossible to ignore. Alinor's outspread wings spanned the night. *Traitor!* She tensed in Titch's direction.

"No," Wren insisted. "He's not. Go. Find a mate. Live free and long."

Titch grabbed her unfalconed wrist, thinking that his helm should serve to deflect Alinor and the rest of him was similarly armored, making the risk acceptable. He had not openly refused Melcia's order. They'd precious minutes before his defection would be noticed, a thing Wren seemed not to take into account. "We've got a better chance if we can get to someplace with more than one way out of it!" He hauled her toward the archway. Wren began to struggle frantically after the first couple of steps. Possibly she hadn't recognized his defection either, till that moment.

"Leave me here!" she insisted. "If she's got *me*, there's no reason for her to come after *you*. Let go!"

Titch ignored her and kept a tight hold. Wren served as a shield from Alinor if he held her to him, and the falcon hadn't room to take flight within the passage. Not much of an advantage, but Titch seized it gladly. He spied a stairway leading up. Around a blind turn, too, and spiraling so that his sword hand would be hampered against the right-hand wall, whereas defenders above would be unencumbered. Couldn't be helped. All the stairways in the castle turned likewise. He was hampered quite enough by Wren, come to that, but he shouldn't need a weapon *yet*. He must hope he wouldn't.

"Titch, there are guards!"

"They're supposed to be keeping the prince safe," he reminded her calmly. "They don't know what's happened. They may let us go past, being neither one of us is the prince. It's a chance." He kept pulling till Wren's hanging back made him stumble and bang a shoulder on the wall. "*Stop it!* We want it to look like we're *supposed* to be here!"

"*You* stop!" Wren demanded. "Leave me here. I deserve to pay for what I did. You don't." She pulled free, slapping at his hand when Titch tried to get his grip back.

Alinor screamed with frustration, and Titch suspected she understood better than her mistress. At least she wasn't going for his face again.

"We're all in this together! She'll figure that out! You can't save me by letting her kill you, Wren." Titch caught her hand again, merciless. If it hadn't been for the Guards ahead, he'd have flung his cloak over her head, thrown her over his shoulder. It was no place for coaxing and pleading. "*Now come on!*"

"Where are we going?" She'd stopped dragging back—too soon to decide whether that was acceptance or only meant to make him relax his grip so she could wriggle out of it.

"Stables," Titch panted. "Soon as we find a way down, but I think we'll do better to go *up* first, no one's apt to be watching for us that way—" He skidded to a halt, seeing the glow of torchlight, peered ahead. "Only two of them. Don't say one word," he admonished. If she fought him *now*, if Wren was the least bit undecided about trusting him or still determined to sacrifice herself, they were undone. Titch cast the thoughts away, tried to pretend he was

Gerein, adept at deceptions having naught to do with sword bouts.

He gathered Wren close as they neared the sentries, grinned Gerein-style at the men as he gave them the password. Evidently, licentiousness was a means of gaining respect—the Guards winked, and actually opened the door for him.

The portal led onto a high walkway, surrounded by stars and doubtless romantic enough to some. Titch staggered as Wren let Alinor out from under her cloak, recovered himself sternly. *Don't look down, idiot!* But he had only the barest notion of their location, and they didn't have an instant to waste on false starts at finding the stables. "Ask Alinor whether she can see the place where the horses are," he begged Wren, feeling sweat start out on his forehead, wanting to drop to his knees, locking his joints so his legs couldn't turn traitor.

"She says they're in the place where she caught the dove, and she can't see that from here because of the walls," Wren reported almost at once. "What's the matter?" She looked closely into his face. "*Oh.* It's not just cliffs?"

Man-built cliffs, Alinor said.

"I'm all right, if I don't have to look down." It was a lie he hoped to make true, Titch decided. "Gray's in the river meadow, but Valadan was in the stable, last time I saw him. Can she see the building from here? Which way should we go?" He wiped his forehead, and the air felt colder, after. He dragged in a lungful of it. "Which side of the keep are we on? That's what I should have asked."

Wren whispered something to Alinor, who hurled herself into the night. She'd do her best, Wren said.

"We have to keep moving," Titch wrestled another urge to lie flat on the walkway. Standing was too risky, he could topple right over. He felt as if the edge were trying to pull him toward itself.

"She'll find us unless we go back inside," Wren assured him. She saw nothing that would conceal them from a falcon, for a little distance.

"Just along here." Titch managed three steps. "We'll

have to go down again somewhere——" His stomach knotted at the thought.

"Don't look down."

"I'm *not*," Titch insisted. "It doesn't help. I still know exactly where I am." Lying to himself wasn't working. There was wind, he could feel it shoving greedily at him, fingering his cloak. Trying to get him closer to the unguarded edge. And then——

Wren abruptly pushed him over against the solidity of the parapet, positioned herself on the inner side of the walkway. They'd gone a dozen somewhat easier steps in that fashion when Alinor returned from her reconnaissance and backwinged onto Wren's shoulder, smashing the leading edge of her wing into Titch's head, perhaps truly by accident between the darkness and their changed positions.

"Where's the stable?" he growled, swiping at his eyes, which watered from the feathers' intrusion.

"Clear the other side," Wren relayed unhappily, while Alinor fussed about her flight feathers.

"That may help." Titch frowned, considered. "If we can get around the walls quick enough, if they're expecting us to be down *there* somewhere—watch where you put your feet, there's a lot of building going on——" And there was a chance, there was still a chance, Titch told himself. The new walls went a considerable way, and part of that was a direction they would find useful. So long as there were no shouts of discovery, they were still escaping.

Alinor, commanded, took wing once more and flapped beside them as they ran, a little ahead, a trifle above, so she could forewarn of trouble. Twice that let them dodge sentries. Then all at once a loose heap of wood and trash warned of a serious work area ahead. Titch headed them for the only visible way down, though the doorway into the tower was dark and none of them had the least notion what lay within. Sounds echoed up as they spiraled down— surely his treachery had been noticed at last, and the pursuit had begun. The clamor was distant, the tower's base mercifully deserted. Titch strove to hold fast to his sense of direction. They were near the stables, but not so near that he couldn't still make a disastrous mistake. All he had to do was lead them right instead of left. Or was that left rather than right? What had Alinor said? He should know the castle well enough to find his way about it drunk, Titch thought. *Gerein* would, certain sure.

To his amazement, Titch realized he could hear music drifting from the windows of the queen's great hall, two floors above in the nearby keep. The dancing proceeded. The prince's absence had not been formally announced. That could mean that not *every* soldier within the stronghold would have orders to stop them on sight, if luck was still with them. How long would it take for Melcia to realize that her Guard wasn't holding Wren prisoner but was helping her to flee? How soon would the alarm be raised?

Had Titch's much-battered nose been working as well as his ears, he'd have been in no doubt about the stable's location. He could have found it by its smell, rather than what seemed blind chance. The dung heap needed clearing rather urgently. He and Wren had to squeeze past it to get to the door of the undistinguished wooden structure that housed those horses deemed best kept near at hand. Titch risked lighting the single lantern that hung close by the door—worth the chance of discovery for the speed he'd gain by seeing what he was doing, though he bade Wren to hide in an empty stall, lest guard or stable hand burst in.

He hastened to Valadan's place and, to his delight, found Gray nibbling hay in the very next stall. The old horse wouldn't be so fleet of foot as the black stallion—nothing that trod the earth could be—but surely they'd do better if he and Wren weren't sharing the same mount. It would free Titch to fight if he had to, and there was none he'd trust with Wren more than Gray, whose brave heart more than made up for his years.

The Guards kept their gear on racks at the short ends of the stable. Titch's personal things were in the barracks, but he could get everything he really needed from the racks before him—shield and a long lance and a formidable war hammer. All of the horse gear, certainly. His sword always hung at his side. Whatever he'd left behind in the barracks he would willingly count as lost—none of it mattered a jot to him. Titch's fingers danced over the straps and buckles.

He wanted to be quick, and quiet, and not let the horses catch fear or excitement from him. Haste could infect them easily, make the most seasoned destrier fractious as an unbacked colt, and start all the others neighing and stamping—

Valadan pointed his ears, but Titch was busy tugging a strap and didn't see the warning, much less heed it.

"Well now, all that fine talk of winning some great lord's favor and getting yourself a knighthood with it—this doesn't seem the way to go about it at all!"

Titch gave a start, and Gray shied away from him in re-action, while the girth went slack and swung free. Titch had his dagger in his hand as he turned—in the narrow confines of the tie stall, drawing his sword would have been impossible as well as obvious. A dagger wasn't much use against a squad of men, but surprise might be—

Gerein was alone. He grinned as the knife caught the lantern light, like a mastiff facing down a puppy's milk teeth. "Is that for me?"

"Depends," Titch answered coldly. "Let me tie you up and gag you, and save the bloodshed."

"Thank you, but I don't think so!"

Titch shrugged. "Suit yourself." He wasn't as sanguine as he pretended—the last thing he wanted was a fight, which would waste precious time no matter how the out-come went. He came up onto the balls of his feet, ready to counter whatever move Gerein made at him, to turn it to his advantage if he could.

"You don't have time for this nonsense," Gerein said tes-tily, not moving a muscle. "No one's thinking you could have made it this far yet, so they just sent one man to se-cure the stables. But five more minutes—"

Titch stared, confused. "You're *helping* us?"

"I'm coming with you," Gerein corrected. "The queen came back into her banqueting hall raving like a mad-woman, there's no sign of the prince, and there's a hue and cry raised for your little witch. I'm sure the Red Queen will reward me today for handing you over, but tomorrow's what concerns me, for once. She's torn her hair, and her fine robes, and she was starting on her face when I left. I hate unstable regimes." He shrugged elegantly. "Assuming I could stand it, it's not safe to tarry here. My oath to Melcia means about as much to me as yours does to you."

Titch flinched. He reminded himself that whatever he'd sworn had been mostly without his knowledge, but his conscience still hurt. He seized the dangling girth strap again and jerked it snug so hastily that Gray grunted with surprise. Another moment sufficed for the bridle—Gray took the bit as if 'twas honey-coated, and there was only the throatlatch strap to fasten after that.

Wren had found herself a pitchfork and was holding it aimed at Gerein's back. The knight turned, saw, and laughed, refusing to take the threat the least seriously. "Put up your weapon, Lady! I think your squire has your steed prepared." He spared a wistful glance for Valadan, then went hastily to a leggy seal-brown gelding two stalls distant, threw a quilted pad and a military saddle onto the horse's high back.

Titch cupped his hands for Wren's foot, ready to throw her up into Gray's saddle, hesitated as his eye took in the finery Melcia had garbed her with when she was an honored guest. "That's not a sidesaddle. Can you ride astride by yourself? Gray will stay with Valadan, I think—"

Wren whisked the dagger from his belt and cut a ragged slit up the front of the fine velvet skirt, from hem to knee. Beneath it, she wore heavy hose. "There are drafts, not to mention *rats*," she said, laughing at Titch's expression of amaze. "Nobody sees what's underneath, and I'd rather not have things crawling up my legs." She put a foot into his laced fingers, went as lightly into the saddle as a cat would climb a fence. "What did you *think* ladies wore under skirts?"

Titch covered his confusion by leading both horses to the door. Behind him, Gerein cursed his uncooperative horse. "Wait for me, won't you? *Stand, you crow's bait—*"

Titch swung up into his saddle and pointed Valadan's head at the bailey. The stallion's ears pricked eagerly.

"You're going to want the password for the gate," Gerein said slyly. "You don't have tonight's."

Titch's turn then to curse, as he realized Gerein spoke the

plain truth. He sat still, halting Valadan, and put a hand on Gray's near rein, as well, to hold Wren in her place beside him. His every instinct told him to make a run for it *now*, but that was very likely to give them away. And like it or not, he was forced into needing Gerein once more.

Gerein caught them up in another moment and vaulted nimbly aboard his purloined steed. "If anyone asks, we're ordered to escort her," He nodded toward Wren. "Best if we don't have to fight out way clear."

"That's the idea," Titch growled. He loosened his reins and both horses went forward.

They might not be able to run, but there was no point to stealth. It wouldn't gain them time, and it would make their claim to be riding escort ring instantly false. Would such an escort ride at night? Not as a general rule, perhaps, but the Lady Melcia had a habit of giving peremptory orders and was lately erratic to extremes. They might pass for an angry whim of hers, *if* word had not run to the gate ahead of them.

The main gate was shut at sunfall and would not be hauled open again until first light, when the town's bakers and laundresses appeared with their goods. But horses were frequently taken to pasture or to water very early, and those went by the postern gate, which was narrow against possible attack but broad enough for a led horse and close to the river meadow into the bargain. The portal in the old log palisade was strait, but tall enough that a horseman could ride out through it, if he chose. As Titch watched nervously, Gerein reported their false mission to the sentries, and the double oaken bars were slowly withdrawn by the junior of them.

"Close the gate!"

The shout came from the parapet above, the shouter unseen but the authority behind the order unquestionable. Titch yanked his sword free on the spot and rode straight at the nearest gate warden. The man went down under Valadan's hooves, taken by surprise and pretty much from behind. His two fellows had more time to react, to let loose of the gate bars and draw weapons. One of them started yelling for help, yipping like a scared dog.

Suddenly a scream rang out from the parapet, and Alinor came out of the dark like a falling star, using wings and talons to distract those men still at the gate. Titch backed Valadan till the stallion's rump held the gate panel wide open and waved wildly for Wren to ride through. A fallen Guard was in her way—Gray balked, snorted, then leapt hugely over the man. Gerein thundered after her, while Titch spun Valadan about to follow.

He caught the flash of steel striking upward from the tail of his eye and leaned over Valadan's right shoulder to beat the upthrusting sword away before it could find a vulnerable leg, or be rammed up into the stallion's belly. He was barely back in the saddle when they plunged through the gate in their turn—Titch's head missed the gatepost by an inch, and his right shoulder brushed it stingingly, but he kept his seat.

He wheeled the stallion about the instant he was through and shoved the panel as far closed as he could with the tip of his sword. He had nothing to bar it with, but mounted men would need to halt and open the postern—which would be appreciably slower than simply riding through it at a gallop. Pity he had nothing to shove against it on the outer side. The man lying inside screamed when the oaken panel struck him. Valadan spun about and gave the gate a mighty kick, which all but slammed it closed before he bounded after Gerein's steed.

Wren was trying to wait for him. Gerein was arguing breathlessly with her and snatching at her bridle, while Alinor dove and screamed to scare him off. Her tactic was working better with his horse than it was with Gerein himself, who held his mount in place with a cruel and practiced hand.

"Come on!" Titch yelled, not wanting any of them to be flat-footed when the pursuit came. He gave Gray a loud *cluck* and a swat with the flat of his blade across the gelding's wide rump as they passed, and Gray broke into a hand gallop. They pounded through the river meadow, scattering knots of grazing horses to either side.

There was a ford somewhere, a broad bottom of gravel with only a foot or so of water running over it. But where?

Deep water would slow them, should be avoided. The night played tricks, and so did memory, just when you needed it worst—

Here, Valadan said calmly, plunging in with his ears pricked sharply. Water sheeted up from his flying hooves, and Wren cried out from behind him, but Gray had never been bothered by water deeper than puddles after a rain shower and went hurtling through after, shod hooves ringing on rocks as he exited. Gerein brought up the rear, sword still in his hand.

The best way to escape would be to get themselves out of sight, Titch thought. Unhappily, they couldn't do that anytime soon. It was a long way to any serious forest, nor were there mountains to aim for. So they'd simply have to run for it, and how long any of them save Valadan would succeed at that was anyone's guess, first two counting for nothing.

Gerein was riding behind, but it wasn't the knight who first detected the pursuit. *Behind us,* Valadan reported unhappily.

"How many?" Titch asked him, his heart sinking but not surprised.

The black ears listened with judicial care. *A score.*

How did Melcia have so many of her Guards left to muster? Hadn't she been winnowing for traitors by wholesale slaughter? There hadn't been a score of horses in the stable, Titch thought—and we took three of them.

They are not twenty together, Valadan told him. *Five or six, and then the others, all riding hard.*

Maybe a patrol had come back, just at the wrong time. All of them knowing the country, too. Titch hadn't been in Josten long enough to say the same. "We can't outrun them, can we?" he asked hopelessly.

Valadan snorted. Gray couldn't, that meant. Titch supposed he could always pluck Wren out of her saddle, and Valadan had proved he could carry the pair of them as fast as the wind, as far as they needed to go. And nothing bad would likely befall Gray, left behind riderless. No such luck for Gerein, however. If they left him, he'd be taken and harshly dealt with. He might deserve it, but Titch wasn't prepared to abandon him to it.

"They're coming up fast!" the knight yelled, having had to ride hard to get close enough for Titch to hear.

For answer, Titch drew back on his reins gently. "We can't run forever," he explained to the stallion, whispering into the ears that flicked back toward him questioningly. "Can you tell Gray to keep going?"

I can. And the white gelding pounded on, a pale blur against the night.

Wren was almost out of sight in a dozen heartbeats, but Gerein got the idea at once and reined in his steed beside Valadan. The dark horse was blowing fiercely, not spent yet, but its first, best speed probably gone out of it.

"There's five ahead of the rest," Titch explained, and Gerein didn't contest the statement, or ask him how he knew. "Think we can take them before the others catch up?"

"No," Gerein answered honestly, and sheathed his sword.

"They'll just all ride us down if we don't." Titch took a firm hold of the grips of his tall shield.

"*She*'s away safe. Didn't you give any thought for what *you'd* do?" Gerein asked bitterly, swinging his shield into position, reaching for his lance.

"I'm doing it." Titch couched his own lance. Their pursuers weren't going to expect the prey to *attack*. The hunter does not anticipate the deer's even halting, far less charging *at* him. Gerein muttered some very unflattering things about Titch's late parents, but he couched his lance and touched his heels to the brown gelding.

They were already well in motion, stirrup to stirrup, when the six riders came over a roll of the ground at them. It was astonishing the advantage the presentation lent them, the way their momentum was increased by the pursuit's sweeping down straight at them. Titch took good aim at the nearest, put his lance-head right in the center of the man's breastplate. The impact splintered the ashen pole of his lance, but not before the unwary Guard was knocked back over cantle and crupper, still looking astonished. He went right into the face of the following horse, which stumbled and could not find its balance before it found the ground in a crashing spill atop its rider.

Gerein swung his weapon to one side just as he closed, letting the long pole catch two riders across their chests. He unhorsed one outright, and the other clung for an instant before his horse managed to shed him. Gerein, in the clear, spun his horse and raced away after Wren.

The remaining riders came straight for Titch. He drew his blade as Valadan spun about to give him the best possible position. He began to trade blows with his attackers, and the horses sidled and backed, shifting for advantage. Valadan was watchful that neither horse got behind him, where its rider could attack unobserved and unopposed. Hard enough to keep track of them both, in the dark, much less keep out of reach and in range at the same time. The stallion danced nimbly, while Titch blocked and struck.

Titch caught one blow glancingly on his shield, swung his blade hastily to block a cut at his head from the other side. Too late he realized the penetrating attack was merely a feint. He struggled to close the opening he'd just made, standing in his stirrups and parrying desperately. The impact of a sword flat across his ribs pounded the breath out of him even if it could do no other harm against bullhide and metal plates, and before he could recover, he'd taken another punishing blow across his shoulders, which knocked him askew in his saddle. Titch couldn't tell which of Melcia's men had struck him, or if both were succeeding now. Valadan reared suddenly to lunge at the other horse, and Titch could not quite match the motion. He tried to cling, but realized he was falling. A blade hacked at him, but he fell wide of it.

The horse could have been running away with her, unresponsive to the bit in its mouth, bolting insanely through the darkness, bearing her to destruction. It didn't matter. Wren didn't want to stop, no matter what lay ahead. She wanted the horse to run as swiftly as Alinor flew, and a thousand leagues distance might not be quite enough, to let her begin to feel safe. The Red Queen's reach was as long as the path from sunrise to sunfall—it could snatch her back no matter how far she ran, where she hid. She must run, or she must hide, or her life, small as it was, was surely forfeit—

No. She was free of that, from the moment she had chosen to return the prince to the shape he had claimed for his own. Had she still believed in the Red Queen's absolute power, she would never have dared work that transformation. The horse pounded under her, its gait growing labored, heavy, though it did not falter yet. A stout heart, but nothing like Valadan's effortless speed, only his command obeyed.

He sent me away so I'd be safe. And faced the whole danger—my danger—himself. They wouldn't be after him, but for me.

And she had agreed, without question, without thought. Let herself be sent. Flight and hiding were habits, the very pillars of her soul. If she let herself be seen, and known—

Wren sat tall in her saddle, felt the gray horse slacken his pace a trifle, perhaps willing to obey her, perhaps weary enough now.

He is buying you time, Alinor said coldly on the wind. *Use it.*

Time to run, to hide herself once more. Could she do that so well ever again? Did she want to? Last time, she had hidden herself *from* herself, a very great deception. It had been needful then. She'd been a child. Children could hide from their fears, and no one blamed them for seeking that refuge. But she couldn't crawl under her bed again, or into the dark at the back of her own mind—she was Savrin, daughter of Kenric and Zorana, the fruit of their forbidden love—and the man *she* loved was facing long odds for her sake, because *she* was the quarry they pursued, not Titch. And he'd die before he let them come at her.

What could you do? She was not sure if the question was Alinor's or her own.

I could throw shadows at them, make a confusion he could escape into. Titch might not be their objective, but Melcia's men would kill him all the same. He was probably alone, if Gerein had found some means to desert him.

"Can you see him?" Wren cried, to her eyes above.

A black horse through black air? I am no owl, whatever broken-beak thinks! But the danger is close enough already. Make this horse go faster. Alinor's wings flickered across the stars, the old moon's ravaged face. *There's still run in him.*

Wren tugged at her right rein, feeling the weight of Gray's head against the bit. For an instant, the sweating horse paid her no attention. She tugged again, twice and thrice. And like a ship under sail, Gray turned in a great sweeping circle and went blowing back the way he had come—only cantering now, but still covering ground.

Alinor swept back to them, protesting shrilly.

"You don't have to follow me, Alinor!" Wren cried over her shoulder. "Anything that has the sky is free!" Could she hear the clash of metal on metal, or was that imagination?

His landing on solid earth cost the remainder of his breath. Titch scrambled up anyway, just in time to be knocked flat by a horse. A hoof grazed his helmet as he sprawled, knocked it askew. His sight blurred, but he could see Valadan trying to come to his side, knew that he could get back into his saddle—that he must. Titch flung away his shield, which was too awkward to use afoot, and only got in his way now. He'd already lost his sword, though, and that he must find. Really wanted to, because it was lonely to be on the ground dodging the other blades that were coming down out of the night like lightning out of a stormy summer sky, with only his bare hands . . .

And all at once Gerein burst into the uneven fray, blade flailing like thunder following the lightning, and Titch's attackers had to start defending themselves once more.

Gerein hurled one out of his saddle almost at Titch's feet—Titch threw himself on the fallen man and wrenched the iron blade out of his hand, hit him twice with the flat of it to teach him the wisdom of staying down, then used the man's sword belt to bind his hands behind his back. He stumbled across his own sword as he worked, and scooped it up gratefully, ready to go to Gerein's aid as the knight had come to his. He whistled for Valadan.

Knight and Guard were striving together like two stags in the rut, fighting stirrup to stirrup, raining mighty sword-blows on helms and shields and hoping for less-armored targets to present themselves. Melcia's man struck out fiercely, and Gerein caught the attacking blade with his own, holding it his prisoner for an instant, then parrying in a fast circle so that the other's blade did his will as well as his own did. Then, quick as a snake's strike, he disengaged and thrust into a new line.

His strategy got him past the Guard's shield. Desperate, the man slashed out and brought his sword-edge down at Gerein's horse, landing a hard blow on its crest. The horse reared with pain and terror, went too high for balance, and pitched over backward—on top of Gerein. The Guard stared an astonished instant at the blood gushing from his wounded side, then clamped a hand to it and tried to ride at Titch, who'd just shoved a toe into Valadan's stirrup. The stallion screamed and lunged to threaten and place his own body as a shield for his master, but the motion prevented Titch from gaining his saddle.

Rather than let himself be cut down half horsed, Titch decided to offer a more elusive target. He dropped back to the ground, stepped a pace back, and raised his sword just as the other blade chopped down. He could defend himself well enough, but he didn't have the reach for a riposte, and the horseman could be sure of that. Titch solidly parried the blow, and as he did, got his left hand as far up the Guard's arm as he could reach, gripped and yanked. The horse trod on his foot as they struggled, but the rider couldn't withdraw his arm enough to slash at him again, and that was as much safety as he'd get, so Titch clung to it, and to the arm. He held on like a bull-baiting dog, till he felt the Guard's balance shift ever so slightly. He smelled the hot coppery tang of fresh blood, knew such a wound had to weaken the man. The Guard's horse was lifting him off his own feet as it tried to circle round him, but Titch held on with the strength of desperation, and all at once the Guard tumbled out of the saddle and fell atop him. They both sprawled, Titch still underneath, trying to keep hold of the man's weapon hand.

Titch squirmed free at last and struggled to his feet, sword ready, but his adversary was done fighting, either swooning from blood loss or dead outright from his wound. Valadan nosed him, snorting, then blew a great relieved breath into Titch's face. Titch clung to his neck a moment, then turned and went to Gerein.

Gerein's horse, bleeding from a deep cut on the crest of its neck, flailed to its feet just as he came near and headed for home, its four legs at least sound. Gerein stirred but didn't copy his steed in rising. Titch knelt down, supposing he'd been stunned or wounded when the horse came down on him. His eyes were squinched shut, and there was blood on his face, but little color *in* it.

"Should have kept riding after all," Gerein groaned through his teeth. "I think I broke my shoulder."

Titch made an inspection, prodded the shoulder, which made Gerein curse, and agreed. "I'm sorry. I let your horse get away." He hadn't been near enough to lay hands on it, but Valadan could have stopped it.

"Good riddance. Stupid animal couldn't even stay on its own legs." Gerein managed to get to his feet, with Titch's help. "There's no other way about it, a knight needs a good horse. It's absolutely essential . . ."

"You can ride behind me," Titch offered. "Valadan can manage double weight a little way." It was something more than double, but he knew the magic-bred horse could handle the task. Whether he *would*, seeing 'twas Gerein, Titch had no idea. He reached for the stirrup.

Valadan threw his head up, snorting, pulling away. Titch stared, disappointed at the show of temper and bad manners, no matter that Gerein had not so long ago stolen the stallion and held him captive to a bit of cruel cold iron. Then he realized that Valadan's attention was fixed on a problem somewhat farther off—which was drawing nearer with every galloping stride the horses carrying it took.

Justice Dispensed

THERE WASN'T TIME to do anything. Not to flee, not to plan an attack or defense. Three to one odds they'd managed, though it had virtually undone the pair of them—but the horsemen coming at them out of the lightening sunrise sky rode in a line abreast, making a show of their numbers and a net of them, as well, lest the prey think to escape the snare. There were close to a score of them, and the banner the foremost bore was the color of blood, save for the black horse that bounded across it, swift as the wind.

"Well met, Gerein," Cullum said deprecatingly, reining in a pace before them. "We are encamped, waiting for day—when we would have petitioned Josten's barbarian queen to hand you over to us for the duke's justice. And with your usual impetuosity, you have ridden into our hands instead."

"Wasn't my idea," Gerein muttered sullenly.

"I'll not ask about the dead men here, or the citadel in flames behind you. It's no concern of the duke's—nor mine."

The wind carried more than a trace of smoke, Titch discovered. He looked at the red sky, realized that part of the glow was not the rising sun at all. The Eral stronghold was in flames. Had Melcia made herself a funeral pyre? Remembering her eyes, he was not surprised at the destruction.

"It wasn't our doing," he said, hoping that was true.

Cullum turned on him. "I have no particular quarrel with you, boy—but you should take better care for the company you keep."

"True enough," Titch smiled without humor. "Last time I fell in with *yours*, you left me for dead."

"You put yourself in the way of our justice. I gave you a fair chance to stand clear, and you chose not to avail yourself of the opportunity. I am absolved." Cullum gestured to a couple of his men. "Mansell, Harn, bind the felon. See you do it well—we want him to reach the duke safely, not injure himself attempting escape."

"He's wounded already," Titch protested. "You don't need to tie him—"

"Don't tell me my business!" the leader snapped. "We've been on this fox chase for months. I've no desire to prolong it further. Someone bring the churl of Kendillin a horse."

Gerein's face was still as an alabaster effigy carved upon a royal tomb. He flinched slightly as his hands were bound, but Titch didn't suppose 'twas pain that gave him his expression of utter hopelessness.

"Falke, fetch the Warhorse."

Titch had utterly forgotten that Cullum claimed Valadan as well as the man who'd reived him from Esdragon. His heart gave a nasty lurch, but there was nothing he could do—even were there not a score of men standing by to dispute his right to the horse, *he* knew the shifty ground such right was based upon, and he could not defend it, no matter had the odds been better in his favor.

It was the Warhorse himself who objected—not with any mild evasion of a hand on his bridle, but with a scream that would have done a catamount proud. He reared and slashed out with both forehooves at a disconcerted Falke, who'd dismounted to approach him. The man threw himself to safety, tripped and fell still within reach, easy prey—but Valadan, prancing and tossing his head, ignored him as if he'd been just another feature of the landscape and made his way to his chosen master's side.

Titch felt as if he'd just had a shield wall form up about him. He patted the dark neck arching beside his shoulder, looked into an eye that was awhirl with dark colors and furious lightnings. "You belong with them," he whispered, confused as much as pleased, not daring to believe.

Do I? Am I not free to choose?

Titch stared at ripples of garnet, flashes of emerald, sparks struck from adamant.

"I'll bring him back," he said across the stallion's back, to Cullum. Something soared overhead, too noisy on the wing to be an owl and too big to be anything else other than Alinor, sent to see what had befallen him. Titch followed the pointing of Valadan's ears with his own eyes and saw a pale blotch against the dark countryside—that would be Gray, and Wren surely with him. "We'll all come with you."

If nothing else, it was a safe escort out of Melcia's realm, and they could still use that, he decided.

No sounds of battle. *Was she too late?* Her poor eyes could not see clearly, even with the aiding light of the sinking moon—that last nail-paring of it. She could see horses, Wren thought, too many horses . . .

He's alive, Alinor told her crossly. *There are a couple of queen's men dead—I don't know what the others are.*

Maybe she shouldn't go nearer. Wren's hands tensed on her reins. Even if those weren't the Red Queen's men—no, he was waving an arm to her. It was all right, somehow.

He was afoot, among mounted men. They could be making him call her into their reach. *No.* He'd die before he did that. And she could see Valadan at his master's side. All was well. He was just beckoning her nearer.

She didn't have to obey him. She could turn the white horse about and vanish into the night. Given the breathing space of a little distance, she had the skills she needed to disappear absolutely.

And where would she go? Where was a wren's place? Not Galvin's empty cottage, she could never bear that, without him. What else was there? She had her name back, and her past—but there was no future in any of that, for her.

He's no future, either. He wants to be a knight, and the gods alone know what he's done to that plan now, with *this* night's work. Where would he have to go, chasing a dream that's farther out of his reach every minute? He's made you no promises, except that he wouldn't let her kill you. You can't go back expecting more than that. You can't cling to him like bindweed, just because you've nothing else.

Arms about her, in otter-shape, in slippery salmon, in

others too dim to remember. He never once let her go. Would seizing a few more days, a few more chances to feel those sturdy arms about her, be so wrong? So weak?

The horse was moving under her, walking slowly down the long hill. She could probably have stopped it with a touch, but Wren did not, and after a few steps it seemed too late for a change of heart. They went down the hill and onto the plain, the white horse trotting with her now, up to the fringe of the knot of horsemen.

The moonlight made all colors shades of gray, but still all Wren saw was Titch's eyes. Their flecks put her in mind of a gravel streambed, and she saw sunlight glance off the rippling water as he smiled at her. She struggled not to set any store by that. *Dark* eyes were honest. Like Alinor's, like Galvin's. Eyes that couldn't make up their minds what color to be—how could they be trusted with anything more?

They were a motley party, jogging in a thin file over hill and dale—Cullum and his men in the sea colors of Esdragon's duke, Titch and Gerein still clad in the dried-blood shades Melcia had found pleasing—though much of Gerein's battle harness had been removed to allow for bandaging his smashed shoulder—and Wren on a white horse in her tattered finery, her falcon on her wrist as if she rode to a heron-hawking.

She and Titch could, Wren thought, have slipped away during any of the nights. She knew minor spells of sleep, of inattention, of hiding what should be seen. But such arts would not work for Gerein, who was manacled with iron, and Titch would not leave him behind to the fate the man had earned. She could go, he had said, when she hesitantly asked. Or he would take her home, after the matter of Gerein was settled.

Wren thought Titch must mean Galvin's cottage beside the marsh, but that could scarcely be home with Galvin gone from it—and besides, it lay within the boundaries of Melcia's realm. But if he meant Crogen, where her father had once ruled? Wren thought she must have grown up near there, but her childhood had been spent inside one castle and another, out of a mortal need for deepest secrecy. One blurred into another, and she knew the names of none of them, nor their locations. She could certainly find Crogen—or Titch could—but it was not her home. Nor was Kôvelir, without Galvin to take her there under his sponsorship. Having discovered her identity, she must now embark on a new quest, for a home, a place to belong. Or do as she did—drift, a leaf on the current.

Journeying into unknown Esdragon did not therefore distress her. One place was like another, except for outward appearances. *All one sky,* Alinor said, seesawing her wings in agreement. They saw no swans, though other waterfowl were plentiful.

Gerein said not one word as they went. His silver tongue seemed to cleave to the roof of his mouth, his chiseled lips to seal. He rode with his chained hands further bound to the pommel of his saddle, staring unseeing between the ears of his borrowed horse. He might be dreaming of escape, but he could not expect it and was doing nothing to obtain it.

Cullum's men plainly despised him. To them, his guilt was unquestioned. They let their disgust show, though they stopped short of abusing him. Such behavior would have been unchivalrous—Gerein's fate was the duke's to decide, his prerogative. No one could hold any illusions as to what they personally thought of him, that was all. Wren shivered and knotted her fingers into Gray's mane. *She* pitied Gerein, but it was another sort of compassion, and she didn't think there was any help tears could give him. She couldn't transform him into a bird, to fly safe away. Even if she could, or would, he'd be broken-winged, and helpless.

Keverne was a proper fortress, and an ancient one—it looked as if its dark walls had grown out of the rock of the headland, living things rather than works of the stonemason's craft atop the marvelously sheer cliffs. Keverne was smaller by half, but it still made Melcia's raw palisade of logs look like a pigsty at the back end of nowhere. The stonework might be mossy with the passage of many years and even more rainstorms, but the great blocks had been cut and fitted so precisely that there were few chinks wide enough to admit a knife blade—and those few turned out to be defensive, arrow-slits made for archers. Keverne's gates were tall and wide and kept oiled well enough to work silently and easily. Every least opening was defensible, but the interior walls were well pierced with windows, the stone framing the casements chased in patterns of vines and birds and animals, some of the openings even glazed with bubbly greenish panes to keep excessively fresh or damp air at bay.

Had they been guests, Titch and Wren would have been conducted to chambers for rest and refreshment, once they'd dismounted within the long narrow bailey and given their horses over to the care of Keverne's attentive hostlers. Instead, Cullum turned to Titch, who still held Valadan's reins, and spoke words with even less welcome in them than his narrow gaze held.

"You are owed thanks for bringing the Warhorse back to the home Gerein stole him from, but if you are expecting more than words, you had best look to your weapons. You may not have shared Gerein's crimes, but you helped him evade us."

Titch ignored the outburst, running his fingers gently along Valadan's lower face, sliding them beneath the bridle straps so he could scratch the places where itch-making sweat collected and dried under the hair. The stallion pressed his head against Titch's chest, rubbed to scratch those spots *he* most favored, all but shoving Titch off his feet with his enthusiasm. "You're home," Titch breathed into the black mane. "It's right, you know it. Every step since we crossed the border, I've felt it." Aloud, he answered Cullum. "Gerein has no friend to stand beside him when he faces his duke. Would I be permitted to do so?"

Cullum's eyes widened with startlement, then narrowed again, all suspicion. "Why would you want to do that?" His sword hand twitched closer to his weapon.

Titch regarded him levelly. "Because there's no one else. And though you won't credit it, Gerein stood by me once."

Gerein's expression was as incredulous as Cullum's. It almost canceled out the stark misery in his eyes.

"As you wish," Cullum conceded gracelessly. Plainly he thought the offer beyond foolishness, perhaps even shading into madness. Most of the riders had gone along to the stables with the horses, but the original handspan that had first accompanied him remained, awaiting their master's command. Cullum signed for them to form ranks around Gerein.

Titch put the stallion's reins into a groom's hands, and he and Wren took up a place at the rear of the column. Wren looked at his still, closed face, wanting to ask him *why* just as Cullum had. Could even the knighthood he wanted to earn demand so much? Such things had been no part of her training, neither as princess nor witch, and Titch, at arm's length away, seemed leagues distant, beyond her reach. He'd think her a fool for asking—or worse, would never even hear.

Had they been guests, still they would have waited till 'twas Duke Rayner's pleasure that he greet them. But the duke was eager to receive the long-sought-for fugitive— word ran ahead of them as Cullum's party made its way toward his audience hall, and they were never once asked to wait or to halt for anyone's questioning.

Melcia's stronghold had been a magpie's nest—hastily thrown up and jammed with Eral plunder. Keverne was ancient glories, less gaudy riches, the great tapestries decking its walls done in shades muted by the weaver's whim or time's passage. Golden threads caught the torchlight but never sought to rival it. Rich dyes impressed but did not flaunt their cost. Many of the great cloths told stories that casual visitors could hope to unravel in their instant of passing by—there were the common representations of hunts and battles. Two wolves ran beneath a moon of silver-wrapped threads on the left-hand wall, while above a doorway—

Titch had barely an instant to look, and that only because he broke step to stare and could do so because he was at the column's tail. The weaving portrayed a black horse in full flight of its gallop, just as did Cullum's banner—only *this* horse had one foot planted upon a winging falcon's back, plain proof that he possessed speed enough to outrun the swiftest-flying of birds. *Valadan!* It had to be! And Titch's heart lurched with the reminder of what he must leave behind in this place, the horse that was never his to possess, that neither birth nor training gave him the slightest right to, but only a hopeless appreciation of.

The doors of the audience chamber were held wide for them by ushers liveried in sea-blue and gray. Within rose a forest of polished stone pillars, opening wide down the center to guide them toward a raised dais. The spot of honor was the room's purpose, and there were no other straight paths through the stone maze, though the outer walls were pierced with tall unglazed windows that admitted the scent of the sea and the sound of waves battering Keverne's lofty cliff. One could walk to those windows—the pillars flanked but did not fence—but attention and feet were subtly directed to the room's distant end.

There was but a single chair crouching upon the dais—simple carven wood, well crafted but hardly to be styled a throne—and one man somewhat past his middle years, seated in it. Cullum halted before the first of the four steps that led up to the ducal place and knelt down, his back straight as any of the pillars and his head unbowed, no supplicant. "My lord duke," he said formally. A nod of the head acknowledged him, signaled him to continue. "You charged me with the taking of this man, Gerein of Kendillin, and I have brought him before you at last, to answer for his crime against your law and your kinsman."

"Well done, my son," Rayner answered in a voice hoarse with years of battle command. He was a square, solid-built man, with a broad square face and eyes light as the gray ice of winter's end. A thin circlet of gold sat on his grizzled hair. He shifted, and Titch saw that his left arm ended at about the elbow. "I feared you lost on this hunt more than once, for I knew you were not one to turn aside from any quarry I loosed you at, and I wondered betimes if I had sent you wisely."

"The quarry was obstinate, my lord. That is all." Cullum smiled, showing all his teeth.

Gerein drew back his own lips. "I am a man, not a

strayed hound!" Cullum swung toward him, hand on sword hilt.

"Once you were my liege-man, Gerein," Rayner said, waving Cullum's wrath aside with practiced ease. "Then you slew my sister's son and fled Esdragon rather than face me. A hound that did as much would die on my knife, but since you are a man, I will give you leave to speak your defense first. What happened between you and the squire Olvan?"

Gerein's trial had begun, with no more preamble. No planning, no witnesses located or prepared. Titch bit his lip.

"He challenged me." There was sweat on Gerein's face, but he kept his voice wonderfully calm. "I accepted."

The duke raised a hand. Two men stepped forward at his beckoning to discuss and agree to the details of the challenge, witnesses after all.

"And you slew him." Another knight related Olvan's fate, the blow and the helmet shattered by it, how surgeons had been too late.

"That was mischance," Gerein protested, white-faced. "I did not intend it."

"You struck him a killing blow," the duke accused. "The witnesses agree, 'twas by your hand and no other's."

"My lord, it was an *accident*! I only meant to knock the boy down, to make him yield the bout." Gerein's tone almost wheedled—would any of them there not do the same, to win victory in a friendly contest of arms?

"You, a seasoned warrior in the flower of his strength and with the wit to know it, struck such a blow to a squire scarce begun his training?" The duke's tone said the matter was not commonplace, but an affront to all chivalry.

"I was not aiming to kill him!" Gerein answered again heatedly.

Duke Rayner stroked his gray-flecked beard, rested his chin upon his hand. "Yet you did just that. And you have left something unsaid here, Gerein. This bout between yourself and Olvan—you would have us believe it was meant to be a friendly contest?"

"Yes—" Gerein was frowning, his face red with outrage.

"It had naught to do with Olvan's encountering you in his unwed sister's bedchamber?"

The hot color fled Gerein's face, running out of it like wine from a shattered bottle. His lips moved, but no silver words came forth.

"If Olvan had only wanted a friendly bout to hone his blade-skills, he would have stopped when you'd beaten him. He knew he did not encounter you as an equal. But he would not yield, would he, Gerein? Olvan had a score to settle with you, and could not for his own honor cease."

"It was an *accident*!" Gerein screamed. "I knocked him down! No more—"

"You slew Olvan," the duke continued implacably. "The witnesses utterly agree on that. You agree you struck him. And there are no witnesses to swear you didn't intend to kill the boy. Your guilt is plain. So is Esdragon's law. The price of murder is death." A silence descended on the hall, as if every witness there feared to breathe. "Gerein of Kendillin, I sentence you—"

"There are no witnesses to swear I *did* intend to kill him!" Gerein shouted. "I demand Trial by Combat!"

There was a second, profound silence, as many an eye went to Gerein's dangling, useless sword arm.

"That is certainly your right," the duke said into the poised quiet. "You may defend your life." His tone was not the least pitying—it was meet that a fighting man die with a sword in hand if he could contrive to do so. It was a fitter end than the headsman's axe, for all the obvious hopelessness in Gerein's present case. "Cullum, the right to meet his challenge shall be yours."

"I accept with thanks, my lord." Cullum's voice was shaded with grim satisfaction, like a sword being whetted on a grindstone. This was the reward for his faithful service, for bringing Gerein back to justice despite months and miles.

It was no less a death sentence than an order for the headsman. Titch found his voice, pitched it to carry past many heads and shoulders. *"My lord—"* He inflected it as a question.

The duke's light eyes searched the faces before him for

the source of the unfamiliar voice. He was helped a trifle in his quest by the astonished looks Titch was receiving from those around him—even Wren. A discreet whisper in the ducal ear evidently told Rayner still more. "The stranger who brought the Warhorse back to us," he said, relieved. "I would bring Gerein to justice for that theft, as well, but now there is no need. A man cannot die twice. We owe you thanks—"

"Grant me leave to defend Gerein instead," Titch interrupted boldly.

"*What?*" The explosive question echoed. The duke was not the only man astonished by the request, and the question was asked many times, by many lips.

Titch swallowed hard and answered the duke. "My lord, if you, as his accuser, are allowed a substitute for the combat, then surely Gerein should be permitted the same courtesy? He is injured; there cannot be a fair fight between him and a hale opponent. Gerein has only one hand to use, and it is not his sword hand." He kept his eye carefully away from the duke's missing arm, lest he give offense. It had likely been a battle injury, one with a high cost.

"Gerein knew that when he spoke," the duke observed coldly. "The combat is by *his* choice." No excuses permitted.

"But to allow so unequal a combat when a man's life hinges on it is ignoble," Titch persisted. "My lord, I beg you, for the value of your own reputation, let me fight in Gerein's place."

Cullum cursed and glared at his liege. "Sire, this is not to be borne—that Gerein cozens every chance-met stranger and gains sympathy for his false tales! Though who'd have thought that any would swallow the lies so wholly—"

The duke waved his son to silence and stared intently at the supplicant. Titch forebore to flinch. He spoke to Cullum's implied question instead.

"Sir, I will undertake it. If I prevail, will I win him his life, as Gerein would for himself?"

"Why should you wish to do this?" The eyes were like a midwinter sky before an ice storm.

"I came to your land to stand as a friend to Gerein,"

Titch explained. "I am a stranger to Esdragon, and I cannot speak as witness to events that fell before I came here. This is the only service that remains to do for him."

"A mad ambition," the duke derided.

"Gerein has stood as friend to me," Titch answered steadfastly. Cullum made a sound of disbelief.

The duke stroked his bearded chin and contemplated honor with obvious displeasure. He wanted the business over and saw too plainly that it was not. "There's truth in your words. I would not have it said that Gerein or any man of mine was treated unfairly, and there may be those would say it of this matter, did they come to hear of it. So—since such seems to be your pleasure—you may fight in Gerein's place, and the combat will decide his fate. But know this—" The eyes went colder yet. "If you prevail, man, still he will be banished from Esdragon."

Hope and despair chased one another across Gerein's features. Outrage marked Cullum's still.

"Only a creature such as Gerein could entrust his honor to a base-born stranger! This man's nothing but a common soldier!"

Titch's face flamed as if Cullum's gauntlet had slapped it instead of merely his words. "My father was a sworn knight," he said, taking plain pride in the plain truth, "till death took him from his liege-lord's service. He wed my mother before lawful witnesses, in Calandra. I will let no man call that base birth." He glared at Cullum, promising that this could very readily become a personal matter between them.

"Who knighted you?" the duke asked, curious despite himself.

"No one yet, my lord," Titch confessed sadly. It was quite possible that Cullum would refuse to fight him on that account. He would follow his duke's lead. Nothing to be done about it, if the two of them chose to seize it.

"Clandara is chaos," Rayner said somberly, using the old name for the land in defiance of its new overlords. "The Eral are unwashed thieves, reivers, and marauders, not fit to judge or able to recognize a fighting man's worth. Be grateful you are not oath-bound to one of them." Something in

Titch's expression made the duke's gaze turn intent. "Or are you, then?"

He might still be allowed to fight for Gerein's life, Titch guessed, but he'd be even less welcome—if such was possible. "I was in Queen Melcia's service briefly, sir," he said truthfully, meeting the duke's scrutiny but offering no more, very conscious of Wren behind him.

The ducal eyebrows rose. "Briefly?" Rayner prodded.

"The queen doesn't require it any longer." Titch continued to meet his gaze, unflinching. 'Twas no business of this duke's and he would not let it be made so.

The duke shrugged at last. "It's not as if she's an ally of *mine*. Cullum, I doubt 'twill spoil your honor to fight this man. He is well spoken and loyal to his friend, if not especially careful in his choice of companions. You will fight for my honor, and for Esdragon's, and doing so in a just cause will never besmirch your sword, no matter who or what you lift that blade against."

Cullum accepted his defeat and smiled coldly. He rested a hand on his sword. "Shall we say sunrise?"

"Indeed." The duke looked at Gerein, shook his head, and glanced back at Titch. "Fool's business should be soon concluded."

"Where do we sleep?" Wren asked softly. *Or sit, or stand, or eat, or even breathe?* she wanted to add, because she was utterly at a loss. She didn't understand what was going on—the trial business was plain enough, but she couldn't fathom why Titch had flung himself into it, and she didn't ask him because she didn't think there was any way he could make her understand it. Gerein had lied to him, sold Titch into mercenary slavery, and even robbed him of his pay for that forced service—Gerein was a petty thief, with a golden tongue and morals of quicksilver: slippery and impossible to hold, for all it glittered brightly. He'd all too apparently committed seduction and adultery and murder, and Wren didn't doubt that he could convince himself that doing even worse, if it served his ends, was perfectly proper. And Titch was going to risk his life just to spare Gerein's, to get him banished alive instead of judicially parted from his head. Did he scry out some good in the man, that no one else in the least suspected? Titch had never mentioned it. He had never hinted that he was going to do this mad thing. He'd just done it.

She watched him fuss over Gray's bad foreleg, rubbing the tendons and wrapping it about just so, as if a few twists of cloth could bring Gray back his long-past youth, the first flush of his strength and speed. And he hadn't heard her question. Wren sighed and wondered whether the piled hay waiting to become horse fodder was as soft as it looked. She had slept very ill on the silk-covered featherbeds Melcia had provided, but just now she thought she could slumber dreamlessly on bare stones.

"I don't know," Titch admitted, just as she'd forgotten what she'd asked. "I've slept most of my life in stables, but I should have asked—we certainly aren't guests here, but no noble lord would refuse a lady lodging. I should have found you a bed." He looked up at her, his eyes bloodshot and particolored as ever. "I'm sorry."

Churl, Alinor accused, slowly raising the yellow eyelid that hooded one dark eye. She settled her feathers again menacingly.

"Stables and hawk houses are both called *mews*," Wren scolded her. "You're perfectly comfortable here, and you know it."

The light keeps me awake. Next thing, I'll be in an early molt. Alinor worked her claws lazily upon the wood of the manger she perched on. Not that she would blunt her talons against the board. Wren smiled at her familiar's deceit. The falcon always stopped short of anything that might compromise her weapons, but she was not above blatant misdirection when she felt guilt was deserved and she was in a position to dispense it.

Titch was looking to his own weapons, laying out sword and dagger to inspect them, then all the pieces of his ragtag, piecemeal war harness. He should be resting, Wren thought. How could he fight if he was bone-weary and sandy-eyed with sleep-lack? But warriors were accustomed to privation, and if his gear was not all it should be come dawn, Titch would count himself shamed.

Now she'd spent a few days in the company of true—and well-equipped—knights, Wren could judge just *how* piecemeal Titch's gear was. It wasn't only the mended bits—some of the paired pieces didn't match one another, and she could see where Titch had added extra holes and straps, made other adjustments to force items crafted for larger or smaller men to fit him. That nasty Cullum's gear was probably all made to his personal measure, and his squire would be the one sitting up all night putting a polish on it, while *he* slept.

It wasn't much, but there was something she could do to even the odds. Wren lifted up Titch's murrey-dyed cloak, the woolen badge of the Red Queen's service. She hated every shade of the color red, and this was the worst of all—just like blood starting to dry. Melcia had costly cochineal for her personal use, but clad her men in the cheaper stuff, the homemade dye.

There was a pail of water standing near—Wren dipped three fingers into it, then began gently drawing them over the cloak, the front and back with graceful gestures and flourishes, like an otter darting through a stream, sporting. She dipped and stroked, dipped and stroked, humming tirelessly betimes, her eyes nearly closed. Though her sight was veiled, she was not in any sense working blind. The inner eye and the outer were not the same. It was in the inner eye that magic dwelt, and she had perfect vision. Her wet fingers signed on and on.

When she had finished, the cloak under her hands was transformed, and dry as a bone. There was no hint of any red left in its threads, but every other color was there, the blues and grays and greens of water, the slatey shades of wet pebbles in a streambed. The hues roved from thread to thread, as unconfined as free-running water, changeless and ever-changing both at once. Satisfied, Wren gave the woolen cloth one last pat and set the emptied pail aside, out of the way.

Then she curled herself up in the sweet-smelling hay and slept.

Trial by Combat

THE NIGHT WAS short, and Titch didn't waste a precious hour of it upon sleep. He polished, shined, oiled—then started in on Gray, so that no smear of dirt should sully the horse's white coat. When he was finished with brushes and comb and hoof file, he began arming them both. The process took longer without a squire's assistance and extra hands, but Titch was used to doing for himself and didn't think of it in terms of inconvenience at all. Somewhere, the duke's champion was doubtless being armed by his body squires, all of whom were doubtless of noble birth. Elsewhere, Gerein was probably sleepless, watching the sky lighten if he had been granted the dubious grace of a chamber with a window.

Titch decided to back the now-immaculate Gray out of the narrow stall. Better to harness him in the aisle, where there was more room and he wouldn't risk scraping fresh-polished leather on rough boards—

The old gelding refused to stir. He wasn't dozing—Gray had every one of his four hooves planted firmly in his bedding, and his posture was rigid. His ears were laid back, flat to his neck.

Titch, weary, was slow to take heed. He clucked encouragement automatically. He pulled back firmly on Gray's bridle, expecting compliance. At last he looked in the direction Gray's ears pointed and saw the black stallion standing in the aisle just behind him, neck arched and head bent to one side, scarlet nostrils flared and teeth bared in a gesture of forbidding that Gray read very clearly.

Titch sighed. He'd seen the stallion put into a comfortable loose box by the duke's own grooms. And like many

289

another clever horse, Valadan was simply adept at undoing a latch with his lips and teeth. No mystery there—the box's door stood wide open, farther down the aisle. Titch went to the stallion and slid a hand along Valadan's neck.

"Foolish," he whispered, taking hold of the sable mane, since the stallion's proud head was bare of bridle or halter. "You don't have any part in this."

Valadan rolled his eyes. Colors swirled inside, like an artist's transcription of a flourish of trumpets. *I am no stranger to combat,* he said.

"You're not mine to ride, either. You keep forgetting that," Titch observed.

It is a waste of breath to forbid me. Put your saddle on my back.

"You'd better do what he wants," a strange voice said. The lantern light wavered, then brightened and redoubled.

Titch's head snapped up, and the last mists of drowsiness left him. A man in Esdragon's blue and gray stood beside Valadan's empty box, holding a horn-paned lantern, low so it wouldn't dazzle Titch's eyes.

"Innis," he introduced himself. "I have been in charge of the stable since Rayner's father gave me the post. So you see, I know this one well." He stepped closer, slid his hand down the slope of Valadan's rump. "The Warhorse. Wind-sired and magic-bred, the pride of the duchy and the dukes. With a mind of his own like no other's. They say even Kessallia's wasn't a match for it."

"Sir, I came by him without stealing him, but I knew he had *been* stolen," Titch admitted. "I know very well what he is. And I have no right to him, except to see him safe back where he belongs." He faced the stallion down, trying to be firm, expecting to be obeyed. "You get back in your box! This is Gray's work."

Valadan stamped a hoof and switched his tail, unimpressed. Gray lowered his head and rested one hind leg, preparing to doze. Titch glared at them both.

"He has arranged it otherwise, I think." Chuckling, Innis produced a bit of carrot and let Valadan have it to crunch. Gray sighed wistfully, and so got his own bit of the treat. "When his last master perished of a wound fever, the duke hoped the Warhorse might heart-bond with one of his sons. Cullum, maybe, the eldest and the best warrior. Or at least Olvan—there was a gallant youth, full of promise as an apple is of juice and near kin to Rayner, being his sister's son. They looked well together, too. But the Warhorse . . . he chooses for himself, and no one knows the how or the why of it. Valadan suffered Olvan to ride him a time or two, but there was no bonding, not like with you."

"But I have no right to him!" Titch protested.

Valadan snorted.

"What's that to do with it?" Innis raised an eyebrow, a dark wing over sea-green. "Anyone with eyes can see it. He's claimed you. There's no one in this land would say you stole him the way Gerein tried to. Your white horse won't stir a hoof without his leave, which he certainly won't give. His mind's made up, and you'd be wise to yield. *I'd* prefer you did. It's nearly sunrise, and I've horses to feed. My grooms are too busy and too excited for the daily routine. Get him out of my way." Innis gave the black neck a pat to take the sting out of his words.

Valadan's great eye turned back to his master. *You see?* he asked, amused.

Titch swallowed a curse around a lump in his throat and picked up his saddle.

Wren started out of sleep, a dream of the sea's edge, and Alinor flying low over the foam. She could hear Titch speaking, and guessed it wasn't to either of the horses. She sat up, combing hay out of her hair with sleepy fingers.

A strange face looked over the partition at her—not a horse's face. Wren gave a startled squeak and shrank back.

"I should like to feed that hay, if you're done sleeping on it," Innis said. "Is that the best our duke could do by way of lodging?"

"I'm not a guest," Wren told him in a tiny voice.

"You should have been." Titch reached a gauntleted hand into the box, assisting her to her feet. "That's my fault, I should have asked. A king's child, sleeping in a stable—"

"I have slept in worse places." She was wrapped in his

cloak, Wren discovered. Maybe Titch hadn't recognized it, since she'd transformed it. Or he'd simply thought the stable chill in the night. That he'd remembered her warmed her far more than Melcia's wool. She slipped the cloak off, brushed stems and seeds of hay away, and held the garment out to him.

"My lady's colors?" Titch asked. He *had* noticed her work.

"I didn't think you'd want to wear the Red Queen's livery anymore." She fastened the clasp for him.

"Its only virtue would be hiding bloodstains." Titch bowed over her hand formally, like a hero out of a ballad. "If I rode today for my own sake, Savrin, I would dedicate the combat to you."

His use of her true name muddled her, and she spoke without thought, from her heart. "I wouldn't want you to!" Wren flushed, wondering whether he'd understood, or if she'd just insulted him to the bone. His clasp on her hands did not waver, nor did his color-flecked gaze.

"You don't have to watch, Wren. Take Alinor out to hunt her breakfast, she's sharp-set enough to want a piece out of me by now!" He wasn't offended. He knew she was afraid for him. "When this is over, I'll come back here, and we'll decide what comes next."

For so long, all she'd wanted was to know who she was. It had underlain all else, like a river that flowed beneath the surface of the earth, hidden most of the time, then breaking through into the light of day. Now she *knew* who her parents had been, but her own identity still seemed elusive— was she Savrin, child of a disastrous love, king's daughter and princess of nothing? Was she Galvin's apprentice, the seal set on his life's work and learning? Or something between, both and neither? She looked into Titch's mottled eyes, with their colors past numbering. Just now they showed mostly shades of green, dapples like damp leaves on the forest floor—and then they were too close to see, as her lips sought and found his.

His arms wrapped about her, startling her. She always forgot the wonderful solidity of him, like earth, or rock—

immovable and immutable. The complete opposite of water, its compliment and heart-mate.

The sea-color cloak wrapped around them both.

She said she would fly Alinor. She politely asked Innis where she might best do so, and let him direct her where some game was likely. Then, as Titch rode to decide Gerein's fate, Wren sent the falcon off alone after her breakfast, and herself trailed after the black horse, at just enough of a distance that Valadan's rider would not suspect her. The Warhorse might spy her, but he would not betray her. The horse knew what it was, to be heart-bonded.

Heart-bonded was easy enough for Innis to say. He wasn't the one had to face the stares as Titch rode Valadan to the place set aside for the combat. From the furious expressions of the onlookers, the only thing that kept the duke's men from seizing Valadan's bridle and hauling the upstart down from his undeserved place was Valadan himself. Hooves and teeth were one thing to face—Valadan's uncanny eyes quite another. There was a rumor that a glare from them could freeze a man's blood, like frosty winter winds.

Not true, but most useful. Valadan agreed merrily.

The duke had sent a mounted page to show them their way; Valadan probably could have found it on his own. The Trial would take place outside Keverne itself, upon the clifftop meadow. There had been insufficient time to set up proper lists, but some loges had been hastily constructed for the ladies who would attend, and for those men who would be witnesses. Many others would stand at the sides, scrambling for a view. No one wanted to miss the show. There had been torches all about, to light the workmen at their tasks, but those were pale things now, more visible by their smoke than their light as the sky about them went from black to gray and then on to a pale blue brushed with lavender at the edges.

Opposite the scant seating, a dozen men-at-arms made a living jail around Gerein. Titch rode slowly up to him, and though the guards did not step aside, he was well above men afoot, able to ignore them if he chose to—which he did. He greeted Gerein.

"Why are you doing this?" the knight whispered, pale and unshaven.

"I've asked myself that." Titch snugged the strap that held his helm in place. "Once I thought—on very little evidence, I'll admit—that you were the truest knight living, straight out of a hero tale." He shrugged. "Now I know better, but I still truly believe you didn't mean to kill that boy. Whatever else you're guilty of, you don't deserve to die for an accident. I can't stand by and watch that happen. I can't let them take vengeance and call it justice."

"Titch, Cullum's come out on top in every tourney I've ever seen him ride in! He—"

Titch wanted to smile at the rather belated attempt to help. Or should he be insulted at the lack of confidence? "He's never had to win or starve, has he? Not likely! Never needed to risk everything he owned, stake everything on his own sword? There *are* advantages to growing up the way I did." Titch grinned mirthlessly. "We're not exactly friends, Gerein. But no honorable knight would allow a man to stand where you do all alone. I can't do that."

He turned then and jogged Valadan slowly toward the misty far end of the meadow. The grass was long and soaking with dew. They passed clumps of flowers in the turf, white daisies with their yellow eyes still squinched shut, tufts of sea-pink already blooming the color of the sunward sky. Titch checked his gear as they swished along through the grass, scattering drops like rain, loosening sword and dagger in their scabbards as Valadan loosened his limbs, snugging straps, easing the shoulder that bore the weight of his shield.

A tinny blast from the horns of the duke's heralds reached his ears. Titch turned Valadan about and faced him toward the field's other end. He'd have preferred to have positioned himself with the sun at his back, but the field was sited so neither fighter could seize that advantage. The loges looked full to overflowing. Cullum had appeared— probably the trumpets had announced him—on a large bald-faced destrier. The horse was barded with quilted cloth—the most minimal of protections, but it made the beast look even more massive than it was.

Valadan snorted. *Large is not swift. Size is not courage.* Titch gave his shoulder a grateful pat, and they took their place on the field.

The marshal bawled the reason for the combat and the rules that would govern the Trial—such as they were. The fighting would continue until one man yielded or looked to be in danger of death, at which point it would be halted by the marshal and the victor proclaimed. The marshal lifted his pale baton of office, glanced first at his duke, then back over his shoulder at the sky. The combatants looked to their weapons, attention on the marshal all the while no matter where their eyes happened to be.

Suddenly gold flashed upward from the dark expanse of grassland. Sunrise. The marshal's baton descended like Alinor hard after a pigeon.

Titch had no need to touch a heel to Valadan's side as a signal—the stallion exploded into a hand gallop at his rider's first slight forward shift of his weight. They flew over the sward, making hoof-thunder.

The morning was still fairly dark, though the sky was brightening and the new-risen sunlight flashed sharply from metal weapon edges and decoration. Titch thought he might be somewhat harder to see than his opponent—the bay horse's white face stood out like a beacon before him, nearer each second. They were close enough to one another now to be thinking about aim. He let his lance drop level. The wind rushed past his cheeks, smelling strongly of the sea.

Time to choose his target. Try to get past the shield, because sending your adversary crashing to the ground on the first pass wouldn't bring instant victory, but it was very unsettling and therefore useful, and a solid hit on the breastplate virtually guaranteed it. Try not to let *his* point get past *your* shield, because he'd be trying the same trick and you didn't *have* a breastplate. Speed and skill, and Titch knew he had the advantage of speed, at least.

Impact, and a couple of loud cracks as they each found one another's shield and rocked with the blows, no harm done except to their lances. They pranced past one another, flung splintered remains of lances safely out of the fighting space, and took up the fresh spears the squires were offering. Titch felt the balance of his and made himself ready, while Cullum fussed more and asked for another.

Valadan arched his neck and pawed at the thick turf, seeming pleased. *I unsettle him.*

"Of course you do." Titch patted the satiny neck. The eye that turned back to him was almost aglow, bursts of color chasing across it as if 'twere a dark soap bubble. Valadan's nostrils flared, ready to puff out fire, like a dragon.

On the second run, Cullum probably thought to catch them flat-footed, scrambling to start first and take control, but Valadan was under way in half a heartbeat, skimming over the now-trampled grass like a nighthawk. The white-faced horse loomed then quickly filled all that mattered of the world. Cullum bore his shield high and hunched behind it so that nothing could be seen of him but those narrow eyes and the bright-polished helm with its decorative plume streaming smokily. The duke's son was very good as a jouster, there was really no getting through a guard like that. It would be lance on shield once more. Titch sat deep, ready for the splintering crash when it came again—they were agreed on breaking only two lances, and he was curious to see just how good Cullum was with a sword, where skill mattered somewhat more than a deep seat and a willing horse—where he couldn't hide so much behind the bulwark of a stout shield.

Valadan accelerated the final three strides, and the impact was more one-sided than it had been on the first pass. Cullum's lance bent and cracked against Titch's shield, throwing Titch back against his cantle—his own spear shattered outright, and splinters of it rained through the air. Cullum's shield cracked, too, though the iron cross-binding held it together. He and his horse were both shaking their heads as they swung about—they might be as rattled as they would get without an actual fall. Titch snatched his sword from its scabbard.

* * *

Wren watched dry-mouthed, jumping at the crack of contact. She was very well aware of being the only one in all the avid crowd—save perhaps for Gerein—who was wishing Titch good fortune. The ladies in the loges might not care to see him slain messily before them, but Cullum was their own, their darling, and fighting for their just cause. He had their hearts.

Titch was doing well enough, so far. Wren wished she had been able to lay a protection upon his cloak, instead of merely altering its color. What did color matter? Each time the riders crashed together, she fully expected to see Titch impaled, but she also had a sense that the jousting was merely a preliminary she was unfamiliar with, that the true fighting—and the true danger—was yet to come.

The sky was, as always, wider awake than the earth. Alinor sailed high above Keverne's towers, soaring out across the still-dim moors. Dewdrops sparkled. There were few other birds flying yet, and the air felt very still. She cut through it cleanly as she explored the seaward reach. The salt water below seemed vaster than the earth it lapped—almost a second sky, beneath her. Alinor climbed, banked, passed through the indistinct, chill edge of a cloud and felt drops of mist gathering upon the feathers of her back.

Her course took her landward once more, toward the tall dark cliffs with their thin fur of dusky green on top. How thick were the bones of the earth! How boring, the same each moment—not like the ever-shifting currents of her world. The creatures struggling upon the cliffs were no more than mites from her vantage.

Her keen eye caught motion, and though that same sight told her 'twas man's business and not hers—which at present was a good chase and a welcome meal—yet Alinor swept nearer, curious and revelling in her freedom and her power. The black horse was a familiar sight—she had seen him often from above. He had a sort of flight of his own, though he seemed to be tragically bound to the dull earth. He was stooping now toward another horse, like a falcon seizing an eagle's prey—like fighting birds, they struck only briefly before passing one another and wheeling for another attack.

If the horse and his broken-beaked rider were there below, then so must her mistress be. Alinor scanned the flock of folk until she found Wren there. It was troubling to see her hemmed by so many, but she seemed to be well, for all her thoughts were troubled and anxious, like the sky before a storm.

Cullum was a clever swordsman. He had reach, too—surprisingly long arms even for a man of his height. He didn't merely bash around, flailing and hoping—if an attack of his was deflected, he did his best to make the backstroke count as he recovered. And Cullum's best was a formidable blend of strength, reflexes, and training. He could think two, three blows ahead. He could hide one feint inside another. He could make an attack he knew would fail, just so he could employ a counterattack after. His smallest parry was a prelude to another offensive move, part of a strategy.

But Titch had lived by his sword, sometimes had lived for nothing else. It made the odds dead even, and might even tip them his way. He had fought bouts with swordsmen of all styles and sizes, whereas Cullum might have sparred mostly with his friends and knightly companions, for lesser stakes.

And Cullum wasn't mounted on Valadan.

Titch never had to spare an instant's attention for guiding his steed. His bridle hand was utterly free to manage his shield, his legs were available to anchor him firmly as he struck and parried. It was as if the stallion's hooves were his own feet—even when Titch might have thought he did not know, himself, where they would be next, the horse was never caught out of useful position. The Warhorse understood fighting. If Titch wanted to get inside that long reach of Cullum's, then it was done. Often Valadan had the taller horse circling to his time, and Cullum had a struggle bending his mount back to his own will and strategy. The beast was a trained warhorse, too, seasoned in battle, but it found standing up to a black thunderbolt who could seemingly be in all places at once difficult and unnerving. Valadan all but nipped at his heels, sheepdog fashion.

The bay sidestepped, backed, leapt forward at its master's urgent command, slipped on the torn turf and went down on its knees. Cullum, flung forward, hurled himself free of the falling beast in an awkward dismount over its right side. Ungainly in the extreme, but he landed on his feet, weapons still in hand, and came back to guard before his horse had even finished sliding on knees and nose.

As the bay lurched back onto its legs, Titch backed Valadan out of the way, then swung lightly out of his own saddle. It was not forbidden for a mounted man to fight against one unhorsed and afoot, but it was unknightly and unfair. He walked warily toward his adversary.

Again, the steely music of one sword ringing against another, with the occasional thump of blade on shield for counterpoint. It sounded rather like a dance held in a smithy. It differed from fencing on horseback—the two men were closer to one another most of the time, and there were no worries about striking a horse with an overwide parry. Overreaching would make a man slip, might leave him wide open to attack, would be unfortunate—but it wouldn't dump him onto the ground.

The fighters circled, closing when either man saw an advantage, a possible opening to be exploited with his blade. Titch held his shield in subtle invitation, hoping to lure Cullum's sword in for a binding circular parry that he could turn instantly into a disengaging attack. Cullum resisted his kind offer, issued one of his own, and they danced another measure or two on the wet grass, feinting and tapping and gesturing with shields. A man could get worn out with such tactics in short order, but they were both fresh, each still taking the other's measure.

Parry. Riposte. Open a new line, he may have forgotten you're close enough to smash his kneecap. He's not using his shield to block as much as he did—is the crack in it getting wider, and will it get worse if I bash it hard a couple of times? Don't try for any other target, just whack the shield?

He's falling back! Careful, he's done that too often, you

know he's not scared, so it's probably a trap—next time you go after him hard, he won't be retreating, just standing station and hoping you won't catch on till his point's rammed between your teeth!

They almost ran into the crowd, except the men parted to give them room. *Watch yourself now. Strange ground. No telling how many worthy knights have died because they stepped into badger holes at an inopportune moment! He's not covering very well to his left. He getting tired, or lazy? Or is it intentional? Work over that way and see—*

They hacked, slashed, parried, thumped each the other's shield. The men were coming down out of the loges to follow after them. Titch's sword arm was starting to ache, a burning sensation that ran up his shoulder and down his back. Cullum would be in like case, so the thing to do was exploit that weariness—Cullum trying to do the same thing to him, so that they actually fought *harder* as the combat took its inevitable toll.

All at once a seagull erupted screaming between them, and Titch realized they'd come within a few yards of the clifftop. Strange ground indeed! He could feel the pound of the surf below, through the earth. He wobbled and let Cullum push him back a pace or two—Titch didn't want to go any farther toward the edge, not to where he'd be forced to realize that safe, solid ground was really high, high up in the clear morning air.

The sun was high enough to become a factor now. It beat down on armor already heated by the sweating bodies within; it shone blindingly. Salt water ran into Titch's eyes, burning like vinegar. He blinked to clear his vision, made a parry by instinct, and caught Cullum's blade. He staggered back, feigning a slip as he gave ground, but Cullum refused to take the bait and go for a quick kill.

Someone was breathing like a foundering horse. Titch thought he'd trade away a year of his life for one sip of cold water, were someone to make him the offer. He got lured by a feint, came out of it wobbling from a blow that probably put a new dent in his helm, but he wasn't truly hurt, and he'd managed to whack Cullum's left ankle hard enough to draw a curse out of the man as he retreated. Too bad it had only been the flat of his blade, bruising but unable to cut through linked mail leg coverings.

Maybe they were done playing now. No more dancing—'twas plain neither one of them would fall down in a convenient faint from the exercise. It was time and past for effective actions, some disabling blows. Cullum was the taller—he kept trying to come over Titch's shield with cutovers and chops at his head from that advantage, while Titch focused his attentions on Cullum's legs. A man couldn't limp with *both*, but it would be amusing to see Cullum trying, he thought wickedly.

When a man got tired in a fight, and tired *of* it, anxious to have it over with, he began to make mistakes. They both committed their share of errors, out of fatigue. Titch's worst was that he let himself get turned around again and then pushed back a pace or two. He was aiming to make easy parries while he caught his breath, defending and defending and defending while Cullum wore himself out against him. Cullum cooperated nicely. And then all at once Titch realized that he could hear seabirds crying *below* him, which meant part of the *sky* was there, as well, or a lot of empty air anyway, because he'd been backed very neatly right to the clifftop's edge, herded like a sheep into an unseen fold. Cullum's panting lips drew into a wider grin of triumph.

Cullum didn't know, of course, that Titch would have thrown himself unarmed and unhesitating onto an enemy's sword to get away from that yawning emptiness. Because Titch *wasn't* unarmed, they crashed shield to shield once more, shoving and striking the shortened blows that were all that such close quarters permitted.

Not being able to step back was just the sort of handicap Cullum must have hoped it would be. His blunder about the terrain cut Titch's options drastically. He could defend—but pure defense inevitably ended in defeat unless one was expecting to be reinforced. Pure defense threw all control of the fight to your enemy, left you forced into reacting to whatever *he* did, refused you plans of your own. The cliff at his back might as well have been a solid wall—Titch knew he had a dozen yards of distance to play with, but while another fighter might have put them to use, *he* couldn't. He couldn't force his feet to take even a single step back, convinced as he was that such a step would be into empty air. He parried and struggled to make his defense into a riposte that gained ground.

Instead, he got shoved back two paces, off balance and still under his adversary's command. Titch understood the tactic. Long fights often resolved into more shoving than striking, whether 'twas shield to shield or blade to blade. He got in a stinging blow under Cullum's shield, whacked the flat hard across the taller man's ribs and hoped for the best, but he had to give ground another step doing it, or get his head taken off—and now he really *was* at the edge. Titch could smell the salt on the wind, taste the spray in the air he gasped into his laboring lungs. If he stepped back again—

He made a frantic effort to break through or past, met Cullum's chopping downstroke with a parry he hoped would throw Cullum's aim aside just enough to let him slip past. If they locked hilts, he could pivot around—

The blades met, struck together ringingly, and something gave without warning. Titch staggered forward off his balance, not pivoting as he'd planned, trying to discover what had gone wrong. He fell, rolled at once and brought his sword up to guard against Cullum's lightning pursuit—and then he saw to his horror that all he held was a handspan of steel, past the brass-inlaid hilt. His sword—his father's sword—had been shorn in two. The remainder of the blade lay shining in the grass at Cullum's feet.

A gasp ran through the crowd, like wind stirring ripe corn. A hundred people sucked in breaths of dismay—one let hers out instead. Wren screamed.

It was half plea, half denial—all grief. Bad enough that Titch should go down to defeat—but Wren saw, as maybe no other there did, how Cullum intended to finish him off, put an end to the upstart with the one thing in all the world that Titch was frightened of. He would fall and fall forever—it would seem like forever to him, from clifftop to sea rocks below—

He wore iron. She couldn't, Wren knew, help him with

magic at all, on account of his armor, his weapons. Tears could do nothing—not even save his life.

Now the men were fighting on their own feet, a slower, graceless affair—falcons killed with a single blow, and Alinor could only despise creatures that could not do likewise. These two humans lacked finesse, though she saw broken-beak make a feint or two that surprised her pleasantly as regarded his skill. The moves were scarcely falcon-worthy, but Alinor called encouragement as she passed overhead, despite herself.

Then disaster! She took scrupulous care never to blunt her own talons against any substance so unyielding as stone or steel—weapons were life, to a bird of prey. One did not abuse them. And broken-beak had just *lost* his, had his lone talon shorn away by his enemy. He held nothing worth calling a weapon now. He was helpless as a chick still in the down. Too bad. He'd fought well, and deserved victory if either man down there did.

She heard her mistress scream, the cry of a falcon who sees her mate in peril. Alinor wavered in the air, struck by the realization. There had been no courtship flight—or she had not recognized it as it happened. But she knew that cry, knew that the broken-beak's death would bring unendurable pain to her lady. He was a worthless, unworthy human tiercel, but he was nonetheless the one her own lady had chosen, and therefore it was her own duty to aid him.

Alinor had height enough for speed—she pointed her beak at the two men poised below her, swept back her wings, and dove. The air whistled between her feathers, a high shrill keening song of death. She saw her target clearly, dropped her talons into position, and struck.

Titch was too dazed by the disaster to think of leaping up, too winded to succeed at it if he had. And fortunately, Cullum was too out of breath to come instantly after him; he would have a moment to digest defeat before the sword was put to his throat, before the baton fell to make it official.

Except he wasn't a knightly foe, not even a noble one.

He was a stranger in this land, without support of lord or family. It occurred to him that Cullum might just boot him over the cliff edge and chance the consequences when he got to them. After all, he'd inflicted a good deal of pain on his opponent, not to mention the humiliation—

Titch saw Cullum's right boot lift. Yes, he'd read those narrow eyes rightly. Didn't matter. There was nothing he could do about it, nothing at all. He heard Wren scream. That was disaster, and regret. She wasn't supposed to be here, watching. She had seen enough awful things—

There was an echoing scream out of the air, and a shadow flashed over. *Alinor*.

Probably Cullum would duck if she stooped at him. That would buy Titch maybe a couple of heartbeats, maybe time enough to scramble back to his feet. And then what? His dagger against Cullum's longsword? Would the marshal stop them first? Alinor was as likely to fly in *his* face as Cullum's, Titch thought, and even if she was joining the battle on *his* side, it was cheating.

Something flashed down out of the sky, not Alinor. It was long, and thin, and bright. A sword.

It landed point-first in the turf and stuck so, quivering. Titch rolled to his feet, snatching at the hilt as he went past, and had barely yanked the point free before Cullum's blade was coming at him. The blow landed on his left shoulder and his whole arm went numb from the force of it, but Titch brought his heaven-sent blade windmilling up with only his right arm, until Cullum's brass-ornamented helm stopped it with a ringing thump. Titch lost his precarious footing then and slipped to one knee, helpless, but Cullum had gone down flat on his back with a clatter. Titch leaned forward, panting, and put his sword's point against Cullum's exposed throat, pressed it lightly against the leather gorget until he was sure it would be felt.

"Will you yield?" he asked formally. His mouth was so parched, he hardly got the words out, but Cullum knew perfectly well what his grunts meant. His eyes were full of rage, but it was a helpless anger. And the marshal's baton came down implacably.

The Knight of True Heart

"No!" CULLUM'S HOWL of protest was echoed half a score of times, punctuated with a cry or two of *"Witch-craft!"* The knight standing closest to Wren discovered that his sword no longer hung easily from his back from its dyed leather baldrick, but was somehow clutched in Titch's gauntleted right hand, a hundred paces distant. Alinor sailed a huge circle coming back to her mistress, scattering men as she passed contemptuously low over their heads, seeming far larger on the wing than she did on the fist. She cleared even more space with extraneous flappings of her long wings as she landed meekly upon Wren's offered forearm.

The instant he'd been assisted to his feet, Cullum thrust off his friends and launched a furious protest, forcing his way to the duke's side. Titch got to his feet on his own and rather warily. No one had tried yet to lay hands on him, but he wouldn't be especially surprised if it happened. He let the sword Alinor had stolen for him fall into the grass and tenderly gathered up the two pieces of the blade that had been his father's. There were a pair of armed men advancing upon him, he noticed, with purpose in the set of their mailed shoulders.

"You were ordered to bring Gerein back for justice, not execution, Cullum. There has been a Trial. However much I may regret its outcome, it is ended." The duke didn't sound especially pleased. Titch supposed he wasn't.

"It's not *right*—" Cullum shouted, refusing to desist.

The two men were closer. So was Valadan, the milling crowd parting before the stallion like grain lashed by a cold wind. Titch measured the distances with his eyes. The

305

duke's men saw, too, and quickened their pace. In the background, Cullum's protests grew shrill. Titch wondered whether he could hold off two men with only his dagger, if he could keep them from taking him without doing them serious harm. Self-defense was valid, but subject to interpretation—and that not likely to go in a stranger's favor.

The sky opened.

Rain was no weighty matter in Esdragon. To be out of doors was to be sprinkled with water at some point, ninety days out of a hundred. But this was a rare deluge, huge drops hurtling out of the sky straight as the sword Alinor had snatched, a rain like a gray mail curtain. It was not only the duchess and her ladies who made great haste back toward Keverne—most of the men were doing likewise, save those to whom the duke was issuing orders regarding Gerein.

"He shall have a sevenday to get himself across our borders. That's ample. If any harm befalls Gerein of Kendillin during that span, I will count it as murder and a slight to my own honor, and it will be so punished." Rayner turned, raised his voice over the rain's drum. "*Gerein!* You are proved innocent of intent to murder by your champion's victory in this Trial, but still you caused Olvan's death, and you are rightly banished from my dukedom. You are free to go whither you will, but you shall never return to Esdragon so long as I or my sons draw breath." Beside his father, Cullum was finally silent, but his narrow eyes held dire promises. "Not if you would keep your life. Begone—and be grateful."

The chains were struck from his wrists. Gerein lifted his unfettered hands, staring as if they were another's, no flesh of his. He looked up from them and saw Titch watching him through the rain. With a disdainful glance at his erstwhile guards, Gerein crossed the soaking grass.

"They took my sword," he said, gesturing at Titch's scabbard, which now held only disconnected shards of steel. "Or I'd give it to you."

"You'll need it yourself," Titch said, raindrops dripping

from the tip of his nose. "Though better if you didn't. Where will you go?"

"Away." Gerein scanned the gray landscape. "It's all away, you know that? Away from wherever you are. Maybe I'll take ship—" And he began to walk away, the duke's men parting for him, while he never gave them another look. Any of them.

There's the thanks you get. If you're idiot enough to do something like this for something as improbable as Gerein's gratitude. Titch shook his head, trying to clear it of cobwebs. His shoulder hurt, and his neck was sore. He was bruised pretty much head to foot, besides being wet to the skin except under the steel cap of his dented helmet. He'd recovered his breath, but he was still sweating almost to match the rain, and his jazerant seemed to weigh a thousand pounds.

Valadan nudged at his chest. The two men were still advancing on him, though hesitating a trifle in their progress. They weren't under their duke's orders, then, but only trying to guess what Rayner might desire be done with this inconvenient stranger. The issue wasn't clear yet, so they were cautious.

If you were on my back, they would not try to seize you, Valadan said pointedly.

"Even if they think I'm stealing you?" Titch yielded to logic and to the weariness in his legs, and stuck a toe into the stirrup. What sense walking back to Keverne's stables through rain and mud, watching over his shoulder all the way? He'd time aplenty for misery—he wasn't likely to be dry for days if this downpour kept up. Gerein wasn't the only one who'd be riding away from Keverne in the rain.

The stirrup and his boot were both wet and slippery. He was nearly too done up to gain the stallion's back. Titch cursed, sighed, and wiped rain out of his eyes as he finally settled safe into his place.

Wren's face was streaming water, but Titch couldn't tell if that was from weeping or only the sheeting rain. Alinor was looking murderous—she wanted to be under cover, only her mistress had not retired to Keverne with the other ladies, but loitered about in the nasty downpour—for which the falcon could only hold Titch to account.

"I thought he was going to kill you!" Wren gasped, clinging to his stirrup while Valadan turned his head back to nuzzle her shoulder.

So did I, Titch wanted to answer, but he shrugged the danger off. "They wouldn't have allowed it. The fight wasn't about that." He remembered the duke's cold, angry face, those eyes like pale stones, and knew he misled her. It wouldn't have been right, but if Cullum *had* slain him, the duke's son would have been granted the benefit of every doubt and certainly never accused of murder. The peril had been all too real.

Titch leaned down to help Wren scramble up behind him, bit back a gasp as her weight pulled cruelly on his bruised arm. She didn't mean to cause him pain. Alinor clipped him solidly across the face with a wing. That pain *was* intentional, but Titch bore it in silence, as well—he knew what the falcon had done for him. "Thank you," he said humbly, when he saw her fierce dark eye fixed on him. Alinor did not respond, save to shake raindrops from her head.

He still wasn't stealing the stallion, Titch reminded himself as they jogged back toward Keverne, all four of them so wet that haste would only have served to spatter them head to toe with mud, as well—just the very opposite, he'd brought Valadan back to his home, his birthplace, the place he'd been stolen from. He'd done Esdragon's duke a service. Perchance such service would cancel out the service he'd just done for Gerein, which Duke Rayner couldn't be liking much. With luck it might bring the scales into balance just long enough for Titch to shift his saddle onto Gray's old back, so that he and Wren could ride away. These moments astride the black stallion were the last such he'd know. Every step Valadan took was a red-hot nail, hammering the reality home into Titch's heart. Losing the horse was hard enough, but doing so of his own will—

Valadan's home was not his, and never would or could be, Titch reminded himself with iron-hard logic that gave him scant comfort. Had things been otherwise, had he not been compelled by his honor to defend a man whose conduct was indefensible ... There was no going back, and Titch might regret the results, but never the action itself. He'd known what the price would be, been keenly aware that there'd be no knighthood for him in Esdragon if he stood by Gerein. Probably there was no real prospect of a knighthood for him anywhere, ever, now. It had been an orphan's desperate dream, too long held to because he'd had too little else to dream of.

So he'd let it go at last, open his tight fist and let the tattered fantasy run away like the rain down his face. Cool reality was that such as he hired out their swords for a crown a year, and lived and died mercenaries, fighting others' fights for gold and loot. He'd have been better off with the stallion as part of his arsenal, but Titch had resolved when they'd arrived that he'd be leaving Valadan behind in this place where the horse had been bred and where the horse at least belonged. It was his own idea. No surprise that it would tear his heart, but he would survive this pain, Titch thought. He could control it. It was only hurting in the present moment because he insisted upon thinking about losing Valadan while he still sat on the stallion's back, dwelling on the knowledge that it was for the last time. If he could stop doing that, Titch thought, he'd be fine. Right as the ever-present rain.

True, his face was wet, but that was only the same cursed rain. He was made of sterner stuff than that—never catch *him* weeping over the loss of a horse that hadn't been his to begin with. He was a practical man, as much out for the main chance as ever Gerein had been.

"We don't have to go with Gerein, do we?"

"*No!*" Titch's laugh, breaking through the dark clouds of his brooding, was Wren's reward for a foolish question. He wrapped an arm about her, even better recompense. "That I can promise you!" he said into her hair. Wren leaned into his embrace, though she knew that made saddling the horse impossible for him. *Only a moment,* she promised herself, but a moment of comfort, content—

"*There she is, my lord!* The girl with the falcon!"

Titch looked toward the stable door. Two men stood with the rain at their backs. Both of them were known to him. One was the chatty Innis, who had claimed charge of the stables and doubtless had a right to be there. The second man was Innis' master, Esdragon's duke.

Wren made a sort of breathless squeak, and Alinor went to her fist as if that had been a signal, then bated impressively, wings and mouth both wide. But it was all show, empty threat—in the close confines of the stable she was helpless. There was no room for proper flights, for attacks. Titch frowned, wondering if there *was* a need, if perhaps he had relaxed his own vigilance too soon, and foolishly.

"Lady," the duke said, not threatening but not friendly, either. He was staring past the displayed falcon, into Wren's pale face. Thinking, certainly, of the part the bird of prey had played in Titch's snatched victory, his own son's defeat, the unwelcome outcome of the Trial by Combat. Thinking Wren had planned it all . . .

"Sir, if you have any quarrel here, it is rightly with me," Titch said, seeking to draw the attack his way. Wren was trembling with more than the strain of holding Alinor in check. Until he knew what this was about, he'd do well to be wary.

"No quarrel, and nothing to do with you," the stablemaster answered impertinently. He shrugged at Titch's dismayed expression, spreading his hands. "Technically, the duke's stables *are* in the charge of the Constable of Esdragon. At your service." He sketched a bow, lifted one corner of his mouth as if in mirth.

"She is under my protection," Titch said, warning in his tone as he adjusted to the news. The man might be laughing at his own expense as easily as mocking Titch, but Innis' office did not alter Titch's own responsibility, nor his response. It only explained why the duke was there, and not some subordinate. And it might not have explained that if he'd had all his wits about him, Titch decided.

" 'King's daughter, sleeping in a stable,' " Innis quoted, cocking an eyebrow as if that explained something more.

"That was . . . a bad jest," Titch protested, still baffled but thinking he'd be wise to deny the words all the same.

What was this about? What did the man think he'd over-heard? Evidence of a royal kidnapping? A princess running off with a lowborn lover?

"No jest, I'll wager," the constable said brightly. "No more than when you called her Savrin. Only the plain—if twisted—truth."

"That remains to be seen," the duke grated.

The constable's attention shifted. "My lord, *you* were the one fostered for half a dozen years in Zorana's household. *You* would have seen her at this very age. What do *you* think?"

"I *think* I had rather the Constable of Esdragon con-cerned himself more closely with his duties to my horse herds!" Rayner snapped. "That was twenty years gone, Innis. How can I say?"

"Perhaps the duchess will better judge? Zorana was her kin, after all—"

"I will not raise my lady's hopes on such premature evidence—her health's not been what it should be since Olvan was killed. This charade today didn't help." The duke's pale eyes fastened once more upon Wren. "Girl, who are you? Answer truly."

Wren's lips trembled. Likewise the rest of her, Titch dis-covered. He put his bruised arm about her thin shoulders and glared at the duke. He thought Alinor looked grateful for the support to her usual position. "What's this about?" Titch asked boldly. "Why—"

"Indulge me." The duke held up his one hand and looked intently at Wren. "Girl, who were your parents?"

Wren stayed mute, shuddering now.

Titch gave her a squeeze of reassurance, and the duke stare for stare. He doubted he could offend the man much more than he had already, but he could try. "This is Savrin, daughter of Kenric, King of Crogen, and his lady, Zorana," he said, presenting Wren formally, with the respect due to her station, whether she claimed it or not. "She is under my protection, and deserves yours, as well."

"Sir, you should put no stock in what he says!" Wren cried desperately, finding her tongue at last, pulling back as if she could distance herself from Titch's words by moving to the limit of his arm's reach. "It was a madwoman proclaimed that birth for me! She may have lied. She may have been mistaken—"

"Do you believe she was?" the duke inquired icily.

Titch, who knew that Wren was at last absolutely certain of her origins, was dumbfounded. Why should she lie, or try to?

"I don't know!" Wren pleaded. Hidden away or transformed all her life, how could she *know*? she wondered. How could she even guess where the truth lay? The Red Queen had believed, and the Red Queen had been mad. There was no evidence beyond that madwoman's word. It would be a very easy matter to deny the truth even now. There would be uncertainties enough to hide herself in, for the rest of a lifetime. And she should seek that escape— Titch was at risk here, too, Wren realized. The new trouble was only to do with her, but his honor would never let him stay safe out of it.

"Zorana was your mother," the duke repeated dispassionately. "Do you know aught else of what she was?"

Wren shuddered once more. She could not repeat Melcia's lies to this cold-iron man. She *would* not. She looked into the duke's stone-color eyes and spoke as her mother deserved, without a quaver. "She was loved by her lord, who was my father."

"Brave," the duke observed approvingly, under his breath. "Child, I am asking of a time before your birth, of a time when your mother was just your age. I thought she might have spoken of her past to you. I meant no insult." Still, his eyes did not warm. He continued. "Twenty years ago, when the Eral reivers were carving up Clandara into parcels, they supposed they could do as much to Esdragon." His empty sleeve attested to the fierce warfare that had settled the question and kept Esdragon from what was now styled Calandra's fate. Rayner had lost the arm before he'd gained the ducal coronet. "The border country became unsettled, unsafe. There were whole families wiped out, slain or taken captive. My duchess lost her youngest sister in such a way—she was carried off into Clandara after the rest of her family perished, and we were not able to get her back, not by arms and not by ransom.

"We did have tidings of her, and so knew that at least she lived. Bards cross all borders freely, and her fate became tasty meat for their ballads. Claimed by an Eral king, who found her face reason enough to cast aside his arranged marriage. Great love, and great cost. An ill end came to her, but she bore a child to her lover first. The woman's name was Zorana, and she called her child Savrin."

Wren felt a cold like springwater creeping up her legs, from her toes to her knees. She would rather that Melcia had lied, whether with madness or malice, than face this. She was dismayed, to find where she had ceased to seek, and trembled ungratefully in the circle of Titch's arm.

"If you are Zorana's daughter," the duke said, "then you are also my lady's only living kin, of what was once a large and noble family. Many an earnest prayer she has sent heavenward, that you should be restored to us. It may seem to you that I offer little of a welcome for an arrival so longed for, but I am determined to spare my lady the grief of false claims and failed hopes. Nights enough she has wept while she thought I slept. Every life brings a share of loss, but her burden is especially heavy to bear. I shoulder what I can of it, for her sake."

"So you believe her claim, Rayner?" the constable asked gently, at his side.

"I believe her better because she has *made* no claim," the duke answered, his mien stern. His expression softened the merest fraction. "And there is something of Zorana in her face. I had not thought to see it again, save in my lady's."

"I don't look like my mother," Wren whispered faintly. All too well, she remembered the nightmare queen consigning her to a watery grave, because her face was so much her *father's*. If face was what they wanted for their proof—

All at once Wren calmed, like water in a lake when the chill wind stirring it dies. What did it matter to *her*, if these utter strangers denied her birth? Keverne was not her home, she'd no reason to want to stay anywhere near it. All to the good, if Esdragon should declare it had no claim on her, should reject her heritage. What had she to do with this girl their bards sang of, this Savrin?

Melcia could tell me who I was, but not who I am, she thought with a flood of relief. *They're not the same at all.* Wren drew in an easy breath. It would be all right. They'd let her go, or they'd send her disparaged away, but that was all one sky—

"Welcome, Savrin," the duke said gently, his decision taken, and lifted her limp right hand in his so suddenly that Alinor had no time to object. "Be welcome to the land your mother was reived from, before your birth. In you, she is restored to us at last. There are lands oathbound to Zorana, which may pass most fitly to her child. I vow those shall be yours, to hold for your own children. Let me take you now to meet my duchess, your aunt—"

So, this cold-eyed stranger had chosen to claim her, after all. The Duke of Esdragon held less terror for Savrin than the Red Queen had, but still Wren pulled her hand from his clasp and stepped back. It was a thoughtful retreat, not a panicked flight, but both Alinor and Titch were disposed to misread her. The falcon screamed excitedly, and Titch interposed one of his wide shoulders in front of Wren and most of Alinor, dropping his right hand to his sword hilt.

"A shattered sword against a one-armed man?" the duke said scornfully. "This is nothing to do with you, sirrah! Would you draw on me?"

"No." Titch kept his hand where it was, and his gaze level. "But you go too fast for her. You took your time, now you must grant the lady the same courtesy." He turned to Wren and smiled. "Sudden as it is, you've found your family."

"I wasn't looking for them."

Titch thought he could guess at her reluctance. "It's not the vipers' nest you've heard of already—your father's kin! That lot never cared about you, didn't mind a bit if you got caught up in the bloodletting over Crogen's precious throne. Good riddance to them!"

Alinor creaked agreement.

"These are your mother's folk," Titch went on. "They've remembered her and kept a place for you, her child."

"And because they deign to claim me, I must let myself *be* claimed?" There was a touch of Alinor's disdain in Wren's gray eyes. "Suppose I don't want to stay here? Suppose I still want to go with you?"

Titch's heart rose into his throat at the notion that she'd cast off such a future to stay with *him*. He shoved it back down, ruthless, knowing what he had to do. "You can't," he said.

"What!" That sense Titch had begun to have from Wren—of a calm stream playing among its sunlit rocks—became a raging torrent tearing its banks under a sky full of lightning. Titch, expecting some such reaction, did not permit the violent flood to sweep him away. He knew how to find bottom and stand firm, knew when Wren needed him to. And she needed that now, though she fought against it—and him—with all her strength.

"I want to stay with you!" Wren gripped his forearm with a force that would not have shamed her familiar. A deep current all but sucked Titch under, to be dashed on rocks.

He managed to keep his footing and get his arms about her. She seemed more disposed to listen when he did that. "There's a home for you here, a future. You know I can't give you that. The road between one tourney and the next, that's all the home I have, Wren. Dirt and dust and cold, bad water and rough company. It's no life for you. You deserve better."

"I don't care!" Such a sudden cascade of whitewater, Titch couldn't see another thing in the room for it—not the duke, not the constable, not even his own Gray, who stood so near he could hear the horse breathing, could smell the hay the gelding munched.

"You might, one day." When she realized for herself what anyone could tell her, how far above him she truly was, by the birth no one denied any longer. She would reach awareness of that, Titch thought, and regret her choice of him. One day, not any too far off. He felt it in his bones, and it stiffened his resolve to do what was best for her, if she would not do it herself. "Stay," he begged, seeking a quiet eddy in the flood, so he could make her hear him. "You won't be trapped. I swear to you, Wren, if you need me, if you send to me, nothing will keep me from coming to you!" *From either side of the grave,* he pledged silently, secretly, fiercely. "But stay here awhile. Your kin want to give you a home. Let them."

"You said I was under your protection." Having tried every tactic she could think of, she was growing frantic as a salmon wanting to be back under the water, tail thrashing in the thin useless air.

"It's yours when you need it," Titch promised. Her eyes were twin lakes, reflecting back the lantern light. "But a duke's protection counts for more than a sword-for-hire's. He's your uncle, Wren. He's an honorable man. He'll keep you safe. Don't worry." *Don't cry,* a man who didn't know her might have said.

He won't take me, Wren realized. *And there's nothing I can do to shift him. He's solid as a boulder that way.* Her narrow shoulders sagged with defeat.

Titch lifted her cold hand to his lips, which were so dry that Wren barely felt them against her fingers. As if he were afraid to touch her now. Yet his grip lingered, as if his arms wanted to go around her, defying his will. Wren trembled, wanting them there, lost without their clasp. And Titch carefully put her hand into the cold-eyed duke's palm and stepped back from her side, away from her new life, all gallant and hopeless.

He'd stay if I could weep, Wren thought wildly, wanting to seize that power. *There's no spell of binding half so powerful as any maiden's tears.* But even if she *could* shed tears, he'd only think 'twas the rain still tickling out of her hair onto her face, down her cheeks. Titch knew too well that she didn't weep for her own sake . . .

Titch led Gray out through the stable's broad door, wondering without real interest whether the torrents of rain had ceased. He had heard the downpour striking the stable's roof, but he could not have said if or when he had stopped hearing it. The cobbles underfoot were wet, but the air was not, and the sky overhead was lightening, even showing raggedy patches of blue. Titch shrugged his shoulders, considering whether his gear might dry that day after all. The wool would steam first, and the leather might develop spots of powdery green, but he had oils and creams aplenty for dealing with that sort of thing. Come nightfall—

Don't think that far ahead, idiot! Titch lashed out at himself. *Not here. Not now.*

Best just to walk, to think of nothing but the putting of one foot ahead of the other. No one challenged him, called out to him—for which Titch was truly grateful. If he concentrated to a sufficient degree, the world became a succession of footsteps, and he had no space to consider hopes and dreams, incomparable horses or the difference between being on the inside and being on the outside, kept there forever by his own open-eyed choices.

Just don't think.

Every step he took hurt some bruise or abused muscle. That should help. Pain canceled out pain.

Wren felt warmth on her face, moisture like a snail's track crawling over her cheek.

I can't weep for myself, she thought, startled, wondering whether she'd learned to shed ordinary useless tears at last. She stared at Titch's back as he walked away from all his hopes, refusing for his pride to let his shoulders sag as if he'd been defeated, limping a little in spite of himself, because he couldn't help it. And in that instant Wren knew that her tears still weren't for her own pain, wrenching though it was. She turned her wet face toward her newfound uncle, who held the chivalry of Esdragon in his hand.

"He is the truest knight you'll ever lay eyes on," Wren said to the duke. "Ask the horse, if you don't believe me."

"Don't weep, child," he said gruffly, and reaching out, brushed her tears away, surprisingly gentle in his touch.

Leaving. Are you leaving me, also?

He'd thought there was something amiss in Gray's clopping behind him, Titch told himself angrily. The cadence was off, more than slightly. He'd feared dimly that Gray was going lame, at best was stiff from standing too long in his stall. But as Titch turned and Gray halted obediently, he saw the truth—there were just twice the number of hooves striking the cobbles that he'd anticipated, just enough out of step to sound false.

"We've been over this ground before," Titch said to the black stallion as it halted before him.

Indeed. Valdan extended his muzzle and gently lipped at Titch's hand.

"No," Titch said, as much to himself in answer to the temptation as to the horse. It was no one's fault but his own that Valadan had followed him—he should have put the stallion into a tie stall. All of the loose boxes had doors with bolts a demonstrably clever horse could draw back in a moment with lips and teeth. Nothing for it; he'd have to tie him somewhere now, before he could stir another step. He looked about the yard for a rope, almost frantic when he could spy nothing that would serve. Later, the grooms could do as they liked, all he had to do was restrain the stallion briefly—

Why do you refuse me? Valadan's head was never held low, but his star-shot eyes were full of sorrow, and his ear position betrayed his uncertainty. *Why do you try to leave me?*

"You belong here," Titch explained patiently. "You *do*. I saw the tapestry. I've heard the stories, the songs. I know what you are."

You have heard but have not listened, Valadan snorted, stamping a forehoof. *The wind blows wherever it chooses.*

"You can't heart-bond with the likes of *me*!" Titch protested.

Is not the choice mine? Valadan's tone was amused.

"Why me?" Titch wailed, a desperate entreaty to the gods of fortune. The horse dipped his head and pawed the cobbles with a forehoof. That was all the answer he gave, and the gods of fortune were even more silent.

Titch glared at the stallion, exasperated. "Choose again, Warhorse. Choose yourself a knight. Choose someone worthy."

Gerein was a knight, Valadan said mildly. *And Cullum is a worthy man, so some say.*

Gods, he was arguing chivalry with a *horse*! And losing,

at that. "Choose yourself a true knight! Take your time, there are plenty of them around. This isn't the Red Queen's realm."

He tried to walk decisively away—he *tried*, but Titch forgot that Valadan could freeze Gray in his tracks just by angling one ear back half an inch; the reins he held jerked him up short in a stride and a half. Titch swore helplessly and shut his eyes with frustration.

And with a step that was like water flowing over slate, the stallion moved himself in front of him, barring Titch's way even supposing he *could* convince Gray to step forward in defiance of Valadan. Those eyes, those impossible eyes, bored into Titch's soul the moment he made the mistake of unclosing his own lids.

You have defended the weak and protected the innocent . . . Little pictures darted like fish within Valadan's eyes, illuminated like sacred manuscripts, in gold, with paints pigmented of ground sapphires, crushed rubies. Titch recognized himself, fighting against a diamond-armored Cullum for no gain save honor, fighting on even with a bare remnant of a ruined sword, never thinking to yield. Then in a heartbeat the scene shifted, to the stomach-clenching height of a battlement, where he was striving doggedly to rescue a swan from those who meant a prince ill. Next Titch beheld himself standing in a flooding river, clutching a terrified otter so that it should not drown, no matter that *he* might himself—

Your heart is brave and pure, and you follow where it leads you . . . *what else does it take to make a true knight?*

"It takes a lord to swear service to!" Titch snapped, so ferociously that Valadan actually startled back.

A pledge of mutual faith? The stallion tossed his head dismissively. *Is that the only obstacle on this path you would walk?*

As if it were a mere trifling thing, a molehill to be skirted or stepped over. Well, how could a horse, even this one, understand that there was no lord would have him now? He was surely foresworn to Melcia of Josten, and he had done Esdragon's duke the sort of service no lord looks for in a new vassal or tolerates long in one he already possesses. "Let me go," Titch begged. "And don't be following after me, either! You belong *here*—"

"So he does."

The duke came striding across the stableyard, stern-faced. Wren trailed him a pace or two, then halted uncertainly. Valadan whickered softly, a greeting.

Titch's heart misgave him. He beat back the feelings of guilt, reminded himself that whatever he'd coveteously desired in his heart, he'd been hewing to the right all along, as regarded this horse. He'd set Valadan free, and he was trying to make the stallion remain where he belonged. It was hard—he knew how things looked. He met the duke's wintery eye, forebearing to flinch. "Sir, I swear to you, I am *not* trying to steal your Warhorse. Only let me put him into some place he cannot let himself straight out of, and I will be on my way." Titch didn't suppose Valadan would cooperate with the process, but he'd have to try. There had to be *some* way—

The duke didn't answer. He was staring at Valadan, and the stallion was staring right back, nostrils flared. "He'll have you out here all day," the duke muttered, dropping his gaze at last. "Why this one, Warhorse? With all my dukedom to choose from?"

Valadan snorted, tossing his sleek head imperiously, and stamped a forehoof. The duke's expression went murderous.

Titch's went desperate. *If I back away, very slowly . . . how far would I get?* Which was the worse peril, the stallion or the duke's guards? There were sure to be guards, even if they weren't in sight—

"I cannot believe a man who would defend Gerein could earn a heart-bond," the duke said. "And yet it stares me in my face. And whether you permit it or not, this horse you think is mine will follow you to the ends of the world. My law cannot bind him, nor your intentions. So he has always been, since a wizard shaped him out of mortal mare and immortal wind, before my great-grandsire drew breath. There's nothing I can do to stop him. Not even a bit forged of cold iron will compel him—"

"If I *ask* him to stay, he will," Titch said quietly. Valadan gave a squeal of distress, and Titch knew he'd been dead-on with his guess. The stallion might not like it, but he *could* be so bidden. Titch looked him in the eye. "You need to stay here, for Wren. You can help her." Valadan snorted fiercely, but his head dipped a trifle. Titch was satisfied with the response.

"You'd yield him up?" Duke Rayner asked, dismayed.

"He doesn't belong to me." Titch held out a palm, letting the stallion lip it, thinking how hard he'd worked, what he'd risked once, trying unceasingly to possess this horse. And how the moment he'd won, he'd realized he'd been wrong the whole time. There didn't seem to be a way to say that. The duke wouldn't understand, and he might not even be able to speak himself. His throat had gone raw, and he couldn't seem to swallow. It was even hard to breathe.

"Principle," the duke mused. "You keep yourself very strait, where that's concerned."

"My father left me three things when he died, sir," Titch replied. "His sword, his warhorse, and his honor. Horses grow old, swords can be broken. Nothing I can do about that. But honor can be lost only if I let it." He thought of the pictures Valadan's eyes had shown him, and suddenly knew he'd kept tight hold of that honor in some slippery places, appearances sometimes deceiving even his own eyes. He touched the stallion's neck once, in farewell; and when he found his fingers lingering, made them let go.

"Could you, I wonder, be so high-principled toward a man who might deserve the honor better than Gerein did?" The duke laid his own hand upon Valadan's crest and scratched the roots of the stallion's shadow-dark mane.

Titch stared, confused. "I don't know what you mean, my lord." He was in no mood for riddles—not while his heart was being torn out of him, thread by thread. He wanted to be gone, even if it was only into the emptiness of what passed for his future. Have this rending over with—

"Could you serve *me*, for instance?" the duke asked, twisting two locks of mane together. "Would you swear to be my liege-man, to uphold my rights and honor as I should uphold yours? Will you do me service in arms, as I require of you in return for the lands you shall hold of

me?" He let go of Valadan's mane and looked straight into
Titch's face as he asked the ritual questions.

Titch's eyes went so wide, he could see nothing at all.
He couldn't speak. He didn't dare breathe, lest the moment
shatter and he realize the truth, that he'd wishfully misunderstood, misheard—

Kneel, Valadan suggested wryly.

Titch did, bonelessly. "Lands and service?" he whispered, disbelieving, his heart beating so hard in his ears that
it sounded like a great river pouring into the sea.

"That's how it works," the duke agreed, still unsmiling
but looking less dreadful and only as stern as one who has
been a warrior all his life. "Cullum will be duke after me,
and you've no friend there—but just now, I've a new kins-
woman by marriage who will require a marriage arrange-
ment of me." He nodded toward the Warhorse. "You come
with high credentials. I will assume you've no objection to
that service, either."

The duke drew his keen-edged sword from its long scabbard and administered the two ritual taps of knighting, one
on either of Titch's wide shoulders. "Arise, Sir Tych, true
knight of Esdragon. And carry your lady's colors bravely."

Titch stood, his sight blurred by tears. He heard a falcon's shrill cry, answered by Valadan's ringing neigh—and
then Wren was in his arms, her own face wet, and as their
lips met he held her tightly and knew he would never let
her go, come what might, whoever she was and whatever
he was.

The land Wren got of her mother's kin was all clifftop
and heather, but it had what mattered: plenty of water and
plenty of sky. The sea below was water ever-flowing, and
there was a fine small castle perched upon the headland,
with stout defensible walls and only one squatty tower that
did not poke too far into the sky for Titch's comfort, though
he seldom ascended it. Alinor claimed its topmost chamber
for her own, and maintained the watch as she tended her
eggs and eventually her chicks. The stronghold was sited
on a bit of coast where Esdragon's duke desired to have a
sharp eye and a strong arm in his service. Alinor provided

the one and Titch supplied the other, willing partners in fealty to the Lady Savrin.

A knight also owed his liege-lord service in arms, when 'twas commanded. And when Titch rode out upon the Warhorse Valadan, when he lifted up his untarnished sword in his duke's cause, it was ever and always under the falcon banner of his lady. Betimes, a living falcon flew escort above, riding the wind.

ABOUT THE AUTHOR

Susan Elizabeth Dexter was born in Greenville, Pennsylvania, on July 20, 1955. She spent her whole life in western Pennsylvania except for the occasional trip to New York and a vacation in England, and is still pursuing her grand design of seeing the United States by following the World Fantasy Convention around each Halloween. She had a very basic education until high school, when she enrolled in a three-year commercial art program at the local vocational-technical school. She spent the next eighteen years slaving in the in-house ad agency of a discount department store chain, doing fashion art and layout while writing in her spare time. Her first book, *The Ring of Allaire*, appeared from Del Rey Books in 1981. In 1992 she made the leap to writing full time.

All those great cover paintings had led her to fantasy, you see. The roots of her addiction go back to her childhood, when fairy tales and horse stories were her favorite literary fare. She next dipped into historical fiction, gothics, and science fiction. At some point she crossed back over into fantasy and knew she had come home.

Susan is fascinated by unicorns, canaries, wolves, carousel horses, pizza, birds of prey, King Arthur, silver rings, Star Wars, Fafhrd, and the Gray Mouser—and of course books. She grows herbs, does watercolors and pastels, creates weavings and soft sculptures. She bought a horse and learned to ride the year she turned thirty. She was an amateur fencer (foil) and has been a member of the Richard III Society since 1983.

DEL REY ONLINE!

The Del Rey Internet Newsletter...

A monthly electronic publication, posted on the Internet, GEnie, CompuServe, BIX, various BBSs, and the Panix gopher (gopher.panix.com). It features hype-free descriptions of books that are new in the stores, a list of our upcoming books, special announcements, a signing/reading/convention-attendance schedule for Del Rey authors, "In Depth" essays in which professionals in the field (authors, artists, designers, sales people, etc.) talk about their jobs in science fiction, a question-and-answer section, behind-the-scenes looks at sf publishing, and more!

Online editorial presence: Many of the Del Rey editors are online, on the Internet, GEnie, CompuServe, America Online, and Delphi. There is a Del Rey topic on GEnie and a Del Rey folder on America Online.

Our official e-mail address for Del Rey Books is delrey@randomhouse.com

Internet information source!

A lot of Del Rey material is available to the Internet on a gopher server: all back issues and the current issue of the Del Rey Internet Newsletter, a description of the DRIN and summaries of all the issues' contents, sample chapters of upcoming or current books (readable or downloadable for free), submission requirements, mail-order information, and much more. We will be adding more items of all sorts (mostly new DRINs and sample chapters) regularly. The address of the gopher is gopher.panix.com

Why? We at Del Rey realize that the networks are the medium of the future. That's where you'll find us promoting our books, socializing with others in the sf field, and—most importantly—making contact and sharing information with sf readers.

For more information, e-mail ekh@panix.com